# Under Enemy Skies

By

# Rebecca Bryn

*'Success is not final, failure is not fatal, it is the courage to continue that counts.'* – Winston Churchill.

*'Vivre libre ou mourir – Live free or die.'* – The motto of the French Resistance.

\*\*\*

Dedicated to the memory of all of those - and there were many - who gave their lives, together with millions more who gave what should have been the best years of their lives, in the battle to save Europe from fascism. Never allow their sacrifice to be forgotten

\*\*\*

**Image and font permissions.**

**Images**

Girl: Depositphotos_4581283_XL.standard licence

Stars: Depositphotos_171625854_L.standard licence

**Fonts**

Cinzel Decorative Regular OFL licence.

Times New Roman MT Pro monotype licence.



**Acknowledgements**

*White Mouse* – Nancy Wake.

*Seducing and Killing Nazis* – Sophie Poldermans

*The Resistance* – Matthew Cobb

Chronology of Repression and Persecution in Occupied France, 1940-44 | Sciences Po Mass Violence and Resistance - Research Network – **Thomas Fontaine**

French Resistance Movements during WWII (geni.com)

# Chapter One

**Near Nancy, France. 1st September 1939**

Bonnie Renard sat beneath the shade of an enormous beech tree, watching damselflies and dragonflies dance above the surface of the river that wound its way in a giant loop around the western edge of Nancy and onward north to the border with Germany. She loved spending time at her grandparents' small farm on the Moselle, walking in the early morning along the riverbank or through the forested hills that rose behind the farm.

Part of her wished she could stay here forever and watch September turn the vines and beech leaves gold and russet, but Dad would be missing her, and she had a new job to start on Monday – she'd got the job with a hosiery firm on the strength of her fluent French and German.

She'd hoped he would come to France with her, but perhaps losing Mum was still too raw to bear his parents' somewhat overwhelming sympathy. He made work his excuse. Mémé and Pépé meant well, they were caring and generous people, but they could suffocate a person with kindness – which was why she was standing under a beech tree watching damselflies.

The old farmhouse wrapped itself around her, homely and comforting. Her grandmother was singing in the scullery and her grandfather would be in soon from checking the ripeness of the grapes and milking the six cows. A small fire burned in the hearth, bacon sizzled in a pan, and a kettle steamed gently. The radio crackled in the corner; her grandparents only nod to modernity apart from the single light bulb hanging on a flex from a beam in the ceiling.

She turned the tuning knob to find a station, and a voice whispered in German. This close to the border, they picked up German radio stations. She turned up the volume and listened.

Her grandmother bustled across the room. 'What's so interesting, Bonnie?'

'Mémé, it's Hitler. He says Polish troops have attacked a radio station at Gleiwitz. German troops have invaded Poland in retaliation.'

Her grandmother huffed out weathered cheeks. 'He's been spoiling for an excuse. He's annexed Austria and is demanding parts of Czechoslovakia – Sudetenland. He's still smarting from Germany losing the war.'

'But that was twenty years ago, Mémé, before I was even born.'

'Bonnie, people don't forget. Twenty years seems like barely yesterday.'

It was more than a lifetime to her. 'So now he's after Poland?'

'So it would seem.'

The German border suddenly seemed too close. 'Suppose Hitler sets his sights on France.'

Mémé clattered plates on the table. 'I would think he has enough on his mind with the countries to the east.' She dished bacon and eggs onto the plates and hacked at a loaf of bread. 'Claude!' There was no answer, so the old lady went to the door and shouted louder. 'Claude! Breakfast!'

Her grandfather hobbled in using a stick. 'I'm not deaf, Aude.' He smiled. 'Smells good, ma chère.'

'Sit yourselves down. What time's your train, Bonnie?'

'Half-past eight from Liverdun.'

'You must eat up then. I'll cut you some bread and cheese for the journey. Claude, we'll need the horse and cart to take Bonnie to the station.'

Pépé stabbed his egg with a grunt. 'The mare's already harnessed and waiting.'

She felt as if she was deserting them. Mémé's dismissal of Hitler might be justified – after all, she'd lived close to the border all her life, but the snippets of news she'd heard recently on the radio didn't fill her with confidence. Treaties were being broken, Hitler was expanding Germany's borders, and tensions were running high.

But what could one eighteen-year-old girl do? She'd talk to Dad. Maybe he could persuade Mémé and Pépé to move farther from a potential danger area.

At the small station in Liverdun, she kissed her grandparents goodbye. From the carriage window, she took a last look at the beautiful, broad, wooded valley with the sparkling Moselle running timelessly through it.

She had an ominous feeling that next time she saw it, things might be very different.

\*\*\*

**Leicestershire, England, later that day**

Antoine Renard waited on the platform at Narborough station. Bonnie hadn't been on the last train, and he'd spent an anxious hour killing time until the next one was due.

He walked to the end of the platform for the fourth time and stared along the tracks towards Leicester. Without his only daughter, he felt as if he had a limb missing, not that he'd let her know that. Since they'd lost her mother, he was determined she'd live her own life, not be tied to him by his loneliness.

He stubbed out a cigarette and fingered another. The BBC announcement of the German invasion of Poland had shaken him more than he wanted to admit, and he was desperate to see Bonnie safely home.

Fighting with the French army during the war had left him with a deep hatred of everything German. He'd lost his only brother, and a cousin, as well as good friends, and he had no illusions about history not repeating itself – the last few years Europe had been dogged with rivalries, swingeing reparations, and bitter disagreements.

A cloud as black as his thoughts smudged the afternoon sky. Would Bonnie be on the train?

The crowd on the platform surged forward as the engine huffed to a halt, puffing steam across his feet. There she was! Thank God! He threw the unlit cigarette in a bin and hurried to meet her.

She waved, dropped her suitcase, and ran into his arms.

He hugged her as if his life depended on it. 'Did you have a pleasant journey, ma chère?'

'Oui, Papa.' She smiled. Two weeks in France had made her second language become her first. 'I had a delay at Paris. I missed my connection, but apart from that, it was a good journey. I told you I could manage alone. I'm not a child anymore.'

'I know you're not. How are your grandparents?'

'They're well. They send their love, and they hope you'll visit before Christmas.'

'I'd like to.' He hesitated, but he needed to treat her like an adult, not the little girl she'd always be to him. 'I'm concerned about them, Bonnie.'

'Hitler? I heard the broadcast about Poland.'

'Yes. He has old scores to settle, and countries are already beginning to take sides.'

'Can you persuade them to come to England until things settle down? They'd be safe here.'

'I'll try.' He stooped to retrieve her suitcase. 'Now, let's get you home.' It was a couple of miles through Littlethorpe to Cosby, and home – to the small brick cottage in the main street, by the stream that ran through the village, and they must walk all the way.

He resolved to bring his parents to England as soon as he could, but he hated the thought of leaving Bonnie alone, and she needed to stay in England and concentrate on her new job.

He looked up into a clear blue sky. He didn't want to disillusion Bonnie about them being safe in his adopted country; Hitler had ordered an air attack on Warsaw, and the man seemed determined to expand Germany's territory.

His mind returned to the battlefields of France. God forbid that should ever happen again.

Sunday woke him with thunder and lightning. For a moment, he was back at the Aisne, seeing his comrades being blown to pieces and listening to the screams of the wounded. He shook away the memory – he was lucky to be alive.

The clock read nine-thirty. He let Bonnie sleep on and busied himself shaving and getting a leisurely breakfast. The radio hissed at him when he turned it on, and he fine-tuned the station to Radio Luxembourg, hoping for something lighter than the usual Sunday BBC fare.

Talk was of the crisis in Europe, something about a treaty with Poland and an ultimatum to Hitler, but the reception was broken and crackling. He tuned back to the BBC hoping for a clearer signal and was rewarded by a sombre voice.

Neville Chamberlain, the Prime Minister, was making an announcement. He got a decent reception in time to catch part of it. *'I have to tell you now that no such undertaking has been received, and that consequently, this country is at war with Germany.'*

'We're at war?'

He hadn't heard Bonnie come down the stairs. She stood in the doorway, small and fragile. Tears sparkled in brown eyes that were so like her mother's.

'We need to be strong, Bonnie. We're as safe here as anywhere, and our government will have learned something from the last war, but we must all pull together to get through this. We will get through it, ma chère.'

'Will it affect Mémé and Pépé?'

'If England sends troops to Poland, it may take attention away from the French border.'

Bonnie's face relaxed slightly. 'I hope so.' She tuned the radio to Radio Normandy. 'If there's any news of France, we should hear it here.'

They kept it tuned to Radio Normandy all day, and at five in the afternoon, their worst fears were realised. President Lebrun's ultimatum with Hitler also expired, and France declared war on Germany.

His trip to Liverdun was now urgent. No one was safe so close to the German border.

# Chapter Two

**Leicestershire, England. September 1939**

Monday brought more news from across Europe. It had taken all Antoine's powers of persuasion to convince Bonnie to travel to Leicester to begin her new job. He switched between the BBC, Radio Luxembourg, and Radio Normandy, while working out which clients he could put on hold for a couple of weeks, and which he couldn't.

He had to think about Yvonne and Rosemary, too; the two women did packing and invoicing for him. If he didn't get orders, they didn't get paid. He would make phone calls from the phone box later, and leave the two women with instructions, so they could keep the business ticking over and access funds to pay wages and invoices.

The news was sobering. China and Japan were fighting, a German battleship had attacked Danzig on the Baltic, annexing the free city into Germany, and the Luftwaffe had attacked several targets in Poland, carpet-bombing Wieluń. Hitler was accusing Poland of border attacks to justify his invasion.

The radio crackled a constant stream of foreboding.

The Italian government had declared a stance of non-belligerence, and several European countries had declared their neutrality. Britain was in a state of flux. The government had announced an emergency war budget, the War Office had ordered a general mobilisation of the armed forces, and a mass evacuation of children from London was being planned. Blackouts were ordered across Britain, which would plunge the villages and cities into a darkness from which he could only pray they would emerge.

The radio hummed and buzzed, and he re-tuned the station. The voice of doom was clearer now. Australia and Newfoundland had declared war on Germany, while the list of those proposing to remain neutral grew longer. All able-bodied men in Britain between the age of eighteen and forty-one were to be conscripted. He was forty-two... his heart thudded; when they'd massacred enough soldiers, he would be next in line, though whether he'd have to fight for Britain or France, he didn't know, and Bonnie would be all alone.

A shocked voice announced the first atrocity close to home. SS *Athenia*, a British cruise ship, had been torpedoed by a German submarine off the coast of Ireland with a huge loss of life.

He could no longer pretend it wasn't happening. England really was at war.

***

'I want to come with you, Dad.' Bonnie resisted the urge to stamp her foot like a spoiled child, but Dad was being unreasonable.

'No. You've only just begun your new job, and it doesn't take the two of us to bring your grandparents home. If you need to contact me, phone the telephone box in Liverdun at seven in the evening. If I need to contact you, I'll phone the one by the village hall at the same time. We can stay in touch that way, and anyway, you'll be more useful here.'

'Doing what?'

'Making blackout curtains, airing the spare beds, seeing our cupboards are well-stocked with food that will keep. Candles for power cuts, a sack of potatoes, order some coal –'

'Anyone would think we were planning for a siege.'

'We're planning for war, Bonnie. With most of the able-bodied men fighting, there'll be shortages, rationing, like there was last time... We need to prepare for the worst.'

'Which is?'

Dad glowered at her. 'You really don't want to know.' He sighed, failing to keep impatience from his voice. 'Just do as I tell you,

Bonnie.' He handed her three pound-notes. 'Go to the shop and see what they have.'

She snatched the notes and a shopping bag and ran from the house. Dad wasn't just leaving her alone, he was going to the border of two countries at war. Suppose he didn't come back? Suppose she never saw him again? Tears blinded her as she crossed the footbridge over the stream that ran in front of the cottages and walked the few yards to the shop. She'd hardly dared to let him out of her sight since mum died, and the thought of losing him as well made her heart race and her body go hot and cold.

'Good afternoon, Bonnie.' The matronly shopkeeper smiled.

'Is it?' She smiled back ruefully. 'Sorry, it's just that Dad is leaving for France, and I'm terrified.'

'Well, he is a Frenchman. I suppose that's where his duty lies.'

'I hadn't thought of that.' Her heart thumped harder. 'He won't be made to fight for them, will he?'

'I wouldn't know, duckie, but I'm sure he'll do his duty. Now, what can I get you?'

'Candles, please, Mrs Sibson.'

'Had a run on them today. I guess folk remember the last war.' She passed over a box of six. 'Anything else?'

'What's likely to be rationed?'

'Everything, duckie.' Mrs Sibson fetched a bag of sugar from a shelf. 'This, for one. You could do worse than buy tinned meat, powdered milk, and some flour.'

She put her pound notes on the counter and took a deep breath. 'Then fill my shopping bag with anything that will keep.'

'That's a might of money, Bonnie.' Mrs Sibson gathered tinned ham, corned beef, tinned fish, spam, a bag of flour, a jar of dried milk, and a packet of suet.

'Dad said a sack of potatoes, too.'

'I'll get Mr Sibson to drop you a sack around. Is that all?'

'It's all I can carry.'

Mrs Sibson totted up the bill and took a pound note. 'Nineteen shillings and sixpence, duckie. That includes the spuds.'

She took the sixpence offered in change and heaved the shopping bag off the floor. Next time, she'd bring two bags or make two trips. 'Thank you, Mrs Sibson.'

'Anything you need while your dad's away, just shout, duckie.'

Her eyes smarted. 'Thank you, Mrs Sibson. That's kind of you.'

'No trouble, Bonnie. Glad to help. Tell your dad we'll keep an eye on you.'

She smiled her gratitude. There were some advantages in still being considered a child at eighteen. She took the shopping home and then walked along Main Street to the phone box by the village hall, fed the slot with pennies, dialled the coalman's phone number, and waited.

'Shilcock's coal merchants.'

Coins rattled as she pressed the button. 'Hello. I want two tons of coal delivered, please.' She gave the address and hung up, assured it would be there the next day.

Perhaps she could do this without dad, with a little help from friends and neighbours. And he wouldn't be away long – it would just feel like it.

\*\*\*

**Near Nancy, France, September 1939**

Antoine patted his breast pocket to reassure himself he had all the necessary papers. New travel restrictions were in force, and he'd had to queue for days at the French Consulate in London for a permit, and then do the same for a British exit permit. The night ferry that carried the train had been suspended the previous week because of the outbreak of war, so he'd crossed the channel to Calais on the SS *Autocarrier*, a car ferry.

The quayside was chaotic, crowded with people and cars. A long line of vehicles waited to board the ferry to England, far more than it could accommodate. The port was bustling with anxious humanity, many of them tourists trying to get home to England, and some of them British soldiers pushing against the flow to board trains into France. Troop carriers disgorged more soldiers and military vehicles into the confusion.

His papers scrutinised, he was waved through and boarded the train for Paris. On the opposite platform, tourists lugging suitcases spilled from train carriages and hurried towards the ferry terminal. He was one of very few civilians travelling into France.

Lines of cars were going north, while convoys of military vehicles drove towards the border with Germany. There was an air of urgency, of brittle determination.

Eight o'clock in the morning, after a night trying to sleep on a bench at Châlons En Champagne, with early autumn nipping at his ears, saw him at Liverdun station.

A cart laden with firewood stopped beside him on the road towards the farm. 'Antoine?' Mum and Dad's elderly neighbour smiled down at him.

'Henri, how are you?'

'Well, thank you. Visiting Claude and Aude?'

'I am.'

'Jump up. I'm going that way.'

'Thank you. You're not leaving then, Henri? Half the country seems to be on the move.'

'I hear there are already a lot of refugees coming in from Germany.' He shrugged. 'Where would I go, and who would look after my animals?'

They'd reached the end of the lane to the farm. 'I'm hoping to persuade my parents to leave.'

'Good luck with separating Claude from his land.' Henri dismissed his concern with a wave of his hand and flicked the reins, urging his horse on.

Mum greeted him with a huge smile. 'Antoine, why didn't you let us know you were coming?' One hug, and she went into mother mode. 'Have you eaten?' Bacon was in the pan before he could say he was starving. 'Sit yourself down. I'll make up a bed. The kettle's not far off boiling...' She wiped her hands on her apron and gave him another hug. 'How are you, Antoine?'

'Surviving. It's hard, but having Bonnie helps, though she reminds me of Sybil every time I look at her.'

'She's grown into a lovely girl. Anyway, I wasn't expecting you. Has something happened?'

He raised his eyebrows. 'War with Germany isn't reason enough to worry about you?'

'It will take more than Hitler to concern us.'

'Mum, you can't ignore the danger. He's bombed cities in Poland.'

'Cities, Antoine. Why would he be interested in a small farm in the Moselle valley?'

'It's a small farm that lies in the path of invading forces when Hitler sends troops. I remember the brutality of German soldiers. I know what they're capable of. Don't think Liverdun's fortified gate will save anyone.'

'Antoine, I'm seventy-five, your father's almost eighty. What threat are we to them?'

'You don't need to be a threat. You're both French, and you're a woman. They...' Visions he'd tried to banish, atrocities he'd told no one about, clouded his eyes. 'You need to leave here, now, with me, and come to England.'

'Speak to your father.' Mum shook her head. 'Antoine, he's not well. I doubt he's up to travelling, whether or not we want to.' She put a plate on the table in front of him. 'Eat up. There's nothing so urgent it can't wait until you've eaten.'

Dad hobbled into the kitchen and sank onto a chair by the table. 'Henri told me you were here. I wasn't expecting you until Christmas.'

'He wants us to leave, Claude. He reckons we're going to be murdered in our beds.'

'Leave? This is our home, Antoine, and my father's before me. I have crops in the fields and animals to care for – responsibilities. I can't up and leave because of one madman. Why do you think the Maginot fortifications were built? To keep out the bloody Germans.'

He winced at *responsibilities*. It had been a bone of contention between them that he'd gone to England to work. He had other responsibilities now. 'It might keep out tanks and give the French army time to fight back, but planes will fly over it, and tanks can go around it not a day's march north. Armoured vehicles could be here in two hours. You're too close to the border. It's not safe here.'

'We survived the last war, and we'll survive this one. The border's no closer now than it was then. If your mother wants to go with you, that's up to her, but I'm not leaving the land I was born on, nor my animals. Not now, not ever. I was prepared to die defending it during the last war, and I'll die defending it now.'

Mum poured another cup of tea and pushed it towards Dad. 'I'm not going without you, Claude. If you stay, I stay.'

Dad smiled. 'There's a shotgun in the larder if it makes you feel happier, Antoine. Your old service revolver is there as well, and we have powerful bolts on the shutters and doors, not that we've ever needed them. There's enough ammunition to put paid to any nosey German who comes snooping.'

He clattered his cup on its saucer. 'I'm not leaving without you both.'

Dad smiled again. 'Looks like we're all staying put then, son.'

# Chapter Three

### Leicestershire, England. December 1939

Bonnie shivered by the phone box in the dark, hoping no one would come along wanting to use it. It was almost seven o'clock, and Wednesday was Dad's day to phone. She'd accepted that she should stay in England to earn much needed money. Yvonne and Rosemary had Dad's hosiery distribution company well in hand, and he'd insisted she spread her wings. Everyone needed socks, and the hosiery company for whom she now worked appreciated her efforts at promoting business in Europe. French troops needed socks as much as the British did.

She and dad had settled into a routine; he phoned on Wednesdays and she phoned on Saturdays, but they both waited by their respective phone boxes for ten minutes every evening, in case of emergencies. So far, there hadn't been any, and she was beginning to think they'd been panicking over nothing. People were calling it a phoney war. Hopefully, it would stay that way.

It didn't mean Britain wasn't preparing at home. Rationing had become the norm. Butter, bacon, ham and sugar were on the list to be rationed, and she'd stocked up as much as she could afford. She was hoping Dad would come home for Christmas.

She kept abreast of the news by radio. Poland had surrendered to Germany, and the Polish government had moved to London, but Hitler's offers of peace had been rejected by Britain and France. The war seemed to be being fought in the Atlantic, apart from the Thames being mined by German U-boats a few weeks before.

For some reason, Jews were being deported from Austria and Czechoslovakia into Poland, and some Czech students had been shot.

According to her watch, Dad should have phoned five minutes ago. Should she phone him? She opened the door, pushed inside, glad to be out of the wind, and switched on her torch.

Something must have delayed him. Visions of Germans in steel hats and aiming rifles, like she'd seen on posters in town, brought her out in a cold sweat. She had to know Dad was all right. Holding her torch between chattering teeth and trying to shield the light with her body, she fumbled pennies from her pocket and reached a numb hand towards the receiver.

The phone rang, and she grabbed the receiver, dropping it with a clatter. A voice called her name.

'Mm ur.' She removed the torch from her mouth and switched it off before anyone spotted it shining. 'I'm here. I dropped the phone. I was about to ring you!'

'I'm sorry, Bonnie. One of the cows had a hard time calving, and Dad needed help. I couldn't leave her until now. Is everything all right there?'

She tried to keep her voice steady. 'Yes. I was worried when you didn't ring, that's all. I'm fine.'

'You don't sound fine.'

'I miss you, Dad.' She missed his warm smile and his blue eyes full of love.

'I miss you too, ma chère.'

'When are you coming home?'

'As soon as I can. Nothing much is happening here. I don't think I need to stay. And if anything kicks off, I can be back here in a matter of hours. Yes, I'll be home as soon as I can – I've been away too long thanks to your grandfather's stubbornness. I've made some good contacts business-wise over here, but I need to reconnect with my English clients.'

Her heart lifted. Beeps meant Dad's money was running out. 'Love you, Papa. Give my love to Mémé and Pépé.'

'See you soon, ma chère.'

She walked home along the main street with a spring in her step. All she needed for Christmas was Dad. A tiny pool of dim light filtered through her fingers, and jaunty music spilled from a blacked-out cottage window.

She sang along to the tune.

*We're going to hang out the washing on the Siegfried Line*
*Have you any dirty washing, mother dear?*
*We're gonna hang out the washing on the Siegfried Line.*
*'Cause the washing day is here.*

***

## Near Nancy, France. December 1939

Antoine packed his bag and checked his papers were in his breast pocket. He'd remained stubbornly determined to ignore his parents' pleas for him to stay. They'd made their decision, and Bonnie needed him. He'd heard the tears in her voice, the worry. As it was, he'd need to be back on the road straight after Christmas taking knitwear samples to British customers he'd neglected. Leicester was renowned for its hosiery and knitwear, and it was his job to find markets for it. He couldn't leave it all to Yvonne and Rosemary, capable though they were.

He checked his watch. Dad was harnessing the horse ready for the trip to Liverdun and the station. He'd miss the place, but it was like he'd told Bonnie – he could be back in a day.

Mum pushed a tin box into his hands. 'Something for the journey, Antoine.'

He kissed her cheeks. 'I'll miss you.'

'Bonnie needs you, too. We've been selfish keeping you here.'

He smiled his thanks. 'I feel torn.'

'I know. Love does that to you, son. It tears you apart. Next time you come, bring Bonnie with you.'

'We'll have to see how things go, but if it's safe…'

'Aude!' The cry from outside sounded urgent.

They rushed out to see Dad clutching his chest.

'Claude, what is it?'

'Pain…' Dad's face was pale, and he was leaning against the horse.

'It looks like a heart attack.' If Dad wasn't faking it.

'Fetch the doctor, Antoine, quickly.'

'Let's get Dad inside, and I'll take the cart.' He helped Dad to a chair and ran back out, lashing the reins to get the old mare into a slow canter. 'Dépêche-toi! Vite!'

He was back with the doctor within twenty minutes, and the man confirmed his fears.

'A heart attack, but not life-threatening if you rest, Claude.' The doctor waved an arm to encompass the farm. 'It's time you retired.'

His mother nodded. 'Perhaps it's a blessing in disguise, Claude. If we can sell the livestock, we can go with Antoine to England and all be together. You know how Bonnie misses her father.'

'No, Madame Renard. Your husband is presently too ill to travel. The journey could kill him.'

'Staying here could kill him too, Doctor.' He paced the room, trying to avoid the inevitable. 'We should have all gone to England when I first suggested it.'

Mum looked up at him. 'It's too late for that now. Antoine?'

Hope of spending Christmas with Bonnie evaporated. *Responsibility* weighed heavily on his shoulders. There was no one else to look after his parents and the farm. He couldn't leave now.

* * *

### Leicestershire, England. December 1939

Christmas morning dawned cold and bright. Bonnie lit the fire in the living-room grate and put a kettle to boil on the gas stove. She'd decorated the house with baubles from the loft, which reminded her of happier days. The first Christmas without Mum was always going to be hard, but to be without Dad as well… She'd never felt so alone.

Pépé was improving slowly, but Dad said it was unlikely he'd ever be fit enough to do a day's work. Mémé would have come to England, but for Pépé. They could all have been celebrating Christmas together, not that there was a lot to celebrate. Rationing had cut a festive dinner to the bone, not that it mattered; she didn't feel much like eating.

She forced down some porridge and a cup of tea, and stoked the fire. At least she was warm, and there were plenty of people in the world who had less than she did. It was the constant uncertainty of war that depressed her.

At eleven o'clock, the pre-arranged time for her Christmas phone call with Dad, she was waiting by the phone box. There was a queue. It seemed half the village wanted to wish loved ones a happy day. Dad would keep trying, wouldn't he?

She stamped her feet. People passed by on their way to church for the morning service. She'd never believed in God, though she tried to take comfort in her mother being in Heaven – it was one of those contradictions she accepted with a shrug.

'Your dad didn't make it home then, Bonnie?'

She turned to find Mrs Sibson standing beside her in her Sunday best. 'No, my grandfather isn't well. He's had to stay to look after Grandma and the farm.'

'Oh, that's a shame. You're all on your own, then?'

She nodded, fighting back tears.

'We can't be having that, duckie, not after the year you've had. There's room at our table when you've made your phone call. Dinner's at one. Don't be late.'

She wiped her hand across her eyes and blew her nose.

Mrs Sibson clutched her to her ample bosom. 'There, there, Bonnie. It'll be all right, you'll see. Nothing lasts forever. Not even wars. Now, I'll be late for church.'

She smiled through her tears. With good people like Mrs Sibson in the world, how could evil people like Hitler hope to win?

The phone box door opened. It was her turn. Her father's voice fled across the miles, along with Mémé and Pépé's. It was so good to hear them all.

'I hope you're eating properly, Bonnie?' Mémé's first concern was always feeding her.

She laughed, happier than she'd felt for months. 'I shall make a pig of myself, Mémé. A kind neighbour has invited me to dinner, and everyone's cooking is better than mine.'

'Have a lovely day, Bonnie. Joyeux Noël. Je t'adore.'

'Merry Christmas to you, Mémé. I love you, too.'

# Chapter Four

**Near Nancy, France. May/June 1940**

Radio Luxembourg had been shut down in September the previous year; Radio Normandy still broadcasted, though for how much longer, with German troops advancing across Belgium, was debatable.

Antoine listened to the BBC Radio broadcast every morning and evening. It kept him abreast of the situation in England and made him feel closer to Bonnie. Churchill had become England's Prime Minister. Could the man change the course of the war? He seemed determined where the defence of freedom was concerned.

Rationing had tightened. Meat was now in short supply as well as many other basic commodities, and rationing looked likely to continue. The war wasn't going well for the Allies. British and French troops had pulled out of Norway, and the Norwegian government was in exile in London.

This morning's news had realised his worst fears. Germany had invaded Luxembourg, dropped bombs on Belgium and Holland, and parachuted in troops.

Out checking on the small flock of Île-de-France sheep, he glanced at the sky. A clear blue, unspoiled by cloud, plane, or parachute. A beautiful, peaceful day with no hint of the burgeoning conflict farther north. The spectre of war dragged his mind back. The German advance had been swift and brutal, and Allied forces had pushed into Belgium to attempt to hold them back.

Today, the thirteenth, the Germans had pushed through the Ardennes near Sedan on the River Meuse, north of the Maginot fortifications, and had set jackboot on French soil. According to the broadcast, they'd met with stiff opposition from French fighters and

Allied aircraft, and bridges on the Meuse had been blown up to try to prevent their advance.

He tried to rationalise his fear. Mum had been right when she'd said cities, not small farms. If his experiences in the last war were anything to go by, the Panzers would either head for Paris, to take the capital, or try to encircle and destroy the Allied forces in the north. He doubted they'd head for Paris and risk their supply lines being cut behind them, so it made sense for them to cut off the Allied forces from their own supply lines.

They were safe enough here, for now, and that was what he had to convince Bonnie of when he phoned her. It wasn't his day to phone, but she'd be waiting by the phone box at seven, and she'd be worrying if she'd heard the news. He picked up the receiver and dialled the operator.

The next day, the Dutch surrendered. British troops fought back at Arras the following week, but Brussels was taken by the Germans, and on the twenty-eighth, the Belgian army surrendered. The Allied forces were encircled. The situation was getting worse by the day, and it was getting more and more difficult to convince Bonnie he was safe.

Mum and Dad were stoical, and he could be no less, but he was deeply disturbed when Amiens was besieged, Calais surrendered, and the British Expeditionary Force retreated to the Channel ports.

The Allies called Operation Dynamo to evacuate troops from Dunkirk, while the Luftwaffe bombed the beachhead, a victory. While he understood the importance of saving hundreds of thousands of fighting men to fight another day, to the French peasants around Nancy, it felt like a betrayal.

France stood alone, and would fall alone to the might of Nazi Germany.

***

Antoine left his parents listening to music on the BBC, a light distraction from the news. Italy had declared war on Britain and France, and Hitler had bombed Paris.

He'd been working on a fence for a couple of hours when the sound of a heavy vehicle made him pause. A visitor? He listened intently. There was more than one. The rumble of engines stopped. Voices shouted something he didn't catch – they must be close by. The unmistakable stutter of a machine-gun came from the direction of the house.

Germans!

He raced towards the house, armed only with a sledgehammer. Three vehicles stood in the farmyard, and soldiers were running in and out of barns. He hid behind a wall, helpless to stop them – the firearms were in the house. A scream came from the nearest barn. Mum?

There was a back way into it beneath loose boarding. He squeezed through slowly and slipped inside. A German soldier had his mother pinned to the floor, stockinged legs spread, and was raping her. Heart racing, he dropped the sledgehammer, grabbed the pitchfork he kept in the corner, and ran across the barn. The man was intent on his pleasure, but Mum turned her head and saw him.

He raised the pitchfork just as the soldier realised he was there. Plunging it down hard, he thrust it through the bastard's back. Screams of agony joined his mother's terrified ones as the man arched his spine before slumping onto her.

He threw the man aside, hoping the bastard died slowly in agony.

'Mum.'

'Antoine.' Tears streaked her face. 'Antoine, they shot your father. He tried to stop them taking me, and they shot him.'

He knelt beside her and held her close. There was little chance his father had survived machine-gun fire. 'We have to get out of here. Can you walk?'

'I'll try.'

He helped her to her feet. A shadow darkened the doorway, and he turned to face it. The soldier raised his machine gun, and pointed.

He threw himself and Mum to the floor as bullets sprayed across the barn.

***

## Leicestershire, England. June 1940

Bonnie waited by the phone box for the third night since German troops had entered Paris. That they'd made for Paris gave her hope that Liverdun had escaped their attention. The French government had declared Paris an open city and fled to Bordeaux. General Pétain had become the new French Prime Minister.

She'd phoned Dad every night and got no answer. She tried to find reasons why that might be. The phone box could be out of order. Pépé might have taken a turn for the worse. Nothing calmed her fear; Dad's silence was terrifying.

Seven o'clock. If there was no answer tonight…

The phone rang and rang. She let it ring for the full ten minutes before hanging up. Biting her knuckle, she considered her options. There was only one. The only thing keeping her in England was her job. She'd phone them in the morning and beg compassionate leave – she was due some holiday. Waiting in Cosby, not knowing what was happening in France, was more than her patience could bear.

She ran home, packed a bag, and gathered together her passport, birth certificate, and all the money she could find in the house. Would it be enough to get her to France? Dad had told her of the new travel restrictions, and that the French Consulate had charged him a shilling for every form he'd had to fill in.

Her parents' wedding photo stood on the mantelpiece. It was the only photo she had of her mother. On impulse, she took it out of its frame and put it in her wallet.

Early next morning saw her pedalling her bicycle towards the station. She left it chained to a post and hoped it would still be there when she came home – if she came home.

The wait for the train was agonising, the journey to London seemed to take forever, and the queuing for travel permits was nerve-wracking, but finally, she boarded the passenger ferry for Calais. It was dark by the time they sailed, and with the ferry blacked-out, the voyage across the Channel was eerie. Only seeing the North Star behind her convinced her they were sailing south.

The port of Calais was in chaos. People milled everywhere, and she had to push her way through the crowds to board the train to Paris, where she would change to go east and then south. Were the uniforms she saw German or French? She sank into a seat and clutched her bag to her chest. There'd be no one to meet her at the station, because she hadn't been able to let them know she was coming.

Taking a deep breath as the train pulled out of the station, she let her heart-rate slow. Military vehicles, lorries, and cars clogged the roads, and an ambulance was stuck in the queue.

Her sense of unease heightened as she approached Paris, but she pushed it aside determinedly. She'd always enjoyed her snatched moment between trains in Paris. She loved the pavement cafes and the sense of fun and freedom. The sight of Nazi swastikas hanging from walls made her blood run cold. She was walking into a viper's nest.

Soldiers patrolled the platforms at Gare de Nord, checking papers. No one took much notice of an eighteen-year-old girl carrying a bag. Hiding behind taller people, she hurried out of the station and along Rue du Faubourg Saint-Denis to Gare de l'Est, to catch the train east. Somewhere in the distance was the sound of gunfire. German military vehicles patrolled the road, and she'd learned what a German uniform looked like well enough to avoid them.

'Die Dokumente!' The thud of boots and a German voice swung her around in panic; a gun pointed at her.

'No!' He only wanted her papers. 'Ja, einen Moment, bitte.' She fumbled in her bag, heart thudding, and brought out her travel permits, thanking God that having spent many happy summers close to the border, she could speak German.

The soldier perused the papers and thrust them back in her face, waving her on with his pistol. Her head swam, dizzy with relief, and she walked as calmly as she could to board her connection to Liverdun.

It was standing room only on the train as people fled Paris and headed away from the fighting. She'd been insane, stupid, to come to France in wartime. She'd had no idea what it would be like, the panic and confusion, the danger. Dad would be furious with her.

She'd deal with his anger after she'd hugged him. The family would all be together for the first time in many months, and that was the important thing now. She'd missed them all so much.

# Chapter Five

**Near Nancy, France. June 1940**

Bonnie walked from the station, the sun burning down on her. Cars passed her going south, piled high with luggage, but no one stopped to offer her a lift. Ahead of her, families walked carrying everything they could. Horses and carts were loaded high, the horses straining in their harnesses. The whole of Northern France seemed to be on the move. Could she persuade her grandparents to move south; they might find that preferable to moving to England, and anyway, retreating north didn't seem like a safe option.

The shade of the trees on the track to the farm were welcome. The roof of the farmhouse peeped between beech trees, and away from the road, there was no sound but birdsong, no movement but the leaves rustling in the breeze. It was almost too quiet.

A strange smell wafted on the breeze, unpleasant and growing stronger. Tyre marks grooved the gravel track, and the gate to the yard stood open. Something wasn't right. The silence was becoming as claustrophobic as the smell.

She hurried forward. The old mare lay on her back, legs sticking out straight, her belly bloated. Farther on were slaughtered sheep and cattle, some butchered. Flies buzzed around her head as she drew nearer, and the stench of death made her retch.

'Dad! Mémé! Pépé!'

No answer. What had happened here?

Dread tightened her throat as she walked through the open front door of the farmhouse. The radio crackled, slightly off-station, but the voice coming from it was definitely German, and the smell was even worse indoors.

A buzz of flies told its own tale. 'Oh, dear God, no… no.' Pépé lay on the floor by the table, next to an upturned chair, one arm outstretched. She turned away and vomited. There was no sign of Mémé or Dad.

She stumbled blindly from the house and across the yard. The barn door swung idly in the breeze. She thumbed tears from her eyes and walked inside. It was dark, but the smell was no better. There was death here, too.

She let her eyes adjust to the dark. 'Please God, no.' She sank to her knees beside the body on the floor. 'Oh, Mémé. What have they done to you?' Bullet holes riddled her grandmother's blouse, stained dark with dried blood. A pair of torn bloomers left little to the imagination. A little way away lay the body of a German soldier, a pitchfork still sticking into his back. It would have taken strength to force the fork into a man like that. It would have been beyond Pépé's strength. Dad's doing surely?

Never had she felt such hatred for another human being. She yanked the pitchfork from the body and plunged it again and again into the corpse, screaming her anger and grief.

'Dad!' She'd never needed her father more, but where was he? He'd have buried Mémé and Pépé if he'd been able. 'Dad!'

She ran out of the barn and across the yard. He wasn't in any of the barns, and the fields were empty of life. What the Nazis couldn't take with them, they'd destroyed, but her father wasn't there. Had they taken him prisoner? Why would they if they could kill him? He must have escaped, but where would he go to hide, and would he come back when he thought it was safe?

Reluctantly, she went back into the house. She couldn't stay there, but she needed food, and she felt the need to cover her grandparents' bodies with blankets, to give them some dignity in death.

What little food was left in the larder had been spoiled. The shotgun and Dad's service revolver were still there in the corner, under the bottom shelf, so Dad must have left in a hurry. She covered Pépé's body, pocketed the revolver and ammunition, and tuned the guttural Nazi voice to another station. It might have vital information.

'*Ici Radio Londres. Aujourd'hui, le gouvernement Français s'est rendu à l'Allemagne Nazie. Le général Pétain a conclu un armistice et l'Allemagne occupe désormais la zone nord de la France.*'

France had surrendered, and Germany now occupied Northern France.

She covered her grandmother's body and prayed to a God she couldn't believe in for her grandparents' eternal souls. 'I love you, Mémé.' They were the last words Mémé had heard her say.

She stood in the yard with tears streaking her face, with no clear idea of where she was going, and not caring if she lived or died, except revenge and hatred burned deep in her heart. Whatever she could do to stop the Nazis destroying her beloved France, she would do. And she had to find her father.

If *she* was missing, Dad would look for her, he wouldn't stop until he'd found her, and she would walk the length and breadth of France to find him.

The sound of a plane flying low and strafing something or someone to the west of her made her take to the forest, and she slipped beneath the beech trees and melted into the shadows. There were sure to be other refugees hiding in the hills and woodlands around Nancy, intent on resisting the onslaught of Nazi tyranny, and she would join them.

*** 

**Near Nancy, France. July 1940**

Bonnie stumbled on, pushing through trees and scrub, moving south – that was where everyone seemed to be heading, and they couldn't all be wrong. If Dad hadn't been taken prisoner, he would try to get to safety, and south as far from the capital as possible, was surely their best option. What would he do then?

She stopped short with a gasp of realisation. He'd know she'd be frantic with worry. He'd try to phone her as soon as he could, and when she didn't answer… Would he try to get back to England, or would he know she'd come looking for him?

He knew her well enough to know she was impulsive, determined, and didn't always stop to think – if she did, she'd probably still be in England, not struggling through trees that whipped her face with their branches and tripped her with their roots.

She brushed aside tears. She needed determination now. Crying over Mémé and Pépé wouldn't help her survive in what was now a hostile country. One thing was certain; she couldn't survive alone.

She pushed on towards a thin plume of smoke rising above the treetops. Woodsmoke. A small huddle of cottages greeted her. She watched cautiously from the edge of the wood. No sound of vehicles. No gunfire. A horse looked over a stable door and goats grazed in a small paddock.

A woman came out of the nearest cottage, and she stepped out from the trees. 'Help me, please. I need help.'

The woman looked up, startled, and then brushed a hand through grey hair. 'Dieu, Dieu, child. Whatever's happened to you? Come along inside.'

'They killed…' Her voice failed her, and she followed the woman inside.

'Sit yourself down, child, and tell me what's happened.'

The woman's kindness broke her resolve. She couldn't speak for crying.

'Take your time. My name's Louise. What's yours?'

'Bonnie. Bonnie Renard.'

'Well, Bonnie Renard. Who's killed what?'

'Germans. They killed Mémé and Pépé. They butchered the animals. Dad's missing and…' The enormity of her loss engulfed her. 'I have no one. I'm all alone.'

'There, there, ma chère. You're not alone anymore. You're not the first refugee to come to our little village.' Louise looked around as if expecting the walls to sprout ears. 'I can trust you?'

She nodded – she felt instinctively she could trust Louise. 'Dad killed a German who raped Mémé. I intend to kill some as well.'

Louise showed no surprise, but nodded. 'We are hiding some Jews who fled Paris when it was declared an open city. They know well Hitler's hatred of Jews.'

'What can I do to help?'

Louise's answer was interrupted by the door opening. Three men surveyed her with piercing eyes.

'This is Bonnie. Nazis murdered her family. Her father is missing. She's come to join us.'

She could sense their mistrust. 'Dad stuck a pitchfork through the spine of a Nazi. I want to kill Germans. I won't rest until we've driven them from France, but I need to find Dad.'

'What does he look like?'

'I have a photo. It's old, twenty years old, but he hasn't changed that much.' She took her parent's wedding photo from her wallet. 'His name is Antoine Renard. He's forty-two.'

The oldest man, tall, dark-haired, and muscular, held out his hand for the photograph. 'His face is familiar. I'm not sure, but it looks very like a man I saw. I can ask around – he may well be with one of the other groups'

Dad was here, and he was alive! 'Thank you.'

The man smiled. 'I'm Raphael. Welcome to our group.'

'Group?'

'People are organising against the occupiers. No one wants them here. We're north of the demarcation line, in the occupied territory, and there are military control posts all along it to stop us crossing. They're occupying everywhere from the Swiss border north and west to Tours and down the coast to Spain. They've taken the industrial heartland, the mines, the iron foundries, and steelworks. The main grain-producing area.' The man shook his head. 'Hitler will force Frenchmen to work for the German Reich. General Pétain signed an armistice, and has moved the government to Vichy, south of the line in the free zone, but he won't let France stay under German rule. The people of France must be ready to fight when he calls on us.'

'I'm ready.'

'It will be dangerous. The Nazis are intent on destroying all resistance, military or otherwise. I shall forget your name, and you will never know mine – as far as the German's know, I am Raphael. You'll need false papers, and we'll call you Vixen. The less anyone knows about another, the less chance of betrayal.'

Louise frowned. 'Is that a bit obvious, given her surname? She looks more like a bedraggled bird with ruffled feathers.'

'Raven, then, as you have black hair.'

It was a good name.

Raphael continued. 'In the meantime, we keep to small groups, and each group has a contact in another to relay messages. We've sworn to do everything we can to hamper the German army and aid the persecuted, even if we must sacrifice our own lives for France. There are those who collaborate with the occupiers. Trust no one, Raven.'

She drew Dad's revolver from her pocket and laid a handful of bullets on the table beside it. 'I swear to stand against the Nazi bastards who slaughtered my family, even at the cost of my own life.'

The man smiled. 'Vive la France.'

She forced a grim smile in return. 'Vive la France.'

# Chapter Six

**Near Nancy, France. July 1940**

Antoine joined a group of men, women, and children fleeing south to try to cross the demarcation line into the unoccupied zone. He'd run from the barn after killing the German and had evaded his pursuers' gunfire. For two days, he'd hidden in the forest, tired and hungry, while moving steadily south. He'd met a kind family who'd shared what little provisions they had and together they'd joined the exodus from the occupied zone. It gave them anonymity – there was safety in numbers.

He needed to find a phone box and reassure Bonnie that he was alive. It had been over a week since he'd spoken to her, and she'd be frantic with worry, but at least she was safe in Cosby.

According to the family, who'd fled from Nancy, the town was occupied by Germans, so he couldn't go there. No, trying to get across the border into Vichy France was his best hope.

The low drone of an engine sounded in the distance. He glanced behind him. Not a vehicle. Scanning the sky, a small dot emerged from cloud and drew closer. Allied or German? He shaded his eyes against the sun as the plane swooped towards them.

The stutter of machine guns exploded into the air, cutting a swathe through the families ahead of him. He dived into the ditch at the side of the road and lay there, heart pounding.

The noise of the engine faded, and he dragged himself from the ditch. 'You bastards!' He shook an impotent fist at the receding dot. Women wailed, children screamed, men wept. Bodies lay where they'd fallen, riddled with bullets. Blood stained the road – innocent civilians maimed and slaughtered.

A small child clutched a wooden toy, his eyes staring upwards unseeing. What chance had he had? A woman held a dead child in her arms, rocking backwards and forwards, moaning. A man knelt beside his injured wife and daughter. The dead were the lucky ones.

Where could they find help? He must try to do something. What if the plane circled around and came back?

'Put your wife and daughter on that cart.' He raised his voice. 'Quickly, get the wounded onto the carts. There must be a village farther on. There may be a doctor.'

They left the dead by the side of the road, made the wounded as comfortable as possible on the carts, and the remnants of the procession picked up their belongings and hurried on.

He followed, stunned by the needless slaughter. Behind him came the sound of a vehicle. He turned. Germans! He was about to dive for cover when a guttural voice yelled. 'Arrêtez ou je tire. Stop, or I shoot.'

He raised his hands and stood vey still. Would it be safer to say he was English or French?

A soldier approached, holding a rifle. 'Die Dokumente.'

'Pardon?' He pretended not to understand German.

'Papiers!'

He fumbled for his ID card and travel permits and held them out, hardly daring to breathe.

The soldier examined them. 'Antoine Renard. An English exit permit.' The man gabbled something to his comrade, who raised his rifle and moved closer. 'Antoine. The old man at the farm where Boris was killed shouted for Antoine when we shot him.'

He had no weapon to kill the bastard who'd murdered Dad. He held his nerve, hoping for an opportunity. 'There must be many Frenchmen called Antoine.'

'But not one carrying no luggage when fleeing south. We chased you from the farm where you stuck Boris like a sheaf of corn.'

The other Nazi put his finger on the trigger of his Luger.

He stopped breathing; he'd never see Bonnie again.

'Nein!' The first soldier held up his hand and turned back to his captive, eyes narrowed. 'We'll make an example of this one. A public trial at a military court and a public execution. We'll show these pigs of Frenchmen what happens to those who attack Germans.'

Poked in the ribs with a rifle barrel, and with a Luger aimed at his chest, he had no option but to get into the back of the military vehicle, crowded with German soldiers. One of them jabbed a rifle butt into the side of his head, sending him reeling.

The driver turned right and headed west. Where in God's name were they taking him? Wherever it was, his days were numbered.

***

**Near Nancy, France. July 1940**

Bonnie listened to the BBC broadcast in Louise's kitchen, surrounded by her new "family". There'd been no news of Dad, despite Raphael asking his contacts, but a lot had happened since she'd left England in June. The Germans had sunk two troopships with huge loss of life. General de Gaulle had formed a government in exile in London and had been recognised by the British as the leader of the Free French in England, though Raphael asserted the resistance and the "Free French" were two different groups miles apart politically.

The German army had occupied the Channel Islands, the Luftwaffe was bombing shipping in the Channel as well as mainland Britain, and controversially, the British navy had attacked the French fleet at Mers-el-Kébir to keep it out of Nazi hands. In retaliation for the French navy's destruction, the Vichy government had broken off diplomatic ties with Britain. Relationships between Britain and Vichy France were now tense.

In Luxembourg, there was open resistance to the Nazi occupation, but *Raven* had already learned to keep a low profile. She'd been beaten for putting an anti-German poster in a shop window calling for people to resist the occupiers. After a man had been executed for having an "anti-German attitude", resistance had gone underground.

The newsreader paused before the next item. *'The Vichy government is debating repealing the 1939 statutory order which makes racist verbal abuse an offense, also known as the Marchandeau law. The law, which provides prosecution "when defamation or insult committed against a group of persons, by their origin, race or religion, will have been designed to arouse hatred among citizens or residents" may be abolished.'*

Louise gasped. 'You know what this means? Pétain is collaborating with the Nazis against the Jews.'

Raphael brushed an anxious hand through his hair. 'It means tens of thousands of Jews are in danger. The Nazis and their collaborators won't stop at insults. I'd thought better of Pétain. What hope has France now?'

Louise's voice trembled. 'Then we must fight on without him, hide as many Jews as we can, and help them get to safety.'

The old woman's determination kindled her fighting spirit. 'But how, Louise? Where in France is safe for them?'

'Nowhere, Raven. Spain is the only safe place now, if we could get families over the Pyrenees. Italy is no longer a safe haven. Switzerland is neutral, but Germany stands between it and England.'

'It will take a lot of organising.' Raphael frowned. 'Bonnie… Raven, you could help here. A young girl like you doesn't get noticed much by Germans. We need more recruits, more groups, a network that is countrywide, so we can work together and set up escape routes.'

'How am I supposed to do that?'

'Large oaks grow from small acorns, Raven. There's a bicycle in the shed. René here has an old Gestetner Cyclograph. He'll reproduce leaflets, calling for volunteers to join the fight. You can distribute them and pass on messages. I'll furnish you with false papers, courtesy of a contact in Nancy, but you'll need a legitimate reason to be on the road.'

Louise nodded. 'I have a store of first-aid materials and basic medicines – she could be a nurse visiting patients.'

'Aren't I a bit young for that?'

'You're not too young to be a volunteer, Raven, doing your bit in wartime by helping out. There are precious few ambulances or ambulance drivers, and anyone needing nursing care would be glad to see you. You can ride a bike?'

'I can. I left mine at the station in Narborough a lifetime ago. I'll do my best to recruit resistors.'

Louise nodded her approval. 'And you can ask about your father as you go. Someone must have seen him.'

She smiled back. 'Then I'll definitely go. I need to find him.'

The next day saw her attired in one of Louise's old black skirts with a white blouse, a black jacket and a black hat. She looked even more like a raven. Raphael hid a pile of leaflets beneath bandages, pills, and potions in a deep wicker basket on the handlebars, and the bicycle tyres were pumped up and checked for punctures.

'Be careful, Raven. And if you are captured, you say nothing. No one must know of any of our group or any of our contacts. Our lives depend upon it, just as yours depends upon us remaining silent under torture. You understand?'

She swallowed hard. Torture? The Nazis had shot Pépé and raped and murdered Mémé. Torture would come naturally to them. 'I understand.'

'And if you have to, shoot first – before they can.'

'Shoot?'

'Under the triangular bandages are a knife, your father's service revolver, and some ammunition. The knife is sharp, so handle it with care. The gun's loaded ready. Use it – on yourself if needs be.'

She nodded numbly, hugged Louise and Raphael, and mounted her bicycle. Heart in mouth, she pedalled along the lane and turned onto the road. She didn't look back.

# Chapter Seven

**Fresnes Prison, Paris, France. July 1940**

The military vehicle rumbled into the heart of Paris, its front-mounted machine-gun swivelling. Antoine looked ahead through a small window, trying to see where he was being taken. Lines of soldiers in green-brown uniforms marched along the streets. No one sat at the pavement cafés, some shop windows had anti-Jewish slogans daubed across them, and those civilians out and about either lurked in shop doorways or walked hurriedly, heads down, as if to avoid notice.

Huge Nazi banners draped walls, and German flags fluttered from streetlights in a desultory breeze. It was as if occupation had ripped the heart and soul from the city.

The driver turned into a street bordered by high stone walls. Behind them, red roofs topped rows of small blank windows. A sign read **Fresnes Penitentiaire**. The vehicle turned in beneath a narrow stone archway, and as the prison engulfed him, the doors closed on freedom. With an abundance of German guards on the journey, he'd had little hope of escape – he had none now.

He was bundled out of the vehicle, prodded in through a door, and handed to a German prison guard, who took him along passages, up several flights of stairs to a small cell, and thrust him roughly inside. The door clanged to with an air of finality, and the key turned in the lock.

He surveyed his surroundings. It was a dark room a little more than two paces across and three long. An iron bed stood along one wall, a small folding table was fixed to the opposite wall, and a cold-water tap, wash basin, and toilet occupied one corner. The tiny, high window was covered with steel mesh and the walls did nothing to dull the shouts of the other prisoners. Guards pounded on doors, yelling at the prisoners to be quiet, but it made no difference. This was to be his home until he was tried and executed.

He slumped onto the bed and held his thumping head in his hands. He must get a message to Bonnie. If he was to die here, she must get on with her life without him. Would they allow him to send a letter? At all costs, she must stay in England. He rubbed ineffectually at a headache and winced at the lump caused by a Nazi rifle. Suppose she'd come looking for him? She hadn't wanted to stay in England, and she was a determined girl, likely to do as she wanted and not what he told her. When he hadn't phoned or answered her calls…

He would write anyway, if he was allowed, and beg her to stay in Cosby. If he knew he'd done all he could to ensure she was safe, he would go to the guillotine with an easier mind.

The light was fading when his cell door opened and a guard banged a metal plate onto the table followed by a tin mug.

'Supper.' The man, French by his accent, turned to leave.

'Wait, please.'

The man turned back his eyes hostile. 'What?'

'I have a daughter in England. Her mother died. I'm all she has. I need to tell her where I am. I need to tell her to stay in England.'

The man shrugged.

'Can you get me paper and an envelope. I must write to her.' He fumbled for his wallet. 'I have money.'

'What did you do to be arrested?'

'I'm going to die, whether they think me guilty or innocent, so I may as well tell you. A Nazi shot my father and raped and murdered my mother. I stabbed him with a pitchfork.'

The guard huffed his disgust. 'I don't hold with rape, even the enemy. I don't have a daughter, but I have a mother. I'll get you your paper.'

'Thank you. My name is Antoine Renard. My daughter is Bonnie. She's only eighteen – still a child.'

'I'm Hugo. If you need anything, ask for me. Not all the guards here are sympathetic to the Germans. Most of us are Frenchmen after all, Antoine.'

'Thank you, Hugo. I shall go to my grave happier for knowing I wrote to her.' He pushed some franc notes towards the guard.

Hugo shook his head. 'That would be bribery, Antoine. I believe in a man being punished for committing a crime, and I uphold the law – French law.' Hugo was as good as his word and returned with paper, pen, and envelope.

It was hard to know what to write.

*My darling Bonnie,*

*I fear I have bad news. Your grandparents are dead, and I find myself in difficult circumstances.*

She didn't need to know the horrific details.

*I have been arrested and may not be able to see you again. If I don't return, please don't come looking for me. I want you to stay in England and make a life without me. France is not a safe place to be. If I survive, then when this war is over, I will return to England. I will find you.*

*I love you so much, Bonnie. Please respect my last wish for you and be happy.*

*Dad.*

He folded the letter and pushed it into the envelope. Hugo had promised to post it in the morning.

He lay back on his bed as the light went out and the cell was plunged into darkness. The voices around him deafened him. Staring into eternity, he prayed for the courage to face his death. Tomorrow could be his last day on earth.

\*\*\*

**Near Nancy, France. July 1940**

Bonnie pedalled along the road trying to ignore the loaded revolver in her basket burning a hole in her mind. Could she pull the trigger and take a life in cold blood? Could she turn it on herself if she was in danger of being captured?

She concentrated on the images she'd take with her to the grave; her grandparents' bodies and the German who Dad had stabbed with a pitchfork. She'd vowed to be prepared to sacrifice her life for France, and if she could kill one German soldier before she died, it could save other innocent victims.

The communes she'd visited so far had welcomed her. Her stack of leaflets, calling on them to resist the occupiers, had been met with enthusiasm. She hadn't divulged her group's location, but she'd made useful contacts and had given her name as Raven. Urging those she met to go out and recruit other people, to form more groups and spread the network across occupied France, she'd agreed mutual places to leave messages that they could visit when safe.

No one had seen her father, and thankfully, no one had required more than a bandage on a sprained wrist.

It was mid-afternoon when she came across the bodies.

She stopped, shocked, and leaned the bicycle against a tree. The road was deserted and there was no sound of approaching vehicles. Even so, she slipped her knife into the waistband of her skirt before kneeling to examine the first body. The cause of death was obvious, for when she rolled the body onto its back, there were bullet holes in the man's forehead.

It wasn't Dad. She let out a breath she hadn't realised she was holding. She needed to make sure none of the dead were Dad.

Someone had taken the time to move the bodies to the side of the road, the dark stains in the road showed they hadn't died by the ditch, so there must be survivors of whatever had happened. Most of the bodies had been shot in the back by what looked like machine-gun fire, as if they'd been mown down while running away.

There were women and children among the dead, even a baby. These had been refugees trying to escape into Vichy France.

Engrossed in her search for Dad, she didn't hear the sound of the motorcycle engine until it was too late. Her hand went to the hilt of her knife as she turned. The soldier got off his bike, removed his cap, and sauntered towards her. He obviously didn't consider her a threat.

He walked up and down looking at the bodies. 'Strafed by our glorious Lufftwaffe judging by the bullet marks in the tarmac. How did you escape unhurt?'

'I wasn't here.' She pointed to her bicycle. 'I'm visiting a sick woman in the next village. I'm bringing her medicine.'

He smiled. 'A good Samaritan.' He moved closer and nodded towards the trees. 'No one knows you are here?'

Her heart thudded, and she let her hand drop from the knife hilt. 'Not exactly where.'

'Then we have some fun, ja?'

'I don't expect I have a choice.'

He laughed. 'No. No choice at all if you wish to live. Come.'

She walked towards the trees, his breath hot on her neck. Beneath the canopy, she turned to face him and ran one hand down his chest, forcing an appreciative smile. 'You are a strong man, such muscles.'

The man puffed out his chest.

'If I am to lose my virginity, I'm glad it is to a virile man such as you.' She lowered her eyelashes. 'You will be gentle?'

His eyes narrowed, and a bulge appeared in his trousers. 'You will not forget your first sexual encounter, I assure you.'

He pulled her to him and planted his lips on hers. She fumbled at his belt buckle, her breath coming in short gasps. He twisted her hair between his fingers, holding her captive, and kissed her hard.

Tugging at his belt with one hand, she pulled her knife from her waistband with the other. Opening her lips to him, and closing her eyes, she plunged the knife into his stomach, ripping upwards as hard as she could.

Her mouth muffled his scream. She opened her eyes to see his startled blue ones staring at her in confusion. She pushed him away from her and pulled out her knife. He dropped to the ground and writhed, moaning and clutching his belly.

Intestines pushed between his fingers through the long tear in his trousers. She turned away and vomited.

He held out an impotent, pleading hand towards her, but she spat in his face. 'The only good Nazi is a dead Nazi.'

*** 

Bonnie left the man beneath the trees and walked back to the road. No one had seen her, and there was nothing to connect her to the murder. Murder... she'd left him alive, but without medical help, he wouldn't survive long. She was a murderer. The feeling of the knife ripping through flesh would haunt her. Her head swam, and she paused to steady herself and let her racing heart slow. No, it was the Nazis who were murderers and rapists – she was defending herself and her compatriots. What she had done was an act of war, but she needed to get away before someone came along and investigated the abandoned motorcycle.

There was nothing more she could do here, and she had work to do and Dad to find. She wiped her shaking hands and the blade of her knife on some grass, remounted her bicycle, and pedalled grimly on.

Ahead, the warm stone walls of medieval houses caught the late sun. Heavily laden carts stood abandoned in the village's main street. She half expected to see bodies strewn across the ground, but there was no sign of a struggle. Had they been captured and taken away?

She knocked on the door closest to the carts. A man's face appeared briefly at a window, bolts were drawn, and the door opened.

She held out one of her leaflets and explained her mission. The man held open the door and motioned her inside, bolting it behind them.

The small room was full of people. Some obviously injured.

'I'm Raven. I saw the bodies back there on the road. Are these people survivors of the attack?'

'Yes. A plane strafed them. Many have bullet wounds. The good doctor here is doing what he can for them.'

'I have bandages. My cover story is I'm a volunteer nurse, though I have no medical experience. You are welcome to what I have in my basket if it will help.'

The doctor didn't look up from his patient. 'Bandages will be very welcome.'

She fetched in what she had and helped the doctor wash and dress wounds.

He straightened and looked at her properly for the first time. 'You're bleeding? Let me see.'

She looked down at herself in horror. *Nothing to connect her to the murder?* Raphael's words cautioned her. *"Trust no one."* These were refugees fleeing south, and this doctor was helping them. Trust was a risk she had to take, and anyway, there was no point in lying – the doctor would discover the truth soon enough. 'It isn't my blood.'

'So, whose is it? Who needs help?'

'Back there on the road, where the bodies were, a German soldier wanted to rape me.'

'Has he hurt you, Raven?'

*Trust no one...* She took a deep breath and prayed she wasn't making a fatal error of judgement. 'No. I stabbed him in the stomach with this.' She drew her knife from her waistband and held it out. 'I think I've killed him.'

A young woman spat. 'Those Nazis killed my baby son. I hope the pig dies in agony.'

The doctor looked towards the window as if expecting imminent discovery. 'He very likely will. How long ago was this?'

'About an hour, maybe less.'

'If he hasn't bled out, the chances are he'll die from sepsis. There's nothing I can do for him.'

'You'd treat a German?'

'I took an oath, Raven. My calling is to uphold life. There are people here I *can* help.'

'Will you betray me to the Germans, Doctor? It was self-defence. He'd have raped me and probably shot me afterwards.' Her voice trembled – would he have? She hadn't actually said *no*, but he'd said she had no choice. 'German soldiers killed my grandparents. One raped my grandmother. What was I to do?'

The doctor shook his head. 'We live in difficult times. We must each do what we must, according to our consciences.'

The young mother got to her feet. 'She killed one of the enemy. I say Raven is a heroine of the resistance. She deserves our help.'

She nodded her thanks. 'I do need your help. As well as recruiting members for the resistance, I'm looking for my father. I have a photograph of him.' She handed it to the bereaved mother. 'Perhaps you could ask if anyone has seen him? His name is Antoine. He killed the German who raped my grandmother.'

The young woman nodded. 'Then he is a hero too. You parents' wedding day? Your father will look like this still?'

'He hasn't changed much. Please ask.'

A girl brought tea and a single slice of bread and cheese. 'It's not much. There are shortages.'

'Thank you. I'm very grateful. I haven't eaten since breakfast.' And she'd lost that vomiting. She pushed the vision of the German's guts from her mind and forced down the food.

A man approached. 'You are Raven?'

'Yes.'

'The photograph. This man, Antoine, was with us when we were attacked by the plane. He tried to help us.'

Her heart leapt. 'He wasn't among the dead on the road. He's alive? He's here?'

The man shook his head. 'He was captured by some Germans who came along later. They seemed to have been looking for him – they knew his name. They took him away – they drove west. I don't know where they were taking him, but your father was alive when I last saw him.'

Dad was alive! Her head swam with relief, the walls and ceiling seemed to fold in on her as the day's events caught up with her, and her vision went black. Strong hands caught her as she fell and helped her to a seat. She held her head in her hands while the room whirled around her. Dad was alive.

# Chapter Eight

**Fresnes Prison, Paris, France. August 1940**

Antoine cringed as the key turned in the lock and his cell door swung open. Please God, they hadn't come for him again. He'd spent what seemed like weeks in solitary confinement, barely allowed sleep, and had been fed a diet of bread and water that had left his guts in turmoil. He'd been interrogated, beaten, and sentenced to death.

'Come. Get a move on.' The German voice mocked him. 'Quickly, you lazy pig.'

The room whirled as he stood. Putting one foot in front of the other was an effort. He'd thought he'd be dead by now, shot or guillotined as others had been since he'd arrived at Fresnes, but the Nazis seemed determined to prolong his suffering. A rifle barrel in his spine forced him onwards to the truck that would take him to the interrogation room at Avenue Foch to be questioned by the Gestapo. How many more times?

At Avenue Foch, the guard motioned him to a chair and stood beside it. 'Sit.'

He sat, his legs too weak to hold him up any longer. 'I can't tell you anything.' Straps secured his wrists and feet, and a bright light flashed on, blinding him. 'I can't tell you what I don't know.'

A voice from behind the light, the owner invisible, shouted at him. 'You are an enemy of the Reich, Renard. We know you didn't act alone when you killed one of our men. You will die for that crime, but before you do, you will tell us what we want to know. You are a communist?'

'No.' The light burned his eyes. He closed them but it still burned his eyelids. Sweat beaded on his forehead.

'Tell us the names of those in your resistance circuit.'

'I acted alone. I don't know any names. Why won't you believe me?' Pain shot across his back.

'The names, Renard.'

'I don't know any names.' The whip lashed again, and he gritted his teeth against crying out. 'I'm not a member of the resistance. I attacked a man who was raping my mother.' His body spasmed and his back arched, while his teeth clamped tight shut. The electric prod was removed and he slumped forward gasping.

His interrogator sighed. 'You're a stubborn man, Renard, but you *will* tell us.'

Sweat ran into his eyes and down his cheeks. 'I don't know any names. Please…'

The chair tilted, and a hand grabbed his hair and yanked his head back. Cold water trickled down his face in a constant stream. He tried to breathe, and it went up his nose. Suffocating, he opened his mouth, and water flooded his mouth and choked him. He couldn't breathe. He was drowning.

'Who is the leader of your circuit?'

The chair tilted upright again, and he spat water and choked a lungful of air. 'Please, I'm not a member of a circuit.'

The chair tilted again and water poured. His lungs were bursting, he had to breathe – he was breathing water, choking, drowning.

'His name, Renard.'

The water stopped, and he coughed and spluttered, shivering now. 'I don't… know –'

'Who are your communist friends? Tell me and you can go back to your cell. You'd like to go back to your cell.'

'I'm not a… communist.'

'Jewish friends, then. You must know some filthy Jews.'

'I don't.' His face burned while his body shivered and his clothes steamed.

'Tell me about your freemason colleagues.'

'I'm not a freemason.'

'Their names, Renard.'

He struggled to concentrate and keep his voice steady. 'I don't know any Jews or communists or resistance members or freemasons. I've been living in England for years. I know hardly anyone in France.'

Invisible laughter mocked him. 'Our glorious Luftwaffe are blitzing London. Are you left or right-handed, Renard?'

He was past making sense of their questions.

'Right, I expect. Remove his little finger, Friedrich. Left hand.'

His left wrist was freed and placed on the table in front of him. His exhausted brain tried to see the danger and failed. What was happening? A sudden, intense pain shot through his hand.

Friedrich held up a bloody finger. 'Tomorrow we'll remove another, and the day after that, another. You get the picture, Renard?'

'Names, Renard. All we want is names of enemies of the Reich.' The invisible voice sighed again. 'You *will* talk, eventually. Take him back to Fresnes and let him reflect on his stubbornness, Friedrich. Tomorrow, Renard.'

***

**Near Nancy, France. August 1940**

Guts spilled across the road, blood spirted, soaking her, and someone screamed. Bonnie woke, sweating and shaking. The scream was hers. Where was she? 'Dad? Dad!'

'It's all right, Bonnie. You're safe here.' The voice was gentle and female.

'Mum?'

'No, it's Louise. You've had a nightmare, Bonnie.'

Reality imploded. Mum was dead, Dad had been captured by Nazis, her grandparents had been murdered, and France was at war. She'd killed a man, ripped his guts open. She closed her eyes and opened them again, praying it was all still a nightmare.

Louise brought her a drink of water and sat on the bed beside her. 'You've had an awful few weeks, Bonnie. Nightmares are to be expected, but you've done good work. You've helped the resistance movement spread. We have contacts in several circuits, and messages are getting through. We've had reports of Nazis persecuting Jews and communists, and of resistance members sabotaging German military equipment, and attacking Nazi soldiers. We've been able to pass on details of troop movements and strengths to London, and we've helped feed and hide several Jewish families and get them to safety. You should be proud.'

'I killed a man.'

'You killed an enemy of France. It was a strike for freedom.'

However she justified it to herself, the feel of the knife going into soft human flesh haunted her, waking and sleeping.

Louise turned on the radio. It was a distraction. London was being blitzed, but the RAF were having some success against the Luftwaffe and had bombed Berlin.

She forced herself to eat breakfast. 'I'll check on the message drops this morning. What messages do I have to pass on?'

'A map of German defences to the north of here and locations of buildings in Nancy occupied by German officers. Also, locations of new guard posts on the demarcation line. Our contact has a contact, who has access to a radio transmitter.'

No names, no locations. It was safer for everyone that way. What you didn't know, you couldn't give away under torture.

Her messages hidden beneath a new supply of bandages, some made from torn-up petticoats, she cycled south along a now familiar route. The bodies had been removed, rain had washed away the blood, and someone had taken the motorcycle. In the late August sunshine, it was as if war had never touched the Moselle valley.

A flurry of whirring wings startled her as pheasants took off and flew across the road in front of her. Something had made them take fright, and it was close enough to the message drop hidey-hole to make her nervous. Had someone discovered it? Were they lying in wait for her? She got off her bicycle. Surely, whoever was there would hear her heart thumping.

A fox trotted across the road, sniffed the air, and disappeared into undergrowth. She let out a held breath and cautiously continued to the message drop. The ruined barn was half-hidden by trees, almost sinking into the vegetation, the windows broken, the door hanging open.

The pheasants had alerted her to the possibility of danger. Pushing her cycle out of sight, she took the loaded revolver from her basket and walked cautiously through the doorway.

Inside was a dusty tin box hidden behind rotting musty hay. She opened it, took out the papers inside and deposited her maps and messages. With luck, the information would get to London and aid the Allies as well as other resistance members in the area.

A sneeze froze her to the spot. She swung around, clutching the precious papers, and pointed the revolver. 'I'm armed. Come out with your hands up.' If it was a German, she'd shoot first and ask questions later.

A dishevelled head appeared from behind a rotting haycart followed by another.

She swung the revolver between them. Why hadn't she just walked away and escaped while she could? Now she had two of them to deal with. Make that three, no four. She had six bullets loaded in the chambers – she'd shoot as many of the men as she could. 'Hands up. Keep them where I can see them.'

Four pairs of hands rose towards the ceiling. The first man took a step towards her, and she pressed her finger on the trigger.' Stop. Don't come any closer.'

'We're British. Don't shoot.'

'British?'

'We didn't get to Dunkirk in time to be evacuated. All of the coast is a forbidden area now, and there are German troops everywhere. It's impossible to get to the Channel coast, so we've been in hiding with various French families while making our way south. We're trying to get out of the occupied zone and back to England. Travelling at night without a guide, it's been slow progress.'

Their English was too good, their accent too British, to be Germans in disguise, and anyway, why would Germans need to hide in a ruined barn? She lowered her revolver. 'I'm Raven. I can take you to a safe house. You'll be fed and hidden while we work out what to do with you.'

The man held out a hand, but both hers were occupied. He dropped it to his side. 'I'm Charles.' He pointed to the other men in turn. 'This is John, Henry, and Roy. If you can help us, we'd be in your debt. We haven't eaten since yesterday.'

'Come with me. Keep your eyes and ears open, and take to the trees if you hear an engine. And keep quiet.'

They followed her like a litter of puppies at feeding time. Hiding the papers under her bandages, she pushed her bicycle back to the cottage that had become her home.

Louise welcomed them all with lunch and coffee, and for once, she was hungry. The British soldiers ate as if they'd been starved, and she was concerned about Louise's larder. Food was rationed in France as well as England. Germans took what they wanted and left little for the locals.

Raphael took the messages from her and sat at the table beside her to read them out.

'We're to meet a family of Jews at the drop barn tonight at eight o'clock. We're to hide them until tomorrow night when we'll receive further instructions.'

Louise looked around the already crowded table. 'We shall have a full house, Raphael.'

She voiced her own fear. 'How are we to feed them all, Louise?'

Louise smiled. 'It's only for one night, Raven. We'll manage. And these men need to move on too.'

Raphael put the letter aside and opened another envelope. '*The man you are looking for is thought to be in Fresnes prison in Paris.* This is about your father, Raven. It has to be.' He read on. '*There is a contact in the prison.*'

'What does that mean? A contact?'

'Someone in the prison is a resistance member. They know we're looking for Antoine. There is hope, Raven.'

Lunch over, and buoyed with hope, she helped Louise with the chores before sitting down with a coffee. She pulled the message about her father out of its envelope hoping to glean something more from it. Raphael hadn't read all of it out. '*The man, Antoine, is being tortured and has been sentenced to death. He has not revealed any names.*'

***

### Fresnes Prison, Paris, France. August 1940

Antoine lay on his bed shaking. Little warmth penetrated the cell through the small window, and he'd spent the night in wet clothes. His finger, or the stub that was left, pulsed agonisingly. Today, he would have to go through it all again. If there had been a way to take his own life during the night, he would have done it.

His cell door opened. No, not so soon. It was barely light. Hot tears stung his eyes and wet his cheeks. He couldn't take any more pain.

'A hot drink, Antoine, and a jacket.' Hugo helped him sit up. 'You look awful, my friend. Drink this. – I have good news. No more torture. The Gestapo have decided you know nothing.'

Hot coffee spilt on his leg. 'They're going to shoot me?'

'No, my friend. They're going to guillotine you.'

He was past caring but... 'That's good news?'

Hugo closed the cell door and sat beside him, helping steady his hand as he drank. 'I am to take you outside this morning to be executed. You must do exactly as I say. A message has reached me from a contact outside. Someone in the resistance is taking an interest in you. I am to take you by a different route and put you on the truck heading for the train going to one of the camps.'

He'd heard of the concentration camps, and none of it was good; few people returned from them. 'A slower death, Hugo?'

'Maybe not. I can't say more, but someone wants you alive. It seems you are a hero of the resistance.'

'For killing one German?'

'So it would seem. News of your exploits must have spread.' Hugo helped him into the jacket. 'It will be cold later. You'll be glad of this.'

He'd lost weight, and the coat was loose on him. 'Thank you, Hugo. Whatever happens to me, I am grateful for your kindness.'

'I must bind your wrists. Not too tight? Come, my friend. It is time. Look afraid.'

'That won't be difficult.'

Not many guards were out and about. The early morning sun glinted off the blade of the guillotine, poised to sever his head from his body, but instead of walking towards it, Hugo led him along a passageway towards the gate. A truck waited inside the compound and was being loaded with prisoners bound for the camp. Their chances of survival were slim, but at least he had a chance.

'Do not lose hope, Antoine. There will be help when you least expect it.' Hugo prodded him roughly with his rifle barrel and raised his voice. 'Up onto the truck, pig.'

He spat at Hugo's feet. 'Filthy collaborator. Rot in hell.'

Hugo winked as he turned away.

The truck pulled out of the prison and turned towards the station. He clung to Hugo's words. *"Do not lose hope."* He didn't know anyone much in France, apart from old Henri, his parents' neighbour, so who was trying to keep him alive?

# Chapter Nine

**Near Paris, France. August 1940**

Antoine was dragged across the platform with other prisoners and bundled into a windowless wagon. If Hugo's promised help was coming, it was too late.

The carriage juddered and swayed. He sat on the floor with his knees drawn up and his back against the wooden wall of the wagon. He'd done this journey east from Paris many times, but he'd never imagined riding the train in a cattle wagon to almost certain death. He tried to imagine the countryside he was travelling through – the fields, woods, and villages. The train would cross the Moselle somewhere between Metz and Nancy, or Nanzig as the Nazis now called it. And then? On towards Strasbourg and the border with Germany.

No one spoke, each lost in their own thoughts, as the train rumbled on. He rested his head on his knees and tried to sleep.

He was woken by a loud bang, a screeching of metal, and the wagon swaying violently. He was thrown across the floor and landed in a heap of tangled bodies. He lurched to his feet. 'What's going on?'

A man crawled to the side and peered through a gap in the wooden boards. 'I can't see much, only hills, trees, and smoke. Wait! There are people running about.'

The wagon door was flung open, and a man stood by the track holding a rifle. 'Out, all of you! Into the woods.'

He hung back, looking for any chance to escape. Nazis had been known to murder prisoners, and this was an isolated spot. Smoke wreathed, and flames leapt from derailed carriages. Had they survived just to be executed, their bodies left for the wild animals? No one would ever know. Bonnie would never know.

'Quickly. Into the forest before the guards arrive.'

'You're French?'

'Stop talking and listen. We're resistance members, and we're not letting the Nazis take any of you to Germany. Go!'

He jumped down, almost falling as his legs threatened to collapse beneath him. He helped an elderly man from the wagon and stumbled for cover. Another man with a rifle grabbed his arm. 'Wait here. We need to stay together, and there may be injured.'

He leaned against a tree, weak and panting. 'Where are we?'

'Not far from the border.'

'Where are going?'

'We have a camp up in the hills. You'll be taken there.'

'Is it far? I'm not sure I can walk. I haven't eaten...' He sank to the ground, unable to stand any longer.

'We'll get you there.' The man frowned. 'You are skin and bone, my friend. The Nazis starved you?'

'Starved and tortured.' He held out a hand with a missing finger. 'I'm Antoine. I'm grateful for your rescue.'

The man didn't divulge his name but stared at the half-healed stump. 'You're Antoine la Fourche?'

He looked up in confusion. 'Antoine Renard.'

'You are the man who stabbed a German with a pitchfork?'

'Yes.'

'Hence the name. Antoine the fork.'

He laughed despite the memory that haunted his nightmares. 'You know about me?'

'Your friend in Fresnes told us about you. He said you had a finger missing. We have an important job for you when you are recovered. Come, I think we are all here now. I'll help you walk.'

The man took his arm, supporting him as he stumbled through the undergrowth and deeper into the forest, walking ever higher into the hills. Wherever they were taking him, and whatever they had in mind for him, it had to be better than a slow death in a Nazi concentration camp.

*** 

## Near Nancy, France. September 1940

Bonnie nursed a cup of coffee. She'd tried to concentrate on the conversation going on around her, but her mind kept wandering. Dad was probably dead by now – executed by the Nazis for trying to protect Mémé.

'Raven?'

She looked up. 'What?'

Louise put a hand on hers. 'Raven, I know it's hard, but we must think of the future now. The future of France. These soldiers need to get back to England, so they can rejoin their units and continue the fight.'

'Sorry. I was thinking about Dad.'

'I know, ma chère. What do you think?'

'About what?'

'You speak French, English, and German, and you know France. You are the ideal person to guide these men to Spain.'

'Me?'

'Yes. You are young, healthy, and female. The Germans won't suspect a girl like you of running an escape route? Why would they?'

It still sounded dangerous, but with Dad gone, she had to use whatever time she had left, and she wanted to make her life count for something. She needed do this. 'How would we get there?'

Raphael tapped a map spread on the table. 'Escape routes have already been set up for soldiers and downed airmen. Most of the way would be by train, but there are places where you'd have to go on foot. Other resistance groups will be told you are coming and will be watching for escapees. I suspect the difficult part will be travelling over the Pyrenees and into Spain. Once over the border, British diplomats will get the men to Gibraltar, so they can be flown or shipped back to England. Our contact in Nancy will arrange false papers for you all.'

'It seems I've been volunteered.'

'You're the best person for the job, Raven.'

John, one of the soldiers, frowned. 'We are trusting our lives to a young girl?'

'She has proved herself, John.'

She nodded, acknowledging the compliment and the trust Louise and Raphael placed in her. 'When do we leave?'

'When we have the papers and money. You'll need money, Raven. I still have some funds, and Raphael is chopping and selling firewood for next winter, but we're hoping sympathetic local residents will help out until we can secure a more permanent supply of cash.'

'We'll also need cover stories. We won't get all the way to the border without being questioned. Life goes on in France, despite the war – people still need to work and travel where they can. We need reasons why we're travelling.'

One of the soldiers scratched his head. 'I used to be a car salesman. I could say I was collecting a new car for a wealthy customer.'

She unclipped a gold chain from around her neck and removed a gold ring with a small ruby set in it. She slipped the ring on her wedding finger. 'This was my mother's engagement ring. It's a bit loose, but I don't think it will fall off. I can claim to be the fiancé of any of these men as needs be. It would give us a reason to be travelling together and allow me to speak for them. I can teach them a few basic French phrases, so they appear French. They wouldn't necessarily be expected to understand German, and not all Germans will speak French.'

Raphael nodded. 'Get your cover stories straight, and I'll get a message to our man in Nancy. We need you out of here and on your way as soon as possible. Now I suggest you all get some sleep while I organise supplies. You'll each also need maps, and compasses, in case you get separated... warm clothes, stout shoes...' Raphael pushed back his chair and stood up. 'But first, I shall cycle into Nancy while it's dark.'

'We'll need weapons and ammunition, Raphael.'

'No. If you're searched, weapons are a giveaway. It will be dangerous, I know, but you'll be safer if you go unarmed. You must take nothing more than a small penknife. Anything you carry with you must match your cover story.'

She took a sip of cold coffee. Louise and Raphael were sending her south defenceless with four men she barely knew and who didn't trust her? Would they come to her aid if she needed them or save themselves?

If she was stopped by Nazis, she'd be like a lamb to the slaughter.

***

**Vosges Mountains, France. September 1940**

Antoine sat on a log by a small campfire in woodland about ten kilometres south of the railway tracks. Germans had been spotted searching the area for the terrorists who'd blown up the train, but he and his rescuers had evaded capture by taking to the hills. Three days of rest and good food had worked wonders, although he was still thin and the stub of his finger pained him.

The broad, auburn-haired, bearded man who'd rescued him from the train wreck had given his name as Florian, not his real name. Florian was looking at him appraisingly. 'We can't wait much longer, La Fourche.'

He'd been introduced to the rest of the group as La Fourche, and he hadn't challenged the name – as Florian had explained, anonymity was essential to avoid betrayal. He understood too well the lengths Nazi interrogators would go to for information. Florian knew he hadn't divulged any names under torture, Hugo had told him as much, but neither man knew that he hadn't known any names to divulge. Would he have betrayed his comrades? Would he have been strong enough to keep silent while they took off finger after finger?

Florian threw a stick onto the fire. 'If the resistance is to survive to fight against Hitler, we need weapons, lots of weapons, ammunition, explosives, and regular supplies – boots, clothing, soap, food, money, and radios. We need proper communications, and codes for various actions and places. We need more maps and support for escape routes – false papers. Thousands of people, Jews especially, are being persecuted. The resistance is doing what it can to get them to safety, but we can't do it alone.'

'I don't see what I can do to help.'

'We have a couple of maps with enemy positions and defences marked on them, plus buildings known to be used as barracks and administrative centres by the German occupying government, all of which would be of use to the Allies. Also, we've marked suitable drop zones for supplies and troops, and a couple of small landing strips in the hills to the south with map references., and we've listed some radio frequencies. We've given these places code names and have listed times when radios will be used for transmitting and receiving. In this envelope is a list of our requirements and where to send them. The drop zones will be attended nightly whenever the weather is suitable for low flying.'

He still didn't see where he came into this. 'And?'

'We want you to take them to London and put them into the hands of British Intelligence. You've lived in England, and you speak good English. Letters and telephone calls are intercepted here. We can't risk such information falling into Nazi hands. It would be a disaster. It would lead the Germans straight to us and destroy our group. They execute anyone showing anti-German attitudes, as you know too well. It would compromise everything we're trying to do.'

'I owe you my life. I suppose this is pay back.'

Florian smiled. 'It's why we took the trouble to rescue you. You came to the notice of the resistance, someone somewhere was looking for you, and when we learned about you from our Fresnes contact, we knew you were perfect for this task.'

'I suppose I can't refuse. How do I get to England? The coast is a prohibited zone, isn't it?'

'We'll take you south from here, keeping where we can to the mountains and the forests. We have a small vehicle, and we know the quiet roads, so not all the journey will have to be done on foot. We can take you down through the Vosges Mountains and guide you through the Jura Mountains towards Geneva. Then you must take a plane to London. We have to get you across the demarcation line into the southern zone. That will be the tricky part. It has checkpoints on all major roads and it's heavily guarded and patrolled.'

'I'll be able to fly from Geneva?'

'No. Switzerland have banned all flights from its soil.'

'So how do I fly?

'A short distance west of Geneva, near Nantua, there is a small field with light aircraft. There is a man who will be willing to take you, for a price. We'll give you money to pay him.'

'How far is Nantua from here?'

'About four hundred and fifty kilometres, at a guess. We'll have to do the last hundred kilometres or so on foot, because we're not going to try to take the vehicle far out of the mountains or that close to the line. It's too risky, and anyway, we only have so much petrol. When we reach more civilised areas, we may need to travel at night. French police in Vichy France collaborate with the Nazis. Don't think you'll be safer there than here. It could take a few days to get there. It will be October soon, and snow isn't unheard of in the Jura Mountains in October.'

'My daughter is in England, and I promised her I'd come home to her as soon as I could. The Nazis took my papers, her photograph – everything.'

'We'll get you new papers and permits – false ones if need be. I regret we can do nothing about the photograph.'

'I'm ready when you are.'

'Good man. We leave as soon as we have the money and the papers.'

He didn't need a false identity or cover story. He'd come to visit his parents, and now he wanted to go home to his daughter. He'd promised her he'd come home when the war was over, and he desperately needed to rest and recover. He'd done his bit for his country in the last war, hadn't he? Once he reached England, and Bonnie, his war *would* be over.

# Chapter Ten

**A train near Dijon, France. September 1940**

Bonnie looked at her reflection in the carriage window and picked imaginary dust from her long black coat. The garment had been donated by a fashionable lady, slim in her youth, but whose middle-age spread had stretched the buttonholes. It had a glamourous fur collar and fitted *Raven* perfectly. The stylish net hat matched it in colour, and along with some lipstick, the ensemble made her feel more elegant than she'd ever felt before.

It matched her cover story – she was recently engaged, and she and her fiancé, who she'd met while in Nancy, were travelling to share their good news with her parents in Perpignan, on the Golfe du Lion, not far from the Spanish border. They were to be married there, which was why three of her fiancé's closest friends were travelling with them. It had been a whirlwind wartime romance.

She fingered her sketchbook and pencil, taken along as part of a small selection of artists' materials to explain her having a large penknife in her handbag – pencils needed sharpening.

Pierre Dubois, Jaques Allard, Gaston Moreau, and Phillipe Boucher studied their false identity papers – she looked from one to another, trying to remember which of the British soldiers had taken which name, and which one she was to marry.

She opened the sketchbook and began drawing idly. She liked drawing people, so she began with her companions. Phillipe, at least she thought it was Phillipe, had a distinctive face.

According to her documents, she was Marie Barbier, aged nineteen and born in Perpignan. For her cover story, she'd stuck to what she knew; she worked for a hosiery company selling socks and stockings across France and had spent two months making contacts in and around Nancy, where she'd met... Pierre. Yes, it was Pierre she was to marry. Dressed in borrowed suits and with their uniforms and boots packed in canvas bags, they all looked very handsome.

Pierre – Charles – was the tallest one, and it was he she was drawing now. He was a striking man with a gentle manner and an engaging smile. a mass of dark hair, a stubble beard, startlingly blue eyes, and high cheekbones. He saw her glancing at him and then down to her drawing and smiled. She smiled back and held out a thumb to gauge proportions.

The seven-hundred-kilometre journey would take most of the day. The four men sat in silence, their faces showing the strain. She'd taught them some basic French words and phrases, but their accents were appalling. She'd told them to follow her lead and let her do the talking, but they were already bored and fidgeting. They'd never sit silent, doing nothing, all day.

On impulse, she tore pages from her sketchbook and handed them to the men along with pencils. Her idea was risky, but less risky than having them break silence. She leaned forward and kept her voice low. 'It's a game I played as a child, a sort of Chinese Whispers, but silent. You draw a small picture at the top of the page and pass it on. The next person writes what they think it is, folds over the picture so it can't be seen, and passes it to the next person. That person draws a picture of what the words represent, folds over the words, and so on. When the page is full, we see what the original picture ends up as.'

Pierre grinned and put his hand over hers in silent appreciation. His hand was warm, reassuring. She smiled, drew a mouse, and passed it to Pierre. His grin widened as he scribbled something on the paper. The picture Gaston passed to her looked like a Yorkshire pudding.

The game continued in silence until it was time to unfold the papers. She began to giggle. Pierre had written Marie underneath her drawing of a mouse, and Jacques' attempt at a likeness of her was hilarious and had been interpreted as a scarecrow. They were all laughing when a guard entered the carriage. She grabbed the papers and hid them – writing in English was a giveaway.

As the guard drew closer, checking papers, she gripped Pierre's hand. He leaned towards her and kissed her, and then drew away, leaving her flushed and breathless. 'Je t'aime, Marie.'

Her cheeks must be scarlet. It was a phrase she'd taught him, as part of their cover story, but... 'Je t'aime aussi, Pierre.' She rested her head on his shoulder – it was what a fiancée would do, wasn't it?

Pierre put an arm around her and kept it there while the guard checked their papers. He made her feel safer than she'd felt since she'd lost Dad. She trusted him instinctively.

She wished her cover story was true. Without Dad, and now separated from Louise and Raphael, she felt very alone. In another life, she'd have let herself get to know Pierre better, except she'd have to say goodbye to him in Spain and would likely never see him again.

The train rumbled on towards Dijon, which was close to the demarcation line between the northern occupied zone and Vichy France. Her heart thudded in time with the clackity-clack of the wheels going over the joins in the rails.

The engine slowed and stopped with a judder, and steam and black smoke drifted past the window. She peered forward through the glass. Ahead was a checkpoint with barriers, and it was crawling with German soldiers. Carriage doors banged open, and armed soldiers moved along the carriage checking papers.

She drew hers from her stylish handbag and held them ready for inspection, trying to stop her hands shaking. Pierre, Jaques, Fabien, and Phillipe clutched theirs in readiness. The forgeries were good, but she was worried about the Ausweis, the travel permits that allowed them over the line and into Vichy France. Raphael swore he couldn't tell they were forgeries, but Ausweis were notoriously hard to get hold of, and they had five.

If their stories weren't believed...

'Die Dokumente.'

Across the aisle, a man was dragged from his seat and marched from the train at gunpoint. She handed over her papers and swallowed hard. Would they have been better to try to cross the line on foot somewhere away from checkpoints, rather than brazen it out relying on her youth and innocence to get them past? It had been a mad scheme to begin with. They'd never get away with it.

The Nazi studied the documents minutely and stared at her. He tapped the Ausweis. 'Wohin gehst du?'

She tried to ignore the sweat beading on her brow and replied in German. It wasn't a language the men would necessarily be expected to understand. 'I'm going home to Perpignan with my fiancé and his friends. We're to be married there.' She reached out and squeezed Pierre's hand again. 'We met in Nancy last month.' She smiled up at the Nazi, her brightest and most engaging smile. 'We are so in love. It will be a wonderful wedding.' She showed the German her drawing of Pierre. 'Do you think it's a likeness? I can draw you if you like?'

He passed the documents back to her without a word and held out a hand for Pierre's. 'Deine Verlobte ist sehr schön.'

Pierre looked at her, and she nodded vigorously, smiling as she translated the German words to French. Pierre nodded and smiled too. 'Oui.' He'd remembered the French for yes if he hadn't understood a word of what she'd said.

The soldier perused the rest of the documents and continued along the aisle. He marched a family with young children from the carriage and slammed the door behind him. The train belched steam and smoke as it moved on, picking up speed. She let out a breath as the checkpoint and occupied France fell away behind them. Others hadn't been so lucky – what would become of them?

Pierre leaned towards her and whispered. 'What did the soldier say?'

She laughed, heady with relief. 'He said you have a very beautiful and talented fiancée, Pierre.'

Pierre smiled and kissed her again. 'I can't disagree with him, Marie.'

Her heart pounded, and not only from the relief of their present escape. She'd sworn she wouldn't allow herself to get emotionally involved with these men.

***

**Vosges Mountains, France. September 1940**

Antoine studied his papers. They were good copies of the originals, and with luck, he wouldn't need to show them until he reached the little airfield, or, if he could offer enough money to bribe the pilot, England.

He checked his waterproof pouch of vital information was secured beneath his coat, patted the pocket that held a borrowed knife, revolver, and ammunition, and counted out the cash before putting it into his wallet. He had no idea if it would be enough to get him to England, but his worry proved the point he must push with British Intelligence, that the resistance needed regular money and supplies if it was to be effective.

'Are you ready, La Fourche?' Florian nodded to the man beside him, who wore a beret at a jaunty angle. 'Renoir here will drive us as far as is safe, then we take to our feet. We can't risk going near a checkpoint.'

He raised an enquiring eyebrow. 'Renoir?'

Renoir laughed. 'They call me that because of the beret, and I like to paint. I don't have Renoir's talent, sadly.'

'Come.' Florian ushered them towards the door. 'We need to be on our way.'

The small car Florian had promised turned out to be a delivery truck laden with sacks of potatoes and coal to be distributed in the locality. It was good cover for being on the road.

The truck whined and grumbled and pulled away with a crunching of gears. Squeezed between Renoir and Florian, he stared through the windscreen into an anxious future. 'How far is the demarcation line, Florian?'

'I would think almost three hundred kilometres.'

'So we're in occupied France almost all the way?'

'Yes, and to make matters worse, Hitler has announced he's annexing the Moselle and settling the eastern part of France from Amiens down to Dole with Germans. Nancy is already overrun with the bastards.'

He shook his head in despair. Pretty villages, peaceful in a gentle landscape, would be taken over by the invaders; families who had farmed for generations would be turned out with nothing or murdered. And what of his parents' farm? It couldn't be allowed to happen. Somehow, he had to get through to England and get help for the patriots resisting the occupation.

Renoir seemed to know the area well; he took small roads, snaking up hills between trees and meadows, going ever higher into the mountains. The villages dropped away, and small farms and isolated houses took their place. Gaps in the trees showed bare hills rising above them and broad settled valleys far beneath them with glimpses of the Rhine sparkling in the autumn sun. It was a beautiful country – a country to die for.

Up there, high above civilisation, war seemed a world away. Why did men have to fight? There were no winners in war.

As they drove south, the landscape became softer, and villages more frequent. Renoir became visibly more agitated the lower they got. 'This is as far I go.' Renoir stopped the truck in woodland. 'I wish you luck, La Fourche.'

'I wish you luck, too, Renoir. Perhaps, when this war is over...' He let the thought hang. There was no guarantee any of them would live to see the end of the war, whoever claimed victory, and he had no intention of returning to France unless it was to settle his parents' affairs. He pushed away thoughts of Nazi victory and bones scattered by wild animals – loved ones he hadn't been able to bury.

Florian pushed open the door, grabbed his backpack from under the seat, and jumped down. 'I should see you in a few days, Renoir.'

*La Forche* followed. It was who he was now until he reached England. They watched Renoir reverse the truck and waved as he drove away. Ahead of them lay a long walk towards Dole and the demarcation line, and a longer walk through Vichy France to Nantua. He mentally checked his pack. Torch, compass, map, water, dried provisions, spare clothes. What had he forgotten? Plasters for blisters. It was too late now to worry.

He slung his backpack over his shoulders and walked on with Florian at his side. It would be dark soon, and they had a long way to go before it got light again. Ignoring the eight o'clock curfew was dangerous, but less dangerous than proceeding in daylight.

First light saw them approaching a small village. They'd walked through Dole by moonlight, and stopped to rest and eat by the church.

Florian paused and looked around. 'The line must be very close now. People will be up and about. We should find somewhere to sleep and cross it tonight.'

The growl of a heavy vehicle grew closer. 'Quick, ditch!'

The ditch proved to be half full of water. Florian growled louder than the coal lorry that had sped past. 'Not one of your better ideas, La Fourche.'

'I didn't know it wasn't a German military vehicle.' He shook cold muddy water out of a boot, grateful he wasn't drowning in it. 'You don't want to be interrogated by Nazis, Florian, believe me. This is nothing.'

'I do believe you, my friend. Now let's find somewhere to sleep, and hope we don't freeze to death.'

They opened the door of a farm outhouse and changed wet trousers and socks for dry ones. Slumped in a corner, he leaned back against the wall and tried to sleep, but sleep wouldn't come. Too much had happened in the year since war was declared, and too much depended on him getting back to England without being arrested.

"*You will talk, eventually.*" Whips lashed his back, electric prods made his spine arch, water filled his throat and nose and threatened to drown him. Agony speared through his hand as they cut off his finger. Mum lay on the barn floor, raped and riddled with bullets. Dad… he'd left without being certain his father was dead, and he'd had no chance to return to the farm. Bonnie was standing by the phone box waiting for a call that would never come. He thrust the pitchfork again and again into Nazi hearts and stomachs.

He woke, shivering and sweating. It was dark. Someone was moving about. 'Florian?'

'I couldn't sleep.' Florian handed him a water bottle. 'I've had a look around. There are Germans patrolling, so we must be close to the line. Come, it's time to try to cross it.'

# Chapter Eleven

**Vichy France, September 1940**

Antoine paused, straining to hear the slightest sound. In the dark, every rustle of a leaf seemed loud and threatening. Every whisper was like a shout. Rather than risk the road, which might well have a checkpoint, they'd taken a farm track, which according to his compass led south. Fields and hedgerows bordered it, and somewhere not far ahead of them was the demarcation line.

Florian had seen German patrols… They walked as silently as they could, trying not to scuff stones underfoot, barely daring to breathe.

A cloud obscured the moon, plunging them into total darkness. Just stars. They daren't risk a torch. A sudden rustle, and something shot across in front of him, brushing his legs. He clamped his lips on a scream. His heart hammered as if it would burst out of his chest. A fox or badger? Whatever it was it had gone. Florian breathed hard at his side but said nothing.

The cloud passed, and they moved on. Florian tapped his shoulder and pointed. Red and yellow posts were stuck at the sides of the track. The demarcation line. Florian indicated a gate into a field. He nodded; a roundabout route by hedgerows and gates would be safer than the track.

They climbed the gate rather than risk squeaking hinges, and took to the field. A beam of light played across the meadow – a patrol! They dived into the drainage ditch and laid low until the light moved on.

'Now's our chance, Florian.' His voice was a shaky whisper.

Florian nodded. 'Make for that gate. Run, and don't stop for anything, until you're sure we're well clear of the line.'

He took a deep breath and ran. Tussocks of grass tried to trip him, something slimy made his feet skid, and the gate seemed impossibly far away. A dark shape moved between him and freedom. A German patrol?

He skidded to a halt and reached for his revolver – no a shot would bring more Germans running. He felt the hilt of his knife and drew it silently from its sheath. The dark shape didn't move, moonlight glinted on the blade. He breathed a challenge. 'Come on, you bastard.'

Blade pointing forward, he moved slowly towards the shape.

'Moooooo.'

He laughed with relief and then clamped his lips shut. Suppose he'd been heard? Florian was by the gate waving urgently, and he ran to catch up.

'Come on, you idiot. Quickly before the patrol comes back.'

Over the gate and into the next field, they ran on. They kept running until their lungs were fit to burst and their legs were on the point of collapse.

Florian slumped to the ground by a hedge. 'I'm done.'

He sank down beside his friend, unable to speak, his legs like jelly. He finally found his breath. 'We made it, Florian.'

They stayed there under the hedge while the moon sank. Tomorrow they must begin the journey through Vichy France.

***

## Vichy France. September 1940

The train rattled on south on its journey down the Rhone valley. Bonnie strengthened a small line on her latest portrait of Pierre to capture his smile. She showed it to him, satisfied at last with her work, but wishing she had a blue crayon to colour his eyes. 'What do you think?'

'I think you've made me better looking than I am.'

'Nonsense.'

'Can I keep it to remind me of my beautiful, talented fiancée?'

She signed the portrait with a flourish, tore out the page, and handed it to him. 'Now I shall have to draw another to remind me of you.'

He smiled that kind, charming smile she'd taken such pains to capture. Lowering her eyes to her sketchpad to hide her embarrassment, she began to draw again. They would soon reach Marseille, where they would leave the train and find an address she'd committed to memory. Before making the onward journey to the Spanish border, they would be sheltered and fed there by members of the resistance who were part of the escape route.

Arriving in Marseille, she asked for directions to the street she sought. Red-roofed houses crowded the narrow streets, the market was busy, noisy, and dirty, most of the population seemed to be shopping or sitting at the pavement cafes, and hundreds of small boats bobbed at their moorings in the harbour. High above the bustle and hubbub stood the Basilica of Notre-Dame de la Garde, and behind the basilica, mountains rose against a clear blue sky.

War didn't seem to have touched Marseille.

They were welcomed by a middle-aged woman with copper hair who gave her name as Colette. 'Come in. You must be tired and famished. You can freshen up in there while I prepare some food.' She pointed to a door and bustled away.

It felt wonderful to wash away the grime of travel. Refreshed, she sat at a large table while Colette placed plate after plate of food in front of her. She'd never seen so much food.

'Please, don't wait. Help yourself.' Colette sat beside her and filled her own plate. 'You must stay a few days to rest. Marseille is wonderful this time of year and with luck, the British Consulate will give you identity papers that will allow you to leave France and enter Spain.' Collette grimaced. 'It may take some time. Since the British sank French ships at Mers-el-Kébir, there has been some unpleasantness – demonstrations, even the telephone line has been cut – the Americans have taken the building under their protection.' She gestured to Pierre and the other three Englishmen, who'd joined them, and swallowed a bite of bread roll. 'You'd be wise not to let any Frenchmen know you are English.'

She'd thought it would be easier once they were in the South of France. 'Is the journey over the Pyrenees difficult?'

Colette wiped her mouth with a napkin. 'You have two options. You can try to find someone to sail you down the coast to Gibraltar, or you can go over the mountains and hope to get through Spain.'

'You mean getting through Spain to Gibraltar isn't certain?'

Colette shrugged. 'The Spanish authorities are not as lax as the French. If you don't have the right papers...' She shrugged again. 'We have no control over Spanish immigration. The British Consulate in Spain will do their best to help, but you may have to insist on being taken to see them. Nothing is guaranteed. I'm sorry. It's the best we can do.'

Pierre cradled a glass of wine in his hands. 'Colette, we are grateful for everything you are doing. Please, don't apologise. We should try to find someone to sail us to Gibraltar. It sounds safer.' He smiled sadly. 'My only regret will be having to say farewell to Marie so soon.'

She could feel her cheeks flushing. 'Your safety is the important thing, Pierre, but I confess... I shall miss you.' More than she wanted to admit. It was never part of the plan for her to leave France, she was always going to have to bid her charges farewell, but somewhere between Nancy and Marseille, she'd fallen in love.

Next day, Colette accompanied them to the British Consulate, but it wasn't functioning. All they could do was give the men a certificate of identity under the American Consulate. It had an impressive seal but otherwise didn't look to be of much use.

They stopped at a pavement café, drank coffee, listened to the conversations going on around them, and watched the world go by. It was a welcome moment of normality.

She pricked up her ears and glanced across at Colette.

Pierre wouldn't understand what was being said, but Colette put down her cup. 'We must go. Now.' She explained as they walked. 'There's a rumour all officers and soldiers from the Seamen's Mission are to be taken to Fort St Jean by the police. It would be well if you left as soon as possible, in case your presence here is discovered.'

They hurried down to the harbour and spent a fruitless few hours trying to find someone to sail them to Gibraltar. According to one sailor, Vichy France had dropped tons of bombs on the island only a couple of nights before and no one was willing to sail anywhere near it.

'It looks like the mountains, then.' Pierre smiled. 'At least I shall have your company a little longer, Marie.'

She smiled back. She'd endure the dangers of the mountains to spend more precious days with him. 'We must pack for the journey and leave as soon as possible.'

Colette was all practicalities. 'We have supplies for the mountains packed ready for escapees. Come, we will have a farewell meal and see you onto the train to Cerbère.'

'Where is that?'

'It's south of Perpignan, close to the Spanish border.'

***

Bonnie took leave of Colette at the station, after promising to spend time with her on her return journey. The thought of travelling back alone was hard to bear, but Colette, as well as Louise and Raphael, would be anxiously awaiting her return.

The journey through the night had allowed them little sleep and had been broken by a wait to change trains at Narbonne. It was early morning, with the sun rising over the Mediterranean, before the train stopped at Perpignan.

A guard walked along the carriage. 'Papiers, s'il vous plaît.'

She handed over her papers and waited anxiously for their return. The guard looked at the American document and handed the papers back. If he'd approved hers, the men's should pass muster. She looked out the train window trying to appear nonchalant while the guard examined them. They were so close to the border; surely, they couldn't be turned back now?

Long heart-thudding moments dragged, but finally the guard moved on, and the train continued its journey down the coast to the border town of Cerbère. The closer they got, the higher the Pyrenees rose, mountain after mountain, stretching away for miles. Raphael had warned her getting over the Pyrenees might be the difficult part.

Pierre leaned towards her. 'That was easy.'

She raised an eyebrow. 'Easy? My nerves are shot. The sooner we get off this train the better – before you lot burst from keeping quiet.'

They left the train at the railway terminal at Cerbère.

Pierre waved at a sign. 'The tunnel is open. We could go under on the train.'

It had reopened after the Spanish civil war. 'I daren't risk it, Pierre. Colette said Spanish border guards are stricter than French ones. No, we either find a boat and someone to sail us to Gibraltar, or we go over, and you keep well clear of border posts, especially Spanish ones.'

Pierre looked crestfallen. 'Yes, miss.'

She laughed and slung her pack onto her back. Leaving the station, they walked to the harbour, but again, as at Marseille, no one was prepared to risk the voyage. With hours of precious daylight wasted, they walked towards the mountains. The road snaked up the hillside, but she daren't take it. A rough track zig-zagged up a rocky slope. She checked her compass and pointed. 'South is that way, so we'll head for that ridge.'

Pierre led the way. He stopped at the top of the hill. 'There are more ridges ahead. If we keep to the high ground where can, we should be able to see where we're going.'

The stony ground made walking on steep slopes, slow, treacherous, and exhausting, and by the time they'd gained the next ridge, the light was failing, there was no moon, and even the young soldiers had fallen silent.

She put her pack on the ground. 'It isn't safe to go on. We should stop and carry on at first light.'

First light was slow in coming. After a fitful sleep, she woke shivering. Pierre had his arm over her waist, and she lay still for a while, happy to be near him and wishing life was different. What was it Mum used to say? *If wishes were horses, beggars would ride.*

The wind had got up and the temperature had dropped. They needed to move before they froze to death. She shook Pierre's shoulder. 'Pierre, wake up.'

He grunted and looked at his watch. 'Five-thirty?'

'The sooner we get going the better. We need to cover some ground before it's fully light. We're getting closer to the border. According to Colette, there are border posts up here.'

'We need to eat.'

'Colette packed supplies. We can eat on the way.'

She took the lead now, the men following her like pet dogs. Her feet slipped and stumbled over the stony ground, but she plodded on, every step closer to losing the man she loved. Why was life so cruel?

The sun was rising as they reached the last ridge and looked down the mountain path and over Spain.

Pierre put a hand on her shoulder. 'We made it, Marie. Thanks to you, we made it. It's downhill all the way to freedom and Blighty.'

She turned towards him. 'This is as far as I go, Pierre.' A lump caught in her throat. 'This is goodbye.'

'Come with us, Marie.'

'I can't. Louise and Raphael are waiting for me, and I don't know if my father is alive or dead. I can't leave France until I know.'

He took her in his arms and kissed her, a tender, lingering kiss. 'I shall never forget you, Marie.'

'Nor me you, Pierre.'

'It's Charles, remember? My name is Charles.'

She wished she could tell him her real name, but too many people depended on her anonymity.

'I love you, Marie.'

'I love you too, Charles. I shall always love you.'

He kissed her again, and when he pulled away, his cheeks were wet with tears.

She wiped away her own. 'Stay safe, Charles.'

'And you, Marie.' Charles turned away and hurried down the slope followed by the others.

She stood and watched them dash down the hillside towards what looked like a farm. People were up and about already – a lot of people. The sound of a bugle tore the silence. Charles and the others had run straight into a Spanish border post. Men ushered the fugitives inside. Would they let them through or take them back to the French?

She slumped to the ground and waited, praying. After a while, Charles and the others came out and were escorted to a vehicle. He glanced up at the ridge before he was bundled into the vehicle and driven away south.

There was nothing more she could do. Clenching her fists impotently, she turned back towards France and let the wind whip away her tears. She'd lost him forever, and she would never love another man like she'd loved him.

# Chapter Twelve

## Vichy France, September 1940

Antoine woke stiff and cold. Someone was shaking him. He lashed out, yelling and kicking.

'It's all right, La Forche. It's me, Florian.'

He stopped fighting. 'Sorry.'

Florian rubbed a sore eye. 'You pack a punch, my friend.'

'Sorry.'

'Stop apologising. Just save your punches for Nazis.' Florian emptied his water bottle down his throat. 'We need to get going and find some water.'

They were well south of the demarcation line and heading for Nantua. It was hard walking. They followed small roads that wound along valleys at night and took to the hills at dawn, finding somewhere to sleep during daylight. The hills rose all around them, rocky and wooded, ridge after ridge that seemed to go on forever.

It was late afternoon. He stretched and rummaged in his pack for food. 'There's not much left. How far to Nantua?'

Florian walked to the edge of the steep ridge and pointed. 'It's down there.'

Below them, a long, narrow lake sparkled in the low sun. Cliffs rose from the lakeside into rugged hills, and small roads zig-zagged down to a town sitting at the lake's end. 'How the hell are we going to fly anything out of there?'

'There's a narrow strip of flat ground over there among the trees. It's tight, but it can be done.'

When he saw the field, he doubted a plane could take off at all. Florian was right when he said it would be tight.

Florian introduced him to the pilot, who was refuelling the plane for its next flight. 'Ghislain, this is La Forche. He needs to get to England, urgently.'

'Good luck with that.'

'I want you to take him.'

'To England? That's a suicide mission. Why do you think Switzerland have banned all flights out of the country, and even then, German fighters are shooting down planes in Swiss airspace.'

'It's important, Ghislain, and you'll be flying over France, not Germany or Switzerland.'

'Occupied France. And we'd need to refuel enroute. Fuel isn't easy to come by these days.'

'You've done the journey in peacetime. You have contacts.'

'What's so important I have to risk my neck and my plane?'

He interrupted the argument between Florian and Ghislain. 'We can pay you.'

'There's no amount of money will induce me to fly to England.'

'La Forche has papers vital to provisioning the resistance. They must be taken to British Intelligence if we're to help push the occupiers out of France, and he has volunteered to take them. He doesn't have wings, Ghislain. You do.' Florian put his hands on his hips. 'If you won't do it for money, do it for France! You think we haven't risked our lives coming here?'

Ghislain smiled bleakly. 'I will do it for France. How can I refuse to aid my country?' He patted the Lysander. 'Lyssie won't let us down.'

'When can you leave?'

'We'd have to fly at night, and for that we need a good moon and clear weather. Full moon isn't for another week, La Fourche.'

'A week?'

'The earliest would be the weekend, Sunday, preferably. Three days at best, and we'll have to pray the good weather holds.'

'If that's what it has to be.' Florian shrugged. 'C'est la vie, La Fourche.'

*La Fourche* wasn't altogether sorry for the delay. He'd barely stopped since his rescue from the train, and he was still weak and exhausted. 'I could do with a couple of days good sleep, Florian.'

Ghislain nodded. 'It will give me time to prepare the aircraft for a long mission, La Fourche. You'll need somewhere to stay. My wife will make you both welcome.'

Ghislain's wife made them more than welcome. After a bath, two nights in a comfortable bed, good food, and clean clothes, life began to feel more normal, but he was impatient to get back to England and Bonnie.

He helped Ghislain and Florian make changes to the Lysander. Ghislain, concerned about refuelling, and having to land at night to do it, had bolted a large long-range fuel tank to the outside of the fuselage. He didn't seem to think it would compromise the plane's handling.

Ghislain had also sourced a machine gun and ammunition – he wasn't intending to be shot down by enemy fire, or Allied fire for that matter.

Sunday dawned clear and fine, and they spent the day pre-oiling the nine-cylinder Mercury engine and greasing the rockers. It was a filthy job needing several gallons of oil that went everywhere. Then they walked the field for molehills or branches that might impede take-off. Ghislain estimated the flight would take about five hours depending on the wind and the moonlight; he'd plotted a course west of Paris, to avoid the occupied capital and keep well away from the border with Germany. They'd be flying low to avoid German radar, without lights and keeping radio silence.

With little light showing from the ground, especially over England, which had a countrywide blackout, they'd be flying blind.

Their last meal was eaten, the light was fading, and the moon, almost full now, hung low in the sky.

Ghislain wiped his mouth with a napkin and pushed back his chair. 'It's time. Come.'

He and Ghislain shrugged into warm jackets and walked out into the moonlight. He still wasn't convinced the plane could clear the trees in the short take-off distance, especially in the dark, but Ghislain seemed confident.

Florian hugged Ghislain and then him. 'Good luck, La Fourche. I hope we shall meet again.'

'Good luck to you too, Florian. Stay safe, my friend.'

They climbed up the wing struts and into the Lysander and slid the canopy forward to close it. Ghislain, in the front seat, primed the carburettor bowl and cylinders, and started the engine. It burst into life, and the propellers began to turn slowly. The engine backfiring, they taxied over the bumpy ground to the far end of the field, so the wind would be behind them when they turned. The trees at the other end seemed far too close. The Lysander gathered speed, jolting and bouncing until its wheels left the ground, and its wings skimmed the treetops.

He held his breath as the fixed undercarriage brushed the branches, and then they were clear. Beneath him, the moon reflected in the lake, above him stars twinkled, and ahead lay blackness, and in the blackness the enemy waited.

It was cold. He was now completely in Ghislain's hands. In the dark, he had no idea of direction or altitude, and with towns and cities blacked out, there was little to indicate either. With radio silence agreed unless in an emergency, he was alone with his thoughts.

Time dragged, and the moon arced overhead. His eyes hurt from straining into the dark to spot enemy aircraft or anti-aircraft guns, and the constant throb of the engine made his head ache. The odd glint of moonlight on water suggested crossing a river, but he had no idea which river. He gripped the machine gun and prayed he wouldn't need to fire it.

At last, the moon rippled on a larger stretch of water. The English Channel? They were flying so low, he could make out the shapes of boats. The plane banked to the right.

The radio suddenly crackled in his headphones. 'This is French Lysander Nantua One approaching England. Repeat, this is French Lysander Nantua One approaching England.' Ghislain gave his position and altitude. 'Request permission to enter British airspace. Over.'

There was a brief silence then a crackling. 'Lysander Nantua One, this is RAF Shoreham. You are heading directly into the flight path of a squadron of incoming Luftwaffe. Bear northwest.' The radio operator gave a heading.

'RAF Shoreham, message received. Lysander Nantua One bearing northwest.' The plane banked again. 'Request permission to land soonest, fuel low, but heading for London. Errand urgent. Over.'

'Received and understood, Nantua One. Once you're safely out of the battle zone, I'll talk you in. Stand by for instructions. Over.'

'Roger, Shoreham. Thank you. Nantua One over and out.'

He craned to see in the pre-dawn light. Flak traces arced across the sky to the east. A sudden flash of light meant a plane had been hit and was diving towards the ocean. British or German? Whoever, he was someone's son.

'Messerschmitt above us at four o'clock, La Fourche.' Ghislain's voice. Ghislain climbed and then turned and side-slipped the Lysander.

A blast of cold air hit him as he slid back the side window and held the machine gun as steady as he could, finger on the trigger. Despite Ghislain's evasive action, the Messerschmitt was heading straight for them. The Lysander banked slightly; he felt a jolt, and petrol sprayed his face. They'd been hit – it was kill or die. He aimed for the Messerschmitt's cockpit and squeezed the trigger. Shots stuttered. He kept his finger on the trigger, spraying round after round, and the Messerschmitt fell away, spiralling downwards.

'One to us.' Ghislain sounded triumphant.

'One is enough. We're leaking fuel, Ghislain. Get us out of here.'

As the sun rose over the Channel, they crossed the coast, and as promised, Shoreham guided them down onto their airfield. The engine spluttered and coughed as the wheels touched down. They'd reached England.

***

Antoine loosened his grip on the machine gun and jumped down onto English soil as Ghislain brought the Lysander to a halt. Next, London, and then home to Cosby and Bonnie.

An air force truck sped towards them across the concrete. Two airmen got out and pointed rifles at them.

He raised his hands. It wasn't the welcome he'd been expecting, but then the British didn't know his mission. 'I'm Antoine Renard, a member of the French resistance. I have documents and information I need to take urgently to British Intelligence in London. This is Ghislain… a Frenchman from Nantua, Vichy France. He risked his life to bring me here.'

The older of the two airmen lowered his rifle slightly. 'The Commanding Officer wishes to speak to you. This way, please, gentlemen.'

The Commanding Officer welcomed them, but he didn't dismiss the airmen with the rifles. 'Sit, please, gentlemen. What is so urgent about this mission, Monsieur Renard?'

He unstrapped the pouch from around his waist and placed it on the desk in front of him. 'This contains maps, co-ordinates, codes, locations of resistance groups, drop zones, and landing strips. I was tasked with bringing it to British Intelligence. The resistance urgently needs supplies, weapons, radios, explosives, money… Every day I delay costs lives.'

The Commanding Officer reached out to touch the pouch and then withdrew it. 'You have papers to prove who you are?'

'My papers were taken when I was captured back in July. The resistance aided my escape and made me new documents especially for this mission. They say who I am, but they're not genuine. I *am* Antoine Renard. I live in Leicestershire with my daughter, and was caught up in the war while visiting my parents near Nancy. I dare say you are wearing a pair of my socks.'

The Commanding Officer looked down at his feet. 'I beg your pardon?'

'I run a hosiery and knitwear distribution company. We supply socks to the armed forces, here and in France.'

The man smiled and then frowned. 'They are very good socks, but I can't let you loose without proper papers. However, I will detail a car, driver, and armed guard to take you to the British Intelligence HQ.' He looked across at the airman. 'I shall telephone ahead to let them know you are coming. Flight Sergeant Jones, arrange a car, please.'

'Yes, sir.' The airman saluted and left.

'Thank you, sir. I appreciate your assistance. France will be in your debt.'

The man waved away his thanks. 'Sergeant Johnson will escort you.'

'One thing, sir. Our Lysander was strafed by a Messerschmitt. We have a leaking fuel tank.'

'I'll see it's repaired and refuelled. Good luck, Renard.'

'Thank you, sir. If I could just say goodbye to Ghislain?'

'Of course.'

Ghislain was standing by his plane looking anxious. 'The fuel tank's like a colander. It's a miracle you weren't killed by flak. Another miracle we got here in one piece.'

'The camp commander has promised to fix it and refuel you for the return journey. Stay safe, Ghislain.'

'I'm not going back, not yet. They need Lysanders to drop inflatable dinghies to downed airmen in the Channel. I'm going to hang around for a while and help out. Then, I shall volunteer Lyssie for resistance work. France needs us, La Fourche.'

Guilt consumed him. 'My conscience won't let me stay in England with Bonnie, will it? However much I want to.'

'You've been through a lot, my friend. You must take time to heal, and you need to spend time with your daughter. You will do what is right for Bonnie *and* France, of that I am confident.' Ghislain hugged him. 'Look after yourself, La Fourche.'

'And you, Ghislain.'

He turned away, a lump in his throat, and accompanied his guard to the car. He had unfinished business in France, but it would have to wait. Bonnie came first.

# Chapter Thirteen

## Near Nancy, France. September 1940

Bonnie had thrown herself into her resistance work with a vengeance – anything to stop her thinking about Pierre. His name might be Charles, but he'd always be Pierre to her – it was Pierre she'd fallen in love with. She had to believe he would get back to England and his unit. She had to believe he was still fighting against the Nazis who were raping her country and its women.

She'd spent a night with Colette in Marseille before travelling back to Louise and Raphael. Goodbyes seemed to be getting more and more painful, for there was no telling if she'd see any of her friends again once she'd bid them farewell.

'Penny for them, Raven?' Raphael looked at her quizzically.

She smiled ruefully. 'Sorry. I was miles away. You were saying?'

'Sabotage, Raven.' Raphael broke a chunk from a bread roll and mopped his plate with it. 'I want you to distract a German guard, while I sabotage something.'

'Sabotage what?'

'Best you don't know. What you don't know you can't tell.'

She put down her spoon. 'You think I'd betray you, Raphael?'

'No, not intentionally, but the less everyone knows the better, for all our sakes.'

'When?'

'Soon, but first, I need to know you can protect yourself.'

'I killed a German.'

'I know. You can blind a man by sticking your fingers in his eyes. A foot or knee in the testicles will disable him long enough for you to get away, and if you can bring a knife into play, do it. A stab to the belly or neck is easier than trying to get a knife between ribs, but all will kill.' He rubbed his ear. 'The main thing is not to hesitate. If you feel in danger, go in fast and hard. You may only get one chance, and yours might not be the only life depending on it.'

'I understand.'

'Good. Eat up. We go in half an hour.'

Her part of the plan involved cycling towards Nancy. Raphael had described a farm, and had given her directions. She didn't know all the roads in the area, but it sounded as if it was close to her grandparents' farm. Anger and loss drove her on. Her knife was in a sheath attached to her belt, and much as the thought of killing sickened her, the deaths of all the Nazis in Nancy wouldn't avenge her grandparents' murders.

She pedalled harder to be at the farm at the right time. It was guarded for some reason, and she had seduction in mind.

The Nazis had to be stopped and any small thing she could do to resist them, she would do. The Vichy government's Sipo-SD branch was targeting "enemies of the Reich", mainly Jews, freemasons, and Communists, who they blamed for France's defeat. In Warsaw, Jews were being moved into ghettos, and in France, Jews were losing their civil rights and having their property and businesses expropriated. Collaborators were no better than Nazis; they were denouncing Jews and Communists, who were being arrested and imprisoned. All across France, those threatened were attempting to flee to safety – like Pierre.

She forced her mind back to the task at hand and pedalled on. Right after two miles and then second left and take a farm track on the right.

She passed a motorcycle and truck parked by the side of the road. Two men were standing by them. One raised a hand in greeting as she went past. Raphael was waiting for her. The sound of engines starting showed they were following. They would stop a hundred metres away and give her time to carry out her mission.

She knew this road. The next farm track to the right led to her grandparent's farm. Her heart thudded. She'd left their bodies covered by blankets. Who knew what she would find now?

A military truck loaded with metal drums stood in the centre of a yard overgrown with weeds. More drums were standing nearby. A fuel dump? One guard, or two? She swallowed and kept her eyes firmly on the truck. Leaning her cycle against the fence, she walked forward. She was here to disable a guard not cry over those she'd lost.

A German in uniform appeared around the corner of the barn. He was a young man, not much older than she was, and he was holding a rifle. 'Halt, der Zutritt ist verboten.'

All thoughts of seduction fled. 'Forbidden? This is my grandparent's farm.'

'This is a forbidden area. You must leave, now.'

She attempted to collect her wits and softened her tone. 'Please, I need to see my grandparents.'

'There is no one here.'

'But where are my grandparents?' She didn't have to fake tears. 'Are they in the house?'

The youth looked around him. 'It's just me and Carl.'

So, there were two of them. She walked closer. 'I'm Marie. Who are you? Do you know where my grandparents went?'

'I'm Gunter. No, I'm sorry, Marie.'

'I bet you do know. I bet you'd tell me for a kiss.'

She could almost see him weighing orders against opportunity. He pulled her around the corner of the barn out of sight of the house. So the other man was in the farmhouse? He leaned in for a kiss, and she loosened her knife from its sheath.

Parting her lips and pressing herself against him, she put her arms around his neck and then sliced the blade hard across the side of his neck. Blood spurted. She hadn't reckoned on so much blood.

She let the youth's body slump to the ground. All he'd wanted was a kiss. The sound of a motorcycle roused her from her nausea. Raphael... There was still a man in the house. She ran across the yard and hammered on the farmhouse door. 'Help! Help!'

The door opened to an older German soldier, whose eyes opened wide at the sight of the blood.

She held the knife behind her hip. 'Help me, please.'

The German hesitated a moment too long. "*Go in hard and fast.*" She brought her arm forward, blade edge upwards and stabbed into his belly, ripping up towards his ribs. The man's guts spilled as he fell. She stood in the doorway, a dead German at her feet, weeping.

'Raven?' Raphael put a gentle hand on her shoulder. 'It has to be done, Raven.'

She shook her head, grief and anger fighting guilt. 'It's not the German. This is my grandparent's farm. Pépé was here on the floor, dead... I left Mémé in the barn. She was dead too.'

'I'm so sorry, Raven. I wouldn't have asked you to come had I known. Jean and I will come back and look for the bodies and bury them for you, but it will have to wait until it's safe. First, let's do what we came for. Let them not have died for nothing.'

She followed him outside. Jean had rolled several of the drums towards their borrowed truck, and he and Raphael loaded it with as many as it could carry.

'What about the rest, Jean? Do we risk coming back for them?'

'No, and I'm not leaving them for the Germans.' Jean tipped over a drum and leaked liquid across the ground. It stank of petrol.

Raphael took a hand grenade from a bag. 'Raven, get the hell out of here. When this goes up, the place will be crawling with Nazis in no time.' He looked her up and down and removed his jacket. 'If they see you covered in blood, they'll arrest you for sure. Put this on.'

She was glad of the warmth. The aftershock of murder had her shivering.

Raphael buttoned the jacket for her, because her fingers were shaking so much. 'You did well, Raven.' He put his finger through the ring on the hand-grenade pin. 'Go, Raven!'

She turned and ran to her cycle as a bright flash lit the yard. Engines burst into life behind her as she pedalled furiously away. Explosion after explosion followed her, but she didn't look back.

\*\*\*

**London, England. September 1940**

Bombed-out buildings stood as stark reminders of Nazi might, streets were filled with rubble, and people picked among it looking for food, possessions, and loved ones. Britain was paying a high price for going to Europe's aid.

The Secret Intelligence Services building on Broadway, near St James Park, towered over Antoine. A brass plaque read **Minimax Fire Extinguisher Company**, and Sergeant Johnson, failing to look convincing as a civilian, marched him into the building. A woman on the reception desk made a hurried phone call, and armed guards arrived and demanded their business.

Sergeant Johnson answered for them both. 'Sergeant John Johnson from RAF Shoreham escorting Monsieur Antoine Renard. You are expecting us. My Commanding Officer telephoned ahead.'

'An intelligence office is waiting to interrogate you, Renard. I'll escort you.'

They accompanied the guard down a dingy passage past small rooms separated by wooden partitions with frosted-glass windows. At the end of the corridor was an ancient lift that took them up to the floor above. Signs read **No Unauthorised Access**.

The guard knocked on a door and a small grill opened. 'Yes?'

'Monsieur Antoine Renard. He is expected.'

The door lock clicked and the door swung inwards. The guard ushered him through.

A man stood and held out a hand in greeting but didn't give his name. 'Monsieur, take a seat, please.' He waved the guard and Sergeant Johnson away. 'Wait outside, please.'

'Thank you for seeing me, sir.' He waited until the door closed before unfastening the pouch of documents from around his waist. 'I have information from the resistance in the Vosges area of France, and requests for aid for the resistance movement. It's all in here.'

The man opened the pouch and spread the contents across his desk. He lifted the telephone receiver and pressed a button. 'Tea or coffee, Monsieur?'

'Coffee, thank you.'

'Two coffees, if you would, Julia, and leave them by the door.' The man studied the reports and maps in silence. A knock at the door made him put down a map. He got to his feet and limped across the room, returning with a tray with two coffees. 'An old war wound. I'm confined to a desk job now.'

'There are all kinds of valuable service, sir.' He took the offered coffee and shook his head at sugar. 'You can see how much the resistance needs weapons, money, and supplies if we're to expand the network. We can do so much – sabotage, mapping enemy positions, leaking Nazi secrets... some of our young women are fearless in seduction.' He left the implication hanging. 'The codes suggested, drop zones, airstrips – with codes and radios, you could get spies and supplies in and out at night using Lysanders. It's how I got here.'

The silence continued. The clock on the wall ticked with ominous lethargy – his heart was beating faster – a lot depended on the outcome of this meeting. The remains of his coffee had gone cold by the time the man spoke again.

'Renard, you would be a valuable addition to the S.I.S. When you go back to France, you could report directly to us via radio and coded messages. We can fly you in at night, using a Lysander, as you suggest.'

'I'm not going back, sir, or not yet. I need to spend some time with my daughter, in Leicestershire. It's where we live.'

'We need to contact your resistance group, Renard, if we're to provide this support.'

'Then you'll need this.' He brought a small envelope from his breast pocket. 'You broadcast this message via the BBC radio at seven o'clock next Saturday evening.'

'And what does it mean?'

'It means that you have received and understood the codes, and that future coded messages will be broadcast by this method at the times it states the resistance radios will be monitored. Basically, it sets up a system of communication.'

'You seem to have thought this through. Very well.' The man stood and reached out a hand to shake his. 'I'm sorry we can't recruit you for the S.I.S. I wish you well, Renard.'

'Thank you, sir. Just one thing. I need to get home, and I have no English money on me.'

The man opened his wallet and gave him a ten-pound note. 'Take it. I can claim it back on expenses.'

'Thank you, sir.' Dismissed, he walked to the door. 'Can you call off my guard dogs?'

'Yes, of course.' The man pushed open the door. 'See Monsieur Renard to the front door, and then your duty is finished. Sergeant, you may return to RAF Shoreham.'

The London air smelled of smoke and petrol fumes, but he breathed it in with a sense of relief. The underground was close by. He hurried down the steps to catch a train to Kings Cross. In a couple of hours or so, he could be home. He couldn't wait to see Bonnie and give her the biggest hug of her life.

# Chapter Fourteen

**Cosby, Leicestershire, England. September 1940**

Yellow leaves drifting from sycamore trees and a bite in the air showed September was already half spent – a bright day, but a foretelling of winter to come. Few people alighted the train at Narborough, and no one was waiting to board. The station seemed eerily quiet.

He breathed in the autumnal smells that mingled with the coal smoke and grease. Damp earth, rotting leaves – God, it was good to be home.

His shoulders relaxed, and he walked out of the station with little more than the clothes he stood up in; to compensate for the weight of the extra fuel, they'd brought little luggage in the Lysander. As there wouldn't be a bus for half an hour, he decided to walk. It was a pity he hadn't left his bicycle at the station when he'd departed for France, but having had luggage, he'd taken the bus from Cosby. There were several cycles in the station yard, securely chained. Bonnie had one just like the blue one.

He couldn't wait to see her. The poor girl must be worried stiff, and he hadn't been able to make the seven o'clock call to the phone box once since he'd left the farm. Had she stood there night after night, anxiously waiting for a call? How many times had she telephoned and got no answer? He was her father, and it was his job to protect her, not desert her. Already, he was torn between staying with Bonnie in England and doing his duty for France. 'Oh, Bonnie, I'll make it up to you, ma chère.'

Leaves bobbed along the brook and carpeted the road with gold. The village seemed different, smaller, quieter. The young men had probably gone to war, and there was an air of watchfulness. Perhaps it was just his imagination seeing Nazis around every corner.

The cottage door was locked, so Bonnie must be at work or shopping. The key was under the flowerpot by the front door, as always, but the plant looked deader than September should make it. Perhaps they'd had an early frost.

He unlocked the door and pushed it open, picking up some post from the doormat. It seemed war didn't stop bills arriving. The house smelled musty, but then he always noticed it when he'd been away for a while. He put the post on the table and made for the kitchen. He needed a cup of English tea and a biscuit if they weren't rationed.

The larder was empty. He frowned. No milk, no biscuits, no cheese in the cheese dish, no bread in the bread bin. Had Bonnie run out of money or was everything on a strict ration? He turned back into the living room, only now noticing how cold the house was. He'd told her to order coal… He should never have left her alone – it was obvious she wasn't coping without him.

He patted his pockets aware he had little money. Mrs Sibson would let him have credit if he hadn't enough, but he needed to restock the larder. He hurried along to the shop.

Mrs Sibson looked at him as if she didn't recognise him and then greeted him warmly. 'Glad to see you home safe, Mr Renard. Has your Bonnie come back with you?'

'Come back? What do you mean?'

'Well, I haven't seen the child for months. I assumed she was with you in France.'

His heart hammered. 'No. I haven't seen her since I left when war broke out. She should be here.'

'Oh well. I'm sure she's all right. She's a sensible girl. She was lonely though, without you. Perhaps she went to stay with relatives?'

'We don't have relatives in England. If she went to her grandparents in…' Dear God, she'd have found them slaughtered. 'No, she wouldn't have done that. I told her to stay in England.' Yet he knew how headstrong she could be. He tried to think, and he wasn't doing a good job of it on an empty stomach and a sleepless night. 'Milk, bread, butter, and cheese, please Mrs Sibson. And a packet of tea. I can survive on that for now.'

The shopkeeper put the items on the counter and totted up the total. 'Your ration book?'

'I've only just got back. I haven't got one yet.'

'It'll be in the post. I trust you to bring it in.'

'Thank you. You're a diamond, Mrs Sibson. I haven't checked the post yet.' He paid and turned to leave.

'She'll be quite safe somewhere, you'll see, Mr Renard.'

'I'm sure you're right, Mrs Sibson.' He hurried back to the cottage. Her passport wasn't in its usual place. How long had Bonnie been gone? He opened the post. Unpaid bills and final demands, and one ration book that was still valid. He recognised the handwriting on one envelope; it was the letter he'd sent to her back in July from Fresnes Prison, the one begging her to stay in England and not come looking for him. She'd been gone since July? If she'd gone to the farm and found her grandparents' bodies, surely she'd have come home. Where was she, and how the hell would he find her now?

He sank onto a chair more worried than angry. 'Oh, Bonnie. We could have both been safe here in England now if you'd stayed.'

He dragged his feet into the kitchen. He needed to eat, he needed a warm fire, and he must sleep. Tomorrow, he would decide what to do.

*** 

Despite his worry, Antoine slept for eight straight hours. The night flying under enemy skies had taken its toll on him mentally and physically when he still hadn't recovered from his imprisonment and torture and the trek to Nantua. His reflection in the mirror showed the ravages the past months had caused. He was greyer, thinner – gaunt almost. He barely recognised himself – it was no wonder Mrs Sibson had looked at him strangely.

He poked the cinders in the hearth, added small sticks to revive the fire, and toasted some bread while the kettle boiled. If Bonnie was in France, then he had to get back there and find her. Getting into occupied France wasn't as easy as it sounded. He'd need papers he hadn't got, and it all took time. He could wait weeks and then fail to get past border guards.

He buttered the toast and took a bite. He should check in with Yvonne and Rosemary and see if he still had a business. Hope flooded through him. Bonnie could be with them. One of them would have taken her in if she'd asked. He gulped his tea and fetched his cycle from the shed.

The small premises he used for his business was in the next village. Yvonne was packing a huge box. It seemed business was booming.

Her face lit with a smile. 'Antoine! You're back. We've missed you.'

He hugged her, kissing her cheeks in the French fashion and making her blush. 'How are you? How's Rosemary?'

'We're well and glad to have work.'

'Have you seen Bonnie?'

'No. She hasn't been near. I've called on her a few times but there was no one home.'

'I think she's gone to France looking for me. Thank you for holding the fort for so long. You have many orders?'

'Enough. It's steady. This order's for the British army. We asked for extra smooth toe seams to make them comfortable for our lads.'

He picked up a pair and examined them. 'Did they cost more?'

'No. The manufacturer said nothing was too good for our boys.'

'And nothing is too bad for the Germans.' An idea formed. 'Small acts of resistance. Yvonne, when Hitler forced Citroën to made trucks for the German army, the boss of Citroën called a go-slow to hold up production.' According to Florian, whose brother worked at the plant, the boss then had the idea of putting special dipsticks in the trucks bound for Hitler's troops. He'd lowered the low-oil mark on them, so the engines ran out of oil and seized. Florian's brother shouldn't have divulged that information, and if he was to work for the S.IS, he couldn't divulge it either, however much he trusted Yvonne. 'If Citroën can sabotage Hitler's trucks, we can do it to his soldiers, but we have to keep this between ourselves and our supplier.'

'I don't understand.'

'I have a contact in the German army requisition department – we used to supply them before the war. If I can persuade him to place a large order – I can quote him a rock-bottom price he can't resist, we'll ask our supplier in Leicester to make socks with really hard toe seams that'll give the bastards blisters. See how they march in those!'

Yvonne hooted with laughter. 'Small acts of resistance. I like it.'

He made the phone calls with a sense of deep satisfaction. The Nazis were always on guard for sabotage, but they wouldn't suspect socks of being sabotaged any more than they suspected dipsticks being the reason for trucks breaking down. It was a small victory.

Happy that the women still had employment, and he had money in the bank, he faced his next decision. 'I need to go back to France to find Bonnie. Her grandparents were murdered by the Nazis, and I don't know where she is.'

'Oh, Antoine. I'm so sorry. Of course you must go. Rosemary and I are fine here. Things are ticking over nicely. It seems war is good for business.'

'Thank you.' He hugged Yvonne again and hurried home.

He'd decided on his course of action. He'd leave Bonnie another letter in case she came home, telling her what he was doing and the address of the Minimax Fire Extinguisher Company in London, where she could find the S.I.S. They'd promised they could get him back into France covertly, and while he was searching for Bonnie, he could turn his knowledge of the country to Britain's advantage against Germany. The British would provide him with a new identity and false papers and get him past the border guards. He would join their Secret Intelligence Service and turn his small acts of resistance into larger ones.

*** 

### Near Nancy, France. October 1940

Bonnie put a log on the fire in Louise's living room and rubbed cold hands together. October had brought a bite to the air and a nip to the fingers. Gloves and hats were the order of the day when cycling from drop point to drop point. She had become the group's courier and messenger, carrying codes and information and taking covert photographs of German military depots and emplacements while on her travels.

Her cover story, that of being a volunteer district nurse, had fooled the Nazis on several occasions. She'd even been asked for plasters for blistered toes and to bandage a soldier's cut arm, injured trying to fix a broken-down Citroën army truck. She'd muttered about the German army being too mean to buy decent socks and ensured she'd got dirt in the cut and made the arm as uncomfortable as she could. With luck, it would have turned septic.

Rina Ketty was singing *J'attendrai* on the radio. *I will wait.*

She'd wait forever for her father. Was he still alive, or had he been executed? Would she have to live the rest of her life not knowing what had happened to him? The letter had said tortured. Its words were burned on her heart. *The man, Antoine, is being tortured and has been sentenced to death. He has not revealed any names.*

Was she wrong to hope? Was she destined to lose everyone she loved? 'J'attendrai.'

'So will we all, Raven.' Louise put a mug of hot coffee into her hands.

'Thank you, Louise. I was thinking about my father.'

'Don't give up hope, Raven.'

The song ended, and the newsreader's voice interrupted their conversation. "*London was bombed again last night. The number of casualties is not yet known. In Vichy France, the government has enacted a law, the Status of the Jews. It defines who is Jewish and precludes French Jews from civil and military service. They are also precluded from working in education and cinema. The Nazi Military Command in occupied France has issued a decree enabling them to confiscate Jewish-owned assets and appoint Aryan administrators for Jewish businesses.*

"*Today, a further law was passed allowing the internment of foreigners of Jewish race in special camps. Several Communist activists have also been arrested by the Vichy police.*"

'Ghettos, camps?'

'Many are trying to leave with what they can carry before Hitler steals it.'

'To Spain, like Pierre?'

Louise smiled. 'You took a liking to Pierre, didn't you?'

'I loved him.'

'Wartime romances, Raven. They're not a good idea. You'd be wise, for your heart's sake, to forget him.'

'I know.' She'd accepted that he'd gone forever, but she'd never forget him.

The door opened, and the flames in the hearth guttered in the wind. Raphael stood in the doorway, blocking out the night. 'Come inside, quickly. You'll be safe here.'

A man and woman herded two small children in front of them. The man put a restraining hand on the little boy's shoulder. 'Thank you. Thank you. You are so kind.'

Raphael closed the door behind him. 'This is Mr and Mrs Abrams and Ava and Jacob. Their shop in Nancy has been seized, and they fear for their children – they've heard about the ghetto in Warsaw, and their cousin's been arrested. They want to leave France. I said we would hide them.'

Mrs Abrams looked round anxiously. 'We can pay you. We managed to hide money and jewellery before the Nazis came.'

Louise smiled. 'We would feed you for nothing, but I can see this problem getting worse, and organising escapes takes money – false papers, permits, train fares, suitable clothing and footwear…'

Mr Abrams nodded. 'We will pay what is necessary. How long will it take to get us false papers?'

'A few days, but you can stay here until they're ready, and then… Ra –' Lousie stopped herself just in time. 'Marie? You know the route over the Pyrenees now, and you've met Colette in Marseille. You're the ideal person to smuggle this family to safety.'

She frowned, looking at the children warming themselves by the fire. 'It could be dangerous, and getting the little ones over the mountains… there might be snow even this early.'

Louise nodded. 'Getting them out of France is down to you if you're willing to try. We'll get a message to Colette, so she's expecting you. I'll mention snow. She may know more than we do and can help you prepare for the mountains.'

'Then I'll do it. Later in the year, it may be more difficult, impossible even, but hopefully, we'll beat the snow.'

Mrs Abrams unclipped a brooch from her blouse and held it out to her. 'To show our gratitude, Marie. Thank you for offering to guide us.'

She smiled. 'I don't need paying.'

'It is not payment. It is a gift. I would be offended if you refused a gift, Marie.'

She took the brooch. It lay warm in her hand and glittered with diamonds and emeralds. It spoke of lives changed beyond all recognition. Tears smarted. 'It's beautiful. I shall treasure it forever.'

# Chapter Fifteen

**England and Scotland. October 1940**

The Special Operations Executive, a subsidiary of the S.I.S, had been formed that summer to send agents into Europe to sabotage Hitler's plans, and they'd sent Antoine to a training school outside London.

He chafed at the delay. Staring at an inkblot on a piece of paper, presumably supposed to show his psychological aptitude for covert operations, he could only see blood. Would saying so mean he'd pass the test or fail it?

'Blood. My daughter's if I don't find her and keep her safe. How long are you going to keep me here doing these bloody stupid tests?'

'I sympathise with your impatience, Renard, but the S.O.E won't send you into enemy territory without at least a remote chance of survival. And training you unnecessarily is a waste of resources.'

'I'm sorry. I'm worried about her, that's all.'

'Then concentrate on your training. You'll have several weeks in Scotland before an intensive parachute training course and instruction in explosives and espionage. There's a lot to learn if you're to be of use.'

'I've passed the test?'

The psychologist didn't smile. 'You'll be informed in due course.'

Dismissed like a small child, he went to the next test, an obstacle course. It was chaotic as each student seemed to have received different instructions, but he got through it somehow. Some of the exercises seemed to have no point at all, but perhaps they tested how good he was at handling stress, or following instructions and obeying orders. Having fought in the first war, he was used to obeying stupid commands, and he was determined not to scupper his chances with more impatient outbursts.

After three days, he was put on a train for Scotland with the rest of his group. A truck met them at the station and took them to a house on Loch Fyne. He jumped down from the truck and retrieved his baggage. Two more men jumped down beside him. Most of the group were French, but Cookie – James Cook, and Buster – Freddie Bussey, Englishmen, had become firm friends on the journey up from London. Both were keen to do their bit for the Allies.

It was a lovely old house with fabulous views of the loch and the rugged hills around it. S.O.E couldn't have found a much more isolated location. The first few days they learned that guerilla warfare was a far cry from military warfare. Operatives must attack and run, keep moving, and gather the best intelligence to plan surprise attacks on enemy weak points, always knowing their escape route, and not dig in and hold ground as they'd done in a military setting.

They learned about handling explosives, grenades, and weapons, and the fact that Lugers, the German weapon of choice, was far superior to the Webley, Colt, or Smith and Wesson which were the British standard issue, and to get hold of Lugers and ammunition whenever possible. They were also taught useful things like how to make duplicate keys, and how to sneak up on the enemy and kill them silently. The vision of sticking a pitchfork into a German rapist's back kept intruding on his concentration.

Then they were taken to Eilean n'a Breac, an island off the Kyle of Lochalsh, for training in recovering parachutes and containers from water. He had no idea whether he was passing the various tests; day and night manoeuvres in the pouring rain left him exhausted, but he plugged on determinedly.

This was now about more than him and Bonnie. Hitler had torn apart his family and his country, and like Cookie and Buster, he would play his part in driving the aggressors from France or die in the attempt.

## Vichy France, October 1940

The train rumbled towards the demarcation line. Bonnie tried not to fidget. Beside her, Mrs Abrams clutched Ava, while on the seat opposite, Mr Abrams held little Jacob on his lap. According to their papers, the Abrams were now the Blanchet family, returning to Perpignan where they were born. Bonnie was their niece, Marie Barbier, the same identity she'd used before.

At least her charges spoke French even if their grasp of German was rudimentary.

'The checkpoint is ahead, Uncle Matis. We'll need to show our papers.'

Mr Abrams nodded, his face pale. He was holding the papers for his entire family, while Mrs Abrams had the family wealth hidden about her body. She'd mysteriously put on weight since arriving at Louise's, and though she'd been generous with her payment for their stay, it was a wonder she didn't rattle.

The train juddered to a halt, and her heart juddered with it. She'd never get used to the fear of discovery. Being suspected of carrying false papers would mean their immediate arrest, and this time there were Ava and Jacob to consider. Guards moved along the carriage checking documents.

The guard held out his hand. Time stopped. Ava and Jacob chatted on, blissfully unaware of what was at stake. The man perused the papers twice, looked them all up and down, and returned them. She tried not to breathe out too loudly.

The guard moved on and Aunt Esme smiled. 'We'll soon be home, now.' How could the woman remain so calm when so much depended upon her?

It was evening when they reached Marseille. Ava and Jacob were almost asleep in their parents' arms.

Colette welcomed them all like long-lost friends. 'Come in, all of you. You must be exhausted. There is food prepared and beds made up. Come and sit down. Let's get these little ones fed and in bed.'

She hugged her friend again. 'It's good to see you again, Colette.'

'And you, Marie.'

No one spoke as they ate, but soon, Colette broke the silence. 'There is no snow on the slopes at this end of the mountains, Marie, so you won't need skis. It's been very wet these past few weeks, so waterproofs and strong boots would be a good idea. I'll see if I can find something to fit the children. I think those I have will be too large.'

'Thank you. I'm glad there's no snow. Rain I can cope with.' She asked the question that had been burning a hole in her heart. 'The British soldiers… they were taken away in a vehicle by Spanish border guards. Have you heard what happened to them?'

'The best information we have about Spain is to demand to be taken to the British Consulate. They will do everything they can to get refugees to Gibraltar and then to Britain. From there, they can go to America if they choose.'

'Do you think the soldiers were taken to the British Consulate?'

'As far as we know, they were.' Colette took a sip of wine. 'We've had no reports of stranded or imprisoned soldiers in Spain or of refugees being returned to France.'

'That's good to know.'

Colette nodded her understanding; the refugees and soldiers she helped became friends, and she needed to know they were safe. Pierre was more than a friend.

'Colette. I have this photograph of my father. I wondered if you could ask if anyone has seen him. He was captured by the Nazis and tortured. I fear he's dead, but I was told not to give up hope. Someone may know something.'

'Leave the photo with me, Marie, and I'll get some copies made while you're away.'

'Thank you, Colette. That would be wonderful.'

Colette sensed her reservation. 'It'll be quite safe with me, ma chère.'

The next day they bade a tearful farewell to Colette. She too, was more than just a friend. She was like a mother to them all.

Again, they had a wait while they changed trains at Narbonne, and their papers were checked at Perpignan. It was lunchtime when they reached Cerbère. The sky was overcast, and the mountains loomed dark and threatening.

'It looks like we'll need those waterproofs. We can try to find somewhere to stay and tackle the mountains at first light, or we can risk a night on the Pyrenees. Dusk comes early now, and it will be cold.'

'We have warm clothes and waterproofs. The sooner we're clear of France the happier I shall be, Marie.'

'Then we'll eat and then set out, Mr Abrams. I'd like to get you down off the mountains and into Spain before nightfall, but it will be slower with the children.' After what Colette had said, she wasn't sure whether it would be wiser to try to avoid the Spanish border post on the far side of the mountains or lead the family straight to it. Much might depend on how the children weathered the journey – a few fat drops of rain spattered on her coat – and on the weather itself. This wasn't going to be a pleasant hike.

They followed the same zig-zag track she'd taken before, and she realised for the first time how vulnerable they all were. Before, she'd had three strong soldiers with her; now she was responsible for one man, a woman, and two small children.

She took a deep breath. She could do this. The sky was leaden, and above and ahead of them the peaks were lost in mist. She consulted her compass, kept her eyes on the ridge to the south, and followed the track.

The rain grew heavier, making the ground slippery beneath their feet and slowing their progress. She paused for a breather. 'It isn't too late to turn back, Mr Abrams.'

'A bit of rain won't hurt us, Marie. Germans might.'

That was true enough. She walked on as the weather closed in around them. They reached the ridge but couldn't see the next one. 'As long as we keep going south, we'll cross the border.'

The rain was coming down in torrents now, turning the track into a stream and making progress difficult. Her feet were soaking, Ava was crying, and Mrs Abrams was struggling to carry her.

'Here, let me take her for a while. Give your arms a rest.'

Mrs Abrams handed the little girl over. 'Thank you, Marie. Just for a while, though. You're doing enough for us without carrying Ava.'

She continued down the next slope, walking in what was now a stream in full spate. All around her, water tumbled in rivulets down the mountainside. She could hardly see ten feet in front of her, and there was no shelter from the storm. What had been a dry valley before, now carried a narrow rocky stream. She crossed it and started up the other side. If it was possible for the rain to become heavier, it did. This was madness. 'We should turn back.'

'I can see the top of the ridge. We're almost there.' Mr Abrams pressed on, unaware there were more ridges to climb before they were across the mountains. She had no choice but to follow him up rough, rocky scree.

They reached the top of the ridge, and she handed Ava back to her mother while she stopped to consult her compass. With visibility so poor, and the track ahead washed away by the deluge, her compass was her only way of knowing which way to go.

She pointed south, down the slope ahead. Was that water she could hear roaring in the valley bottom? 'With this amount of rain, the water down there will be a torrent. It's too dangerous. We can either stay here and hope the rain eases or go back.'

Ava was still crying and holding out her arms to her father. Mr Abrams put Jacob down. 'Here, let me have her. You take Jacob for a while, beloved.'

She looked around her for some landmark she might remember, wishing she'd taken more notice of the shapes of rocks last time. She'd been more occupied with Pierre than the route. 'We could all do with a rest while we decide whether to go on or go back.'

A low rumble turned into a tremor and became a roar. Water cascaded down the valley ahead of them, carrying with it rocks and debris. Going on was no longer an option.

'We have to go back, now.' Rain poured down her neck, plastered her hair against her face, and filled the inside of her boots. The rain and clouds made it feel like dusk, not late afternoon. 'At least moving, we'll keep warm. If we stay put we'll die of exposure.' She turned to check her compass, but the stones and wet earth shifting beneath her feet made her jump aside onto a slab of firm rock.

Mrs Abrams screamed. 'Jacob!'

The child had been standing by his mother, but now... the ground was moving, and Jacob was tumbling down the slope.

'Landslide... Over here, quickly – it's a landslide.'

Mrs Abrams threw herself after her son and disappeared beneath a torrent of water, soil, and rocks. Mr Abrams flung Ava into her arms and half ran and half leapt down the slope after his wife and son.

Clutching Ava, she watched in horror as their bodies were tossed over and over and pounded by rocks until they disappeared from sight. Sobs racked her body. How could anyone survive that?

She slumped onto the rock that had saved her life and unbuttoned her coat. Ava was crying and shivering, and the child needed what body heat she could provide. The scree slope settled and stilled, the odd rock tumbling and resettling as if in apology for the deaths it had caused.

There was no way back and no way forward. She sat in the torrential rain, cuddling Ava close while the light failed and darkness stole her soul.

# Chapter Sixteen

**Eastern Pyrenees, France. October 1940**

'Marie… Marie…'

'Dad?' No, not Dad. He didn't know her as Marie. Bonnie opened her eyes. She'd had a nightmare, and she was shivering with dread and cold. Dad was dead, wasn't he? Her mind was numb.

It wasn't yet light, though dawn bled night from the eastern sky, and it was still raining as if it would never stop. She was soaked to the skin. She tried to move, but her body felt heavy and stiff, her throat was parched, and her legs were weak. The events of the previous day flooded back. 'Oh God… Ava? Ava!'

She sat up carefully, and fumbled with her coat buttons. 'Ava?' The little girl's body was still warm against hers. She felt for her pack. Most of the baggage had slid down the mountain along with Mr and Mrs Abrams and little Jacob. Was there any chance they were still alive? As soon as it was light enough, she'd try to get down the slope and see if she could find any trace of them.

This was all her fault. The Abrams had been her responsibility. Why hadn't she been more forceful and insisted they turn back?

'Ava?' She had water in her pack and food. She laughed, hysteria threatening; there was water everywhere. Ava stirred weakly. 'Thank God.' Had she the strength to carry the little girl all the way back to Cerbère?

She tried to stand and failed, weak and light-headed, struggling to think. *Eat, Bonnie. You need to eat.* She listened to her inner voice and ate, but she let Ava sleep. It would be an hour before it was properly light, maybe longer.

Lights danced before her eyes, and tears mingled with the rain on her face. It would be a miracle if she got herself to safety alone, never mind carrying Ava, but she must do this or die in the attempt.

Lights danced again, and she blinked. There *were* lights, a line of them, and they were coming up a ridge to her west. The wind blew a faint sound towards her. 'Marie…'

'I'm here!' Her voice was a croak. She tried again. 'I'm here!'

'Marie…'

They hadn't heard her. Somehow, she must attract their attention. She forced herself to her feet and stood, wobbling, clutching Ava to her chest. She waved frantically. Stupid, they wouldn't see her in the dark. A torch – she had a torch in her pack. Fingers fumbled and shook. Would the torch work? She clicked the switch and a beam of light shone out. Her brain tried to figure the distress signal. She should know it. She did know it. Clicking the torch on and off, three short bursts, three long, and three short, she spelled out S.O.S.

The line of lights moved on up the ridge. She clicked on the light again and waved the torch, making the beam dance. She yelled and waved the torch again. 'Over here!'

The lights paused. Someone had heard or seen her? She repeated the S.O.S signal.

'Marie! Marie! We're coming.'

She sank to the ground as her legs gave way. Ava mewled softly. It was a miracle the child was still alive; she desperately needed warmth. The torch beam dimmed. No! No! Not now! She switched it off to save the battery, praying it would work again when the rescuers were closer.

The lights disappeared. 'It's all right, Ava. They'll find us. They must find us.' The lights bobbed along the top of the ridge, closer. She flashed her torch again.

'We see you. Keep flashing the light.'

She could count them now. Five lanterns swinging and bobbing. 'We're here.' She flashed the light again.

Figures were silhouetted against the lanterns. Five figures, trudging towards her through the rain. She struggled to her feet again and stood to meet them.

'Marie, thank God you're safe.' Colette hugged her. 'It was on the radio – a metre of rain in twenty-four hours in the Eastern Pyrenees and more to come. Vernet-les-Bains has been virtually destroyed, and there are rivers flooded and bridges down. Hundreds are dead both sides of the border. We knew you'd still be up here, even if you got the Abrams safely off the mountain and into Spain. We travelled overnight – we had to drive miles out of our way to get here.'

'You shouldn't have risked your lives for me.' She brushed tears and rain from her eyes. 'Mr and Mrs Abrams and Jacob were swept away in a landslide. They're down there somewhere.' She opened her coat to reveal Ava. 'She's cold, she's dying, Colette. We have to get her to safety. We should never have come. I should have turned back.'

'No one could have predicted this, Marie, It isn't your fault. Can you walk?'

'I don't know.'

'Let me take Ava.' Colette unbuttoned her own coat and took the little girl. 'Marcel, help Marie. The others can look for the Abrams, though it's doubtful they'll have survived.'

'Let me help you, Marie.' Marcel put his arm around her waist and supported her, a staff in his other hand for balance. 'If you can't walk, I'll carry you. I'll get you to safety, I promise.'

She leaned against him, grateful for the support and glad of a strong arm and comforting words. 'Thank you, Marcel. Thank you from the bottom of my heart.'

Dawn lightened the sky in the east as they half slid and half stumbled down the muddy scree. The track was completely washed away, the ground still unstable, and it was hard to find solid ground.

The other three men fanned out across the mountainside, searching. One of them waved his lantern. 'Over here!'

'Are they alive?' Marcel held her upright as they crossed the slope to where the Abrams lay.

A tiny foot stuck out of mud. Mr Abrams lay on his back, eyes open and washed by the rain. Mrs Abrams lay half-buried in a tangled heap a few metres away, her limbs at unnatural angles.

She closed her eyes and crossed herself. They'd never stood a chance. 'God have mercy on their souls.'

Marcel held her close. 'There's nothing we can do for them, now. Their bodies will be recovered when the weather breaks. Come, Marie. Let's get off this mountain and save the one we can save.'

She looked up into dark eyes full of compassion. Marcel had done more than help save her life; he'd made her feel safe for the first time in months and had given her hope for the future.

***

**RAF Ringway, Manchester, England. November 1940**

The large house in Bowdon, near RAF Ringway, would be Antoine's lodgings for the next stage of his training.

Cookie slapped him on the shoulder. 'Home, sweet home for the next two or three weeks. Can't wait to get started, Renners.'

Their driver cautioned them. 'Unload your baggage and come straight back. There are formalities to complete, and I'm to deliver you to the airfield.'

At the airfield, they were greeted by a man in uniform. 'Welcome to the RAF Special Duties Service, gentlemen. I'm Corporal Brian Backhouse, your jump instructor.'

He saluted from habit. 'Antoine Renard. This is James Cook and Freddie Bussey. We're all anxious to get started, sir.'

'Good. Muir will take photographs of you for your identification papers, and you'll be issued with boots and kit. Training begins in one hour.'

'An hour?'

'No time to waste, gentlemen. The lives of brave men and women resisting Hitler in Europe will depend upon you.'

Muir shook their hands. 'Call me Frank. I shall be taking photos of each of you for your documents. False and real. You'll be assigned names, and cover stories. I also take photographs of jumps to improve safety, so you'll see me around the place. Sadly, we've had a couple of fatalities.'

'No one expects jumping out of a plane to be safe.'

'We aim to make it as safe as we can. It takes a lot to train an S.O.E agent.' Frank took his time, taking three photos of each of them. Satisfied, he sent them to supplies, where they were issued with boots, protective headgear, uniforms, webbing harnesses, and knives to cut paracord should they get hung up in a tree. Jumping from a plane looked even less safe.

Happy that they were properly kitted out, the supplies clerk pointed them in the direction of a bomber standing on the runway. 'Your instructor will be waiting.'

Corporal Backhouse stood by the Whitley bomber with a group of young men all dressed in the same uniform. 'Good, we're all here. Each instructor has a stick of ten men. You ten are mine.' He turned to the Whitley. 'She's an old bird, and not ideal for the purpose, but she's what we have.' He gestured to a hangar. 'The northside hangar houses Avro's experimental department, so we hope for better things to come; we build planes here as well as fly them and jump from them. Now, come and familiarise yourselves with the Whitley.'

He climbed the short ladder. It was cramped inside, with just enough room for ten men to sit five-a-side with their knees drawn up. Their comfort was obviously not a priority. The rear turret had been removed and a round hole, about three feet across, cut in the floor and fitted with hinged doors.

'As you can see, the exit hole is almost three feet deep, and you will have to exit through it carrying a parachute. Following my instructions closely will prevent you "ringing the bell" – which is smashing your face on the way out and possibly getting a broken nose and concussion. Jumping isn't all about how and where you land.'

Parachuting held far more dangers than being dropped over enemy territory. He could be hospitalised or killed before he even left the airfield.

'Are you listening, Renard?'

'Yes, sir. Sorry, sir.'

'Good. Your life will depend on it as much as it will depend on the girls who make and pack your parachutes. Now we'll have a look at what you'll all be wearing, especially the webbing and how the parachutes fit, so you know what to expect when we begin proper training. Learning how not to break your neck or ankles when you land is the first lesson. We'll continue in the training hangar.'

Inside the hangar, wooden staging replicated the exit hole in the Whitley bomber. The platform had just enough room for the stick of ten men to sit.

Corporal Backhouse interrupted his thoughts. 'First, we'll try some exits and landings without the parachute. It's only a drop of about eight feet, and it's onto padded mats, but you need to perform a clean exit, and a shoulder roll to break your fall. 'I'll demonstrate.'

The corporal showed them the right and wrong ways, and then it was his turn. He sat on the edge of the hole, back ramrod straight, his hands ready to push himself off. Eight feet suddenly looked a long way down. He launched himself into the air and hit the ground feet first, bent his knees and rolled.

'Good. Next!'

They jumped again and again until they could land and roll in any direction, for as the corporal explained, there would be wind direction and parachute drag to account for as well as uneven ground, and that was if they didn't get blown into trees. Corporal Backhouse handed out leaflets with diagrams. 'Study these tonight. Tomorrow, we'll try some exits wearing your parachute packs. Now get some sleep. We've a lot to get through tomorrow.'

'Corporal, when do we get to make a proper jump?' Cookie asked the question no one had voiced.

'When I'm happy you stand half a chance of not breaking your necks and legs. First, you'll jump from a tethered balloon. Day jumps and then night jumps. Then, if you pass that stage, you'll parachute onto a landing site at Tatton Park from the Whitley, again there'll be night jumps, bad weather, winds, and targets.'

He'd been anxious to get back to France. Now, three weeks of parachute training, followed by a couple of three-day courses in explosives and espionage, seemed far too short a time to learn how to parachute from a Whitley bomber and stay alive in Nazi occupied France.

# Chapter Seventeen

**Marseille, France. November 1940**

Bonnie walked along the quayside of the old port. Although the nights were growing cooler, the days were warm, much warmer than November in England would be. The sea was as blue as the sky, and boats bobbed at their moorings; the wealthy yacht owners seemed little troubled by war.

It had taken her a fortnight to recover physically from her ordeal on the mountain. The journey home to Colette's had been made difficult by flood water, burst riverbanks, and bridges being washed away. Trains had been cancelled or diverted, and they'd spent hours on a station platform… she wasn't sure where.

Recovering emotionally would take much longer, but seeing Ava improving daily helped. Colette had taken Ava to her heart; childless and widowed, the woman had begged to keep her. *Marie* was only too happy to agree; she didn't need to be constantly reminded of her folly by the little orphan, and Ava needed a stable home. Colette would make a wonderful mother. She'd given Colette the brooch for safekeeping – it didn't feel right to keep it when it would be the only thing Ava had of her mother, and its value might mean the difference between the child eating and starving. Her family's wealth was buried with her mother on the Pyrenees.

They weren't sure how old the child was, but had guessed around two, and had acquired false papers for her in the name of Ava Blanchet, her date of birth two years before the day the landslide killed her parents and brother. When Ava was old enough, Colette promised, she'd tell her about her parents, but for now, the little girl was safer being French and not Jewish.

Marcel had been a tower of strength since her ordeal on the mountain; he'd carried her the last mile into Cerbère, and since then had barely left her side. He'd taken her to the local bars and pavement cafes, and they'd drunk Spanish absinthe and coffee and pretended life was normal. She was only alone now because she had a decision to make, and Marcel being with her would only make that decision harder.

Colette had showed the photos of Dad to various people she'd met, including Marcel, but no one recognised him. She'd introduced her as Marie Barbier to Lieutenant Ian Garrow, who'd helped set up the escape and evasion line over the Pyrenees. Ian had managed to avoid being captured after the surrender of the Highland 51$^{st}$ Division at Saint-Valéry-en-Caux on the Normandy coast in June. He'd tried to escape to the Channel Islands after France surrendered, but had walked to Marseille with some other British soldiers and had handed himself in to the Vichy government in August. Although interned by them, he was allowed to roam Marseille, and had recently begun working with other British in the city to aid the escape of other internees and British soldiers and airmen stranded in France.

It was Ian's idea that she become just part of the chain, the link that brought escapees from the Nancy area to Marseille, and handed them over to someone else for the journey from Marseille to the Spanish border. Marcel had volunteered to be the "someone else". It meant she would see him briefly when handing over escapees.

Pierre had been her first love, and she'd never forget him, but she was still only nineteen, and she didn't want to live the rest of her life alone; she'd seen what loneliness had done to Dad. Marcel had saved her life; she owed him her loyalty. If seeing him for a few days each month was all she could have, then so be it. The war wouldn't go on forever, and if they both survived… maybe… if Marcel was the right one.

She'd made her decision. They could be dead tomorrow, so she'd live for today.

***

## RAF Ringway, Manchester, England. November 1940

Antoine adjusted the parachute on his back and looked over the edge of the open cage suspended beneath the tethered balloon. He'd practised for this so many times. He'd practised flight drills while hanging from the hangar roof in a parachute harness, learned to control his parachute while being blown by a huge fan, and had learned to land in water, courtesy of a huge vat full of very cold liquid. In theory, he could untangle his cords, cope with colliding with another parachutist, and land safely even when being swung in the air.

Now, faced with leaping into thin air, he wasn't sure he was ready. An ambulance parked a respectful distance away didn't give him confidence.

'Go!'

His training kicked in, and he exited the cage as he'd done so many times from the mock-up. The Tatton Park landing zone hurtled toward him at terrifying speed. Wind rushed past his face, the parachute was taking forever to open, and the jerk when it did almost made him faint with relief. He swung from side to side. He mustn't pass out. He still had to land.

His feet hit the ground harder than he'd expected, he landed awkwardly, bent his knees and rolled into an undignified heap. He knelt on his hands and knees and kissed the grass, elated to be alive. He'd done it!

'You all right, Renard?'

'Yes sir. I think so.'

'Good. Clear the landing site for the next jumper.'

He gathered up his parachute and hurried to a safe distance to watch the next man jump.

They repeated the exercise several times over the next few days, but although he managed some clean landings, he approached every jump with trepidation. So much could go wrong.

At last, the day came for them to jump from the Whitley. Corporal Backhouse pointed at a map of Tatton Park on the wall of the hangar. 'This is the drop zone as you will see it from the air. Take note of the key features.' He tapped the centre of the map. 'This is your target. Your first jump will be done solo, and then you'll go again and jump as a stick – all ten of you one after the other. You need to keep your distance from one another while staying as close to the target as possible. If you don't break your necks, you'll advance to jumping with packs, weapons, and at night. To earn your wings, you'll need to execute four passable jumps from the Whitley. Any questions?'

No one answered.

'Good. Kit up, and let's get this jump under way. Report to me at the Whitley at eleven hundred hours sharp.'

Eleven o'clock saw them packed into the Whitley like sardines, one end of their static lines attached to a bar above their heads and the other to their parachute bags. As he fell, the static line would pull open the bag and deploy the parachute – at least that was the idea. The Whitley taxied, gathered speed, and took to the air. The jump light was red. He was second to jump and sat opposite number one, Cookie.

Cookie looked as nervous as he was. Backhouse opened the doors to the jump hole and a blast of cold air rushed in. 'Take your positions one and two. Wait for the light to turn green and go on my command.' Backhouse gave a rare smile. 'Remember your training, and you'll be fine. Good luck.' The light turned green. 'Number one, go.'

Cookie launched himself through the hole, and the light turned red and then green again. 'Number two, go.'

He followed Cookie, falling and falling, and then the jerk that meant the parachute had opened, and time to look around.

Everything looked so small. Cookie was a hundred yards or more to his left. The target area was ahead and to their right, wind from the left would carry him past the target. He pulled on his left cord and steered slightly to slow his approach, closer to Cookie.

The wind was gusting, swinging him from side to side as he descended. It was going to be a difficult landing. Below him, Cookie hit the ground and rolled, right on target, while he drifted off to the right and touched the ground, rolling, fifty yards or more off target, but he was down.

The plane circled Tatton Park and came in for another sweep. More jumpers floated down like thistledown.

In a few days, after his course in explosives and espionage, he'd be doing this for real, and fifty yards off target could land him in the midst of Nazi troops. He had three more attempts to get it right.

Two more jumps carrying weapons and body armour, amid dropped containers, and it was time for the night drop.

Cooped in the small space with dim bulkhead lights, his mission began to feel all too real. They were to drop as a stick, all ten one after the other. It was a clear night, the stars twinkling in a velvet sky. Through the jump hole, all was dark, villages and towns blacked out, so it was impossible to see where they were. Ahead, two rows of three bonfires lit the landing target.

This is what it would be like. Dropped over France, with valuable supplies and radios, aiming for a small drop zone lit by the resistance, not knowing if Germans were lying in wait.

Bonnie was in France, somewhere, and this was his passport into the country.

The light turned green. 'Go!'

He launched himself into the icy November wind and fell.

***

## Near Nancy, France. November 1940

Bonnie had bid Marcel and Colette a fond farewell and returned to Louise and Raphael's home in the forest near Nancy. A lot had happened since she'd been recuperating in Marseille. Hitler had annexed the Moselle and Alsace, and the area around Nancy was crawling with German forces. He'd created a forbidden zone to the north and east of the country to prevent the return of any who'd left during the exodus and to stop people leaving for Britain. With letters and telephone calls being intercepted, getting information out to England was going to be harder and harder.

Raphael turned up the radio. There'd been a huge demonstration against the German occupiers in the Place de l'Etoile in Paris, and he was keen to learn more. *"French police have arrested about a thousand people. Many are imprisoned in Romainville, on the outskirts of the city, and some have been sent to camps in the Reich to serve their sentence."*

'Damn Nazi collaborators. You'd think the French police would take the side of the French, not the bloody Germans.' Louise wasn't normally given to swearing.

Raphael put a hand on Louise's arm. 'You can't blame people for kowtowing to the Germans. They shot Auguste Gras back in June. Anyone found to have an anti-German attitude can be arrested, tried by a military court, and executed. I fear for the thousands of protesters arrested in Paris. It takes a brave person to stand against Hitler. God alone knows if those sent to the camps will survive.'

*"Last night the Luftwaffe blitzed Coventry, destroying the cathedral and large parts of the city. The death toll is not yet known."*

Coventry wasn't far from Leicester. Why destroy a cathedral? Her thoughts turned to Dad, as they so often did. 'Do you think my father is still alive?'

Raphael looked sombre. 'I don't know, Raven. We can only hope.'

'I read the rest of the message – the part where it said he'd been sentenced to death.'

'I didn't want you to see that. Raven, there was a member of the resistance in the prison. They knew of the sentence, so if they could get him out, they would have done.'

She smiled her thanks. 'If he's alive, he'll be trying to find me. I know he will.'

'Where would he look?'

'England, I suppose. That's where he told me to stay.'

Raphael put his head on one side. 'And if he went and you weren't there?'

'I expect he'd come back to France, somehow, and go back to my grandparents' farm. He'd have expected me to go there, but he'd know what I'd have found.'

'And what would he expect you to do then?'

'I don't know.'

'Join the resistance and avenge your grandparents?'

'I don't know.'

'Return home to England?'

'Possibly. I have no other relations in France. Anyway, he probably thinks I'm still in England.'

Louise bit her bottom lip. 'Raven, if your father is alive, and he's looking for you, he may be trying to get back to England. He may even be there waiting for you.'

'I suppose.'

Louise put her elbows on the table and rested her chin on her hands. 'You've been through a terrible ordeal, child. I think it's time you went home. You owe it to yourself to see if your father's there.'

'But…'

'No buts.'

'I have work here with the resistance. I'm part of the escape line.'

'And there are still families trying to escape. You could go with them.'

'But...'

'It would mean going over the Pyrenees and into Spain. Could you do that after what happened to the Abrams?'

She tried to push from her mind the image of Jacob's little leg sticking out of the mud, but the thought of finding Dad was seductive.

'That weather was a freak, Raven. It isn't likely to happen again. Though the longer you leave it, the more likelihood of snow.'

'It feels like abandoning you.'

'We have information that needs to get to London that we can't trust to a letter. You'd be working for France against Hitler if you delivered it.'

Put like that, she could hardly refuse. She'd see Marcel again in Marseille, but for how long, and would it be for the last time?

# Chapter Eighteen

**Occupied France. November 1940**

It was a few days after full moon, the take-off from RAF Stradishall being delayed because of days of bad weather. After an anxious wait that night, kitted-up and ready to go, the Whitley, with Antoine on board, had taken off forty minutes before midnight. They'd flown low-level to avoid German radar, via Holland to drop another agent, and were now approaching the Vosges Mountains in France.

S.E.O had used the information and codes Antoine had delivered to message Florian and his group to set up the time and co-ordinates for the drop. And it wasn't only a trained spy they were parachuting into a group where he was known and trusted, it was containers of desperately needed food, weapons, explosives, general supplies, money, and radios.

With the annexation of the Moselle and Alsace Départments into Germany, and the Vosges Départment now in the *Zone Interdite*, the zone prohibited for the return of refugees and in which German farmers must settle, life for the resistance group would be perilous.

Nancy, also was in the forbidden zone, and so was his parents' farm near Liverdun. A German family would own it now, what was to be Bonnie's inheritance and security stolen, and the thought tied his stomach in knots more than his imminent plunge into occupied France.

'There's the drop zone, Gervais.' The navigator pointed to his right.

*Gervais DuPont* was the name on the false identity papers S.O.E had given him. He opened the hinged door on the exit hole and peered down as the plane banked to line up with two rows of bonfires that marked the zone. The only person parachuting, he'd have to kick out the heavy containers before he jumped himself. He braced himself against the side of the plane ready to kick.

'Containers, go!'

He kicked, one, two, three, four… Parachutes opened beneath him floating their precious cargo to the ground.

'Going around again. Good luck.' The plane flew lower, every minute of delay a moment when the German military could hear them or spot them. The last container out, he sat on the edge of the hole, legs dangling.

'Go!'

He pushed off, dropping through the hole into the night. The parachute opened with a reassuring jerk, and he drifted towards the bonfires.

He hit the ground and rolled. Before he could sit up and gather his parachute to bury it, a man pointing a rifle was silhouetted against the moon.

He froze, heart thudding, and then held up his hands in surrender.

The man walked towards him, rifle raised, ready to shoot. He couldn't see the man's face, but he heard a muffled laugh. 'Welcome home, La Fourche.'

He got to his feet and held out a hand. 'Good to see you, too, Florian.'

Florian embraced him. 'Let's get these bonfires put out and the containers loaded into the truck before the Nazis home in on us. There's a stream over there, and I brought a couple of buckets and a spade. Renoir's with the truck. He'll be pleased to see you. It's been a while.'

They doused the fires, and located the canisters and buried the parachutes by moonlight before dragging the containers to the truck.

Renoir helped load the supplies and throw tarpaulins over the canisters, and hastily shovelled coal on top of them. He threw the spade into the back of the truck. 'Let's get out of here.' Renoir drove along a narrow lane without headlights to guide him. The moon was all they needed. He drew to a halt outside a barn with tall double doors. The doors opened, a light was quickly extinguished, and Renoir drove the truck inside.

Someone shut the doors behind them and relit the lamp, and Renoir turned off the engine. 'Welcome to our winter quarters, La Fourche. Come and meet the rest of the group.' He introduced them one by one. 'Lucas, Zacharie, Juliette, and Adolf – on account of the moustache. La Fourche has brought supplies.'

Eager hands unloaded the containers from the truck, overjoyed at the contents.

'Radios and batteries.' Adolf connected wires and twiddled knobs.

'Boots. A pair of size thirteens as requested.' Zacharie removed his worn-out boots and put on the new ones. The old ones had holes in the soles.

'Explosives, ammo, lamp oil.' Lucas carried the boxes of explosives to a safe place away from the small fire in the centre of the barn.

'And food. Tinned stuff, dried fruit…' Juliette held cheese to her nose and breathed in. 'And cheese. English cheese, but cheese nonetheless. And bacon!'

'Rifles, pistols, medical supplies, warm clothing… and money. Lots of money for false papers and bribes.' Florian smiled. 'You did well, La Fourche.'

He smiled in return. He owed these people his life, and he'd done something towards repaying them. Tomorrow would be soon enough to discuss the targets the S.E.O had set them.

*** 

**Near Nancy, France. November 1940**

Bonnie had a week before her next trip south – it would take that long to gather the information together that she was to take to

England – and she was determined to use the week to do some serious damage before leaving France for what could be the last time. There was an extra burden added to her shoulders; the Nazis had passed a law legitimising the taking and execution of hostages in the occupied zone in retaliation for the attacks and sabotage the resistance was carrying out.

Any anti-German action could now result, not only in the arrest and death of the culprit, but in the death of a hostage, anyone who'd been arrested, and imprisoned, and held on whatever pretext. She was risking more than her own life, and she must weigh every decision carefully.

'We can't let this stop us, Raven. It's what they want, to scare us into lying down, so they can trample us. There are going to be casualties, it's unavoidable, but if we do nothing, the whole of France is a casualty.' Raphael was right, but it didn't make things easier. 'We must be more subtle. Make things look accidental rather than sabotage.'

'What do you suggest?'

'Instead of blowing up fuel dumps, we put water and dirt in the petrol drums or in the vehicle's tanks when they're left unattended. Hammer thorns and nails into tyres. Loosen wheel nuts and radiator hoses... anything that will harass them without being too obvious.'

Louise's face lit up. 'Not just the military. We target the industries in the area who supply vehicle parts, clothing, boots, weapons, and transport to the Germans– anything they rely on. We hamper production and distribution. I could get a part-time job in Nancy at one of the firms that supply the army. With the men fighting, there's work for women. There must be something I can quietly sabotage, and I'm sure I won't be the only one doing it.'

That night, they were out as soon as it was dark equipped with everything they needed for sabotage. They'd had a message that a number of Citroën trucks, bound for the German army, were parked up nearby. It was too good an opportunity to miss.

Shielding torches with their hands, they crept through the trees. Ahead, in a clearing, the moon shone on six trucks. Raphael held up a hand and motioned to his left.

A guard lounged against one of the trucks, smoking a cigarette.

She nodded. They'd discussed this possibility, and her job was to distract the guard. Hopefully, there would only be one.

She hurried towards the German. 'Bella! Bella! Where are you? Bella, come here!'

The guard swung his rifle towards her. 'Halt.'

She ignored him. 'Have you seen a dog? She's black, tan, and white, about this tall. She went off after a cat, and she hasn't come back. I have to find her.'

'No. I haven't.'

She swung around, shining her torch into the trees. 'I must find her. Can you help me look for her?'

'Go away.'

'Please?'

The guard narrowed his eyes.

'If you help me look for her... Bella! Bella!' She walked away from the trucks, paused at the edge of the trees and looked back. She was losing her touch. 'Please, help me. I can't go home without her.'

The guard hesitated and then shone his torch towards her. 'Where have you looked?'

She pointed away from the trucks. 'I haven't looked that way.' Out of the corner of her eye, she caught sight of Louise pouring water from a can into a fuel tank. Raphael had opened the bonnet of one of the trucks. She led the guard farther away and into the trees. The longer she kept him occupied, the more damage Raphael and Louise could do, but she was putting herself into danger, and she didn't want to have to stab the man if she could avoid it.

She continued calling for her phantom dog, all the while listening for Raphael's signal. He'd said he'd need twenty minutes, and it suddenly seemed a dangerously long time. She kept ahead of the man, luring him on in a wide circle.

'What's that?' The guard grabbed her arm. 'Listen.'

She tensed. A dog barked. The signal. 'That's her! She's over there. Thank you for helping me.' She planted a huge kiss on the guard's cheek and broke loose, running towards the barking. 'Bella, I'm coming.' More barking.

She met Louise and Raphael a few hundred metres farther on. 'Done?'

'Done. Let's get home, before that guard realises he's been conned.'

\*\*\*

## Vosges Mountains, France. November 1940

Antoine outlined his plan. 'It carries a huge risk, but our main mission for the moment is to disrupt Nazi communications and power. They've laid miles and miles of dedicated phone lines, linking strategic places – airfields, ports, command headquarters. Men have been executed for cutting cables to the north, but now Moselle is annexed, we find ourselves right on the border with Germany, and we're also on a direct line between Paris and Munich, and between Vichy and Berlin.

Renoir nodded. 'And our group is ideally placed to sabotage them.'

Florian rubbed his beard. 'Do we know where they are?'

'I have a map and a compass.' He spread out a silk handkerchief printed with place names and intersected by lines. 'It's rough, but these are the main phone lines. Any of the dedicated lines we cut will be a bonus, because they'll have to be repaired and that takes time away from the war effort, but these will cause most disruption.'

Renoir stared at the map. 'Are they guarded?'

Florian grinned. 'The Nazis are forcing French farmers to patrol the lines at night, but by early morning most of them are drunk on wine and asleep. If we pick our time and place, we should be able to cut the cables and escape without being seen.'

Renoir waved a hand at the map. 'Some of these lines are several miles away. How do we get there unnoticed, La Fourche?'

'Bicycles. They're quiet and show less light than the truck.'

'And our cover story if we're intercepted?' Florian wanted every detail clear – it was a risky operation.

'We ride a little distance apart. We're French farmers patrolling the lines.'

Renoir hooted with laughter. 'I love it.'

Florian smiled, but he had one more question. 'What if we meet with real trouble?'

Renoir shrugged. 'It has to be every man for himself. Agreed?'

'Agreed.'

Florian nodded. 'When do we go, La Fourche?'

'About two in the morning. Most of the farmers should have drunk a good amount by then, and anyway, most of them would probably turn a blind eye to us cutting the wires, as long as it's our necks and not theirs on the guillotine.' He'd escaped the guillotine once, thanks to Hugo and this group, and here he was about to risk it again.

Renoir got to his feet. 'I'll organise some bicycles if you can find large wire cutters.' He paused. 'We can't take a ladder.'

Florian nodded. 'Good point. Lucas, can you make up a pair of climbing spikes to strap on over our boots?'

'Will do. We'll need rope, and a long strap to hold onto, as well. There'll be some horse harness suitable for that.'

Juliette brushed back her hair in a gesture that reminded him painfully of Bonnie. 'I'll see to that. There are halter ropes we can knot together, and a girth will be strong enough and long enough for the strap. There'll be something to buckle to it to make a loop.'

His mind wandered to Bonnie as it often did. Despite asking everyone he met, no one knew of a young girl called Bonnie Renard. If she was working for the resistance, she too might have false papers and a codename. How would he ever find her?

He wrenched his mind back to the task at hand. 'Good. I suggest we report back here in a couple of hours and try to get some sleep. It's going to be a long night.'

It would also be a dangerous one.

# Chapter Nineteen

**Near Sainte Die des Vosges, France. November 1940**

Antoine cycled along the road with his bicycle lamp shielded to show only the ground immediately ahead of him. There was little moon, the night being overcast, and it was cold with a stiff breeze. In the distance, Florian's rear reflector caught his headlight sporadically, giving him only a vague idea of how far ahead his friend was. Renoir and the others followed at intervals. Each of them carried an essential item, ready to throw them into a ditch should they run into a German patrol. Juliette brought up the rear as lookout and the only one with a bicycle bell to ring as a warning.

According to his map, one of the main Nazi phone lines was just ahead of them through the silent, sleeping town and on to the next junction. Florian was already there, a shadowy shape at the side of the road, waving him down. 'This is it, La Fourche.'

They hid the cycles in a hedge and waited for the others. When Juliette arrived and declared the all clear, they set to work. As the youngest and fittest, Zacharie was tasked with climbing. Lucas and Adolf produced the climbing spikes and fastened them onto Zacharie's boots while Juliette kept watch.

Florian handed Zacharie the girth. 'Ready?'

Zacharie nodded, looped the girth around the pole and his waist and held onto it with both hands. 'Give me a leg up, La Fourche.'

He and Renoir gave Zacharie a shove, and with the halter ropes looped around his waist, the young man began to climb. Once at the top of the pole, Zacharie loosed the ropes, lowering one end towards the ground. Adolf attached the wire cutters to the rope and Zacharie hauled them up.

Would he see enough in the moonlight to determine which was the new wire and which the old. Cutting the wrong one would disrupt communications for everyone, not just the Nazis, though with telephone calls being intercepted, they were of dubious benefit. *Trust no one.* That's what S.O.E had taught him, and yet he did trust his group. Hadn't they saved him once already?

'Hide!'

Juliette's voice brooked no argument. Zacharie slid down the pole, and fumbled with the buckles on the girth strap. They all dived into the hedge as headlights lit the place where they'd been standing.

The vehicle screeched to a halt a few metres farther on. 'Jemand hat den Draht durchtrennt!' German soldiers piled out of the vehicle and inspected the wire that hung loose onto the road. One waved a commanding arm. 'Ausbreiten. Finden Sie sie!'

They couldn't stay where they were. He tapped the nearest shoulder and gestured across a field. The message was passed on, and silently, they crept through the hedge and along the hedge bottom. The Germans would find their cycles, but with luck, the group would escape with their lives.

No one spoke. Heavy breathing and the rustle of dead leaves were the only sounds. Thankfully, the Germans didn't have dogs, or they'd have had no chance of escape. Once on the far side of the field, they scrambled through a hedge. *"Every man for himself."* He couldn't desert a woman to the possible clutches of Nazi interrogators. He paused to ensure Juliette was safely through, clasped her hand tightly and ran.

It was almost light when, footsore and exhausted, he and Juliette reached the barn that was home. Florian and Adolf were already there. Lucas arrived half an hour later, but daylight crept through the holes in the window shutters, and there was still no sign of Renoir or Zacharie.

***

**Near Nancy, France. December 1940**

Bonnie spent the rest of the week distributing explosives and messages on her cycle. She didn't know what they were to be used for, or what was in the messages, but a railway bridge had been blown up and a truck reputed to be delivering food to a Nazi barracks had been destroyed. Rumour had it the food was being distributed among the resistance.

Louise set plates on the table. Four more plates than usual.

'We have guests?'

'One of the groups has been compromised by an informer. Four members of the resistance are being hunted by the French police. They're to be turned over to the Nazis. They've been passed from safe house to safe house, but –'

'They're here? You're hiding them? What if the person informs on us?'

'Yes, we're hiding them, and it's a risk we must take, but tonight, you catch the train to Marseille. You're to guide them over the Pyrenees, make contact with the British consulate in Spain, and take them and the information we've gathered to England. When the dust has settled, they can return with new identities but somewhere away from here. This is your chance to find your father if he's in England.'

It made sense to get them out of France for a while and quickly. 'And if he isn't there?'

'What you do with the rest of your life is up to you, Raven.' Louise hugged her. 'Whatever you decide, I wish you well. Just get this information to England without delay...' Louise hesitated. 'There are dozens of German tanks hidden in the forest under camouflage netting. Among other information, you'll be carrying photographs and co-ordinates. It's essential the British destroy the tanks before they do too much damage.'

'I understand.'

The four guests entered the room and introduced themselves. Sol, L'Escargot, and Christos – code names – and a young woman, Danielle.

'I'm Marie.' It was the name on her papers, and the name they would need to call her. 'I'm to be your guide.' She could sense their mistrust in one so young. Her last trip would hardly inspire confidence if they knew of it. 'I've guided soldiers over the mountains. I know the route and the safe house.'

Louise came to her aid. 'You can trust Marie with your lives, and she's coming with you to England, so she's hardly likely to compromise your safety. Do you know who informed on you?'

'No.' The four looked at one another uneasily.

*Trust no one.*

The older man, Sol, held out a hand in greeting. 'We're grateful for your help, Marie.'

Louise bustled around bringing food. 'Eat up. The train leaves in two hours. Raphael will drive you to the station.'

Over supper, they worked on their cover story and the names on their papers. They decided to use the story she'd used with the soldiers. One of them was to be her fiancé, and they were travelling to Perpignan to be married. It was where her papers as Marie Barbier stated she was born, so she could say she had family there. Danielle was her best friend, and the other men were her fiancé's best friends, which was why they were travelling together.

Sol made a game of it by casting lots, and Christos won the right to be betrothed to her. He looked particularly pleased with himself, and spent the next hour getting to know her better. Not that she gave away much about herself that was true. She only hoped she could remember the falsehoods.

With the documents and photographs strapped around her waist in a waterproof pouch, and hidden under her black winter coat, she crossed the station platform. Laughing and giggling with her new friends, and arm-in-arm with Christos, she negotiated patrolling police, and they boarded the train.

They found a carriage close to the toilets, and she watched for approaching guards. If she could get the four escapees to Marseille, they could leave the hunt behind. She glanced at her watch. The train should be leaving any minute. Through the window, she could see armed French police. It was illegal now for a Frenchman to own a gun, and the German authorities had access to the gun registry, so they'd know who hadn't turned in their weapons, but that didn't stop the men of the resistance from carrying them. Raphael had suggested Sol, L'Escargo, and Christos didn't carry revolvers, but that didn't necessarily mean the men weren't armed.

She didn't know these men. She didn't know how they might react to a threat. The police were making for the train. 'Quickly, into the toilet and lock the door. Don't come out until I tell you.'

There was only room for three, so as girls were viewed with less suspicion, Danielle stayed with her in the carriage. Heart thumping, she engaged in what appeared to be casual conversation. 'Don't look up. Pretend to be touching up your makeup.' She got a small mirror from her own handbag and tidied her hair with a shaking hand.

Danielle attempted to add lipstick, not the best idea as she couldn't hold still enough to apply it. She gave up and found a comb instead. A policeman approached and Danielle fiddled with her hair. 'Can I borrow your mirror, Marie?'

'Papiers.' The officer was abrupt. No please. Or thank you.

She remembered to breathe as the man perused her documents and then Danielle's. 'Where are the men I saw you with?'

Her carefully rehearsed story wouldn't wash. 'Men? Oh, those men. I don't know. We met them at a bar in town, and they kindly walked us to the train. I don't know who they are or where they were going.'

'And the reason for your journey?'

'We're visiting my parents. They live in Perpignan.'

He turned to Danielle. 'And you?'

'My parents are dead. Marie invited me to have a holiday with her. It's so kind of her, don't you think?'

The policeman grunted and returned the documents.

She smiled her thanks while her heart raced. The train was held up for half an hour while the police checked documents, but finally, the police left the train and it pulled out of the station. She knocked on the toilet door. 'It's Marie. You can come out now.'

There would be other searches at other checkpoints, but for now, they were safely away from Nancy.

All too soon, the demarcation-line checkpoint loomed. She leaned forward. 'Remember our story. Christos and I are to be married, and we are travelling together for the wedding in Perpignan. We all met in Nancy, if they ask. The wedding is to be next Saturday.'

Sol, L'Escargot, and Danielle nodded their understanding.

Would she ever get used to trying to get through checkpoints on false papers? If her charges were caught, they'd likely be imprisoned, possibly sent to camps in Germany, or executed. She might be executed herself. She couldn't fail. 'Whatever happens, stay calm.'

The train slowed to a halt and German guards threw open the doors and jumped aboard. Sol put his hand to his jacket pocket. Did he have a revolver? There was no time to caution him. A guard demanded their papers and the reason for their journey.

She explained for them all, waving a hand at Christos, opposite, and showing her mother's engagement ring.

The guard took Sol's papers. Beside her, Sol was fidgeting; his hand was in his pocket.

The guard frowned and started rechecking the documents. On impulse, she leaned across and kissed Sol hard on the lips. Too late, she realised he wasn't her spurious fiancé.

The guard looked as confused as Sol. She couldn't make matters worse, so she jumped up and kissed the guard, and then L'Escargot, and Christos. 'I'm getting married! I love everyone!'

The guard smiled and returned Sol's papers. 'Enjoy your wedding.'

She slumped back into her seat, feeling weak and dizzy. The three men looked slightly bemused.

'I had to do something. Sol looked as if he was about to draw a gun.'

Sol brought a packet of cigarettes from his pocket. 'I was going to offer the officer a cigarette, but the kiss was very welcome, if unexpected.'

'I panicked.'

Danielle came to her rescue. 'No way would I have kissed any of these reprobates. I think you were very brave.'

She laughed and accepted a cigarette to calm her nerves. 'I should have asked this question earlier – are any of you armed?'

'No. We were warned against it, but it leaves you feeling vulnerable.' Christos smiled. 'We were right to trust you, Marie.'

The rest of the journey passed without incident, and they arrived at Marseille Saint-Charles station with a feeling of huge relief.

Would Colette be there to meet them?

A familiar figure was walking along the platform, searching the crowds disembarking. 'Marcel!' She waved and ran into his arms. He kissed her, making her heart thump. She hadn't realised how much she'd missed him. She wanted to hold him close and never let him go.

Sol and the others joined them. Christos pretended jealousy. 'Do you kiss every man you meet, Marie?'

Her cheeks were hot with embarrassment. 'This is Marcel. He is my real fiancé.'

Marcel raised an eyebrow. 'Am I?' He swung her around and kissed her again. 'That's fine by me, Marie.'

# Chapter Twenty

**Vosges Mountains, France. January 1941**

Antoine sat in a corner in an abandoned cottage, the owners having fled south months before and it not yet having been taken over by German immigrants. He was cleaning his Colt Super pistol. Weapons were in very short supply, but the British had managed to buy some Colts from America, and some had found their way into S.O.E agents' hands.

Juliette held out a mug of coffee and perched on a chair beside him. 'You've been captured by the Germans and imprisoned – what do you think will happen to Renoir and Zacharie?'

He rubbed the pistol barrel harder. 'I've been trying not to think about it.' She waved the mug again, and he put down his pistol and took the coffee. 'They'll be taken somewhere to be interrogated, probably Paris, as I was.'

Juliette put a hand on his arm. 'I know this is hard.'

'It's all right. We need to face the fact that that they're either dead or captured, and we haven't heard that they're dead. They'll be tortured until they confess to being members of the resistance and betray us all.'

She nodded. It was why they'd moved from the barn to the cottage. 'Do you think they'll betray us?'

'They'll question them for hours under bright lights until sweat blinds them. They'll stop them from sleeping, give them electric shocks, pour water in their mouths and noses until they think they'll drown, and do that again and again. And if that fails…' He held out his left hand to show his missing finger. 'They start cutting off fingers, one at a time.'

Juliette frowned. 'You stood all that, so if you didn't crack, why did you only lose one finger?'

'They decided I didn't know anything and condemned me to the guillotine.'

'You held out then.'

'Juliette, I'm no hero. I didn't know anything to tell. If they'd taken off every finger and all my toes, I couldn't have told them anything of use.'

'Would you have done, to save yourself?'

He smiled grimly. 'That's a question that keeps me awake at night. I hope I would have held out to save my friends, and for France, but I was so exhausted, terrified, and confused. I don't know.'

She studied the liquid in her mug. 'It's the risk we all take.'

They sat in silence for a while, each with their own thoughts and fears.

Florian was bent over the radio set. He'd sent a morse-code message to a contact in Paris and was waiting for a reply. The radio emitted a series of staccato beeps. 'I've had a reply. Renoir and Zacharie were executed yesterday.' He slumped onto a chair at their side and held his head in his hands. 'I'd known Renoir since school. Zacharie was my cousin.' His voice broke into sobs.

'I'm so sorry, Florian. They were good men, and I know what they would have suffered.'

Juliette had tears streaming down her face. 'They wouldn't have talked, would they? I mean, if they were executed, does that mean they didn't give us away? Wouldn't they have sent them to a camp...' Her voice trailed off.

Florian looked up. 'Is that all you can think about? They gave their lives for France, and you think only of yourself?'

'I'm sorry, Florian, but it isn't just me I'm thinking of. It's all of us and our ability to resist if we're compromised. This only makes me want to fight on to avenge them.'

'I'm sorry. You're right. This affects us all.'

'You're both upset, Florian. And yes, Juliette is right. This makes us more determined, not less. We have more cables to cut, and we'll cut each one for Renoir and Zacharie and the hundreds of others who've already sacrificed themselves for our freedom. The Nazis won't win, not if the people of France and Britain stand against them.' St Paul's cathedral had been damaged in the blitz. The people of England wouldn't soon forgive that.

Florian sniffed back tears. 'So when is our next target?'

He needed revenge, focus – they all did. 'Tonight, we head south a way. The phone line linking Vichy to Berlin passes quite close.' He spread out the handkerchief with the phoneline network printed in ink and pointed to a thick line running roughly southwest to northeast.

'How do we get there?'

'We managed to recover three of the cycles. If we can requisition a couple more?'

'I'll get Lucas and Adolf to see to it, La Fourche.'

'Good. We'll leave at midnight.' He put his Colt in its shoulder holster and brought out his Fairbairn Sykes to sharpen the edge. He had another small fighting knife concealed behind the lapel of his coat. The matchbox in his pocket held tiny binoculars, various handkerchiefs were maps, and the heel of his shoe held a cyanide pill he had no intention of taking – he had a daughter somewhere, and he was determined to stay alive for her.

Muffled in coats, boots, and scarves against the frost, and armed with climbing spikes and belt, as before, they left the cottage a few minutes after midnight. It was a new moon and black as pitch with stars twinkling. Somewhere a dog barked and was answered by another. The white ghost of a barn owl glided feet from his face and disappeared into the night. Had he been foolhardy to suggest tonight when there was no moonlight, and they'd need torches and lamps?

He pedalled along the lane between high hedges and sparse woodland, the light from his headlamp lighting a small yellow pool on the road. Behind him, Florian's cycle squeaked – he hadn't thought of oiling it. Hopefully, there was no one to hear at midnight.

It took an hour to reach the line drawn on his handkerchief map, but he was certain this was the place. Their cycles hidden in the trees, they approached the telegraph pole. This time, it was Lucas climbing while Juliette kept watch. There was no sound of any vehicles, no headlights strobing through trees.

Lucas adjusted his head torch and shinned up the pole like a squirrel. The beam of light played across the road and trees as he got himself into position and lowered the rope. 'Send up the cutters.'

'Coming now.' Adolf gave a tug on the rope and Lucas hauled them up, cut the wire, and shinned back down the pole.

'Done., La Fourche.' Lucas sounded pleased with himself.

He smiled into the darkness. 'For Renoir and Zacharie. Now, switch off that torch, Lucas, and let's get out of here.'

He led them home with Juliette cycling beside him. They'd struck another blow against Hitler, and escaped unhindered, but how many loyal, innocent Frenchmen would pay for their deed with their lives?

***

**Pyrenees, French/Spanish border. January 1941.**

Bonnie, Danielle, Sol, L'Escargot, and Christos spent three days in Marseille with Colette and Marcel. As always, war seemed far from the city, and life resumed an appearance of normality. They were precious days, with little Ava toddling around after her and Marcel like a young puppy, and the time to leave for Cerbère and the Spanish border came all too soon.

The photographs Colette had shown people of Dad still hadn't brought forth results, but as Colette reminded her, trust was hard to come by, and no one gave information willingly. The possibility of finding her father seemed farther away than ever; England, despite her not wanting to leave Marcel indefinitely, seemed her best option, and anyway, she'd promised to deliver messages to British Intelligence.

Sacrifices had to be made – the fight against Hitler came before love.

Marcel walked them to the station to board the train for Perpignan and Cerbère. 'I shall miss you so much, Marie.'

She clung to him. She'd lost Pierre, and now she was losing Marcel. 'I'll come back if I can. I'll write.'

'I'll wait for you, mon amour.'

She kissed him, tore herself from his arms, and ran across the platform to where the others waited with their luggage.

Waving from the carriage window as the train pulled out of the station, her heart broke all over again.

She stared out of the window as the train rattled down the coast, and finally, she slept. They showed their papers at Perpignan, changed trains early in the evening and arrived at Cerbère in the dark. The days were short now, and Colette had arranged for them all to stay overnight at a safe house in the town.

The house was terraced and old, and in a narrow street. They were welcomed by an elderly couple, the Cuveliers, who fed them and directed them by candlelight to a loft which had a number of mattresses and blankets.

She lay awake, remembering the Abrams, the torrential rain, and the landslide. This time, she must make it over the mountains and take Danielle, Sol, Christos, and L'Escargot safely to England. She couldn't fail, not again.

She woke to the sound of someone moving about. Sol was folding his blanket. 'It's morning, Marie. I smell breakfast. The others have gone down already.'

She threw on the few clothes she'd removed the previous night, having felt shy about undressing in front of three men, and followed Sol down the steep, narrow stairway. It was barely light.

'Come, eat.' The old lady smiled and piled food onto plates. 'There is plenty, and you need flesh on your bones, young lady.'

'Thank you. You are so kind.'

'It is nothing. When you have eaten, we will fetch what you will need for the journey.'

'Thank you, again.' She hadn't realised how hungry she was. Food seemed more plentiful here.

There was no sound but the scraping of knives and forks on china plates, but finally they'd eaten every scrap.

'There are few hours of daylight. You must not waste time. Your equipment is here. Dark goggles, snowshoes, ski poles, warm clothing.'

'Ski poles, snowshoes?'

'There is snow on the mountain. I have packed food. Denis will take you as far as he can in his van. He is fetching it now. You must hurry. Go, before people are up and about and you are seen.'

The growl of a vehicle stopped outside the door, and bidding Madam Cuvelier a hurried farewell, they piled into the back of the old Citroën van. It bumped along the road for half an hour before it rattled to a halt.

Monsieur Cuvalier flung open the rear doors. 'This is as far as I can take you. From here, it's on foot.'

She climbed out and squinted in the bright light. Ahead of her and towering above her were the Pyrenees in all their snow-covered glory. 'Oh, hell.'

Sol threw their equipment out onto the road and jumped out after it. 'Where now, Marie?'

She pointed. 'Up there. Over the ridge, and the next ridge, and the next, and on into Spain.'

'Jesus.'

She offered up a small prayer for their safe journey and took a deep breath. 'We'd better get started. We want to be off the mountain before dark.' She'd spent one desperate night on the Pyrenees, and she was terrified of having to spend another. She forced a smile for Danielle's sake. 'We'll be fine. Let's get these bags unpacked. The sooner we start, the sooner we all reach Spain and safety.'

# Chapter Twenty-One

**Pyrenees Mountains. January 1941**

It was bitterly cold with an icy wind. Bonnie zipped herself into a thick, insulated snow suit and donned tinted goggles and thick mittens. The Cuvaliers had provided clothing for each of them that fitted reasonably well, as well as packs with food, Thermos flasks of hot drink, emergency flares, and basic first aid supplies.

Monsieur Cuvalier pushed Spanish currency into her suit pocket. 'There is also the telephone number of the British Consulate. I wish you all the best of luck. I shall wait here for a couple of hours in case you have problems and decide to return.'

'I can't thank you and your wife enough, Monsieur Cuvalier.'

'We do it for France and for the resistance. Safe journey, my friends.'

She shrugged her pack onto her back and slung her snowshoes over her shoulder. She would need them all too soon. They walked along the stony track, moving steadily uphill until they hit the first of the snow. The higher they climbed, the deeper it got, except where the wind had blown the exposed places clear and drifted it into the hollows.

She stopped as her feet sank into soft snow. 'I think we need our snowshoes now.' She looked up towards the first ridge. Flurries of snow blew from the top and down the slope reminding her of the landslide that killed the Abrams. Was she leading these souls into danger or to safety?

They did as she told them, trusting that she knew what she was doing. She owed them the truth. 'I've not traversed the mountains in the snow before, in fact, the last journey ended in disaster – torrential rain caused a landslide. Three people were swept away and killed. I almost died. I would have done if my friends hadn't rescued me. This is a dangerous undertaking.'

Sol adjusted the strap on his snowshoe and straightened. 'Yet you are prepared to do it again.'

'My life is my own to risk, and I have my own reasons for wanting to reach England. Yours are not mine to sacrifice. You need to be aware of the dangers.'

Sol shrugged. 'I've crossed mountains before – skied in the Alps before the war. It doesn't look too deep or powdery, and we're reasonably well-equipped. I'm for going on.'

Christos and L'Escargot agreed, but whether that was from bravado or commitment, she wasn't sure.

'Danielle?'

'I'm terrified, but I can't go back on my own. If you all go on, I shall.'

'Then if we're all ready?'

Snowshoes took some getting used to, and it was a while before she settled into a steady rhythm that wasn't energy intensive. The poles helped her keep her balance, and the exertion kept her warm. They reached the top of the first ridge and started down the other side, half walking and half sliding in places. Snow had drifted into the valley bottom, and without the snowshoes, they'd have sunk up to their waists.

She prodded the snow with the ski poles to find the shallowest places, crossed the dip and trudged slowly up the other side. Halfway up, she stopped, struggling for breath. 'I think we should take a short break.'

'Over there looks to be out of the wind.' Cristos pointed to a craggy outcrop.

She'd expected the trail to have changed, given the landslide and flooding, and the snow blanketed anything she might have recognised, but the outcrop looked horribly like the place she'd sheltered with little Ava, drenched and frozen.

Shivering, she pushed the memory away and turned towards the shelter. Huddled together, they ate bread, cheese, and fruitcake, and drank hot coffee.

The sky was dark and ominous, the light failing although it was only three o'clock in the afternoon, and flurries of snow melted against her cheek.

Sol picked up his pack and got to his feet. 'We shouldn't stay still too long.'

She was glad of Sol's presence. He was a strong man, and the mountains called for strong men.

Together they topped the next ridge, and the next which had a knife-edge drop on the far side, only to see another. She removed her mittens to consult her compass, and her hands felt frozen almost immediately. 'We're on course. That's the last ridge. Once over that, we're in Spain.' She replaced the compass safely in her pocket and pulled her mittens back on.

The wind howled along the ridge, blowing a blizzard into their faces and freezing her cheeks. Turning aside to find a way down, and trudging on, she couldn't help thinking of her first trip over the Pyrenees. By the time she reached the last ridge, she could barely see for tears.

'Is that Spain?' Danielle pointed across the land spread out below them. Lights twinkled in the dusk.

She couldn't answer. This was where she'd said farewell to Pierre. The border post beneath them was her last sighting of him, and now she was as much in the dark as to their future as any of them.

'Marie?'

She gulped and removed her goggles to brush away tears. Snow blinded her, and she replaced them hastily. 'That's a Spanish border post. If we head for it, and our papers aren't in order. we run the risk of being turned back into France.' The possibility didn't bear thinking about. 'Or they may take us to the British Consulate, which could save us weeks of walking.'

'Surely, no one would be inhuman enough to turn us back into the mountains in this weather and at night?'

'You think we should head for the post?'

'We need shelter for the night. Would they deny us shelter, whatever they decide to do with us later?'

After a brief discussion, they decided to head for the border post. In the event, it wasn't a decision they'd needed to make. A border patrol had already spotted them, and a vehicle was waiting for them at the bottom of the track.

The border guard, an untidy man wearing a uniform two sizes too small for him, waved a rifle at them and motioned them into the ancient truck. They may have survived the snow and freezing weather, but their lives were now in Spanish hands.

***

## Spain. January 1941

The guard took them to the guard post, which was more like a fort, and made them sit in a small room. An officer came in and began questioning them.

Bonnie shook her head. 'We don't speak Spanish.'

The officer ignored her and directed his questions at the men.

Annoyed at being ignored, she got to her feet. 'We don't speak Spanish. We demand to see the British Consulate. Britain. Gibraltar, yes?'

'Gibraltar? British?'

'Yes. British. Escape – escapado France over Pyrenees.'

'Escapar?'

'Si, escapar Vichy France.'

'Papeles.' He held out his hand imperiously. 'Documentos de salida!'

'He wants our papers.' She placed hers on the officer's desk, anxious not to annoy him further, and the others did the same.

L'Escargot frowned. 'Spain is a neutral country, isn't it?'

Sol shrugged. 'It's supposed to be, but it collaborates with the Nazis.'

Danielle's face blanched. 'You mean we're prisoners? Marie?'

'Not yet. Stay calm, Danielle.'

The officer checked their papers and said something they didn't understand. He kept the documents but took the five of them to a long room set with a table and chairs and gave instructions to a soldier.

The soldier waved them to chairs. 'Alimento, si?' When they didn't answer, he pretended to eat.

She nodded. 'Food. Si. Gracias.'

Other soldiers arrived and took their seats. Food was more than they'd expected. Did this mean the Spanish army would help them?

After their meal, they were taken to a room with camp beds. She and Danielle seemed to be causing the commanding officer a problem as the only women in the fort. In the end, two camp beds were moved into what was little more than a large store cupboard. She didn't care. She was dry, fed, and not freezing, and she felt as if she could sleep forever.

Next morning, after breakfast, they were put into the truck under armed guard, and the vehicle rattled and shook as it bounced along a rough track on bald tyres.

They passed half-starved donkeys and mules carrying machine guns and mortars. It seemed this truck was the only vehicle they had, and it was falling apart. The lorry grumbled to a halt in a small village, and they were bundled out. A heated conversation ensued between the soldiers and the local Guardia into whose care they were dumped. It seemed no one knew quite what to do with them, and the army was eager to get rid of the responsibility.

The Guardia made them sit outside his office while he made some telephone calls. They heard the words *Consulado Británico* which sounded hopeful.

She swatted away a fly; the weather was much warmer here, and flies buzzed around the rubbish and piles of donkey dung. After France, Spain seemed a dirty and untidy country. At length, they were taken to a small room and locked in.

'Is this it?' Christos tried the door but found it firmly bolted. 'You realise they could keep us locked up until the end of the war, and then what?'

Sol was equally pessimistic. 'I suppose it depends who wins and whether we survive that long.'

She slumped against the wall and put her head in her hands. Was this what had happened to Pierre? Was he languishing somewhere in a Spanish gaol?

She mustn't give up – she had information she must get to England. 'Unless they take us to Figueres – there's a British Vice-consul there according to Colette. The phone number! How could I forget the phone number Monsieur Cuvalier gave me.' She pulled it out of her pocket along with a bunch of notes. 'I'll give it to the Guardia, and if needs be, we'll try bribery.'

It was next morning before the door opened and daylight flooded in. Again, they were fed and given red wine to drink. They washed under the village pump, with a shotgun pointing at them, and relieved themselves in the privacy of a ruined building. There didn't seem to be any other sanitary arrangements, a fact the flies obviously appreciated.

A lorry rattled to a halt with a squeal of brakes, and again they were bundled inside and driven away under guard.

'Where are you taking us?' The guard appeared not to understand. 'Figueres? Barcelona? Gibraltar?'

The guard nodded. 'Figueres, si.'

She breathed her relief. 'Figueres, gracias.'

By the time they reached their destination, every muscle in her body ached from the bouncing and shaking of the lorry. They pulled up outside the *Jefatura de la Frontera*, the police station, where they were hustled inside and thrown into a guard room with some other unfortunates – mostly refugees from the Spanish Civil War returned from France.

After a while they were taken to see the *Jefe*. The man glared at them and muttered a few words. She picked out some, and her heart thudded. *Campo de concentración.*

'No! Here, I have the phone number of the British Consulate. Telephone him, please! British!' They weren't but the Jefe didn't know that as they had no documents now. In desperation, she pushed her few notes of Spanish money across the desk to him.

The man pocketed the cash and took the paper and perused it. He waved them away, and the guard marched them back to the guard room.

This time, she couldn't raise a shred of optimism. The phone number had been her last hope. They had no documents, no means of identifying themselves, and no money. All that lay before them now was the prospect of spending the rest of the war in a *Campo de concentración* – a concentration camp – and if they were suspected of working for the resistance, the chances of them surviving to the end of the war were doubtful.

# Chapter Twenty-Two

**Vosges , France, January 1941**

Antoine blew hot breath on his fingers and replaced his woollen gloves. It was the coldest winter in living memory, and yet he and the rest of his small group were out in the dark with nothing but moonlight to guide them. He was about to put what he'd been taught about explosives to the test.

Squatting by the side of the railway track, he laid an improvised satchel charge, a small bag containing explosives and a pull detonator, against the track and reeled out a line to what he hoped was a safe distance. According to the coded message he'd received earlier in the evening, the train was due to pass in about half an hour and was carrying steel from the steelworks in the Moselle Valley to a major weapons factory controlled by the Nazis.

He hunkered down in a ditch to await the train. A little farther along the track, the others waited with the truck, ready for the next target of the night. Shivering, he jammed his fur hat down over his ears and pulled up his collar. Nothing seemed to keep out the cold.

Ten minutes... twenty... twenty-five... He strained his ears to catch the first sounds of an approaching train. Thirty minutes... thirty-five... There! The rumble of the train was unmistakeable and approaching fast. He held the line taut. Closer, closer. Black smoke trailed across the moon, and the huge shape loomed. Closer, closer... he yanked the line to set off the explosive charge and leapt out of the ditch and up the bank.

The sound of the explosion was almost drowned by the thundering of the locomotive, but a bright flash showed it had gone off. Had it done its job? The train reached the breach in the rail, and then everything seemed to happen at once. With an ear-splitting screech, the engine jumped the rails and careered along the ditch, followed by trucks full of steel bars. One of trucks fell on its side, cascading steel where he'd been waiting just moments before and pulling more wagons onto their sides. The noise was deafening.

Not needing to see more, he ran along the top of the bank to where the others were waiting. He arrived breathless. 'It's done. It'll take ages for them to clear that and repair the track.'

'We heard it.' Florian's tone was grim. 'Heads will roll for this. Let's make sure they aren't ours. We still have work to do.'

S.O.E would have called it collateral damage. For every act of sabotage, or Nazi soldier killed, a hostage would die, and the fact didn't sit easy with him.

They drove on through the night. The train wouldn't reach the weapons factory tonight, but they intended to be there. It took them about an hour to reach the factory. There were bicycles in the yard, and lights shining through windows showed a night-shift was working – if French workers, they'd be on a go-slow or doing other small acts of sabotage. Lucas donned thick rubber gloves and heavy rubber boots. Florian handed Lucas heavy duty wire cutters with the handles wrapped in more thick rubber. They hadn't tried cutting a live power cable before, and Lucas had drawn the short straw.

The first challenge was reaching it. Juliette drove the truck close to the wall beneath the power cable and leapt out, leaving the engine running.

Adolf hauled at the extending ladder. 'Give me a hand, La Fourche.'

Together, they wedged the ladder against the side of the truck's bed, leaned it up the wall, and pushed up the extending part. Would it reach?

Lucas put his foot on the bottom rung. 'Stand clear. I may have everything insulated, and be standing on a wooden ladder on a truck with rubber tyres, but I don't want to take any unnecessary risks.'

'Be careful.' Holding his breath, he watched his friend climb and reach the top; Lucas leaned to one side, arms outstretched holding the cutters – there was a flash, the lights went out in the factory, and the ladder wobbled. He rushed to steady it, and held it as Lucas scurried down.

The ladder packed away, they jumped in the truck, and Juliette rammed her foot on the accelerator. The lorry lumbered forward, and they roared away into the night.

***

## Figueres, Spain. February 1941

Figueres bore the marks of the Civil War. There were bombed out buildings, a heap of scrapped cars riddled with bullet holes, and a guard on every road out of town. Bonnie and her friends had been given the freedom of the town while the Jefe waited for instructions from Madrid, but had been forbidden to leave it, not that there was much chance of escape.

Cataluña had been on the losing side, and had taken harsh punishment. The Catalau tongue was forbidden in public, as were their traditional festivities. Food was scarce, and awful, and prices meant basic supplies were beyond ordinary people. Figueres had suffered a quick death and was now slowly decaying. Franco smiled down from posters across town, and propaganda was strongly anti-British; Gibraltar was a thorn in the Spanish side.

There was also a strong Nazi presence which accounted for the propaganda.

They'd considered trying to smuggle themselves out in a lorry, but with no money and no papers, appealing to the British Consulate seemed the best option.

Eventually, the Vice-consul, a Mr Whitfield, arrived. He frowned when they introduced themselves. 'You're not British.'

L'Escargot shook his head. 'No, we're French, but we are resistance fighters being hunted by the Nazis in France, and we need to get to England. We hope, with new identities, we can go back to France to continue the fight.'

Perhaps her living in England would help. 'I'm trying to go home to England. I live there with my father – in Leicestershire.'

'You have no papers?'

She shook her head. 'The border guards took them. We have no money either.'

The man sighed. 'You are lucky not to be in prison or a concentration camp. There are well over a million political prisoners, and I spend much time trying to free them and get them out of Spain. And it isn't just political prisoners the Nazis are targeting - thousands of Austrian Jews have been transported to Poland. I fear hundreds have already been killed by the Nazis there.'

She exchanged a glance with the others. It made returning to France urgent if they were to save any French Jews from the same fate. 'We've heard nothing from the English Ambassador, and we've been held here for three weeks.'

He nodded. 'Everyone here is suspected of being a Communist. I know as little as you do, but I shall make enquiries on your behalf.'

'Thank you.'

A few days later they were accompanied to Gerona, and confined to a hotel, forbidden to communicate in any way with the outside world. Someone must have been paying for their keep. The Consulate?

She and Danielle distracted the hotel staff, while Sol snuck behind the desk and telephoned the Consulate. He came back with a smile. 'They say to sit tight and not do anything stupid. They are trying to get us out.'

'At least they know we exist. I was beginning to wonder.'

It was another fortnight before their gaoler arrived with orders. 'You are to go to Madrid by train, via Barcelona. Collect your belongings. The train leaves in one hour.'

She stuffed her few possessions into her backpack and hurried down the stairs after the others. A car waited to take them to the station, where they were dumped on the platform.

Their gaoler saw them onto the train. 'You will be met at Barcelona by Consular staff.' With a stiff bow, the man was gone.

At Barcelona, they caused an argument between local police and the man from the Consulate, and were escorted to yet another hotel and forbidden to leave. They were joined by other refugees and prisoners released from the gaol at Figueres. Herded onto a train for Madrid, the next morning, and met by a member of the British Embassy, and lodged in another hotel for the night, they finally boarded a train crammed with British servicemen and arrived in Gibraltar.

The island bore the marks of war with buildings destroyed by bombs. They might not be truly safe, but at last, they were on British soil.

***

## London, England. March 1941

The voyage from Gibraltar to the Port of London had taken several days in a converted fishing trawler, now armed with two three-inch guns. With U-boats causing losses to convoys, Bonnie was relieved to step out onto solid ground.

London was in ruins. The blitz had wreaked havoc with docks, buildings – even St Paul's Cathedral was damaged. The spirit of the Londoners, however, wasn't dampened. Everywhere people were shovelling rubble and clearing the streets. Bodies lay shrouded in sheets – bodies dug from the rubble of what were once homes.

The British servicemen were making their way back to their units, which left her, Sol, L'Escargo, Christos, and Danielle to find British

Intelligence, hand over her messages, and ask for documents with new identities. Her friends were as eager to get back to France and continue fighting as she was to get home to Cosby and hopefully reunite with her father. If she still had a home.

The Minimax Fire Extinguisher Company looked like any other business offices. She told their story to the receptionist unsure if she was even in the right building.

The woman nodded, appearing convinced of the truth of it, and made a telephone call. An armed guard arrived. 'Come this way, please.' He led them down a long passage and knocked on a door. He waited for permission to enter and pushed open the door. 'Some escapees from France, newly arrived from Gibraltar, sir. They have letters of introduction from the British Embassy in Madrid.'

The man stood and extended a hand in greeting. 'Come in. What can I do for you.' There was no name plate on his desk, and he didn't give his name.

Bonnie handed him the documents she'd carried hidden beneath her clothing for all those weeks. 'Information from the resistance near Nancy. We got out over the Pyrenees in January, so I don't know how much is still relevant – we've been held for weeks in Spain.'

'Thank you. Sit, please.' He read the documents and looked at maps and photographs. 'These are most useful. Now, it didn't take five of you to bring these?'

In turn, the others told their stories and professed a desire to return to France under new identities.

The man turned to her. 'And you, miss?'

'I've been working as a guide on an escape and evasion line through Vichy France and over the Pyrenees, I brought these people here, through Spain, but now I'm going home to Leicestershire to find my father.'

The man frowned slightly. 'You have no official form of identification. I would need to know who it is I am letting loose in England.'

'My name is Bonnie Renard. My home address is Main Street, Cosby. You can check that.'

He rubbed his chin. 'Renard... I'll make some checks. In the meantime, I shall have you escorted to lodgings. You'll be photographed and informed when new papers are ready for you.'

Another night confined to another hotel. A car arrived to collect them the next morning, and they were escorted into the office of the nameless man.

He smiled when they entered. 'These are your new identities.' He handed documents to Sol, L'Escargot, Christos, and Danielle. 'We are eager for you to resume your work for the resistance. Therefore, you will be flown into France at night. You'll have to wait for a clear night with sufficient moonlight for a plane to land, so you'll be taken to an airfield to await the first opportunity.' He turned to her. 'Miss Renard, these are in your real name as you intend remaining in England. Should you wish to return to France to rejoin your comrades, we can arrange that. You are doing valuable work there.'

'Thank you.' She hesitated. 'We have no money. The Guarda took everything we had.'

'I'll see you have funds before you leave. I wish you all luck, and I hope you find your father, Miss Renard.'

Dismissed, they were escorted back to the reception area. The woman at the desk gave them envelopes containing several pound notes.

'I suppose this is goodbye, Marie.' Danielle had tears in her eyes.

'I suppose so.' She hadn't realised how close they'd all grown and how much she would miss them.

Sol hugged her. 'Thank you for bringing us safely here.'

Christos and L'Escargot couldn't speak for tears. She hadn't seen a grown man cry since Dad lost Mum.

'Stay safe, all of you. Please be careful.'

'And you, Marie… Bonnie. Perhaps, we'll meet again when this is all over.'

'I hope so.' But as they were led away for their journey to the airfield and then France, she knew she would never see them again.

# Chapter Twenty-Three

**Cosby, England. March 1941**

Bonnie stood in the corridor as the train approached Narborough station. Being alone, after months of constant companionship, had made the loss of her friends all the keener, and she couldn't wait to throw herself into Dad's arms. He was alive, and he would be there – she refused to allow herself to believe otherwise.

Her bicycle was where she'd left it, still chained to a post, but there it had to stay; she'd lost the key to the padlock, long since. She hurried the two miles to Cosby muffled against the cold but savouring the familiar sights. Drifts of snow nestled under shady hedgerows spoke of a winter as cold as in France. The stream running through the centre of the village was swollen with meltwater but hadn't yet overtopped its banks. Many of the houses had high doorsteps to keep out the frequent winter floodwater.

The door to the cottage was locked, but the key was under the flowerpot as usual. The house was freezing, and an icy chill settled in her stomach. If Dad was here, he'd have had a fire going. He could be at work, or away showing his samples to customers. Yes, that would be it – Yvonne and Rosemary would know where he was.

The niggling feeling that he'd come home, found her gone, and had gone looking for her refused to leave, but that was better than the other feeling she was failing to ignore, that he'd gone to the guillotine in Fresnes prison six months earlier.

She shivered. First things first. A fire, some food, and a hot drink. She fed the electricity meter and witched on the radio to lessen the oppressive silence. Vera Lynn's voice filled the room. *"We'll meet again..."* The song faded to be replaced by the news. Reports of U-boat attacks on convoys in the Atlantic and bombings in London and Liverpool did nothing to cheer her – she'd witnessed the destruction and the heartbreak. There would be a lot of people who would never meet again.

The fire alight, she looked in the pantry. If Dad had been here, he'd been gone for a while. A lump of green mould probably used to be Red Leicester cheese, and a bottle of milk had separated and solidified. Her heart sank. He wasn't here and hadn't been for months.

She still needed to eat. She had a little money left, so she crossed the road to the shop.

'Bonnie!' Mrs Sibson came around the shop counter and hugged her. 'Have you seen your father?'

'No. He isn't here. Do you know where he is?'

'I haven't seen him since, when would it be... September time. He was worried because you weren't here.'

'September?' Her heart thudded. 'Are you sure it was September?'

'Yes, quite sure.'

'So he's alive! Thank God! He was condemned to the guillotine in August. He escaped! The resistance rescued him!' She danced around the shop and hugged Mrs Sibson. 'Dad's alive.'

'He didn't stay long, duckie. Here one day and gone the next.'

'Did he say where he was going?'

'Not a word. Didn't he leave you a letter or anything?'

'A letter?' She hadn't thought to leave him one. 'I didn't think to look.' She bought some basic provisions and ran back across the road. She should have left him a letter, back in June, instead of taking off for France without a thought, but then she hadn't expected to find her grandparents murdered and her father missing.

The envelope was propped up in front of the clock where she shouldn't have failed to see it. She opened it with shaking fingers.

*My darling Bonnie,*

*I had hoped to find you here, but Mrs Sibson tells me you haven't been here for months. If you have been to France, you'll know that your grandparents are dead and the farm is now in German hands. I am returning to France in the hope of finding you there, but I am joining the Secret Intelligence Service, a branch of the Special Operations Executive, and hope to return to France covertly to continue helping the resistance.*

*If you contact the Minimax Fire Extinguisher Company at 54 Broadway, Westminster, London, they will be able to get a message to me, so I know you are safe.*

*Please, do as I tell you this time, and stay in England.*

*I love you.*

*Dad.*

She reread the letter. Minimax! The nameless man had repeated *Renard* as if he'd heard it before, but he hadn't said anything. He knew where Dad was, he must do.

***

## London, England. March 1941

She'd waited by the phone box in Cosby at seven o'clock, just on the off-chance that Dad was near a phone box, and she rang the one near the farm but without much hope. He wouldn't have remained at the farm, and if he was back with the resistance, he could be anywhere now.

She'd stayed long enough to have a bath, write Dad a letter, check on Rosemary and Yvonne, pack clean clothes, and draw money from the bank in Narborough before catching the train back to London. Staying safely in Cosby, when her friends and father were risking their lives daily for freedom, wasn't an option.

She walked out of the St James Park underground station and across to the Minimax building. She accosted the woman on the reception desk. 'I was told you could get me back into France.'

The woman feigned ignorance. 'Who told you that? We sell fire extinguishers.'

She glanced around, but she was the only person there. 'The intelligence officer I saw a couple of days ago. He said if I wanted to return to help the resistance, he could fly me back in. Tell him Bonnie Renard is here, and I demand to know where my father is.'

'Wait, please.' The woman made a phone call, shielding her mouth and speaking quietly.

She waited, tapping her fingers on the reception desk. She needed replacement papers in the name of Marie Barbier, and transport, and she needed them now.

A door opened and the nameless man smiled at her. 'Come this way, Miss Renard.'

She followed him along the same passage but to a different room behind frosted glass walls, her bravado fading. This man could have her arrested and imprisoned as soon as help her.

'Sit down, please.' The man sat opposite her behind a large mahogany desk. 'You want to return to France?'

'I want to know where my father is.'

'Your father?'

'You know very well who I mean. Antoine Renard – I know he's been recruited by you. Where is he?'

'I don't know.'

'He's one of your agents, and you don't know where he is?'

'He's in France.' The man steepled his fingers and seemed to come to a decision. 'This is classified information, but as you ran an escape and evasion line, I am trusting you with it. He was parachuted into France in the Vosges area, but it doesn't mean he is still there.'

'Vosges isn't that far from Nancy.' She bit her lip aware she might give away information that could compromise Louise and Raphael. *Trust no one.* 'Our family farm is near Nancy. I understand the Germans have taken it.'

'I'm afraid they have appropriated much that belonged to Frenchmen. Land, crops, industries, resources – anything of use to the Nazi regime.'

'Dad said you could get a message to him, so he knows I'm safe.'

'We can send a message, but I can't be sure he'll get it.'

'Can you try?'

'It will have to be in code. What would your father recognise as being from you?'

She rubbed a finger across her lips. 'He'd know who Mrs Sibson was, but I need to tell him where I shall be. I need something… Got it. When I was little, I saw a sparrow and told Dad it was an eagle. He used to tease me they were Cosby eagles.'

'So what would you want to say?' The man reached for a pad and pen.

'Mrs Sibson says the rare Cosby Eagle has been seen nesting in the forest near Nancy. The single chick is waiting for the parent bird to return to the nest.'

The man finished scribbling and nodded. 'The BBC radio broadcasts messages at seven each evening. If your father is with his group, they'll be tuned in and listening. I'll get the BBC to broadcast this a week from tonight. Now, I assume you want to return to France?'

'Yes. I was known as Marie Barbier by my group. I need new French papers in that name, and I need transport to as near Nancy as you can get me.'

'I can get you flown in at night, by Lysander, the same as your friends, but if you miss this full moon period, you'll have to wait until the next. That is out of my hands.'

'I understand. Thank you. Our group desperately needs money if we're to survive.'

'I'll arrange that for you.'

'French francs?'

'It can be done.'

'One more thing. If Dad is working for the S.O.E, he'll have false papers, a false name... how will I find him?'

'He is using the name Gervais DuPont, but divulge that to no one.' He made a brief phone call. 'I'll arrange money, your papers, and a photograph and have you escorted to RAF Shoreham to await a flight. Someone will escort you to your accommodation for this evening and collect you in the morning.' He stood to shake her hand. 'I wish you luck, Miss Renard.'

\*\*\*

**Nancy, France. March 1941**

Waiting for the weather to clear had Bonnie fretful and impatient. The Lysander was fuelled ready to go at a moment's notice, but while the days were cold but sunny after a wet few days, night fogs prevented it from taking off. In another three days, there wouldn't be enough moon to land by.

Coded messages flew backwards and forwards between Louise and Raphael and RAF Shoreham. Raphael had cleared some scrub to enlarge the clearing in the woods. He'd paced it out, and the Lysander pilot assured her he could land and take off again in the distance. In daylight, perhaps, but at night with a waning moon?

The thought of being stuck in England, impotent to help her friends or aid escapees, for another two to three weeks minimum, and then be at the mercy of the weather again, was driving her to desperation.

On the seventeenth, the skies cleared somewhat, and a hurried message was sent to Louise for a weather report.

The reply came back almost immediately. *"Clear. Will light fires at midnight."*

The Camp Commander gave her the thumbs up. 'It will be down to the pilot whether he feels able to land. If not, I'm afraid he will have to bring you back.'

She was ready to throw herself from the plane, but the man would never let her fly if she admitted that. 'I understand.' She smiled. 'Then, I hope not to see you again. Thank you for your help, Commander. I appreciate it.'

He laughed. 'I wish you a safe journey.'

Her pilot, a skinny young man called Geoff, shrugged into his parachute. She looked around for hers, but apparently passengers didn't get one. Throwing herself from the plane became a less attractive option.

The pre-flight checks seemed to take forever, but at last they slid the canopies closed and taxied along the runway. The airfield dropped away and stars twinkled above a thin layer of mist. Soon, moonlight reflected brokenly off water and the dark shapes of ships floated beneath her.

They kept radio silence and flew without lights. This way they hoped to cross France unseen and drop down into the forest west of Nancy. Her job was to keep her eyes open for enemy aircraft and search the ground for the landing fires when they reached Nancy.

The little Lysander droned on through the night. Geoff banked it in a loop and pointed. Below them, the moonlight picked out a broad river. The Moselle. Geoff followed it south until it made a wide loop.

He shouted above the noise of the engine. 'There's Nancy. The landing strip will be pretty much due west among the trees.'

Geoff banked the plane again and swung west.

She peered into the dark, nothing but skeletal trees. 'There. I see a fire.'

He came around and lined up on two rows of three bonfires. 'I'm going to attempt a landing.'

Flying low over the treetops, he dropped the Lysander into the clearing and the wheels touched the rough ground, bumping them along almost into the trees at the other end.

Geoff kept the engine running but jumped out. 'I'll need a hand turning this around.'

Raphael and Louise helped them turn it, ready for take-off.

Geoff climbed back into the plane and waved. 'Good luck, Marie.'

'Safe journey back, Geoff, and thank you.'

They watched as the Lysander trundled along the airstrip and took off, its fixed undercarriage scraping the treetops.

She let out a deep breath as it disappeared into the night.

Raphael was already dousing the bonfires. 'Quickly, we must get away from here before the place is overrun with Nazis. Someone is bound to have heard the plane.'

The fires smothered, they hurried back to Louise's home, taking a roundabout route. As always, the cottage welcomed them, and as always, there were strangers hiding there, waiting to be guided south to Spain and eventual safety.

# Chapter Twenty-Four

**Vosges Mountains, France. March 1941**

Antoine bought supplies from local chemists and hardware shops to replenish his bomb-making stores, wondering how long it would be before the Nazis caught on and banned sales of the stuff. Having carried out several night forays to cut more telephone cables as quickly as they were repaired, destroy some lengths of railway track, and stop production temporarily in three factories by cutting power lines, the group now had a bridge in mind.

It was an old bridge with crumbling masonry, not large or even on a main route, but it was used regularly by Nazi troop carriers and lorries taking provisions to a nearby house that the Germans had requisitioned for army barracks and officer's accommodation.

The home-made satchel bomb packed more explosives than usual, but he still wasn't sure it would do the job. He frowned. 'Don't spoil the ship for a ha'porth of tar.'

Florian looked at him with a puzzled expression.

'It means don't penny-pinch and ruin it. It was one of Sybil's favourite expressions.' Her name fell awkwardly from his lips. He hadn't spoken of her since coming to France and hearing it aloud brought a lump to his throat and an ache in his chest.

'Sybil?'

'My wife.'

'I didn't know you were married. You've never mentioned her.'

'She died – it will be two years ago come Friday. Cancer.'

'I'm sorry, La Fourche. You must miss her.'

'I do. More than I can say.' He added more charge to the satchel bomb. Part of him was grateful Sybil hadn't lived to see the world at war. She'd been such a positive force in his life, so bright, so happy. *La Fourche...* All this was so foreign to her memory – he couldn't imagine that anything but conscription would have wrenched him from her side. Killing the German soldier who'd raped Mum had made him a fugitive and lost him his daughter as well. He tied the top of the improvised satchel and looped the string to make a shoulder strap. 'This one is for her and Bonnie.'

There was little moon, so they were forced to use small handheld torches and the lamps on their bicycles to light their way. The sound of water over rocks chuckled in the still air. The bridge was ahead of him, frost on the road glittering in the light from his bicycle lamp like stars in the heavens.

He leaned his bicycle against the bridge parapet and looked for a good place to lay the bomb. Would it work well enough to blow a hole in the bridge? 'I'm going to take a look at the centre support. If I can weaken that, it should collapse if not immediately. With luck, when it does, it will take a lorry load of Nazis with it.'

'That would be better than blowing the bridge now.' Florian's voice was grim with a note of bitter determination. Renoir and Zacharie's deaths had hit the man hard, and he was hell-bent on revenge. They all were.

'Keep your ears pricked. I'm going to climb down.' He slung the satchel bomb's strap around his shoulder, leaving Florian, Adolf, and Juliette on the bridge, and climbed over the wall and down the bank into the stream. Cold water around his shins made him gasp, but he waded on. Torchlight played on the ripples from above – Florian, no doubt, lighting his way.

The central support had loose stones where the cement had washed away over the years, and no one had bothered to repair it. He scraped out more cement with his pocketknife and pulled the stone out, hoping the structure wouldn't collapse while he was under it. If he could weaken the support, a few heavy lorries should do the rest.

Carefully, he placed the bomb in the hole left by the stone and played out the line that would trigger the detonator. He placed his feet with care; stumbling over a rock could wrench the line and bring tons of masonry down on top of him. Not to mention… 'Get off the bridge! If this goes off…'

The torchlight wavered and disappeared, and he waded to the bank. Back on dry land, he looked for a safe place from which to detonate the bomb. There wasn't one. He just had to hope the line was long enough, and he was far enough away.

'God protect us.' The words were muttered but fervent. He pulled the line, and there was a vivid flash, a deafening explosion, and shooting pain before all went black.

***

Antoine drifted in and out of consciousness, not sure which was which. He could hear voices over the ringing in his ears, but it was still dark. He was lying on something soft, and he was warm, so he must be indoors. How had he got here? His last memory was of cold water and pain. The bridge. The explosion. His head hurt, and he felt sick.

'He's awake.'

'Wherr um.' He tried again. 'Where am I?'

'You're back at the cottage. The bomb went off better than you expected. You were hit with flying rubble.'

'Why is it so dark?'

'You were hit on the head.'

Panic flooded through him. 'I can't see.'

'It's all right.' Juliette's voice was close, calm, and comforting. 'The doctor says you have concussion. You have a nasty cut, and we had to bandage your eyes.'

He forced his hand to obey him and felt the bandage. 'But I will be able to see?'

A warm, soft hand held his. 'The doctor says to keep the bandage on for another day.'

'That doesn't answer my question, Juliette.'

She sighed. 'He hopes you will. Nothing is certain, mon cher.' Warm lips brushed his cheek. 'Try to sleep, La Fourche.'

'But the bridge blew?'

'It's still standing, but as far as Florian could see by torchlight, the masonry was weakened. We can only wait and see.'

'You've warned the resistance and locals to keep off it?'

'Yes, of course. Now rest. I'll bring you some soup when it's cooked.'

'What time is it?'

'Almost seven o'clock.'

'Morning or night?'

'Night.'

Not being able to see isolated him, but he could still hear. 'Can you turn on the radio?'

'Florian's doing it now.'

Music faded, and the BBC newsreader's familiar voice spoke. *'The Luftwaffe have bombed the Avonmouth area of Bristol, causing damage and civilian casualties. The German submarine U-100 was depth-charged and sunk by British warships when it attacked convoy HX112. U-99 was scuttled off Iceland. Liverpool and Birkenhead were both targeted today, and the British vessel Rosaura is reported sunk off Tobruk after striking a naval mine. Yugoslavia has voted to join the Tripartite Pact and side with the Axis powers.'*

The news ran on, little of it good.

'*Now for some messages to our troops. Mrs Sibson says the rare Cosby Eagle has been seen nesting in the forest near Nancy. The single chick is waiting for the parent bird to return to the nest.*'

He forced himself up on one elbow. '*Mrs Sibson? The Cosby Eagle chick?* That's a message for me from Bonnie! It has to be! She's here, near Nancy – only a few miles away. If she's in the forest, she must be with the resistance, with another maquis cell. I need to find her.'

Gentle hands held him. Juliette's soft voice calmed him. 'You're not fit to go anywhere, La Fourche. If she's sent you a message, she's letting you know she's safe. When you're up to it, we'll help you find her. I promise.'

He sank back against his pillows, exhausted. 'I can't wait to see her.'

The silence told him *seeing* her might be a hope too far. Tears soaked into his bandage. She was so like her mother, and the thought of never being able to see her beautiful face again crushed his soul.

***

**Near Nancy, France. April 1941**

Bonnie listened to the radio and the BBC broadcasts every evening in Louise's living room, but if Dad had heard her message, he hadn't replied to it. He must have realised it was from her. Who else would know of Mrs Sibson and the Cosby Eagle?

She tried to concentrate on the newsreader. '*An ancient bridge over a stream near Sainte-Michel-sur-Meurthe collapsed today, plunging two German troop carriers into the water. Three soldiers are reported killed and many more injured. The bridge...*' A loud cheer from Louise and Raphael drowned the rest of the report. Any Nazi death was a cause for celebration, and the chances were, the collapse was down to maquis sabotage.

While she shared their jubilation, a part of her regretted how hardened she had become to death and killing. War had changed her in ways she didn't like, but while she still blamed herself for the Abrams' deaths, it was Hitler's attitude to Jews that had forced them into that tragic decision. Hitler who had killed her grandparents. Hitler who had stolen her father.

'The authorities haven't blamed the maquisards. Hopefully, that means there won't be reprisals.' Louise echoed her own hope.

*Maquisards*, members of the rural resistance, so called because maquis meant underbrush, and many of the maquis bases were hidden in the wooded hills, and protected and provisioned by the farms and villages that surrounded them, just as Louise and Raphael's was. She smiled, unable to hide her joy at three Nazi deaths, while wishing one of them had been Hitler. 'However it happened, it's another victory for France. Wait. Listen!'

'*A mob of Nazi collaborators has attacked two synagogues in Antwerp. The Vlaams Nationaal Verbond, Flemish National Union, the Volksverwering, the People's defence, the Anti-Jewish League, and other pro-Nazi anti-Semitic groups burned two synagogues in the Oostenstraat, and smashed the windows of Jewish-owned shops before looting them.*

*The attacks happened after the showing of a film produced by the Nazi Ministry of Public Enlightenment and Propaganda, which showed Jews as parasites bent on world domination.*'

She looked at Louise and Raphael in alarm. 'It's getting worse and worse. Hitler is determined to turn everyone against the Jewish people.'

'And he's already deported thousands from Austria to camps in Poland or forced them into ghettos.' Raphael shook his head. 'It will happen here before long, mark my words.'

'Then we must step up our efforts to get them out of France.' She hadn't told them of the long delays she and the escapees had endured in Spain. 'I'm willing to escort them to the safe house in Marseille. Colette and Marcel will arrange for them to be taken on through Spain. That in itself isn't easy – the Spanish aren't helpful, as I discovered, but the British Consulate will do all they can, and there are ships to take escapees to England.'

'We'll put the word out. The more people we can help, the better.'

She was determined to do her part. 'If I could get to London, so can others.'

The radio droned on with depressing news. She was about to turn it off when the message came through '*On a lighter note, an update for ornithologists on sightings of the Cosby Eagle. The adult male bird has been seen circling over the hills south of Nancy, searching for prey.*' She let out a whoop of joy. 'Dad got my message. He knows where I am now. He's here in France, and not far away.'

Louise hugged her. 'I'm so happy for you, Raven. *The hills south of Nancy.* The Vosges? There is a maquis cell in the Vosges Mountains. *Searching for prey.* He's working for the resistance?'

'He's working for British Intelligence, Louise. They're the ones who would have got the BBC to broadcast the message. He's quite likely to be with the maquis.' She would find out where his camp was, and she *would* see him again, but she must be patient. She and Dad both had vital work to do to help bring down the German occupiers and save those in fear of their lives, and she had to be very careful not to compromise his cell, the safehouse in Marseille, or Louise and Raphael.

# Chapter Twenty-Five

**Near Nancy, France. May 1841**

Bonnie and her father had sent messages to one another via drop points and the couriers who worked the area between Vosges and Nancy. Both agreed that the future of France came before personal desires, hard though that was. They might not be able to meet yet, but they could communicate, and that meant a lot to her. She no longer felt alone.

She dropped her latest message and picked up one for Raphael.

Back at the cottage, Raphael read it. 'Damnation. The Nemrod cell has been compromised. Several members have been arrested. They're being tried before the Greater Court in Paris.'

'And we don't doubt they'll be found guilty. Hitler is good at passing laws to legalise murder.'

Louise dried her hands on a towel. 'And to discriminate against Jews and "Aryanise" their property.'

Raphael nodded. 'I'll move the radio transmitter again. We can't risk the Germans homing in on it. I think we should move our drop point as well. See if you can find a suitable place, Raven.'

'It's not long since it was moved, but I'll leave a message in the old place saying where the new one will be.'

'The Nazis are getting more determined to stamp us out.' Louise looked around her living room. 'Do you think we're safe here?'

Raphael looked from her to Louise. 'It shows we're successfully being a thorn in their sides. However, I think we should be more careful how we approach the cottage. We must take different routes, maybe hide some of the more frequented paths with brushwood.'

Louise smiled. 'I'd hate to leave here, and there's plenty of dead wood and branches in the forest we can use.'

'We should use branches to brush out our footprints as well. Anything to hide our whereabouts.'

'Can we risk listening to the BBC, now, Raphael?'

'We need to listen for the coded messages, but the Germans are jamming the signals. Perhaps, for now, it would be safer to listen to Radio Paris, Raven, though I'll miss the music and sketches.'

Louise got to her feet with a huff and turned on the radio. 'Not that we can believe what the Nazis say. The BBC is more likely to tell us the truth, and they cheer me up.

'It's all propaganda. One side refutes what the other says. What are we to believe?'

*'In one of the first major trials of a resistance group, all of the accused have been condemned to death. The trial on Rue Saint-Dominique took place today. Acts of sabotage against the German occupiers will result in execution by shooting.'*

Condemned to death, as Dad had been. No one spoke, but determined expressions showed they weren't afraid to die for France should it be necessary.

*'Upon a request by the German authorities, French police today arrested more than three thousand seven hundred Jews, mainly of Polish origin, and transported them to Pithiviers and Beaune-la-Rolande camps south of Paris. They will be processed and deported to Auschwitz in Poland.'*

Raphael's knuckles showed white. 'It's begun. First Jews in Austria and now here.'

'Can we do nothing to stop it?'

'There'll be groups nearer the railway routes preparing for sabotage as we speak – you can be sure of that. We three can only do so much, Raven.'

'I'll do more journeys.'

'It will become more dangerous both to hide them and guide them south as more Jews try to leave and the Nazis step up their searches and surveillance.'

'I don't care. I owe the Abrams... I owe it to little Ava.'

Louise put a hand on hers. 'It wasn't your fault, Raven.'

'Maybe not, Louise, but I won't let Hitler kill more Jews without saving as many as I can.'

'Neither will I. The day after tomorrow, you'll head south with a family. They are arriving tonight, and I hope to have their false papers tomorrow. Now, I must prepare food. I'm sure they'll be hungry.'

\*\*\*

## Vosges Mountains, France. May 1941

Antoine's sight had gradually recovered, though he still had headaches. He listened to the news when he could, cheered and depressed according to how the war was progressing. The battlecruiser HMS *Hood* had been sunk by the German battleship, *Bismark*. It was a blow to the Royal Navy, but he'd cheered at the news that HMS *Ark Royal* had sunk *Bismark* three days later, off Iceland, while the Germans had been attempting to break out of the Denmark Strait to attack Allied merchant shipping.

The French still hadn't forgiven Britain for sinking their ships at Mers-el-Kébir, killing more than a thousand French sailors the previous year. Collateral damage to avoid the fleet falling into German hands, didn't comfort the bereaved nation however necessary it may have seemed to the British.

Now, miners in Northern France had gone on strike against working conditions, and it wasn't only costing the Nazi war machine thousands of tons of coal, it had boosted the resistance movements morale by protesting against the collaborative employers who sought to repress them.

The German administration was increasingly targeting Jews, communists, resistors, Gaullists – anyone who made a stand against them or whom they considered undesirable. The maquis' men and women were all in constant danger of arrest or betrayal, but it didn't stop him considering the matter at hand.

The convoy of arrested Jews had yet to leave Paris for Poland, and they didn't know which route they would take – Metz and Saarbrucken east, or farther south, passing Nancy to the north, and on via Strasbourg.

If deporting Jews, resistance hostages, and political prisoners was to be a regular occurrence, a major disruption was needed. Blowing up a small road bridge or train tracks was one thing, blowing a substantial railway bridge would be quite another.

He spread a map on the table and traced a finger along a railway line. 'Here is about the closest place to us.' He jabbed the map. 'The railway crosses the Canal de la Marne du Rhin and La Zorn River west of Saverne. We'd need a truck to get there, but if we could blow one of those bridges before the train reaches it, it would hold up a convoy and give the deportees a chance of escaping.'

Florian studied the route. 'We'd need to be sure the train didn't go off the bridge, La Fourche, and kill everyone. Someone would need to warn the train driver with red flags or lights. It's a long, slow journey, and the train might well reach the bridge in the middle of the night. It could be a disaster.'

'That's a wise precaution.' He added red flags and lights to his list of requirements. 'Lucas, Adolf, can you "requisition" flags and lights from the station as soon as possible?'

Lucas leapt to his feet. 'Consider it done.'

Florian pointed a grubby finger. 'That looks like a tunnel after the bridges. Could we block that somehow?'

'It would take a lot of rubble to hold up a train for long. A bridge down would be more disruptive.'

Florian still sounded doubtful. 'We don't know when the train will leave. We could already be too late, or we may be standing guard over the bridge for days and they take a different route. We need more information.'

Juliette stood. 'I'll get a message to Hugo in Fresnes. He may have contacts in the other prisons who'll know.'

He smiled. 'Hugo saved my life. I never got the chance to thank him properly.'

'Then I shall add a message that the little bird he set free is alive and well.'

He reached out a hand to hers. 'Thank you, ma chère.' He turned back to Florian. 'If we can stop one convoy it will be worth it.'

'Agreed. I shall check over Renoir's truck and load it with a few bags of coal. With this strike, coal is in short supply. It's excellent cover.'

He folded the map. 'I'll prepare some explosives while we wait for a reply. I'm not sure what kind of bridge it is. If it's stone, it may be more than I can blow without more supplies.'

It was late when Juliette hurried into the room. 'The convoy is due to leave Paris first thing in the morning. Hugo's contact didn't know the route.'

Florian got up from the table. 'Then we must go tonight and take our chances. Just make sure it's the biggest bang you can make, La Fourche.'

***

The Zorn valley was narrow and steep-sided, and early morning mist rose from the river. The river, canal, road, and railway all ran alongside one another, but the railway crossed the canal and the river at this point before entering a tunnel under the mountain.

Antoine cursed beneath his breath as Florian parked the truck. 'It's a stone bridge and a big one at that.' Five arches spanned the river while the sixth crossed the canal.

'You can only try, La Fourche. One arch may not be beyond your explosives. It worked before, eventually.'

'That was an ancient bridge that was in a bad state of repair already. This is a different proposition altogether.'

'Do your best. No one can ask more of you than that.'

He picked up his satchel bombs, he'd made two for double effect, and walked along the towpath towards the bridge. A line of barges pulled by horses travelled east laden with steel, coal, and grain. French steel, coal, and grain bound for Germany.

He fisted his hands. There was rationing in France, and people in Paris were starving with ration cards and nothing to buy in the shops, while the Nazis stole the very food from their children's mouths. Rural folk didn't eat well, but with vegetable gardens and a few chickens and animals, they fared better. The maquis, constantly forced to move around the wooded hills from camp to camp would have starved too but for the farmers and villagers who brought them food they could ill afford. It was their way of standing together and resisting the occupiers.

There was nothing he could do about the barges, and looking at the sturdy construction of the underneath of the bridge, it didn't look as if there was much he could do about that either. Just mangling the track or blowing a crater in the ground wouldn't hold the train up for long if it wasn't derailed, and they couldn't risk that with innocent people aboard.

A shaggy carthorse led by a man lumbered under the bridge a few metres ahead of a barge loaded with steel, and he stood aside to let them pass. The canal was narrow beneath the low bridge with only room for one barge and not a lot of headroom. The bow of the boat drew level with him, and on impulse, he threw himself onto it as it passed. Keeping his head and body low, he planted his bombs, and pushed himself clear. Running, pulling the line as he went, he dived to the ground as a huge explosion sent lumps of metal crashing against the underside of the bridge.

A woman screamed, horses broke free and galloped off in panic. Lumps of masonry fell from the arch and splashed into the water, and the barge sank slowly to the bottom of the canal, totally blocking the waterway.

He picked himself up off the ground, head ringing. That had been a shave too close. A woman was floundering in the water, yelling and trying to save a dog.

He waded in and helped her out and then pulled out the dog by the scruff of its neck. It shook canal water all over him. 'Are you all right, madame?'

The woman dripped in front of him. 'No, I'm not! My barge has sunk. What happened?'

He looked up at the bridge, which was stubbornly standing despite the scars of war. It had been a small hope his ploy would work. 'I'm sorry, but you were taking steel to Germany.' He waved an arm at the laden barges crowding behind her. 'Steel, coal, machine tools, spare parts, food…'

'I have to earn a living.'

'Steel to build weapons and tanks to kill Frenchmen and our allies. Be grateful you and your dog are alive, and your man and horse aren't hurt.'

Gruff shouts sounded behind him. He turned to see angry bargees running towards him, shaking their fists. He'd blocked their only route east through the Vosges Mountains, and they were far from happy about it. He took to his heels, praying Florian had the truck's engine running, and fled along the towpath.

He'd gambled to save three thousand Jewish lives and lost.

# Chapter Twenty-Six

**Near Nancy, France. June 1941**

Bonnie had run several missions south with people trying to evade the Nazis. Airmen shot down over France, Jews, communists, and resistance fighters needing to escape Nazi clutches. There seemed no end to people desperate to leave occupied France.

The more journeys she made, the more nervous she'd become, and the more she hated leaving Marcel, fearing she'd never see him again. She needed a new cover story in case some guard checking the train recognised her from a previous mission, and to that end, she'd contacted Yvonne and Rosemary in Leicester – a request for two dozen pairs of assorted styles of socks and stockings, a price list, and an order book, to be sent to M. Barbier, care of the Post Office in Nancy, shouldn't raise the suspicions of any nosey Nazi.

She cycled into town, hoping her package would have arrived. Her new cover story was actually the truth. She was going to be a travelling saleswoman, showing samples of her father's wares to prospective purchasers and existing clients. It was totally reasonable that her father was away fighting for France, and she was trying to keep his business going. She felt bad about leaving her employees in the lurch, so if she could send some new contacts to them, it would help assuage her guilt. She was not only helping them and the resistance, she was helping the family funds, and it gave her the perfect excuse to make regular journeys south by train.

Had she considered every aspect of her plan? She could carry the sample hosiery easily in a small bag. She would have an order book printed with the company name – Dad's name wasn't mentioned on it as far as she remembered, and if it was, she could cross it out and insert Marie Barbier to match her papers.

She could take cash or cheque deposits, cheques made out to the company and forwarded to Yvonne and Rosemary, and cash, she could use herself; she wasn't sure if she was allowed to send money out of the country under the new regime.

She would post the order, the women could dispatch it to the address in France, and new clients could pay the balance direct to England on delivery of the order.

All businesses operated on trust, and with copies of orders and invoices as well as the samples, she would appear a bona fide business to German guards.

What about existing clients. They'd be a source of easy repeat orders, but they knew Dad. What if they were collaborators? Was she overthinking it? They didn't know where Dad was, that he was a maquis, or what his false name was, and they'd never met her. They would believe she was Marie and was working for Monsieur Renard.

Who was going to bother to check the fine details, anyway? As long as she stuck to the same story, convincingly, she'd be fine.

The parcel had arrived, and she put it in her bicycle basket and pedalled home again. She opened it on the kitchen table. There were socks but no stockings. Yvonne had penned a letter.

*My dear Bonnie,*

*I have sent what I can. Clothes rationing has just begun in England, and silk and nylon are particularly hard to come by as they are needed for parachutes. However, I have some stock of socks, though they may not last long unless I can get some on the black market, and of course there's an extra cost as you will see from the price list. Everything is so expensive because of the war.*

*Rosemary and I are both well, thank you for your enquiry, and I hope you and your father are too.*

*Best wishes*

*Yvonne.*

That had dashed her hopes of making much money, but as long as she had samples and paperwork, she should pass scrutiny at checkpoints, which was her main objective. She could make up false orders and invoices.

She threw the letter on the fire before anyone who shouldn't saw her real name. One day, she'd be Bonnie again, not Raven or Marie, but for now –

'Raven, there's another family needs picking up.'

'Going now, Louise.' She hurried out of the house. The family would have been passed from safehouse to safehouse all the way from Paris, and she would meet them in an old barn a couple of miles north of Louise's home. From there, they'd take a circuitous route along hidden trails, removing their tracks as they went.

They were daily more careful as further members of the resistance were arrested, and either deported to camps or executed. Some had been tortured into giving up their comrades, and it was more and more difficult to know who could be trusted.

In April, Pat O'Leary was arrested when his boat capsized, and he had to swim ashore. He ran part of the eastern escape route, bringing agents in and taking escapees out on feluccas to bigger boats sailing between Marseille and Gibraltar. He'd been imprisoned in St Hippolyte du Forte. Colette had been distraught, not just because she liked the man, but because he knew a lot of names and safehouses in the Marseille area if he broke under torture.

She tried to push thoughts of betrayal from her mind as she knocked on the door of the barn. The Vichy government was carrying out a census of Jews and their property in both zones – it could only mean they intended to arrest more people and make it easier to steal their assets.

The door opened a crack.

'It's Marie. I've come to take you to a safehouse.'

The door opened wider to reveal the frightened eyes of an elderly man, a young woman, and a boy.

She glanced around. 'I'm alone. Come, quickly.'

She led them away from the barn and into the trees. 'Walk carefully, and keep to hard ground. We must leave no trace.

It took three miles to cover the two miles from the barn to the house, back-tracking, leaving false trails, covering their tracks and trails, but at last they reached home. She ushered them inside. Another family to feed, more false papers to arrange, more heart-stopping checkpoints and guards demanding papers.

It was worth it to see them safe to Colette's, where she'd hand them on to Marcel to take to the Cuvaliers, who'd prepare them for the journey over the Pyrenees with a fresh guide – only the Cuvaliers knew who. June was a better time to cross than December, but Spain would be unbearably hot, and the thought of possibly being incarcerated for weeks in a Spanish prison in the heat and flies of summer didn't bear thinking about.

Her mind was drawn back to Marcel. They'd have a day together, maybe two, before they must part again. She couldn't wait to see him.

\*\*\*

## Marseille, France. June 1941

As always, the family she guided over the demarcation line to Marseille had become friends. Much as Bonnie had tried to distance herself emotionally from them, Avis, James, and Raymond had wormed their way into her heart. She didn't know their real names, any more than they knew hers, but those were the names on their documents.

It was weird, getting to know people on a long journey that had so much at stake for them all, and yet never really knowing them at all.

Her new cover story had worked like a charm – she'd almost sold one guard a pair of socks. Avis and James had their own cover story, and professed not to be connected with Marie although they shared a carriage. Raphael had insisted on it to help protect her, and she was grateful for his care. She was needed for future missions.

The train pulled into the station in Marseille, and she threw open the carriage door.

'Marie!' Jumping up and down and waving his arms at the far end of the platform was a familiar figure.

She waved back, resisting the urge to abandon her charges and run into Marcel's arms.

He ran along the platform towards her, dodging around people in his haste to reach her. 'Marie…' He held her close and kissed her, a long, passionate kiss that made her heart feel as if it would burst.

'Marcel…' Breathless, she introduced her friends.

'I have a car. This way, quickly.' Marcel grabbed a couple of their heaviest bags and led the way.

Once safely in the car, she relaxed. 'Is everyone well?' It was a pointed question.

Marcel nodded. 'Nothing has happened since you were last here.'

'And O'Leary?'

'We think he escaped.'

He hadn't betrayed them? 'You think he can be trusted? You don't think he was allowed to escape?'

'I would trust him with my life, Marie. If he'd cracked under torture, we'd all be arrested by now, and if he didn't crack, he won't betray us now.'

'I hope you're right.'

Marcel put a hand on hers. 'Garrow trusts him, Marie, and I trust Garrow.'

She'd heard the name Garrow before but hadn't enquired further; the less she knew the better.

He parked the car a few streets away from Colette's house, and they took a detour before knocking twice and then twice again on her front door. The door opened almost instantly, and he hurried them all inside.

'Marie! Thank God.' Colette hugged her tight. 'This never gets any easier. Every time, I worry until you're here safe, and Marcel is like a lost puppy when you're away.'

She laughed and squeezed Colette closer. 'Well, he'll have me all to himself until you have the documents for Avis, James, and Raymond.' She turned away as she introduced her charges. 'You're safe here with Colette. She is a diamond among women. I am blessed to have two mothers – Louise and Colette.'

Avis looked surprised. 'Louise is your mother?'

'No, sadly my own mother died not so long ago, but Louise has been like a second mother to me.'

'Louise?' Marcel was curious.

'A woman at a safehouse I use.' She wanted to say more, to tell Marcel all about Louise and Raphael and their home in the forest near Nancy, but she couldn't. It was so unfair she couldn't share that part of her life with the man she loved. Maybe one day, when it was all over, and she and Dad had been reunited, she and Marcel would share stories and tell their children about the heroes of the resistance.

Her cheeks flushed hot. They'd lived for the moment and hadn't dared to discuss the future or marriage, let alone children. Their view had been *eat, drink, and be merry, for tomorrow we may die*, but she wanted there to be a future beyond tomorrow, beyond war, and she wanted it to be with Marcel.

Colette interrupted her daydream. 'You'll not have heard the news. O'Leary is in Marseille.'

'He is? Where?' Marcel flushed. 'Sorry, I shouldn't ask, but I'd like to meet him.'

'It's an open secret. He's at the Seamen's Mission with Garrow.'

There were several safehouses in Marseille, it was a jumping-off point for Gibraltar either by sea or over the mountains. The Seamen's Mission was one of the largest; it operated under the cover of being for needy seamen, and it hid soldiers, downed British pilots, and sailors rescued from torpedoed ships, all pretending to be civilians, and all eager to do their duty and return to Britain and serve any way they could.

With such devotion to duty, how could Britain and France fail to boot the Nazi occupiers from French soil?

Colette hadn't done with her news. 'Also, Jean Moulin is in Marseille. He's collecting information to take to de Gaulle in London. We are small groups working with little knowledge of one another. Moulin hopes to convince de Gaulle of the importance of the resistance work and link us with the London Free French. He hopes a more unified organisation will be more efficient.'

It was another of the names she'd heard; another resistance fighter she'd never met. These were important leaders, all putting their lives at risk for France and with the best of intentions, but was unifying the movement advantageous or dangerous?

*Trust no one.*

# Chapter Twenty-Seven

**Vosges Mountains, France. June 1941**

June was proving to be a wet month. Antoine turned his back to light drizzle as he waited alone for the expected drop – he'd drawn the short straw to come out and get wet. A message had come through that there would be "*birds migrating south*" to the usual drop point. Plural sounded like several more mouths to feed.

The sky was overcast, blotting out the moon, which made the drop all the more unusual and perilous. It was down to the pilot to decide if it was safe for agents to jump. He consulted his watch, which glowed faintly in the dark. Time to try to light the bonfires he'd laid earlier. He shook a generous splash of lamp oil from a can onto a large handful of dry tinder and struck a spark on his lighter, holding his breath. The flame caught, and he fanned it gently, before moving on to the next – six in all in the usual two rows of three to guide the pilot in.

Thunder rumbled in the distance, and lightning briefly threw the trees into bright relief. *Please, God, don't unleash a downpour now.* He searched the sky, listening intently. Was that thunder or the sound of a plane? Surely, the pilot would have aborted the mission.

His neck was stiff from looking up, and rain dripped down his face and neck. This was madness. A bright flash lit the clouds. A plane!

He threw more lamp oil onto the struggling bonfires which flared with increased vigour.

The plane was flying low to get beneath the cloud cover and German radar. Too low? Would parachutes have time to deploy properly?

He forgot to breathe.

A white cloud mushroomed above him, then another, and another, and the plane banked away west, the sound of its engines fading. Either that was all the men who were jumping, or the pilot had gone around for another approach.

Another flash lit the parachutes as they drifted to the ground. He frowned. There weren't any men. Three containers hit the ground and were enveloped in collapsing cream silk. That explained the risk with parachuting in bad weather, but what was so urgent the pilot risked his own neck?

He wouldn't find out standing there in the wet. He bundled up the parachutes and hid them in a deserted badgers' den, concealing the entrance with dead wood. Two of the containers were metal cylinders, probably containing arms and ammunition. The other was a large wicker hamper – S.O.E expected them to have a picnic in this weather?

As long as it contained food, he didn't care.

He loaded the cylinders onto Renoir's truck with a sigh. It would always be Renoir's, no matter that he was dead. He went back for the hamper, hurrying now for fear of Nazis mad enough to be out in the rain.

It was heavy and was making an odd noise. He loaded it quickly and jumped into the truck out of the rain. S.O.E was sending their food live now?

Back at the cottage, they opened the containers. Ammunition as they'd hoped, tinned and dried food, another radio, and a large bag of corn. They eyed the hamper uneasily. A soft churring noise was coming from it.

Juliette unfastened the leather straps and opened it cautiously. 'Pigeons?'

Florian rubbed his hands together in glee. 'Fresh food! Tasty cooked in a good Bordeaux.'

Juliette pushed Florian's hand away as he reached for the neck of the nearest bird. 'Wait. There's an envelope taped to the inside of the lid.'

'I don't need a recipe.'

'Shush, Florian.' She opened the envelope and read the contents. 'They're not for eating. They're carrier pigeons. Homing pigeons.' She lifted one out and held it upside-down. 'These little cylinders are to put messages in. We put the cylinders around their legs, let the birds go, and they fly home to England. German radar won't pick up these little fellows.'

'That explains the corn.'

'There are instructions as to their care. We need somewhere to keep them, La Fourche.'

A bird flapped into the air and perched on top of the kitchen dresser. He closed the lid on the hamper before Juliette gave them all names or they escaped. 'I'll knock something up. There's wood and chicken wire lying around.' Leaving the others to capture the escapee, he slipped out to the shed. He couldn't stop grinning at the downcast expressions on his friends' faces when they'd realised pigeon in red wine was off the menu.

*** 

## Marseille, France. June 1941

Disturbing news had come from the Vienne, an area to the north of Marseille that had been cut in half by the demarcation line.

Bonnie looked across the table to Colette and Marcel. 'A thousand?'

Marcel nodded. 'That's what the man said. Over a thousand communists rounded up and arrested in the occupied zone and thirty-three in the Vienne. The Nazis are calling it *Aktion Theoderich*. It comes straight after Hitler attacked the Soviet Union.'

'And the French police helped the Nazis? What was their crime?'

'Communists believe all private ownership of land and assets is theft. Germany's landowners and businessmen want to stop them gaining political influence – many of the rich are Nazi supporters. The arrested were members of a trade union or the Communist Party. Some are suspected of sabotage, producing anti-German leaflets and newspapers, or providing secret meeting places.'

She lifted her hand from the pile of leaflets she'd promised to circulate that morning as if she'd been stung. 'And they're in prison?'

'At the moment, they're in the camp at Chauvinerie in Poitiers. '

'That's a concentration camp for gypsies, isn't it?'

Marcel nodded. 'And Jews. From there, many have found their way to Drancy.'

Colette shuddered. The name, like Auschwitz, Mauthausen, Sachsenhausen, and Bergen-Belsen made them all uneasy. 'And none return from these Nazi camps to tell of the conditions there. We shall have a flood of communists joining Jews trying to escape. You're going to be busy, Marie.'

She chewed a thumbnail. 'The Germans will be all the more watchful now. So far, I've been lucky bringing families south. Our passes have held up to scrutiny. I've managed to distract guards with seduction, or portraits, or by trying to get orders for socks.' Some of the guards had complained of sore feet and uncomfortable socks and had actually asked to take one of her samples. 'Hiding in the train toilets when passing the checkpoint has also worked, but I can't help feeling our luck might have run out.'

Marcel leaned forward and put a hand over hers. 'What can we do to help you, Marie?'

Colette put her hands on the table and pushed herself to her feet. 'I have a contact in Vienne who runs a small business taking livestock from the local markets to the abattoir. He has a pass because his work means he has to cross the demarcation line with his cattle truck.'

'You think he would take our escapees?'

'I think so. He already runs weapons and messages across the line, but it would be a greater risk for him, Marie.'

'Breathing is a great risk. Everything we do is a great risk. If the Nazis discover this safehouse...' The unfinished thought hung between them like a death sentence. 'Contact him, Colette. I'm willing to take the risk if he is.'

Marcel squeezed her hand. 'I'm so proud of you, ma chère, but please, be careful.'

She smiled. 'I will. I just hope we don't have to share the truck with cattle.'

***

## Near Vienne, France. August 1941

'Ugh!' Bonnie flinched as a wet tongue slapped across her ear and cheek. She pushed the bullock's nose away and wiped her face on her sleeve. 'Stop it.' The young beasts were curious and skittish – not the best travelling companions.

As she'd feared, her new route over the demarcation line in a cattle truck necessitated sharing the truck with livestock. Five communists had fled Paris and found their way to Louise's door. As always, they'd been welcomed, fed, hidden, and transported south. They'd left the train north of Vienne and been met by Dion, Colette's contact, who was to take then to the nearest station south of the line to continue their journey.

The truck stopped bouncing along the rough road. Were they at the checkpoint already?'

She peered through a gap between wooden planks. A Citroën lorry in German livery had broken down by the side of the road. 'Get down, hide at the back among the cattle.'

The men did as she bid them, and she squatted beside them, praying the bullocks wouldn't move apart and betray their presence.

Usually, they were waved through with a cursory inspection if it was obvious there were cattle in the truck.

'We are requisitioning this lorry.'

'But, you can't. It's full of bullocks for the abattoir.'

A long, pointed stick poked through one of the ventilation gaps, jabbing the nearest bullock and stirring them all into motion.

Someone shouted in German, and light flooded in as the rear ramp was lowered. Looking between the bullocks' legs, she could see two Germans.

Dion, who was driving the lorry, was arguing. 'If you let these bullocks escape, there'll be no catching them. Do you want cattle all over the highway? Close that ramp.'

Darkness descended and she breathed again.

'We are still requisitioning this lorry. Ours has broken down – damned inferior French vehicles. We need to get to Valence.'

There was a silence but for the disturbed bellowing of the cattle, and the truck bounced forward again. She peered out of the gap again but couldn't see if Dion had been left behind. She couldn't see any Germans either.

One of the men stood between two bullocks. 'Are the Germans in the cab? Oh, Lord help us.'

She steadied herself against the wooden lorry side. 'Shush, Valence is south of the line. With luck, they'll abandon the truck once they get to their destination. What would two Germans want with a load of cows?'

'Fresh meat?'

'God, I hope not.'

The truck bounced on for what seemed like an age but was probably only minutes. It came to an abrupt halt amid shouting, before moving on again. What the hell was happening.

At length, the rear ramp banged down and the bullocks, wide-eyed and frightened, made a dash for freedom. The stench told her they'd arrived at the abattoir.

Dion smiled at them and pointed. 'You can get out now. The station is half a mile that way.'

***

**Near Nancy, France. August 1941**

Bonnie moved the radio yet again. As she'd feared, the occupying force had increased the pressure on Jews and the resistance. New laws had been passed in July that prohibited Jewish people from having radios, moving house, or going out in public at certain times. Many had no income, and all were desperate to escape the Nazi regime; they were being hunted down and deported.

The military tribunals that tried people suspected of anti-Nazi actions were becoming ever more severe. Prison sentences and death sentences were handed out for the least infringement. Hundreds were being sent to Reich prisons.

More terrifying still was a report of the mass murder of Polish scientists and writers. Hitler, it seemed, was determined to stamp out anyone capable of intelligent independent thought who might speak against him.

She and Louise and Raphael huddled around the radio in the deserted barn a mile from Louise's cottage. The roof leaked, and they'd had a job finding a dry spot.

Louise held up a hand to stop the conversation as the radio crackled into life. "*The Parisian Municipal Police have today arrested more Jewish men in retaliation for acts against the German military authorities. Some four thousand are being taken to the new Drancy camp in the suburbs, where they will be held as hostages.*

"*AktionT4, the Nazi euthanasia programme for institutionalised people with disabilities, has been suspended in Germany after the Bishop of Münster led a widespread protest against the euthanasia of the incurably sick and those in psychiatric hospitals.*

*"Following the shooting of Alfons Moser, a German naval cadet, at Barbès-Rochechouart station in Paris, the military administration announced that all French citizens detained by the Germans be considered hostages, and therefore are liable to be shot. The murder of Moser was in retaliation for the execution of Samuel Tyszelman for taking part in an anti-German demonstration. One hundred and fifty Parisians will be shot in reprisals."*

Louise held her head in her hands, shaking it in denial. 'When will this madness stop?'

Raphael thumped the table with a fist. 'It will stop when every German has been driven from France. It will stop when Hitler is six feet under the turf. He thinks this will stop us resisting! He is wrong. We will fight to the last for a free France.'

She put an arm around Louise's shoulders. 'We'll make every death count, Louise. They are sacrificing their lives for their country, just as we are sacrificing ours. They will not die in vain.'

# Chapter Twenty-Eight

**Near Nancy, France. September 1941**

Bonnie cycled along the lane through the forest, pamphlets hidden beneath the medical supplies in her bicycle basket. Appalled by the shootings of Parisians, Louise had had them printed secretly in Nancy. They were bound for a drop point used by neighbouring resistance cells and were to be passed along a chain to the good people of Paris.

She hoped Louise's rousing words would kindle the flame of resistance in the hearts of those who stood by and did nothing while good men died for them.

As she pedalled, she considered the ever-darkening days, and not because autumn had arrived. How often had she longed to be in the forest when the leaves turned to yellow and gold, and mist swathed the Moselle Valley. Despite Hitler, the world was still a beautiful place.

Hitler dragged her mind back to the reality of life in occupied and "Free" France. The Vichy government had committed themselves to the execution of six communists, and they'd passed a new law, creating a State Tribunal for the judgement of "acts against the people's security" with no appeal.

In occupied France, things were even darker. The parliamentary representative of Amiens, and two others, had been guillotined. Jews were to be forced to wear yellow stars with *Juif or Juive* written on them and were forbidden to leave their town without written consent – getting them onto one of the escape lines that ran south through France was now next to impossible.

Another decree had been signed concerning seditious communist movements in the occupied territories that required the execution of fifty to one hundred communists in reprisal for every German soldier killed. Military courts had been ordered to sentence the perpetrators of acts of resistance to death. Reprisals after the attack on German soldiers by resistance members in Paris would be swingeing.

The only bright pieces of news were that the British had bombed Berlin, and the United States were on convoy duty after a German submarine had fired on the USS *Greer*. President Roosevelt had ordered his navy to shoot on sight; America had joined the naval war against Germany and Italy.

She pedalled on grimly determined. What she was doing now was punishable by death. What Dad was doing, what all the resistance cells were doing, was punishable by death, and yet here she was extolling others to resist and risk execution. Tears rolled down her cheeks and blurred her vision.

All she longed for now was to be able to go home and live her life in peace, but she couldn't. Unless all France rose against their oppressors, and the Allies were victorious... She refused to contemplate defeat. France as a German state didn't bear thinking about. Punishable by death or not, she would deliver these pamphlets.

\*\*\*

### Vosges Mountains, France. October 1941

Antoine smiled as Juliette smoothed Jean's ruffled feathers. She named every pigeon that arrived and swore some of the birds dropped were those she'd released the previous month with messages.

He fastened the little cylinder around Jean's leg. The pigeon churred softly and cocked its head on one side while surveying him with black, beady eyes. 'Good luck, Jean.'

The message, short and to the point, warned of the growing reprisals against the resistance. *"German Lt-Col Holt, Nantes, shot. 48 hostages shot in reprisal. 50 hostages shot, Souges, for another killing. More arms req'd, urgent. Vosges."*

'Bon voyage, Jean.' Juliette released the bird into the October morning, and they watched it circle before winging its way northwest. Juliette turned to him as Jean became a black dot high in a threatening sky. 'Do you think she'll make it, La Fourche?'

He put an arm around her. 'She has a better chance than any of us, ma chère.' She was safe from pot shots from the ground as long as she flew high. Birds of prey were another matter entirely, but there was no point worrying Julliette with that thought. 'I'm sure she'll make it.'

Juliette looked up at him and smiled. He smiled back and brushed his lips across her hair. He hadn't thought he would love again after Sybil, but despite his determination not to form relationships with people he could lose at any moment, he'd fallen for Juliette.

Florian came out of the cottage, a sober look on his face. 'I've been listening to the BBC. There's been a massacre of Jews in Odessa. With the anti-Jewish laws here in France, the restrictions on their movement, and the census... the police and Gestapo know exactly where to find them. I fear for them – I fear for them all.'

\*\*\*

November brought yet more drizzle, making everything that wasn't close to the hearth damp. Antoine sat on a low stool, cleaning Lugers liberated from German soldiers who'd fallen foul of Florian in the wood, one eye watching Juliette feed grain to six pigeons in a coop in the corner of the room.

'You'll make them too fat to fly, Juliette, and that grain has to last.'

She pouted. 'They're not here long enough to get fat, La Fourche.'

That was true enough. The birds were proving invaluable couriers, though they couldn't always be certain the birds had arrived safely. He went over the news from Britain in his mind. The RAF had carried out heavy night bombings on Berlin, the Ruhr, and Cologne but had sustained substantial losses. *Ark Royal* had been sunk, and there was fighting in Moscow.

Juliette's face was painted with a smile.

He arched an eyebrow. 'What are you smiling about?'

Juliette laughed with glee. 'I forgot to tell you – I have a friend in Nancy – she works for a laundrette the Germans use for their shirts and undergarments. I saw her when I cycled into town yesterday. She says she put itching powder in the wash. Can you imagine them all scratching for days?'

He joined in her merriment. 'Added to socks that rub their toes, they should be feeling pretty miserable.'

She frowned. 'Socks?'

He tapped the side of his nose conspiratorially. 'Trust me. I know my socks. Special German order. Hopefully, they are hobbling by now.'

'Anything to make life more difficult for them.'

A lilting German waltz ended, and a guttural voice announced the news for Radio Paris, wiping the smiles from their lips. "*Three soldiers of the Reich have been killed and five injured in an explosion in a Parisian bar. Be assured the Judeo-Bolshevik enemies of France and Germany will pay the price.*"

Every German death was a victory, but the price would be high in the Jewish and communist communities.

Florian's voice was grim. 'Then we'd better try to distract them.'

'What do you have in mind?'

'A major attack on the main rail routes or some engines. The Gestapo will send more soldiers to guard the railways, and that takes men from other duties. If we can get whole police battalions diverted to protect the railways as well, it will give any targeted Jews and communists time to hide or make their escape.

'Tonight?'

'Yes. As soon as it's dark.'

He nodded. 'Then I'll prepare some explosives. If we can't stop the bastards from shooting hostages, at least we'll make sure their deaths count for something.'

They'd pinpointed two locations for maximum disruption to the German war effort and a distance from villages in the hope of preventing punitive attacks on the villagers. That night saw them driving with blacked-out lights towards the railway. He climbed a fence and carried the satchel bombs down the bank to the track. Juliette stood guard nearby, Adolf and Lucas were on sentry duty a hundred metres in either direction, and Florian waited in the truck, lights out, engine running.

Kneeling by the side of the rails, he positioned the bombs by the points to disrupt two lines at once and do the most damage. He paid out the pull-cord and backed away to a safe distance. He motioned to Juliette to go back to the truck, pulled the cord, and ran. The explosion sent soil and rock and bits of wood and metal into the sky.

He reached the truck at the same time as the others, shoved Juliette up into the seat and climbed in after her while Adolf and Lucas jumped into the back.

Florian grinned. 'Vive la France!'

The engine roared, the dim lights lit the road immediately in front of them, and the truck trundled on towards their next target.

\*\*\*

**Marseille, France. November 1941**

Bonnie sat in the car near the station with Colette and Marcel, two escapees huddled in the boot. The town was swarming with police and Gestapo, and it could only mean they were looking for people to arrest.

Their escape line had been compromised in occupied France, and several couriers, safe-house keepers, and organisers had been arrested. Some had fled south, like her two escapees in the boot, who hoped to get to Gibraltar and go on to London. She, and Louise and

Raphael had escaped attention so far, and had continued their work with even stricter security.

Ian Garrow, who'd headed the Marseille group, had been arrested and imprisoned, and the Seamen's Mission had been closed down by the police, on orders from the Gestapo with more arrests. Pat O'Leary had taken over Garrow's duties with the headquarters in a new location.

'Do you think it's safe to go to your home, Colette? Will they search houses?'

'I think we'd be safer to drive out of town for a while. Then, if they search my house, they won't find anyone. I must be careful – there are those who would denounce me.' Colette consulted her watch. 'We'll go down to the Old Port. O'Leary said there should be a felucca called *Seawolf* willing to take escapees out to the boats. If we hang around for a while, we might be able to get these two souls to safety rather than risk taking them back to the house.'

Marcel started the Citroën's engine and jammed it into gear. 'After Garrow's arrest, I'm not sure the harbour is any safer than the house, but we'll give it a go.'

The port was ancient, built to withstand attack and defended by the twin forts of St Jean and St Nicholas, and the old houses that bordered the water huddled together. The huge Transbordeur bridge, an aerial ferry, spanned the water, the blue sea reflecting a sky that was more like summer than winter. A stiff breeze cooled the air and rattled the rigging on the moored boats. Out in the harbour, wind filled the sails of small craft.

Marcel parked the car. 'There's a felucca coming into port now.'

Colette looked where Marcel pointed. 'I think it's time for Marie to use her womanly charms. See if you can get passage for our "luggage", Marie.'

"Marie" tidied her unruly hair and opened the car door.

'Be careful, ma chère.' Marcel leaned across and kissed her.

She smiled. 'I will.' She walked along the quay and waited for the felucca to moor. *Seawolf* was painted on its bow. She waved to the man aboard and stepped closer.

He looked slightly puzzled. 'Do I know you?'

She glanced around. The quayside was busy and ears were in abundance. 'No, but I have a favour to beg.' She lowered her voice. 'Police and Gestapo are everywhere, and I have "luggage" I need to get to Gibraltar. O'Leary said you might be able to help me. Please?'

He nodded. 'Luggage, you say. How many pieces of luggage?'

'Just two.'

'And when would this be?'

'Now. The poor souls have been cooped up in the boot of the car since we arrived on the train. They must be stifled.'

'Bring them to me, one at a time, and they can board *Seawolf* and lie low under this tarpaulin until I sail. At least they'll have fresh air. '

'When do you sail?'

He shrugged and smiled. 'When I have sufficient luggage.'

She hoped that wouldn't be too long and kissed both his cheeks. He smelled of the sea. 'Thank you. I am in your debt.'

One at a time, she escorted the man and his daughter along the quay and onto the boat. 'I wish you both good luck.'

'Thank you, Marie.' The man followed the girl under the tarpaulin and the sailor took the felucca out a little way and dropped anchor.

They were as safe there as she could make them. Her part in their journey was over – they were in other hands now.

# Chapter Twenty-Nine

**Near Nancy, France. December 1941**

Christmas looked to be a sober occasion. The killings of three German soldiers in an explosion in a Parisian bar, and the shooting of a German in Brest, had brought the feared reprisals. December had opened with a mass round-up of Jews and communists in Paris and the imposing of a billion franc fine on the Jewish community there. A thousand Jews and five hundred young communists had been arrested. The flow of desperate families trying to escape France was never-ending.

Bonnie nursed a mug of hot soup in front of the fire. Louise and Raphael sat beside her – as much her family now as Dad was.

She looked at the radio. Listening to "enemy radio stations" was punishable by imprisonment, but she was desperate to know what was going on in the world, facts Radio Paris, which was all Nazi propaganda, would never tell her. 'Dare we have the radio on, Louise?'

Louise switched it on and turned it to a low volume. Not that there were houses nearby, but anyone could be walking past who might denounce them. Life was a constant fear of being discovered.

They all listened in silence.

*"This is BBC Radio Londres. Malta has been bombed again, now it has been bombed more than a thousand times. Conscription in Britain has been increased to include eighteen to fifty-year-olds and women are now being enrolled in the fire service.*

*"Today, Britain declared war on Finland, and the Japanese have bombed the United States naval base at Pearl Harbour. Attacks were also carried out on the US-held Philippines, Guam, Wake Island, and the British-held Malaya, Singapore, and Hong Kong.*

*"The naval base was attacked by Imperial Japanese aircraft launched from six aircraft carriers. All eight United States battleships present were damaged, and four were sunk. Almost two hundred US aircraft were destroyed and more than two thousand Americans are feared dead with many more wounded. Vital infrastructure was also badly damaged.*

*"The British government has declared war on Japan."*

They looked at one another, stunned. Raphael was the first to speak. 'That will stir things up. I can't see the Americans standing by and not declaring war on Japan.'

'And Japan is an ally of Germany, so –.'

'Hush, Raven. Listen.'

*"Hitler today signed the Nacht und Nebel, night and fog, directive to eliminate all anti-Nazi resistance activities in Western Europe. This will force military judges in the occupied territories to condemn to death those accused of certain acts within a week of their arrest."*

She went hot and cold and swallowed bile. 'Certain acts? Everything we do is anti-Nazi. Does this mean without trial?'

Raphael shook his head. 'I don't know. It sounds as if being arrested is enough for the death penalty. I doubt Hitler cares whether we're guilty as long as he's passed a law to make his murder legal.'

Raphael was right about stirring things up. The next day, Japan declared war on the United States and the British Empire, and the United States Congress declared war on Japan. Over the next few days, Germany and Italy, siding with Japan, declared war on the United States, who retaliated by declaring war on Germany and Italy.

The whole world seemed to be fighting, but Raphael was jubilant. 'With America joining us against the Axis powers, how can we lose? Japan made a huge mistake bombing Pearl Harbour.'

Their good mood didn't last long. Ninety-five hostages, mostly communists, were shot in reprisal for the Paris bar explosion. Many were Jews from the Drancy camp, and some were taken from

Romainville Fort, Compiègne and Châteaubriant camps, and the prisons of Fresnes, Fontevrault, and La Santé.

As she had feared. Christmas was a sober occasion.

***

## Vosges Mountains, France. January 1942

Antoine paced the small room. 'There must be more we can do than blow railway tracks and cut power and telephone lines. Ninety-five hostages shot, and a thousand Jews arrested for the deaths of four Germans.'

Florian lounged in an old, sagging armchair. 'What do you suggest, La Fourche?'

'Whatever we do, there'll be reprisals. We're playing with other peoples' lives, and yet... we can't sit by and do nothing while Hitler spreads his evil.'

Lucas twiddled with the knob on the radio, and it crackled into life.

Florian held up a hand. 'Speak of the devil.'

Hitler's strident tones filled the room with hated guttural German. He was speaking at the Berlin Sportpalast. The speech dragged on, Hitler becoming vehement at the mention of Churchill. His tone hardened when he spoke about Jews. It was difficult to hear with the crackle of the radio, but they caught most of it, despite German being their second language.

*"They are our old enemies as it is, they have experienced at our hands an upsetting of their ideas, and they rightfully hate us just as much as we hate them. We are well aware that this war could eventually only end... they be out-rooted from Europe or that they disappear.*

*"They have already spoken of the breaking up of the German Reich by next September... The war will not end as the Jews imagine it will, namely, with the uprooting of the Aryans, but the result of this war will be the complete annihilation of the Jews.*

*"Now for the first time, they will not bleed other people to death, but for the first time the old Jewish law of 'An eye for an eve, a tooth for a tooth,' will be applied... and they will be used as food for every prison camp, and... the hour will come when the enemy of all times, or at least of the last thousand years, will have played his part to the end."*

He stopped pacing and looked at Florian. 'The complete annihilation of the Jews?'

Florian ran a hand through his hair. 'He's rounding them up and arresting them, sending them to camps… Who knows what goes on in these camps. No one ever comes back to tell us.'

'You think he's murdering Jews in these camps?'

'It could be. He has no scruples about shooting people, especially Jews.'

'So, they'll die whether we kill German soldiers or not?'

'Almost certainly. Hitler hates Jews. Why else has he passed all these obscene laws against them. It's clear, now, he wants them all dead.'

'Then I think we need to check these Lugers and ammunition you acquired, and go and kill some Nazis.'

They drove down from the mountains towards Neufchâteau, hid the truck on a narrow track in the woods, and walked through the trees to the road. It was still early, so the road was quiet, but it was a main route between Nancy and Dijon, and German military vehicles passed along it daily.

He brought his Luger from his shoulder holster and pushed a pre-loaded magazine into the grip. 'We stay hidden behind the trees and aim for the front tyre. They'll think they have a blow-out. When they get out to change the wheel, we strike. Understood?'

Adolf nodded. 'Understood.'

'The more Nazis we can get, without showing ourselves, the better.' He weighed a grenade in his hand. 'If it's a troop carrier, I'll lob this at the truck, so stay well clear, and be ready to mop up any survivors. If it's carrying goods, they may be goods we need more than they do, so we'll kill the driver and any passengers, capture the truck, and hide it and the bodies somewhere they won't easily find them. Either way, I aim to make a difference, and I don't intend we leave any witnesses.'

Lucas pushed a loaded cartridge into his pistol grip. 'No witnesses. Understood.'

'And remember, take any Lugers and ammo you find.'

'What if there's other traffic on the road?'

He whirled around. 'I thought I told you to stay with the truck, Juliette. This could be dangerous.'

Juliette smiled innocently. 'Did you? I must have misheard.'

He sighed, exasperated. Women could be so difficult to protect. 'We'll have to judge it best we can, and act quickly. We don't want innocent travellers involved.'

Florian waved his pistol. 'I suggest we spread out. Only fire if the last person has missed the tyre, that way we won't waste ammo, and one bang will sound more like a tyre blowing and arouse least suspicion. Who's the best shot?'

Adolf pointed at Lucas. 'Lucas can split a bullet on a knife edge.'

'Lucas one end of the row then, and I'll take the other end.' He had no qualms about his own accuracy. He'd done well in the training sessions. 'Spread out but keep one another in view, stay out of sight of the enemy, and keep your ears open.'

His breath wreathed in front of him. Frost sparkled on the road, and mist rose in the early morning sunshine. He shivered, as much from the thought of killing other humans as from the cold. The Nazis who'd killed Dad and raped Mum had shown no compassion. Thousands of innocents were being butchered without mercy. He took a deep breath and committed himself to murder.

The rumble of a heavy vehicle grew closer. It was coming from Lucas's direction. He held his Luger at the ready.

An army truck rattled into view. There was a bang and the front tyre exploded. The truck swerved and came to a halt close to the narrow verge. He held his breath. Move too soon, and their attack would be uncovered before they knew how many Germans they had to contend with. *Wait… wait…*

An overweight German dropped down from the passenger door. He kicked the deflated tyre, cursing loudly. 'Otto, give me a hand to change the tyre.'

Otto, the driver, walked around the front of the vehicle. He too kicked the offending tyre. 'I'll get the jack and pump. You get the spare wheel.'

No one got out of the back of the truck, so it seemed it was just the two of them. To wait and let them change the wheel or shoot now? It was still early with no other traffic. He signalled wait and watched his signal being passed on.

While Otto and his passenger huffed and puffed with wheel nuts and a handpump, he shivered. The odd vehicle had passed, showing no sympathy for the broken-down lorry. If another German vehicle came by…

At last, Otto kicked the reflated tyre and disconnected the pump. 'That should last us all the way to Vichy.'

*Now.* He gave the signal, and five simultaneous shots dropped the two Germans like sacks of flour.

They erupted from the trees, bundled the bodies into the back of the truck, and jumped in. Florian at the wheel, they roared along the road and turned onto a track through the wood to where they'd left Renoir's lorry.

He jumped out. 'Adolf, Lucas. Get these bodies out and hide them in the wood. Florian, let's see what this truck is carrying.'

In the back were wooden crates and metal boxes. Some were stamped **Luftdichter Patronenkasten.**

He whistled. If he'd thrown a grenade into that lot, it would have blown the lorry sky high. 'We've hit the jackpot. Airtight cartridge boxes. Let's get all this into our truck and get the hell out of here.'

Cartridges, rifles, Lugers, and grenades bound for Vichy? He and Florian ran from truck to truck, arms aching as they carried the heavy boxes. Lucas and Adolf returned and helped. Juliette had the engine running ready to move at a moment's notice.

The German truck emptied, and its equally valuable petrol syphoned into their tank, they piled into Renoir's lorry, and Juliette accelerated away.

Thousands of rifle cartridges and Luger magazines, and hundreds of weapons denied to the Nazi regime, would bolster the resistance for months to come. As they bowled along the road back up into the mountains, a jubilant Lucas burst into a song the rest of them quickly took up.

*'Hitler has only got one ball*
*Göring has two but very small,*
*Himmler is rather sim'lar,*
*But poor old Goebbels has no balls at all…'*

# Chapter Thirty

**Near Nancy, France. March 1942**

Bonnie walked through the forest breathing in damp air and the smell of new leaves and spring grass. Buds were breaking on the trees, and a green haze clothed some of the low shrubs. Primroses, wood anemones, and snowdrops shone like tiny gems in the clearings, each one a bright memorial for those who'd sacrificed their lives for France, pale beacons of hope for the future.

The world *was* still a beautiful place.

It was silent but for a distant blackbird and the robin perched on a branch above her head, singing his heart out. She smiled, the little bird cheering her. She was glad he was untroubled by war. 'Thank you, robin.' A squirrel scolded her and scuttled up a tree trunk. 'Good morning to you, too, squirrel.'

All too soon, she turned her steps towards home. Louise would need help getting breakfast. Her brief respite over, her thoughts turned back to reality. The Germans were in retreat on the Eastern Front, which was good news – Hitler blamed the weather – but war raged on in the Pacific and the Atlantic.

Conscription was in force in Canada, and the United States now had air-force bases in Britain. War had spread its evil to every corner of the world and seemed to be blossoming rather than fading.

According to information received from other groups, Jean Moulin, the former mayor of Chartres who'd escaped to England, had been parachuted back in to try to unify and co-ordinate the resistance. If it improved the flow of information across France, it would be a good thing, but the groups relied on secrecy for their safety. She wasn't sure how unifying them would work.

Nazi authorities were hunting resistance members all across France. They'd had word a couple from western France were heading their way. She was hoping to pick them up from the derelict barn in the forest later that day and get real news of other parts of France, not what Radio Paris would have them believe.

Louise was fiddling with the radio. 'I'm sure the signal from London is being jammed.'

'Keep trying. We need to know what's going on.' She shook off the feeling of impending isolation and put the few brave primroses she'd picked into an empty fish-paste jar. They brightened the breakfast table with a dash of hope.

The radio burst into life, crackled and went dead. Another burst of life, more crackles.

*"RAF bomber moonlight raid on Billancourt... hundreds... Renault Motor Works... nightshift... destroyed... casualties. Salmson factory... motors, magnetos... No warning... damage."*

Her jubilation was tinged with sorrow. 'Some of those casualties will be French workers trying to make a living to survive, not just collaborators.'

Raphael nodded and sighed. 'They gave their lives for France. I fear they won't be the last to die if Britain targets facilities taken over by Germany.'

She brushed a finger across a pale primrose petal. The deaths of over a thousand French sailors on ships sunk by the British to keep them from German hands still rankled across France. How many more must die?

Juliette bustled with breakfast, trying to lighten the mood. 'Can you set the table, Raven?'

She fetched cutlery, cups, plates, and bowls and made a pot of coffee. 'Have you had a message about the two we're expecting?'

'No, nothing more. You'll have to go straight after breakfast and wait around, I'm afraid. I'll pack you a sandwich or two in case they're late. You're skin and bone already, without missing meals.'

Food was becoming scarcer – they'd all be skin and bone if Hitler had his way. 'Just a little. Don't use your rations up on me.'

Louise smiled. 'Someone left half a cheese on our doorstep last night.'

Her heart skipped a beat. 'Someone who knows we're part of the escape line?'

'If they meant us harm, Raven, we'd have had the Gestapo on our doorstep, not cheese.'

Louise was right, of course, but the fear of discovery ran deep.

After breakfast, she cycled to the meeting place at the derelict barn. She hadn't slept well and had been up and out early. Making herself as comfortable as she could against musty stooks of straw, she settled down for a long wait.

'Well, who have we here?' The voice sounded French, not German.

She opened her eyes to find a tall young man looming over her, the barrel of his revolver pointing at her head. 'Marie. And you are?'

He lowered the weapon and smiled. 'To you, Fleur.' He turned to the door. 'It's all right. You can come in.' A young woman slipped through the narrow opening. 'This is Lys.'

She snorted a laugh. 'Fleur-de-lys. Very good. Were you followed?'

'I don't think so. The woman who brought us here was very careful.'

She got to her feet. 'It's quite a walk, I'm afraid.'

Wheeling her bicycle, she led them along twisting paths through trees, hiding their tracks as they went. She itched to ask questions, but she must wait until they were safely back at the cottage. The trees opened out into a clearing, and the sun sent shafts of light through the trees and across the rough walls of Louise's cottage.

The small meal Louise provided eaten, her curiosity got the better of her. 'We're desperate for news. Apart from Radio Paris and what we can catch of the BBC, we hear next to nothing of what's going on more than a few miles away.'

Fleur cradled his mug in his hands. 'You'll have heard of the attack on the Renault factory.'

'A bit.'

'We heard the bombers going over. There were nearly two hundred. It was a moonlight night, and they were flying low, so we saw some of them. We weren't sure where they were heading, but they dropped illuminators, and we could see from them, and the terrific explosions, that they were near Paris. It made sense that they were targeting the industrial sector at Boulogne-Billancourt.'

Lys took up the story, 'They dropped hundreds of bombs. We saw very little anti-aircraft flak, so they must have come in under the radar and taken the Nazis by surprise. Losing the facilities at Renault and Salmson will hit the German war effort hard.'

'And we aim to hit it even harder.' Fleur tapped his breast pocket. 'I have vital information that I must get to British Intelligence in London. We can't trust it to a letter.'

'We have a radio –'

'No. You can't send drawings and maps by radio.'

She was intrigued. 'Drawings? What of? Sorry, I shouldn't ask.'

'Since you are going to get us out of France, you should understand the importance of what we're carrying, of not being caught. Near Nantes, on the west coast at Saint Nazaire, the Germans have submarine pens. It's a vital base for their operations attacking convoys in the Atlantic. If Britain could destroy the base –'

'You have drawings of the submarine pens?'

He nodded. 'Another agent is also carrying copies by a different route, but one of us must get through. Our group was compromised, we're being hunted, so we need new identities.'

The weight of responsibility was on her shoulders – a twenty-year-old waif of "skin and bone" carrying sock samples – and nothing must compromise the escape line. 'I understand. Raphael will sort the false papers, and I shall get you over the demarcation line and to a safe house in Marseille. From there, someone will take you on to Spain. The British Consulate will get you to Gibraltar, and from there, a plane or fishing boat will take you to England. It's a difficult journey, and it could take weeks, but it can be done, and someone will guide you.'

'You know this for certain?'

'I've done it myself. The escape line was set up to aid people like you. I've been a guide for a while now.'

'How did you get back into France?'

'British Intelligence flew me in by Lysander, but they also parachute agents in.'

'Then we put ourselves into your hands, Marie. Thank you.'

\*\*\*

## Marseille, France. March 1942

Bonnie dried herself on one of Colette's bath towels. Soaking away the stress of the journey and the smell of cow muck from Dion's cattle truck had been as much a necessity as a luxury. Marcel had offered to come and scrub her back... She wasn't quite ready for that degree of intimacy yet, though she longed to be closer to him – the thought made her cheeks and neck hot. Part of her wanted the security of marriage, and part of her wanted to grab the moment before it was too late. Perhaps it was as well he had to leave with Fleur and Lys before she'd weakened. She hated saying goodbye to him.

Shivering in the outhouse, she put on clean clothes and began emptying the tin bathtub with a bucket to pour down the drain. The house in the old part of Marseille had no inside conveniences other than a sink and cooker. The bathtub emptied and hung on a hook on the wall, she hurried back into the warmth of the living room.

Colette greeted her with a glass of mulled wine. 'Come, there's something you must see.'

She followed Colette through a door and down a passage. She'd never been into this part of the rambling old building before. At the end was a door and beside it a row of shelves full of books. The shelves looked homemade and new.

'This door leads back into the kitchen, but I keep it locked as there's a cupboard the other side.' She put a hand on a book. 'What I'm about to show you must remain secret. Only you, me, and Marcel know of it, and it's only to be used in dire emergencies. Some houses were searched last time you were here. If that happens again, we have a safe place behind here.'

'I shall tell no one, Colette.'

'I know, ma chère. It's why I trust you with this secret. Marcel made the shelves.' She pulled at a book and two spines hinged outwards to show a narrow gap. 'You put your hand in here, and you can feel a latch. The latch opens the door to the cellar. The shelves swing out on hinges, and you can pull them and the book spines closed after you, so no one can tell the door is here.'

She demonstrated and pushed open the cellar door, closing the shelves behind her. Steep steps led down into a dimly lit room with damp stone walls.

She shivered. 'It's cold down here.'

'Cold is better than captured or dead, Marie, and I shall provision it with food and water.'

She couldn't argue with that, but she made a mental note to grab a warm jacket in her flight to safety. It was good to know they had a safehouse within a safehouse. She prayed they'd have no cause to use it.

All too soon, she had to leave amid hugs and tears. Leaving Colette didn't get any easier, but she'd arranged a time to meet Dion and his cattle truck for the return journey and didn't want to miss her train north.

As always, Louise and Raphael were relieved to see her safely home; for her part, she was torn between what had become two branches of her own family.

Raphael seemed agitated. 'We've had a message, Raven. I'm not sure what it means. If we are at La Pont de la Meurthe southwest of Luneville at midnight tonight, we can have a large basket of Grenadier apples.'

She frowned. 'Apples? Grenadier is a lovely cooking apple. We have an old tree in the garden at Cosby.'

Louise pulled out a chair and sat at the table. 'Raphael thinks it's code for something.'

'It could be... Grenadiers don't store well. You're right, Raphael. Whoever it is can't be offering us apples. They'd be rotten by now.'

'Well, it's too far to cycle, Raven. Must be twenty-five to thirty kilometres. Can you borrow a car, Raphael?'

'That's the trouble. There's no petrol – a car is useless. If we want to know what these apples are, it's bicycle or nothing.'

The message intrigued her. 'Twenty-five kilometres is not so far. I'll go. I can sleep when I get back.'

Louise wasn't convinced. 'Suppose it's a trap?'

Raphael shook his head. 'The call sign was correct, and surely if it was a trap, they'd offer us more than apples for a twenty-five-kilometre journey with petrol shortages as they are.'

'I shall go.' Her tone brooked no argument. 'If all we get is apples, then we'll make a huge pie.'

And if it was a trap?

She had a knife, revolver, and ammunition.

# Chapter Thirty-One

**Vosges Mountains, France. March 1942**

Antoine counted the remaining stock of weapons, explosives, and ammunition. They'd split their ill-gotten gains into piles, some to keep hidden in the coalhouse and some to be distributed among the nearest resistance groups, and had spent weeks hiding them in caches in wooded areas, digging pits and burying them or covering them in dead brushwood or piles of logs. It wasn't an ideal way to store them, but it was too dangerous to keep such a large stock at the cottage, and hopefully, it wouldn't be for long. It had been over a month since their capture of the German lorry and its cargo, and they'd heard no news of it being missing or found. He hoped it was safe to surface; the sooner they got rid of some of it into safe hands, the better.

Florian surveyed the last cache with satisfaction. A dense thicket of spiny blackthorn, white with blossom and already leafing up, made an ideal if prickly hiding place. He sucked a jabbed thumb. 'The rest can stay in the truck. I've arranged to meet someone from the Jura Mountains cell near Lure this afternoon.'

'And if we're stopped?'

'Camouflage, La Fourche. We have coal sacks. Grenades and ammo will look suitably lumpy in a sack.'

He ran a careful finger down the sharp edge of the machete he'd been using to slash dead branches. 'If we cut a load of firewood, too, we can say we're doing our good neighbour stint delivering coal, kindling, and logs to our new German neighbours.'

By three that afternoon, he and Florian were driving south towards Lure. It was a journey of some fifty kilometres, and they kept mainly to minor roads through woodland, bog, and open fields. This part of France had been reserved for German settlers, as had his parents' farm near Nancy, and was close to the region annexed by Germany two years earlier. His suggestion about being "good neighbours" to Germans had been no joke. Collaborating, or appearing to collaborate, was a vital part of staying alive in occupied France.

Florian stopped the lorry a hundred metres from an isolated cottage and backed off the road a short way. 'This is our rendezvous.'

'It should be safe, but I'll check it out.' He patted his pocket gingerly. He had a grenade in it, a loaded Luger in his shoulder holster, and a knife strapped to his shin beneath his trousers. It only took a careless word from the group he'd contacted to betray them.

'Stay out of sight as long as you can. Be careful.'

He didn't need telling. He used the cover of trees and hedges to creep closer to the cottage. There didn't seem to be anyone around. He was about to try to see through a window when the rattle of a van made him shrink back into the undergrowth.

Two men got out of the van and walked towards the house, looking furtive. Either they were resistance or Germans, and whichever they were, he must confront them if this transfer was to be done safely. He drew his Luger and stepped out of the bushes. 'Stay where you are. Hands above your heads.'

'Ne tire pas! Don't shoot.'

He lowered the gun. A German would have pleaded in his native tongue or have been carrying a loaded weapon and shot him before speaking. 'I think you are expecting me.'

The men lowered their hands. 'You have goods for us?'

'We do. Our lorry is a hundred metres this way.' He waved the gun in the direction of Florian and the truck. 'Bring your vehicle and back it off the road.'

A sack of grenades, a crate of weapons, and a box of ammunition loaded into the van, the men shook hands.

'Vive la résistance.'

'Vive la France.'

***

## Mont-sur-Meurthe, France. March 1942

Bonnie pedalled towards her rendezvous, her bicycle basket already half full with a loaded revolver and medical equipment, the medical equipment her cover story for being out in the middle of the night, should she be stopped, and the revolver in case a Nazi didn't believe her. Killing a man didn't sit easy with her, but being killed sat worse.

A thin crescent moon gave little light, but her lamp threw a beam across the road in front of her. She winced at the tiny squeak the bicycle had developed and which sounded horribly loud in the silence of the night. She must ask Raphael if he had oil.

The bridge at Mont-sur-Meurthe, as far as she remembered, was about a hundred metres ahead, and sound travelled as did light. Acutely aware this could be a trap, she ditched the cycle in trees by the river, pocketed the revolver, and took to her feet.

Rounding a bend in the road, keeping to the grass verge and using the cover of trees where she could, she approached the bridge revolver in hand. Lights shone from the far side, lighting her way and giving her no chance of a covert approach. Whoever was waiting was unnervingly sure of themselves, but then they would see anyone coming from fifty metres away and doubtless had rifles aimed at her.

To go on or go home? Something about that message had made her decide to come. She held her revolver in her hand and walked into the beam of the headlights.

'Stay where you are. Hands in the air.' The speaker couldn't be seen against the glare of light.

She stopped and raised her hands, her finger on the trigger, ready to aim and shoot. 'You can't be offering Grenadier apples in March. Grenadiers don't keep.'

'Who says?'

'I do. I had a tree in my garden in Cosby.'

A dark figure emerged from the light. 'Bonnie? Bonnie Renard?'

'Papa?'

'Bonnie!' The man started forward.

'Papa!' She dropped the revolver, broke into a run, and flung herself into Dad's arms. 'Papa…' Tears blinded her.

'Oh, Bonnie, ma chère, ma chère.' He hugged her, almost squeezing the breath from her body. He let her go at last and held her at arms' length. 'You look well. Where are you living?'

'I'm at a cottage in the forest west of Nancy. Louise and Raphael are like family to me.'

He turned her towards the headlights. 'Come and meet Florian. And where's your transport? You surely haven't walked?'

'My bicycle is in the trees, a way back. I have a basket for the "apples".'

Dad put an arm around her. 'Grenades, not Grenadiers. We liberated some from a German lorry a few weeks ago. We also have weapons and explosives. We're distributing them among other cells as best we can.'

'I'm part of the escape line down to Marseille and across the eastern Pyrenees. I don't travel armed when I'm escorting escapees. Raphael doesn't consider it safe for any of us if I was stopped and searched. It doesn't mean a few grenades and weapons wouldn't be useful to have though. Raphael isn't averse to a little sabotage.'

'Then we'll fill your basket and your pockets.' He turned. 'Florian!'

A man jumped down from the driver's door. 'Who have we here, La Fourche?'

'Florian, this is my daughter.'

'Pleased to meet you, er… Bonnie?'

'My code name is Raven, and my documents have me as Marie Barbier.' She raised an eyebrow at Dad. 'La Fourche?'

Dad shook his head. 'The incident with the German and the pitchfork.'

She nodded, not wanting to bring up the tragic end to her grandparents lives any more than he did. The image of their bodies and the dead German was one she'd never forget. 'It's a good name.'

Florian put his hand on the driver's door. 'We should get loaded before we attract unwanted attention. What transport have you brought?'

'A bicycle with a large basket. Over there.'

She retrieved her revolver, and Florian drove the truck to where she'd left the bicycle. She handed all but a small amount of her medical supplies to Florian to make room in her basket. Loaded with hand grenades, four Lugers and boxes of ammunition, and her pockets bulging, it was time to leave for home. She didn't want to leave Dad. 'Where are you staying? Where can I find you if I need you?'

'We have a camp in the Vosges Mountains, but we need to move around. Send a message that the raven needs help, and I can meet you wherever you say, whenever. Just send a message, and I'll be there, I promise.'

Her cheeks were wet with tears. To find him after so long and have to leave him so soon. 'I love you, Papa.'

'I love you too... Raven.' He hugged her as if he would never let her go.

'La Fourche, we must go.'

'Stay safe, Papa.'

'And you, ma chère.' He thumbed away her tears and kissed her cheeks. 'This war won't go on forever. We shall meet again when we've driven the Germans from our soil.'

'It can't end a moment too soon, Papa.' The lorry's headlights dimmed as Florian started the engine, and she turned her bicycle for home and pedalled into a night blurred by love and heartbreak.

*** 

## Near Nancy, France. March 1942

Nothing could dampen Bonnie's spirits. She'd seen her father again and had run into his arms, a little girl again, running to him when he'd come home from work to be scooped up and swung around. It could have been the poor light from the lorry, but he'd looked older and thinner – but then three years of war and rationing had taken their toll on all of them. It had been so good to see him safe and well.

She sang as she prepared vegetables for supper from the root clamp in the garden. Louise had worked hard to grow food for them and had stored it over the winter to eke out between the three of them and was already planning this year's crops from saved seed.

Radio Paris played a German waltz, listening to it was a necessary penalty of trying to keep up with the latest repressive measures to be forced upon the citizens of occupied France, Jews especially.

*"Yesterday, a convoy of eleven hundred and twelve Jews left Compiègne in third-class carriages for Auschwitz, a labour camp in Poland. Many were arrested last August and in December. The deportation is a reprisal for attacks carried out against the occupation forces. A detachment of German soldiers under the command of Hauptsturmführer Theodor Dannecker accompanied the train."*

Raphael tuned the radio to the BBC. 'It won't be the last convoy. Hitler is determined to rid the world of Jews. Let's hope the BBC have better news.'

*"Earlier today, acting on information received, British commandos launched a raid on the port of Saint Nazaire, France."*

'Isn't that what Fleur and Lys were carrying information about?'

'Shush, Raven.'

"*HMS Campbeltown, filled with explosives, rammed the dock gates, while commandos destroyed vital parts of the port infrastructure. Several Germans were killed when they boarded the ship, thinking the attack had failed. A time-delay fuse detonated a huge explosion that has caused immense damage to the port and U-boat pens. Regrettably, British commandos suffered heavy losses to secure this victory. Shipping in the Atlantic carrying vital supplies and troops will be safer thanks to their sacrifice. God bless them and keep them.*"

She bowed her head. 'God bless them and keep them. Perhaps, this means Fleur and Lys got through safely. I pray they did.'

It was good news, despite the terrible losses of men, if shipping was safer. Two days later came news of a RAF bombing raid on Lübeck. An estimated four hundred tons of bombs and incendiary devices had been dropped on the city causing vast destruction, injury, and loss of life. Much of the medieval city was in ruins – a civilian target, as Coventry had been. German sources said three churches had been destroyed and almost fifteen hundred buildings totally destroyed with thousands more damaged.

Hitler would have his revenge. No one in England would sleep easily in their beds, and the hostages already held in France were as good as dead.

# Chapter Thirty-Two

**Vosges Mountains, France. April 1942**

Antoine put down his knife and fork and switched off the radio. Hitler, enraged by the RAF bomber raids on Lubeck and Rostock, had announced the Luftwaffe would target civilian centres other than London. The war in the Pacific rolled on, and in France, the resistance had attacked the German headquarters at Arras, to the north, one of a series of attacks on Nazi installations and personnel. In retaliation, Hitler had announced the deportation of a thousand communists and ordered a number of hostage executions.

Florian didn't mince his words. 'The RAF raid on the Gnoms-Rhore aircraft engine factory will cause more deportations and executions. The jumped-up little psychopath's dangerously insane.'

Adolf wiped goose fat from his chin – the goose a gift from a nearby farmer, a rare treat, and Juliette wisely hadn't asked what it had died from. 'I can't argue with that, Florian.'

Lucas grunted in agreement. 'That was a wonderful meal, Juliette. Thank you. La Fourche and I will do the dishes. La Fourche?'

'Yes, indeed, Lucas.' He stood and began collecting plates wiped clean with bread. 'These will hardly need washing.'

Juliette laughed. 'I shall be checking you haven't just put them in the cupboard.'

He smiled. He loved to hear her laugh and see her smile. She brightened all their lives at a time when there was little to smile about.

A knock at the door had them running into the kitchen after clearing the table of all evidence of more than Juliette living there. Juliette waited until they'd shut the kitchen door before answering the knock.

His ear to the door, he listened intently. The voice of the visitor was brusque with a German accent. He hadn't heard the sound of a vehicle, so the man must be reconnoitring the area on foot, and he wouldn't be alone. He drew his loaded Luger from his shoulder holster. Putting his finger to his lips, he motioned to Florian, Lucas, and Adolf to arm themselves and scout outside. Weapons and ammunition were stashed behind a kitchen dresser and accessible through a large hole in the back panel chewed by rats.

Armed, his friends slipped silently through the rear door and past the kitchen windows, Florian to the left and Adolf and Lucas to the right.

He put his ear back to the door. Juliette was insisting she lived alone since her husband had died, and she knew nothing about stolen weapons or hijacked lorries. Was this a random visit, or had someone connected the hijacking to them?

A tap on the kitchen window made him turn on his heel. Lucas held up three fingers and pointed right. Three soldiers, so four in total. They could kill four soldiers with the element of surprise. Opening the window carefully, he whispered instructions. 'I'll take the one inside. You take care of those outside.'

Lucas nodded. 'I'll tell Adolf and Florian.'

His Luger wasn't silenced, so he couldn't remove the threat to Juliette without alerting the rest of the Germans. He gave the others time to get into position, took a deep breath, tried to ignore the thumping of his heart, and turned the doorknob slowly.

He pushed the door open a crack. Juliette had her back to him. The German soldier was pointing a Luger at her chest and threatening to shoot her. He had one chance to do this. Raising his weapon, he took aim through the crack.

The door creaked. The German swivelled to face him. Juliette dived to the floor. The gun sang, and the German dropped in a heap. Outside, gunshots erupted. He ran to the front door and threw it open, ducking back inside as machine-gun fire strafed the front of the house.

'Stay down!'

Juliette crawled across the floor to a shelf where a Luger was kept ready-loaded and positioned herself under the window.

'Stay down, Juliette.' More gunfire and then silence. 'I'll check the back of the house.'

Florian helped a bleeding Adolf into the kitchen. 'Adolf took a shot to the shoulder, but we got the bastards.'

'Where's Lucas?'

Adolf shook his head. 'He's dead, but I got the fucker who shot him.'

***

**Near Nancy, France. June 1942**

Twenty-four hostages had been shot the previous month as a reprisal for the derailment of the Maastricht to Cherbourg train near Moult-Argences that had killed twenty-eight German sailors and injured several others. The following night, the train had been derailed again with more loss of German life. Twenty-eight more hostages had been shot. It was a war of attrition both sides were hoping to win, and Hitler was increasingly determined to grind all resistance into the ground.

Bonnie walked through the woods trying to assimilate the latest Nazi atrocity. She stooped to pick a posy of late bluebells and orchids and laid them by a pile of stones beneath a tree. It wasn't a grave or even a proper memorial, but she felt the need to mark the deaths of the people of Lidice and Ležáky in Czechoslovakia.

Reich Protector Reinhard Heydrich had been a hated man, the founder of the organisation that rooted out resistance to the Nazi Party using arrests, deportations, and murders. The man had been assassinated, probably by S.E.O agents, and the people of Lidice were targeted because they were suspected of harbouring local resistance partisans.

She sat by the small memorial and let her tears fall. According to the radio broadcast, all one hundred and seventy-three men over the age of fifteen were shot and the women and children deported to the Chelmo extermination camp. Lidice was burnt to the ground and the ruins levelled. The tiny village of Ležáky hadn't fared any better. For the crime of having a radio transmitter, linked to a S.E.O operation, all thirty-three adults had been shot and the buildings destroyed.

Radio Berlin had issued a stark warning to any village in an occupied country aiding the resistance.

*"It is officially announced: All men of Lidice, Czechoslovakia, have been shot. The women deported to a concentration camp. The children sent to appropriate centres. The name of the village was immediately abolished."*

***

## Vosges Mountains, France. June 1942

Antoine considered the news, both encouraging and worrying. There'd been a thousand-bomber raid on Cologne, and Rommel was facing tough resistance in Tobru. At home in France, Jews were forced to wear a yellow Star of David, and people were disappearing under the new Nacht and Nebel *"Night and Fog"* decree.

Adolf flexed his injured arm, rotating the shoulder gently. The wound was healing but he still had pain and stiffness. 'People wear the yellow star at their peril. I've heard reports of Jews being gassed to death in these damned camps.'

Juliette sat on a chair with a thump. 'How can any human do that to another, whatever they think of their race or religion?'

Florian shook his head. 'It beggars belief, yet I think Hitler is capable of doing anything. You only have to think of the poor people of Lidice.'

Juliette rubbed a hand across her forehead. 'Thank God for people like your Raven and the escape lines, La Fourche.'

He smiled. 'She's a very brave young woman, her mother would be so proud of her, but I do worry about her.'

'Of course you do, but it sounds as if she has good friends. We must all make sacrifices.'

His smile faded. 'Lucas gave his life.'

Tears glistened in Juliette's eyes. 'He died to help save me.'

Florian leaned across and put a hand on hers. 'Any one of us would have done the same, Juliette, as you would for us.'

Juliette nodded and wiped her cheeks with her hand. 'We must go on, or all our countrymen and women's sacrifices will have been in vain.'

Adolf switched on the radio, doubtless hoping to lighten the mood. The news was mixed. A thousand-bomber raid had been carried out on Bremen, British ships had been lost in a convoy despite the destruction of the submarine pens, and the United States had deployed troops in Europe. The deportation of three thousand Jews from the internment camp at Drancy had been followed by two more of the same number from Pithiviers and Beaue-la-Rolande. For the first time, women were among the deportees.

'Nine thousand Jews in less than a week. How's Hitler planning to feed so many or look after them?'

Florian raised an eyebrow. 'You think he'll feed them? You think this is just hostages being taken in retaliation for attacks on Nazis?'

'He really does intend to eradicate them, doesn't he?' Juliette was distraught. 'How long before he sends children to these camps? How many will die before we can stop him?'

\*\*\*

**Near Nancy, France. July 1942**

Bastille Day had passed with little celebration in Louise's cottage. Bonnie paced the small room. It was airless even with the windows open, inside almost as hot as outside, but she couldn't sit still. More and more convoys of Jews were leaving France on trains heading for

Auschwitz, and Jews from the Warsaw ghetto were being sent to a new camp at Treblinka. It was becoming terrifyingly apparent that victims were being selected not because of their political views, or because they were hostages to the resistance's "good behaviour" but because they were elderly or unfit to work. Rumours of gassings and mass murder sent a chill down her spine.

She stopped pacing, her muscles taut. 'Do you think the rumours are true, Raphael?'

'Nothing would surprise me anymore, Raven. Hitler is tightening the noose. If we're not to endanger our families, the resistance must be extra careful.'

'Our families?'

'Hitler's latest decree. Family members of "terrorists" on the run will be taken as hostages.'

'How can we hope to keep resisting when he murders whole villages and threatens those we love in retaliation?'

'That's the very reason we must keep on, Raven. What is life going to be under a regime that can do that? France will be a slave nation – Hell, all occupied Europe will be slaves to Nazi Germany. Hitler would be so power-crazed...' Raphael shook his head as if the prospect was too awful to contemplate.

'You're right, of course.' They'd had this conversation before, but she'd needed reminding why they were fighting and risking so much, why she'd been torn from her father, her only remaining family, and she'd never forget it was Hitler who'd murdered Pépé and Mémé. It was one more reason that for the foreseeable future, no one must know she and Dad were family.

Louise came in from outside mopping her brow. She plonked a basket on the table and fanned herself with a crumpled handkerchief. 'There's barely a bit of shade out there unless you're under a tree. It's too hot for gardening.'

'Sit down, I'll get you a drink, Louise.' She poured water from a jug into a glass and handed it to Louise. 'I'll help you in the garden this evening when it's cooler.'

Louise gulped the water and passed her the glass for a refill. 'I was talking to Madeleine Tirel – she was passing on her way to Nancy. Apparently, there's been a huge round-up of Jews in the Paris area by French police.'

Raphael spat his disgust. 'Because of damn collaborators denouncing neighbours and shopkeepers.'

'She said it was mainly foreign Jews, not French citizens.'

'They're still people.'

'Yes, of course they are, Raven. I wasn't suggesting they weren't.'

'Sorry, Louise. This heat is getting to me.'

Louise sighed. 'It's all right, ma chère. This heat, this war, is getting to us all.' She accepted the second glass of water. 'According to Madeleine, who had it from her brother in Paris, British and American citizens weren't targeted, but our new Prime Minister, Pierre Laval, ordered children be arrested with their parents for "humanitarian" reasons.'

'Children? When has Hitler or the Vichy government showed any humanitarian compassion? Laval is no better than Pétain.' Raphael banged the table with a clenched fist. 'The children will end up in concentration camps.'

Louise nodded. 'Thousands of people have already been taken to Drancy, and we all know that's a transit camp for Auschwitz. The rest are being held at the Vélodrome d'Hiver.'

'The rest? How many have they arrested?'

'Madeleine didn't know, Raven, but she said it was well over ten thousand men, women, and children.'

Bile rose in her throat. 'I've seen the velodrome in Paris. It has a glass roof for winter use. It'll be stifling crowded with thousands of people, and I doubt the Nazis will provide food and water, let alone sanitation or medical help for the sick.'

'Madeleine says they've been there five days already. Her brother reckoned they'd separated the children from their parents and they were going to be deported to Auschwitz.

What sin had these children committed? What sin had any of them committed except in Hitler's eyes?

# Chapter Thirty-Three

**Vosges Mountains, France. October 1942**

Antoine shaded his eyes as a plane flew high above him. The United States air force had begun flying daytime missions over France a couple of months earlier, while the British flew at night, but he couldn't make out if this one was American or German. He hoped it was an Allied plane and it would arrive safely at its destination and make it home again. So many didn't after raids on factories, arsenals, and submarine docks.

Hamburg had been bombed, but a raid by British and Canadian forces on Dieppe had ended in an Allied disaster; most had been killed or captured by the German defenders. Luxembourg had been annexed by Germany, and Jews had been massacred at Stanislau in Poland. Eighty-eight hostages had been executed at Mont-Valérien fort, in Paris, in retaliation for the deaths of eight Germans when grenades were thrown at the Luftwaffe.

The battle of Stalingrad still raged, though Hitler boasted on the radio that Stalingrad would fall to Germany. The British appeared to be making ground at El Alamein, in North Africa, but both fronts seemed a world away to life in the Vosges Mountains with Florian, Adolf, and Juliette.

Pétain, Chief of State of Vichy France, and Prime Minister Laval had concocted a new and worrying law the previous month, the *"Law of 4 September 1942 on the use and guidance of the workforce."*. Innocuous though it sounded, it meant that able-bodied men and young, single women could be conscripted to work for the government, and that meant for Germany. With the German workforce being called-up for military service, labour was needed, and thousands of Frenchmen were being torn from their families and sent to work in Nazi Germany.

In the previous months, volunteers had been called on with the promise of the release of a French prisoner of war for every three volunteers, but now more and more forced labour was being demanded by the Nazis, and any one of them could be seized and sent into a life of slave labour.

The plane diminished to a dot and disappeared behind cloud, so he cast his eyes down to the road that ran along the valley below. A convoy of trucks was winding its way south. Looking back along the road, he thought he could see tanks following them. He frowned. Where were they all going? Vichy, like the truck they'd hijacked back in January?

He shrugged, unable to second-guess the Nazi military mind, and turned down the slope and into trees. He made this journey once a week to make sure badgers and foxes weren't digging up the remains of the four Germans they'd shot, stripped of their Lugers, rifles, ammunition, and uniforms to hinder identification, and buried. Lucas had a grave nearby, marked with a small silver fir sapling, growing straight and true – like Lucas.

He stopped by the grave of his friend. Lucas, Renoir, Zacharie – all gone. Could he have done anything differently to have saved them? Juliette would tell him not to torture himself over what couldn't be changed, and it was sound advice, but doubt ate at him.

'I'm sorry, Lucas.' The words were painfully inadequate.

A rustle of dead leaves froze him for a second before he dived for cover behind a large beech tree. He watched, breath held, as two bedraggled men hunched up the hillside between the firs and beech. They didn't look like Germans, unless they were deserters dressed as civilians.

Drawing his Luger, he stepped out from behind the beech. 'Stay where you are and put your hands on your heads.'

The two men stopped in their tracks. 'Don't shoot.' Their voices held no trace of a German accent.

'You're French.'

'Yes. We're trying to escape the draft to Germany. We want to fight for France, not work for the Nazis. We were hoping to join the maquis.'

Could he trust them? He lowered his pistol but didn't re-holster it. 'I can take you to the maquis.'

One of the men held out a hand. 'I'm Alain. This is Baptiste.'

He didn't shake it but checked them over to ensure they were unarmed. 'Come with me.' He led them by a tortuous route, backtracking several times until he was sure they were lost, before arriving at the cottage.

Opening the door, he shepherded them inside. 'These men wish to join us.'

Florian turned from poking the fire, the poker still in his hand. 'You trust them?'

'No, but let them tell their story, and we'll decide then whether to let them join us or bury them in the forest.'

*** 

### Near Nancy, France. November 1942

Bonnie cycled along a lane through the woods on her way to a new, safer rendezvous point to collect the family of a resistance worker. The increased deportations and transports of forced labour meant more and more people were attempting to escape the occupied zone, and the threat to families of captured resistance workers meant some were sending their loved ones to safety. She'd spent more hours cooped up in a cattle truck than she cared to think about, and the smell of cows made her nauseous.

All was not bleak however. Rommel was in retreat at El Alamein, and the United States were victorious in Guadalcanal, not that she was sure where those places were. What gave her most hope was the four hundred French resistance fighters who'd help the Allies defeat the Vichyist XIXth Army Corps in Algeria. The resistance was making a real difference in all the occupied countries.

The track opened onto the main road that followed the Moselle south. She took a deep breath, recited her reason for being on the road, and pedalled on; she wouldn't be on the road for long, and the route back with the family would be different.

The rumble of vehicles grew louder behind her. She pedalled furiously, head down – after all, she had a sick child to attend...

The military staff-car passed her and sped on. She wobbled as a troop carrier almost clipped the mirror on her handlebars, the soldiers in the back of the truck waving and jeering as it passed. A quick glimpse in her mirror showed a long line of military vehicles. They were obviously not interested in stopping a young girl on a bicycle, and were in a hurry to get somewhere, so she pulled into the side of the road to let them pass.

London would want to know about troop movements, so she counted the lorries, estimating the number of men in each one. Something big was about to happen with this many on the road south.

She was about to remount her bicycle when several tanks rounded the bend and lumbered past her with remarkable speed for such heavy vehicles. One of them swung its gun barrel menacingly in her direction before growling past.

This road led to the demarcation line near Dole, not far from Dijon. Why would tanks, troops, and armoured vehicles be heading there? She'd ensure a message was sent to London.

Mounting her bicycle, she took a track back into the woods and arrived at a woodsman's shelter. It wasn't so much a cottage as a lean-to thrown up against nothing very substantial. The sound of sawing and the smell of newly sawn timber showed the area was in use. She approached cautiously, one hand on the knife she'd taken from her basket and pushed under her belt. A man was thrusting a long saw backwards and forwards to another man in a sawpit below him.

The man stopped sawing. 'Can I help you?'

'I'm Marie.'

He nodded. 'The family are in the shack. They'll be glad to leave, I think.'

She smiled briefly. 'I'll go and introduce myself.'

The inside of the shack was dark and smelled of damp and fear. 'I'm Marie. I've come to take you to a safe house and then to Marseille.'

A young woman tore herself from her husband's arms. 'I'm Lili, and these little ones are Anna and Elyna. This is my husband, Mylan.'

'I was told three people.'

Mylan nodded. 'I'm going back. I wanted to see my wife and daughters safely into your hands. You –' The man's voice broke and recovered. 'You will take care of them?'

She pushed away memories of the disastrous attempt at crossing the Pyrenees, and the tiny foot sticking out of the mud. 'I shall deliver them safely to Marseille. I trust the man who will take them on to Gibraltar. We've done this trip many times now.'

'Thank you, that's reassuring.'

The children were younger than she'd hoped. 'We should leave now. It's a long walk and daylight is precious.'

'Yes, of course.' Mylan hugged his little girls and kissed his wife. 'Stay safe. I shall find you when this war is over. I love you.'

She had tears in her own eyes as the family parted, knowing they might never see one another again. She'd had to say goodbye to her father, and much as she'd come to love Marcel, and hated having to leave him, a part of her heart still wept on a mountaintop in Spain, knowing she'd lost Pierre, her first love, forever.

*** 

Next morning saw Bonnie and her charges trudging towards the station with tired legs. The walk back to Louise's house the day before had been too far for the children and only accomplished by her wheeling her bicycle with Anna on the seat and little Elyna sitting in the basket on top of medical equipment, a knife, and a loaded Luger.

Without her bicycle, she and Lili would have to carry the little ones when they tired. Marseille seemed a long way away.

Two women travelling with two young girls didn't attract the attention of the police or Nazi guards, and their false papers were almost brushed aside without a glance.

The train slowed, ready to stop at the usual station north of the demarcation line. She grabbed her small overnight bag in one hand and Anna's hand in the other. 'Quickly, Lili, this is where we leave the train.'

Lili picked up Elyna and her own luggage. 'Is it far, now?'

The train rattled to a halt. German soldiers were flooding the platform from the carriages behind them. She bit her lip, trying to keep calm for the sake of Lili and the girls. 'Transport will be waiting to take us across the line and onto the next station.'

'Thank goodness. Elyna's getting heavy.'

She forced a smile, grateful Anna was capable of walking. She wasn't at all sure how Lili and the girls would take to being crammed into a cattle truck. She led them out of the station to where Dion usually waited, except he wasn't there. Instead, there was a line of troop carriers.

Minutes passed, and it became obvious Dion wasn't coming. 'I expect Dion is worried about attracting attention with all this military activity. We'll walk. It isn't that far.' How the hell would she get them across the line unseen? She'd cross that bridge when she got to it. At worst, they'd be refused entry into Vichy France. She'd find a way around it somehow and get her charges onto the train again.

The checkpoint was just ahead now. Vehicles and soldiers were marching towards it. Perhaps they could lose themselves among the crowd. The barrier was raised, the guard post empty. Men and vehicles passed through unchallenged.

She caught the arm of a soldier striding past her. 'What's happened? What does this mean?'

'Haven't you heard?' The soldier grinned down at her. 'The demarcation line has been torn down. We've invaded Vichy France. All of France is now occupied by the glorious German army.' He threw off her grip. 'Get out of my way, woman, before I'm tempted to despoil these two little cherubs.'

She dropped his arm as if burned by hot coals and pushed Anna behind her. *All* of France was occupied. Marseille was no longer a 'safe' haven.

# Chapter Thirty-Four

**Vosges Mountains, France. December 1942**

Antoine mulled the latest message from London and the S.O.E. He'd been tasked with destroying several railway engines in an attempt to stop or slow the increasing numbers of Jews and other *"enemies of the Reich"* being deported from the Drancy internment camp, near Paris, to what, if reports were to be believed, were suspected of being death camps for the extermination of men, women, and children.

Germany kept up the pretence of resettlement to the east and labour camps to work for the Reich, but the reality, if it was true, was barbaric.

The route passed near Metz, which at about one hundred and twenty kilometres, was far enough away for them not to be immediately suspected, and hopefully not close enough to Nancy and Bonnie to put her in the way of retaliatory Nazis.

It wasn't an area he knew well. It was close to the border, and now annexed by Germany would be crawling with Nazis. How on earth were four Frenchmen supposed to blend in with Germans unnoticed?

He slapped his forehead as he realised the obvious answer. They still had the German uniforms taken from the four they'd buried. He spoke German fluently, and the others knew enough to get them by, especially if they were armed. People didn't tend to argue with a German soldier if he was pointing a Luger at them.

With luck, they could get close enough to the train engines to lay charges. The next problem brought him back to earth. Railway engines were massive, the quantity of explosives needed to permanently disable them would be huge, and the same ploy wouldn't work more than once. He needed to destroy them all on the same day, and preferably set charges to go off within minutes of one another – he needed a station.

He poured coffee and put his problem before Florian, Juliette, Adolf, Alain, and Baptiste. The two newcomers had proved their worth over the last month and were now trusted members of the group. The numbers of the maquis in the mountains had been swollen with escapees from the work draft, and the resistance was becoming a force to be reckoned with. The danger now was the German army turning their attention to the maquis.

Alain frowned. 'They deport the Jews in cattle wagons. I've seen them being loaded in Bobigny. You need to target goods trains.'

Baptiste nodded. 'And if they aren't carrying deportees, they'll be carrying French goods to Germany for the Reich.' He spat the last word.

Juliette sipped her coffee and put down her cup. 'What about a marshalling yard? There's one near Metz.'

Florian rubbed his chin. 'Suppose we pretended to be inspecting the engines? The Germans would do that, wouldn't they? We could get close enough to lay the charges.'

Alain looked up from his coffee. 'All we need to do is blow the boilers.'

The effect of scalding water and shrapnel made him cringe. '*All* we need to do? How would we do that?'

'Simplest way is to jam a safety valve and over-pressurise the boiler, or lower the water level to expose the crown sheet of the firebox. The firebox will explode and rupture the boiler. I've seen the effect. It's catastrophic.'

'We wouldn't need explosives?'

'You could throw dynamite in the firebox, but you wouldn't run fast enough to escape the blast.'

'How do you know all this?'

'I worked on the railways for a while.'

'And you could help us pose as inspectors and show us how to do it?'

Alain nodded. 'I can do it if you distract the engine driver long enough for me to build up a bit of steam.'

'It sounds dangerous, and it would have to be done in daylight.'

'It would, but I'd know when to jump ship. Uninterrupted, I could set two or three on the path to destruction before the first one goes up.'

'Then we do it. We only have four uniforms, so I suggest Adolf stays here with Juliette.'

'Why me?' Adolf pulled a face.

'I think we four are a better fit for the uniforms, Adolf, and your arm still isn't right. And I don't like leaving Juliette here alone. If we leave as soon as it's light tomorrow, we can get the job done and home before dark.'

Juliette cleared away coffee cups. 'I'll give the uniforms a brush over and hope I can darn the bullet holes and get rid of the bloodstains.'

'Thank you, Juliette. You're an angel. What would we do without you?'

She smiled. 'Starve, probably, and run out of clean coffee cups.' Her smile faded. 'Just be careful, La Fourche. I don't want to be without you, either, not any of you.'

*** 

## Metz, France. December 1942

Florian parked Renoir's truck around the corner from the entrance to the station. Alain wanted to try to identify deportation trains to disable in preference to engines in the goods yard, but he wasn't sure they would stop at Metz. After ten hours locked in a cattle wagon travelling from Paris, it was possible the guards would be humane enough to offer the prisoners water.

Antoine pushed a cartridge into his Luger. 'It's all a matter of confidence. Think like a Nazi. Arrogant, impatient, superior, entitled – speak as little as you must and wave your pistol in people's faces. If you need to shoot someone, do it, but try to make sure they're German.'

Baptiste's face was grim. 'I've never killed a man before.'

'It isn't easy for any of us, Baptiste, but I think of the Nazi who raped my mother and killed my father. I stuck a pitchfork in his back. I have no regrets.' He did still have nightmares. He holstered his gun and straightened.

Alain led the way, looking every bit a Nazi. He pointed to a long train of wagons standing on a track near the station platform. 'I'll try that one. Baptiste, you engage the driver and fireman, while I carry out the "inspection". Keep them busy but stay at a distance from the trains. When the boilers explode…' He didn't need to finish the sentence. 'Florian and La Fourche, wait for me here.'

Alain and Baptiste sauntered towards the train. He and Florian watched the people on the platform. There would be injuries, deaths even, and some would be innocent bystanders.

Alain returned after a few minutes, leaving Baptiste to occupy the driver and fireman. 'La Fourche?'

'I'm ready.'

He followed Alain to another engine, and ordered the driver and fireman down from the engine. Leading them away from Alain, he engaged them in conversation. 'The inspection won't take long. I'm sure you can make up the time and keep to your schedule. Where are you bound?'

'Francfort-sur-Maine and Dresde.' The accent suggested the driver was German.

'Not a train going to Auschwitz, then?'

'No. They don't stop here. They stop only once and in open country. The train is well-guarded to make sure no one escapes.'

They had little chance of stopping an Auschwitz train mid-journey unless they destroyed the tracks, which were soon mended. 'What are you carrying?'

'The driver waved a hand at the cattle wagons. 'Cattle – to feed the people of Germany.'

He laughed through his anger. 'Better than feeding the damned French.' He glanced at the train to see Alain jump down and motion to Florian to follow him to a third engine. Baptiste was still waylaying the first crew. How long before something exploded? Suppose it didn't? He should have brought dynamite and satchel bombs and timers.

'Indeed. Who cares if they starve?' The man's laughter brought him back to the moment. 'Germany grows fat and victorious on the backs of the labour of our stupid vassals.'

How he wanted to punch the man's insolent face. Instead, he continued talking until Alain waved, which was the signal to leave. 'I won't hold you up any longer, my friend. It seems the inspection is over. Heil Hitler.'

The man returned the salute and hurried back towards his engine.

He attempted the assured saunter of a German officer as he made his way towards the truck, ordering bystanders away from the trains as he went. Any locomotive out of action was a blow to the occupiers, and this was a ploy they could use again even if they couldn't target the deportees' trains themselves.

As he joined Alain, Florian, and Baptiste, a huge explosion shook the ground. He turned to see metal flying through the air amid a cloud of overheated, scalding steam. People were screaming, running, bleeding, and the tubes that had been inside the boiler looked like some ferocious, twisted, nightmare animal that had burst out of the front of the engine.

Alain grabbed his arm. 'La Fourche, come. We must leave – now!'

As they hurried towards the truck, another explosion rocked the station followed closely by a third. Florian jammed the truck into gear, floored the accelerator, and the old truck rumbled away from Metz and the terrible destruction they'd left behind.

He shook his head in appalled denial. There'd been women and children on the platform, and he hadn't been able to warn them all. His voice was as bleak as his heart. 'Collateral damage?'

Florian nodded, his expression grim and his eyes fixed on the road ahead. 'It's the price we pay for freedom.'

***

## Marseille, France. January 1943

Marseille in January was far warmer than winter in Nancy, but since the occupation of the southern zone, the relaxed atmosphere of the summer pavement café culture had been replaced by winter wary silence – apart from the sound of Nazi boots on the hard ground and the gentle flapping of German flags with Hitler's face on them.

Outside France, the war was going better for the Allies. Rommel was trapped in Tunisia, the Soviets had the Germans encircled at Stalingrad, and the Japanese were losing the battle in Guadalcanal. Berlin had been bombed two nights running, and there'd been an uprising in the Warsaw ghetto.

On the other jackboot, Nazis had arrested hundreds of people in Normandy; more unfortunate souls to be deported east to the labour camps of Germany, and the Vichy government had ordered all Jews to have their identity papers, ration cards, and work permits stamped with "Juif" or "Juive". With the yellow star and the stamp, they were now unarguably identifiable.

Bonnie sighed as she walked along the street towards Colette's home, the blue door with its peeling paint and dolphin knocker as welcoming as ever. Her own lot was much better than the Jews, but she had a personal decision to make that affected her future. Marcel was expecting an answer before he left with the two British airmen, who'd been shot down north of Paris and had been passed from safe house to safe house until she'd brought them to Colette's home.

Could she bear to refuse Marcel? Mind made up, she knocked twice and twice again. Marcel opened the door and smiled, and she walked into his arms. 'I love you, Marcel.'

'Then tonight, you'll come to my room?'

She shook her head. 'I want to wait until...'

'Until what? The war is over?'

'Until we're married.'

His mouth spread into a wide grin. 'You want to marry me?'

'I want to be married before I sleep with you.'

'Then let's marry, now, before – before it's too late, and we regret wasting precious time together. I want to marry you, Marie. Stay here and arrange it while I take the airmen to Spain. I can be back here in a week, God willing, and we'll marry as soon as we can.'

'Then it's time to be honest. The mayor will need our real names, our addresses, and proper proof of identity before he can legally marry us.'

'Of course he will. I have no problem with that. I'll go first. My real name is Maurice Auclair.'

She smiled, relieved to have someone she could share reality with at last. She'd pretended to be someone else for far too long. 'My name is Bonnie Renard. My papers are sown into the lining of my coat.'

He kissed her forehead. 'Thank you for trusting me.'

'I trust you with my life, just as I trust Colette.'

'And I trust you with mine.' His lips were firm and passionate, his arms strong, and she desperately wanted to forget her decision to wait until they were married.

# Chapter Thirty-Five

**Marseille, France. January 1943**

Bonnie hurried towards the station to meet Marcel off the train. Her feet had barely touched the ground since she and Marcel – she still had trouble thinking of him as Maurice – had decided to get married. Arranging the wedding was going to take longer than she'd imagined, and Marcel would be disappointed with her news.

There was endless paperwork to be completed, and to be legally married, she needed her real identity papers. – a copy of her birth certificate and proof of her address, neither of which she had – she'd entered France under a false name, and the papers sewn into her coat didn't include her birth certificate, which was in a drawer back in England, and how could she prove Cosby was her home?

Documents could be forged, but how good would a French forger be at English documents? And she lived with Louise and Raphael now, but giving their address might put her friends in danger if she was arrested.

She pondered the wisdom of revealing her true identity to the mayor. *Bonnie Renard* wasn't being hunted by the French police or the Gestapo; to all intents and purposes, no one of that name was of any interest to the authorities. Except Dad had been arrested and had escaped… How common was the name *Renard* in France? How trustworthy was the mayor? He was a Frenchman all too aware he and his family lived under German rule.

Dodging people hurrying in the opposite direction, and trying to convince herself she was dreaming up danger when none existed, she wondered if it wouldn't be safer to marry as Marie Barbier, or better still, postpone the wedding until after the war – it couldn't last forever, could it?

Despite the difficulties, however, thoughts of the forthcoming wedding had brightened a dark time. Colette insisted on paying for everything and thought of something they absolutely must have for the wedding meal at least ten times a day. It would be a small affair, given the few friends they'd been able to make while keeping a low profile in Marseille, but Colette was determined to make it perfect.

How could it be perfect when she daren't tell Dad or Louise and Raphael for fear they'd put themselves in danger to be with her? No, if the wedding went ahead, it must be her and Marcel's day, with Colette there as one of the witnesses. Perhaps, after the war, they could have a church wedding with all their friends and family present. She and Marcel had talked far into the night about their family and friends far away, and how delighted they would be when they learned of their marriage.

She reached the station and paced backwards and forwards along the platform. Gestapo officers marched imperiously towards her and demanded her papers. She handed them over, ever-nervous, despite Marie Barbier having passed inspection on numerous occasions – the forgeries were good.

The papers returned, after heart-stopping seconds, she resumed her pacing.

Louise and Raphel were used to her stretching her visits to Marseille by a day or two, to spend time with Marcel, but she'd been with Colette for a week now. She needed to get home before they began to worry at the delay. When they finally met Marcel, he would be her husband. There must be a way. There had to be…

If the wedding went ahead, the honeymoon would be short, and with their escape-line work taking priority, and Marcel based in the south, time together would be limited, but when she was in Marseille, they would make the most of every second. They were already making plans for life after the war when they *would* be married.

The train pulled into the station, and she peered over heads, searching for his familiar figure. People met loved ones, hugged, and carried luggage away to live their own lives.

The crowds thinned, the train gathered steam and moved slowly forward with a clank of couplings. Marcel hadn't come.

\*\*\*

Bonnie tossed and turned in her bed. She couldn't eat or sleep, worrying about Marcel and what might have befallen him.

Colette tried to calm her fears. 'Anything could have happened to delay him. I dare say there's snow on the Pyrenees to hinder them, and there are Germans everywhere. He might have had to lie low or find a different route. Since the occupation, everything has changed, and people are frightened. Everyone must be more careful.' Colette hugged her to her motherly bosom. 'He'll come. I'm sure of it, Marie.'

She met train after train to no avail. Unable to leave without knowing Marcel was safe, she sent a message to Louise and Raphael that she was delayed. No one in the escape line seemed to have heard anything about Marcel for several days, and it was a week before an anonymous message was posted through Colette's letterbox.

Marcel had been captured and taken to the Compiègne transit camp, north of Paris.

Tears streaked her cheeks. He could be held hostage, deported to Auschwitz, or even executed. *Dear God, let him be alive. Bring him home to me.*

There was nothing she could do but wait for news that would probably never come. People disappeared without trace every month, it was part of the Nazi agenda to demoralise the resistance, but she mustn't give up hope.

She mustn't ignore her escape-line work either. Marcel wasn't the only one in danger. People – families – depended on her. Reluctantly, she hugged Colette and left for the journey north to Louise and Raphael.

Bonnie travelled south again with a heavy heart. Three resistance workers, known as Matiss, Aristide, and Guy, who'd escaped the spate of arrests in Normandy, had made their way south to Nancy and been brought to Louise and Raphael's home. Nowhere in France was now safe for men hunted by the Gestapo, and it had taken days to get them false papers for their journey to Spain.

She wouldn't spend long in Marseille, now that Marcel wasn't there. Colette would have organised someone else to take the men on to the Spanish border; the escape route must be kept open, the whole resistance network was deeply committed to it, and it took precedence over personal needs.

Life seemed colourless without Marcel, every day a grey drag of time Louise and Raphael had tried to lighten. They'd been supportive, as they always were, but she longed to send a message to Dad; *the raven needs help*. He'd have come, and she'd have cried on his shoulder and welcomed his strong arms around her, but it would have put him in danger, and she couldn't bear the thought of losing another person she loved.

She sat in the carriage, looking out of the window and letting the chatter of the three men wash over her. She hardly looked up when a guard asked to check her papers, and she took them back checked without even a thank you.

Marseille station arrived too soon. He wouldn't be waiting for her on the platform. The train slowed to a halt in a scene of frenzied activity. Gestapo and French police were everywhere, shouting and waving their arms. Hundreds of people crowded the platform, some carried bundles over their shoulders. Children cried, and women tried to comfort them, while keeping fear almost concealed behind masks of calm. They were all being herded into cattle wagons.

She motioned to her charges. 'Keep your heads down and follow me. Don't attract attention to yourselves.'

Going to Colette's could be dangerous. She caught the arm of a young mother who pushed past her to board the train they were leaving. 'What's happening?'

'Get away from here. There are thousands of police and Germans. They came with loud hailers before it was light. They're evacuating the area north of the Old Port. They're going house to house, checking papers, looking for Jews and resistance workers. They've arrested hundreds. Nowhere is safe.'

'Where are they taking all these people?'

'I heard a policeman saying they were going to the camp at Compiègne and then to the transit camp at Drancy.'

And then to extermination camps if what Raphael feared was true. She grabbed Guy's sleeve. 'Get back on the train.' With luck, she could get the men to Cerbère, and the Cuvaliers, but she'd have to take them over the eastern Pyrenees herself. There was no Marcel, and going to Colette's was impossible with police everywhere. Thank goodness Colette had a safe house within the safe house where she could hide with Ava.

*** 

**Pyrenees, France. January 1943**

News of the round up in Marseille had already reached the Cuvaliers. They greeted Bonnie with anxious hugs and showered her and the three men with typical hospitality.

The meal wasn't lavish, but it was wholesome and welcome.

Monsieur Cuvalier, finished with the important task of eating, sipped wine. He put down his glass. 'We were expecting Marcel, but it's true? He's been captured?'

She nodded, trying to swallow sobs. 'We've heard nothing more. I daren't go to the safe house in Marseille, so I don't know if he's alive or dead.'

Madame Cuvalier looked up from her plate with an expression of understanding. 'Ah, you were fond of the boy? It's hard losing those you love, but such is the madness of war. Such is the inhumanity of those who start wars and leave others to fight them.' She spat her disgust. 'You won't see Hitler out on the battlefield with his troops.'

Monsieur Cuvalier nodded. He'd obviously heard his wife's tirade before. 'So, who is guiding these stout men to Spain, Marie?'

She put down her knife and fork. 'I am.'

'It won't be safe to use the route over the Eastern Pyrenees, not with Germans and police checking everyone.'

'How will we get to Spain then?'

'There's a route over the Central Pyrenees. It goes from Saint Girons-Esterri in Ariège. It's a much higher, harder trail, and this time of the year, it won't be easy, but it avoids all the official checkpoints and German patrols.'

'How long will it take us?'

'To Alos d'Isil, in Spain, four days there and four days back, God willing. We'll equip you best we can, and I'll take you as far as I'm able in the Citroën.'

'Thank you.'

First light next morning saw them equipped with bulging backpacks, warm clothing, and skis and ski poles.

Monsieur Cuvalier loaded everything into the van. 'You'll have to learn how to ski when you hit snow. Just try not to break a leg.'

Matiss examined the skis. 'I've done a bit of skiing. I can give the others some tips.'

She looked from the blue of the Mediterranean to the sun-kissed, snow-covered peaks of the mountains behind the town. Memories of mud slides and death and cold flooded back. Men died every year buried by avalanches. Matiss's knowledge could save her life.

It wasn't only her life at stake. If these men were caught, they were dead. If she was caught, she was dead, and the Gestapo was hunting down families of resistance workers as well as destroying whole villages. Everyone she loved was in danger.

She forced a smile. 'We'll be careful.'

'You won't be alone up there. A lot of people use this route despite its difficulty.'

'That's good to know.'

Monsieur Cuvalier closed the van doors on Matiss, Aristide, and Guy, who sat on the floor with the equipment. She sat beside Monsieur Cuvalier and watched the mountains loom closer as they drove west.

He stopped at a bridge over the river that swept through the village of St Girons and unloaded the van. He helped her on with her backpack and slung the skis over her shoulder. 'This is where we part company.' He pushed a map into her hands. 'I'll look for you here in eight days' time, Marie.' He smiled as he shook the men's hands and then hers. 'Good luck.'

The path led them through woodland and climbed steadily. Below lay villages, according to the map, Eycheil, Lacourt, and then Alos. Above them, and where the marked trail led, was Col de l'Artigau. It grew colder the higher they climbed. The bitter wind nipped her nose, and she was glad of the woollen hat over her ears, but as long as they kept moving, she felt warm.

The light was failing as they descended into a valley and climbed again to the hamlet of Aunac. They were welcomed cautiously, not the first to arrive that day. They ate a frugal meal from their provisions and found a corner in a room in a small cottage. Even with a fire burning in the grate, it would be a cold night.

Beyond the curtained window, the mountains waited. Tomorrow the climb would be harder, steeper, and colder. They would meet snow for the first time.

# Chapter Thirty-Six

## Central Pyrenees, France. January 1943

Bonnie struggled uphill under the weight of her pack and skis. The eastern route had been hard, but the climb had now become much more difficult, and the cold and altitude of the Central Pyrenees made every breath raw. Now, the third day since they'd left Monsieur Cuvalier, they'd hit snow. She stopped to gain her breath and looked up at the massif of Mont Valier almost three thousand metres high, its peak piercing the clouds. Somehow, according to the route marked on the map, she had to get these men over that.

She was beginning to wonder why she was leading these men on a route she knew no better than they did, especially when Matiss was an experienced skier. The truth was she felt responsible for them, and anyway, the escape line needed information taking back on the new route for those who would cross after her.

Eyes smarting, she fixed landmarks in her mind and donned her dark glasses. Matiss helped her adjust her skis and showed her how to use the ski poles and how to "walk". Marks left by earlier escapees showed the trail clearly, and far ahead of them, men moved like black ants against the snow.

The route wound up and down through rocky terrain and into a valley before climbing steeply again. She pushed forward, one foot after the other, grateful Matiss, Aristide, and Guy had shared some of the heavier items to lighten her load.

Her breath wreathed in front of her, blown away by the wind. A sharp crack made her look around, and a heavy weight knocked her to the ground and pinned her there, struggling to breathe, and her legs twisted at unnatural angles.

'Stay down!' Matiss put a hand on the back of her head, forcing her face into the snow. 'Don't move.'

'Wha –' She couldn't speak with a mouthful of snow.

Another crack, and the weight rolled off her. Turning her head to one side, Matiss's eyes stared into hers. The snow beneath his head was crimson with his blood. *Stay down...* She lay still. *Don't move...*

Gun shots, shouting, screams, and moans. She couldn't see what was happening without moving, and Matiss had given his life to save hers.

*Don't move.*

She closed her eyes, unable to bear the accusing blue eyes of her dead friend. She'd never noticed before that they were blue like Pierre's.

The sound of skis swished closer. Rough hands turned her over, and she stayed limp and lifeless, eyes closed, letting her head and legs flop to one side and trying not to breathe. 'Merde!' The man's voice was as brittle as the icy air.

*Shit* seemed an odd thing for a murderer to say. Had he not intended to kill a woman? An assassin with a conscience?

The voices moved away, and she risked a shallow breath. Her face burned with cold, and she was shaking. If she stayed still much longer, she'd freeze despite her warm clothing. She opened her eyes cautiously. The assassins had gone.

Warily, she removed her skis and rolled onto her hands and knees. Matiss was obviously dead. No one could survive a bullet in the back of their head. Two more bodies sprawled across the snow. Guy wasn't moving, and a trail of deep crimson showed Aristide had tried to crawl towards her before he died.

She turned back to Guy and held her dark glasses over his mouth. No mist formed, so he wasn't breathing. Undoing his jacket, her fingers shook and fumbled. She couldn't feel a heartbeat, and his shirt was wet with blood. She'd read something about resuscitation. She grabbed his forearms and raised his arms above his head and then crossed them over his chest. She could see his chest rising and falling as she repeated the movements, but he still wasn't breathing.

Snowflakes brushed her cheek, but she carried on, determined not to lose another man, woman, or child. Snowflakes became a blizzard, blinding her and covering the bodies with a mantle of virginal white. The price of freedom grew as the light failed, leaving her marooned with three dead men two thousand metres up in a snowstorm.

\*\*\*

## Vosges Mountains, France. February 1943

Antoine added sticks to a small fire in the middle of the barn. Smoke puthered up and drifted out through a convenient hole in the roof – convenient if it didn't rain too hard. After the comfort of the cottage, it was a harsh reminder of reality. The toilet was a hole in the ground amongst the undergrowth, and Juliette was doing her best to cook in a cast iron pot suspended on rusting metalwork over the fire. They had managed to bring basics and bedding but slept close to the fire to keep warm. Spring couldn't come too soon.

It was recent news that had forced them to change their hideout yet again. He nursed a mug of hot coffee. 'This new Milice force could be even more dangerous than the Gestapo or the SS.'

Juliette sat cross-legged beside him on the floor. 'What makes you say that?'

Alain butted in before he could answer. 'I've heard they torture people to get confessions, La Fourche.'

'So do the Gestapo.' He shuddered at the memory. 'The Milice is dangerous because they're ordinary Frenchmen, promised extra food and exemption from forced labour if they join and hunt down Jews and the resistance. Some feel justified in targeting us, because of family killed in Allied raids – they think collaborating is safety and revenge. Some are criminals who've been promised their sentences will be commuted. These people have little to lose and much to gain. Worse, they know the locality and the dialects of their area, and probably where the maquis are likely to be holed up. They can infiltrate more easily than Germans.' He looked from Alain to Baptiste to Adolf and Florian. 'Any one of us could fall prey to Nazi promises.'

As one, his friends shook their heads and protested their loyalty to the resistance.

'I know. I trust you all, but food is getting scarcer, and a starving man, or a man who sees his family starving, will do things he wouldn't normally entertain. We must be more vigilant than ever.'

Baptiste stared into the flames. 'Men will flock to join them. This could be disastrous for the resistance.'

Florian poked the fire with a stick, sending sparks flying. 'And they'll be keen to prove their worth. Not all will realise Nazi promises mean nothing. We're French – worthless… expendable.'

'We shouldn't even have a fire. The smoke will be seen for miles.'

'Juliette, we'll freeze without a fire and hot food.'

Adolf took the stick from Florian's hand. 'Perhaps we should let the fire die down and not light it again until after dark. Agreed?'

They all nodded.

Florian shrugged his coat collar higher. 'We should take turns to do regular patrols in pairs. Anyone we don't know who comes close dies. Agreed?'

Again, they all nodded.

Florian got to his feet. 'I'll go first. Who's coming with me? La Fourche?'

He grabbed his coat and followed Florian outside. They'd taken the fight to the Nazi regime, and now the Nazis and the Vichy regime were bringing the fight directly to them. He put a hand to his throat. The noose was tightening.

\*\*\*

## Central Pyrenees, France. February 1943

Bonnie crawled out of the tent into a crisp, bright morning. The flimsy canvas had kept the worst of the wind from her, but it had been a cold night. She hurt all over, and her legs felt as if they belonged to someone fifty years older. Only long shadows thrown by three low humps in the snow showed the violence of the previous day.

Survival was now her first concern, and after a hurried meal of dried fruit and icy water, she rifled the men's packs for food, donned her skis and pack, and started back down the mountain. There was nothing she could do for her friends, and feeling guilt at having survived and "stealing" dead men's food wouldn't keep her alive. Matiss had given his life for hers. She shivered. She needed to be down beyond the snowline before the few hours of daylight were spent.

The sun was high in the sky when she spotted a small group of skiers coming along the valley towards her. She gripped the handle of the knife she always carried in a belt pouch beneath her coat. There was nowhere to hide, and she couldn't outrun them.

The leader stopped beside her. 'What are you doing up here by yourself? Are you all right?'

'I was with three friends. We were ambushed.' She waved vaguely in the direction from which she'd come. 'They're up there. All dead. Shot.'

The man stared up at the mountain behind her. 'I heard the Milice were targeting the escape routes. This one has been fairly safe until now.'

'The Milice?'

'A new paramilitary organisation tasked with destroying the resistance. It appears to be a law unto itself – torture, executions. It seems we've become quite a thorn in the side of the Nazis.'

'The Vichy government allows this?'

'Prime Minister Laval is rumoured to be the head of the organisation, and the Secretary General is running operations. They're after resistors and the maquis as well as rounding up Jews.' He spat into the snow. 'Damned collaborators.'

Dad was with the maquis. The sun was setting, and she still wasn't below the snowline. 'I must go. Be careful up there.'

'Thank you for the warning. Good luck.'

She set off again. She would have to spend another night on the mountain, and when, if, she reached the bridge at St Girons, it would be two days at least before Monsieur Cuvalier came looking for her.

***

## Marseille, France. February 1943

Bonnie nodded sleepily to the rhythmic sound of the train rattling along the track towards Marseille. The trek back down the mountain had taken a day longer than she expected and had sapped the last of her energy. Even two nights of blessed warmth and comfort spent with the Cuvaliers hadn't bolstered her spirits. She'd tossed and turned, waking from nightmares bathed in sweat.

How many more Frenchmen would die before every Nazi was banished from France?

'Papers.'

The sharp request jolted her awake, and she fumbled for her papers. The man wore a uniform with an insignia she hadn't seen before; not SS, or Gestapo, or French police. He stared at her for a long moment and returned her documents without a word before moving on. Behind her, a voice hissed. 'Milice.'

*Milice.* The murdering scum who'd shot Matiss, Aristide, and Guy, and would doubtless have killed her had they not taken her for dead. She stared out of the window to hide her fear from the man's penetrating stare.

The sky to the east was laden with low dark cloud that did nothing to lift her heart. She'd left Marseille without seeing Colette, and she was desperate to know where she was and that she was safe.

A man in front of her got out of his seat and opened a window to look out. A faint acrid smell wafted in. She sniffed. Smoke from the engine probably.

The closer they got to Marseille, the darker the sky and the stronger the smell. By the time the train pulled into the station, it was evident there was a serious fire not far south of her, somewhere near the Old Port. Colette lived in one of the narrow streets of old Marseille, north of the port. Many of the safe houses were reputed to be in that area, it being difficult for the authorities to police the winding alleys and streets.

She grabbed her meagre possessions and jumped from the train, hurrying along the platform and out onto the street. A few streets south she was met by barricades, police, and a scene of utter destruction. Clouds of dust and smoke rose from ruined buildings. An air raid? Only bombs could do this much damage.

A loud blast sent tons of rubble flying into the air, and a building collapsed in slow motion and a cloud of dust. Her brain struggled to understand. The occupants of the north of the Old Port had been evacuated, some sent to camps... This wasn't an air raid: this was the Nazis and the Vichy government destroying what they were sure was a hotbed of French resistance.

The police motioned her away, but when they weren't looking, she ducked under the barricade and dodged between piles of rubble that had once been homes, trying to remember the way to Colette's when everything looked so different. Some houses were virtually unscathed, some had flames licking at their roofs, and others stood with their interiors bared to the world, pictures still hanging on walls that would never again ring to the sound of children's laughter.

Recognising a house, she turned left, climbing over rubble. This was Colette's street. She hurried along, looking for the blue door with peeling paint and a dolphin knocker.

'Dear God.' The door stood askew in a broken frame. Half the house had collapsed, and the rest looked precarious. 'Oh, Colette.' She had to know if Colette and Ava had escaped or if they were trapped in the cellar.

Taking a deep breath, she squeezed past the door and walked carefully along the rubble-strewn hallway. The back of the house was less damaged, and the bookcase Marcel had made was still intact. The two book spines that hinged out to reveal the catch to the cellar door had been ripped off and lay on the floor.

She pushed her hand through the gap and released the handle.

# Chapter Thirty-Seven

**Marseille, France. February 1943**

It had been over a week since Bonnie had fled Marseille. Colette would have had food and water, and the cellar had a grill for delivering coal, so she'd have air. Heart thumping, she pushed open the door to the cellar.

'Colette? Ava?'

It smelled of something worse than damp. The lantern wasn't hanging on the hook at the top of the stairs, so gingerly, she edged down into darkness. As her eyes accustomed themselves to the little light falling through the grill on the pavement, she could make out shapes.

'Colette? Ava?'

Her hand caught the top of the lantern, which was standing on a small table. Fumbling for the lamp oil and matches, she managed to refill the lantern and light it, as much from memory as sight. Lantern light chased shadows into dark corners. Colette lay sprawled on a straw mattress, her dress up around her waist, her knickers looped around one leg, and her limbs akimbo. It was obvious she'd been raped.

Ava lay at Colette's side. She turned away and vomited. What kind of monster would do that to a child? It would have been better if she'd been killed on the mountain with her parents. What kind of man would do this and leave them to die?

Holding her hand over her mouth, she forced herself to look closer. He hadn't left them to die. Colette and Ava had been violated and then shot.

She stumbled back up the stairs, sobbing and gasping for breath. How long had they suffered in terror? How long had they been lying there undiscovered?

The house shook as more explosions sent buildings tumbling to the ground. Masonry crashed to the floor only metres from her. She ran out into the street. All around was devastation, the narrow streets filled with rubble, hundreds of houses razed to the ground, the safe houses gone, and their occupants almost certainly arrested or dead. The escape line in Marseille was finished – Colette and Ava were gone forever.

The only thing left to her now was to escape Marseille and go home to Louise and Raphael to lick her wounds.

A figure dressed in dark clothing was making its way across the rubble, apparently unconcerned at being spotted. Police? Unarmed but for her knife, she hid in the open doorway of one of the few houses untouched by dynamite, praying he would walk past without seeing her.

Something about the figure was familiar. She stepped from the shadows. 'Marcel?'

He turned to face her. His eyes widened. 'Marie? I thought you were –'

'They're dead.' She ran into his arms. 'Colette and little Ava are dead.'

He crushed her to him. 'You're alive. How did you survive?'

'I wasn't here. I came looking for them. The house has been dynamited. It's…' She sobbed on his shoulder, her arms flung around his neck. 'You were captured. I thought I'd lost you. How did you escape?'

'It's a long story.' He pushed her away and took hold of her hand. 'Come. We must get away from here. It isn't safe.'

'But what about Colette and Ava?' She slumped onto a pile of rubble, and Marcel sat beside her. She looked at him properly for the first time. He'd lost weight, but then so had they all. His hair was

270

unruly, and he'd grown a stubble beard. Sunlight filtering through the dust shone on the badge on his lapel. It was a sword and a stylised "V".

'Milice?' She got to her feet and backed away from him. 'You're a member of the Milice?'

His eyes begged her understanding. 'I had no choice, Marie. I was tortured, starved, and threatened with deportation or execution. They offered to commute my sentence if I joined. They promised me rations, freedom, purpose.'

She shook her head in denial. 'You're a collaborator.'

'The Germans are our masters. The escape lines are finished, and the Nazis are here to stay. It's time the resistance accepted that – if they're not wiped out, how will France ever be at peace?' He walked towards her. 'We must be on the winning side, Marie, if we're to survive. I can protect you. I love you.'

Her heart ached. 'I love you, too, but...' Some of what he said made sense.

He held out his arms and she walked into them. She'd missed him so much, and she understood his decision, even if she abhorred it. So many people had sacrificed their lives, and she couldn't, wouldn't, betray their memory.

The sound of running feet preceded a deafening roar and the rumble of a collapsing building close by.

'Merde! We must go.'

*Merde...* Slowly, pieces of a jigsaw fell into place, and it all began to make sense. "*I thought you were...*" What? Dead, because he thought he'd shot her along with Matiss and the others? And the hinged book spines that revealed the latch to the cellar. Only she, Marcel, and Colette knew of it, and Colette would have shut the door after her and pulled the books back into place.

'It was you.' Her voice trembled. 'Up on the Pyrenees. The ambush. It was you!'

'Rooting out resistance is my duty, Marie. This is your chance to escape it. I *can* protect you once we're married.'

Married? He seriously thought she would still marry him? Tears ran down her cheeks. 'Collete and Ava. You betrayed them. Please tell me it wasn't you who raped them.'

'I told the soldiers how to open the door. I didn't stay to see what they did.' He clutched her close to his chest. 'Please, we must leave here. It isn't safe.'

Coward.

Collaborator and coward.

Traitor, collaborator, and coward.

*Traitor…*

Dear God, she'd told him about Louise and Raphael and that Dad was with the maquis in the Vosges mountains. How much more had she told him? Enough for him to find them or direct Nazis to them?

*Trust no one.*

If Marcel had had no choice, neither did she. 'I loved you, Marcel.' The words came out in a sob. He bent to kiss her, and one hand caressed his back while the knife in her other hand slid between his ribs close to his spine.

His lips parted and his eyes widened in shock. 'Marie…'

'My name is Bonnie Renard. Marie is dead, Maurice.'

He slumped to the ground, and she pulled out the knife and wiped it on his Milice uniform.

He wasn't breathing. His heart wasn't beating. She'd killed the man she'd loved – the man who'd brought her down from the mountains and saved her life after the Abrams had died.

Slowly, she stumbled away from the ruins of her life, numb and beyond grief.

One thought percolated the cold void in her mind. Suppose he'd already betrayed Louise and Dad? Was she too late to warn them?

The station was only a few shattered streets away, and the sooner she left Marseille for good, the better. She broke into a run careless of attracting attention. She had a train to catch and no one was going to stop her.

***

**Vosges Mountains, France. February 1943**

Antoine pulled up his coat collar around his ears and squinted against the sunlight reflected from the latest fall of snow.

'There, see?' Baptiste pointed down the slope, beyond the snow-laden trees.

'Got them.' Black ants crawled across the valley below. 'Milice?'

'Could be.'

'They may not be after us. Keep an eye on them, and I'll warn the others to be ready to move.' The snow crunched beneath his feet as he tramped back to the barn.

It was little warmer inside the barn than it was outside. Juliette sighed, but as always, she packed her precious cooking equipment into a bag, ready to move at the first sign they'd been compromised.

Florian got to his feet. 'I'll make sure the truck is ready to go.'

'Alain, Adolf, it might be an idea if you scout around to the south and east, Baptiste and I will keep watch to the west and north.' He hurried back to Baptiste. The ants were moving steadily along the valley, taking the easiest route. 'They look as if they know the area. Locals, do you think?'

'Local doesn't mean they haven't joined this damned Milice, and what would they be doing up here in this weather?'

'And if they come this way, we've left a trail of footprints straight to the barn. There's no way we can disguise them.'

Baptiste kept his eyes on the moving ants. 'They could be resistance members coming to join us.'

'Possibly, but do we dare take the risk of letting them close?'

'They're heading this way. What do we do, La Fourche? There are too many to fight, even if we could pick some off at a distance. And I don't like the thought of shooting people who might be loyal to the resistance.'

'Then we move. Alert Alain and Adolf. I'll help Florian and Juliette load the truck.'

'See you back at the barn.'

He hurried back to the barn, hoping the truck would start and could get through the snow, otherwise, they'd have to dump most of their possessions, and flee on foot to somewhere less accessible. Somewhere the Milice couldn't follow. There were shovels and sacks in the barn that would come in useful.

Florian was fiddling with the radio. He looked up when the door banged against the barn wall. 'I was hoping for some news.' The radio crackled into life. A small voice rose above the crackles. '*The raven needs help. Bridge as before, urgent.*'

'That's Bonnie!'

Adolf hurried into the barn. 'There are skiers to the south heading this way.'

'And to the west. That settles which direction we go. Bonnie's sent a message. She needs me. We'll head northeast and then west to the bridge at Mont-sur-Meurthe.'

'But we need a safe house, La Fourche. In this freezing weather…' Alain's concern was met by murmurs of agreement.

'You can go where you want, but if my daughter needs me, I shall go to Mont-sur-Meurthe if I have to walk every damned step alone.'

Juliette put a hand on his arm. 'We're in this together, and we stick together. Once we see what Bonnie needs, we'll decide what to do.' She looked from face to face. 'Agreed?'

'Agreed.'

The old truck chugged into life as they loaded the last of their possessions, and the precious radio transmitter, and jumped aboard.

The barn had become a home of sorts, and every move left him with a pang of regret and a feeling of insecurity. Not this time. The Raven – Bonnie – had asked for his help.

*** 

## Mont-sur-Meurthe, France. February 1943

Bonnie approached the bridge cautiously. It was dusk and freezing cold with a biting wind, and snow on the hills, and there was no sign yet of Dad. Forewarned, Louise and Raphael had left the cottage in the woods, having hidden signs of recent occupation in the loft, and were staying with a friend near Nancy until they felt it was safe to return. If Marcel – Maurice had betrayed them, members of the Milice would act quickly, and they'd surely lose interest in an obviously abandoned house.

Her message to Dad hadn't been for her own comfort, much as she needed it; she may have compromised him, and it was the fastest and surest way she could think of to get him away from danger.

She shivered and began pacing to keep warm. Dusk turned to darkness lit only by the moon. It was enough to stop her wandering off the road and falling in a ditch or worse.

She stopped and cocked her head, listening, straining to hear above the chuckle of the river. A vehicle was approaching. She shrank against the stonework of the bridge. Lights swung around a bend and dimmed. The engine went silent.

It must be Dad. She walked forward. Moonlight glinted off the water and shone on the bonnet of a truck. She stopped, uncertain. A group of people stood at the side of the vehicle.

One of them walked towards her. 'Bonnie?'

'Papa!' She ran forward and almost fell into his arms. The emotions of the past days welled up, and she couldn't speak for sobbing.

'Oh, Bonnie. What is it? What's happened?'

She shook her head, unable to speak.

'He held her hands. You're freezing. Let's get you in the truck and out this wind.' He helped her into the back of the lorry amid bundles and boxes of stores and cans of petrol. 'You've met Florian before.' He pointed to each of the others in turn. 'This is Juliette, Adolf, Alain, and Baptiste. This is Raven, my daughter.'

Juliette moved aside so she could sit beside her. 'You poor thing. Tell us what's happened.'

'I…' She swallowed a sob. 'I killed him. Marcel, the man I was to marry. He betrayed us, and I killed him. Colette and Ava, the escape line – Marseille's in ruins. They raped little Ava and shot them both. It's finished, over, all gone.'

'Slow down, Raven. You killed a man?'

She turned bleary eyes on the speaker and tried to gather her thoughts. 'He joined the Milice after he was captured. I was afraid he would compromise Louise and Raphael and Dad. I daren't let him live, but I didn't know if he'd already betrayed you. I came to warn you.'

Dad nodded. 'We saw men near our safe house, but we weren't sure they were Milice. Then I got your message, and we decided to leave anyway. What about Louise and Raphael? Are they…?'

'I warned them. They're hiding out with friends until it's safe to go back.'

'And you? Where are you living?'

'Nowhere. I came to warn you.'

Juliette shook her head. 'Then we're all in the same boat. We can't spend the night in the truck. We'll freeze to death. What are we to do, La Fourche?'

'You said Marseille is in ruins?'

'The Nazis dynamited the streets around the old port and arrested the resistance leaders. The escape line is finished, the safe houses gone. I came… home.' She burst into tears again. Home was the people you loved, and Dad was all she had left.

'These friends of Louise and Raphael – would they take you in?'

'I expect so.'

'Can you take us there?'

'Yes, but –'

'No buts, ma chère. You need somewhere to stay.'

The bicycle thrown into the back of the truck on top of everything else, the truck ground on towards Nancy, and she directed them to the village Louise had described. 'Louise said the house with the big chimney on the edge of the village. She said I'd be sure to recognise it.'

Florian stopped the truck. 'This one?'

'It could be. I'll ask.' She jumped down and knocked on the door. A matronly woman in a white apron answered her knock. 'I'm looking for Louise.'

'And you are?'

'Raven.'

The woman smiled. 'And I'm Sofia. Louise has been pacing up and down worrying about you. Come in, child.'

She hesitated and pointed to the truck. 'My father and his friends have been forced out of their safe house by the Milice. They have nowhere to go.'

'I expect we can squeeze in one or two more, Raven.'

'There are seven of us.'

'Seven? Well, child. You'd better tell them to come in. We'll all have to squeeze up a bit, though. Go on. I can't stand here on a cold night with the door open.'

She ran back to the truck. 'This is the right house. Sofia says you are all welcome to stay. We have a home again, Papa. We have a home.'

# Chapter Thirty-Eight

**Near Nancy, France. May 1943**

Bonnie had the kitchen to herself for once and was taking the opportunity to sweep and wash the floor. The house near Nancy was a rambling old place, with small windows and a tiled roof; three storeys' high and built of mellow brick, it had room for a large family and servants and was blessed with a sizable vegetable garden. As they weren't the only guests, and Sofia had a daughter, Simone, large was just as well.

It had soon become apparent that the three girls who shared a bedroom on the top floor worked from home in a less than savoury occupation. As Sofia explained, they entertained German soldiers, elicited useful information during pillow talk, and got paid into the bargain.

It made coming and going without being seen hazardous, except that Dad and his friends had brought four German uniforms with them in their flight from the mountains, and soldiers were commonplace in the area. As most of their resistance activities took place at night, the whorehouse made a perfect cover for their comings and goings.

Not so fortunate, were the escapees who were restricted to the cellar. Since Jews had been forbidden to leave their home towns, forced to wear yellow stars, and have their papers stamped with Juif or Juive, it had been increasingly easy for the Gestapo to round them up, and increasingly difficult for the Jews to escape arrest, especially as the Gestapo demanded lists of Jews' addresses from the local préfets. Now more than ever, they needed the escape lines.

A lot had happened during the months since the destruction of old Marseille while she'd wallowed in her own grief and anger, and nursed her wounded heart. Many leaders of the resistance had fallen

278

prey to Gestapo raids in Paris, Marseille, and Toulouse, Pat O'Leary among them. She'd thought the escape line finished forever, but a woman who called herself Françoise had re-formed it using Toulouse as a base. Toulouse was closer to the Central Pyrenees than Marseille, but that route was difficult and dangerous, as *Marie Barbier* had found to her cost.

But Marie was dead and gone; Raven determined to find a new way to help the resistance. She clenched and unclenched her hand to rid herself of the feel of the knife as it slid between Maurice's ribs. It was a memory she would take to her grave.

*Trust no one.*

Would she ever be able to trust again?

She pushed the memory deeper and closed the lid on the box containing the lives she'd taken, looking instead to the future. Realising the importance of the resistance, the O.S.S, the British Office of Strategic Services, had sent agents to France to help the S.O.E agents rally support against the German occupation, and Jean Moulin headed newly merged groups under the Conseil National de la Resistance and recognised de Gaulle as leader of the movement.

The Allies were bombing the Ruhr industrial area, and every German loss seemed to result in ever greater reprisals. Thousands were deported to Mauthausen, Sachsenhausen, Ravensbrück, and Sobibor death camps; rumours said those not used for hard labour were killed on arrival. After the Jews rose in protest in the Warsaw Ghetto, fourteen thousand were killed and forty thousand sent to death camps. The numbers were staggering and mounting daily; Hitler was hell-bent on extermination.

The resistance to German occupation ground on relentlessly throughout Europe. In occupied Belgium, partisans had attacked a railway convoy and released hundreds of Jews being sent to Auschwitz. Dad and the other men were laying plans to carry out a similar attack and rescue mission in France. Somehow, Raven must stretch her clipped wings and learn to fly again.

Michelle, one of the girls from the top floor, padded into the kitchen in slippers, filled the large kettle from a tap in the kitchen, and yawned. 'I'm making coffee. Do you want one, Raven?'

'Coffee? Real coffee?'

Michelle smiled and winked. 'One of the perks of my line of work. German soldiers often bring black market gifts when they lust after your body. How did you think we had a supply of rationed goods when most of the people in this house don't have ration books?'

She always felt slightly embarrassed talking to the "girls", as if the sleazy side of them would taint her somehow. She hesitated. Michelle had worked the night before and slept late. Everyone else was already out and about. Coffee was coffee, wherever it came from. 'If it's no trouble.'

Michelle brushed dark hair from her face and put cups on the table and Nazi beans in the grinder. 'I know what you did, Raven. I don't know how you could kill someone, even a German, never mind the man you were supposed to marry.'

She swept harder, pushing dust and dirt onto a dustpan as if sweeping away the crime. 'The Germans were enemies – they'd have killed me without a thought. My fiancé was a traitor. I had no choice.' Her tone was harsher than she intended.

The noise of the coffee being ground drowned the distant sound of anti-aircraft guns and briefly interrupted the conversation. 'I wasn't criticising.'

'Sorry. It still hurts, that's all. The betrayal, I mean.'

'You shouldn't sit around moping, Raven. You should be helping the resistance.'

The accusation was too close to the truth not to hit a nerve. 'I'm not moping, and it was helping the resistance that forced me to murder the man I'd loved. What do you suggest I do, become a prostitute like you? Sleep with the enemy?' She regretted the outburst as soon as she'd said it.

'Why not?' Michelle leaned her hands on the table and stared at her. 'You think I do it for pleasure or reward?' Michelle spat on the floor. 'I do it because I hate Germans. I do it to gain information for the resistance. I do it for France because my body is the best weapon I have. I do it so you can drink fucking coffee!'

'I'm sorry. I didn't realise. Ignore me.' Shame burned her cheeks, and she leaned on her broom. 'How can you bear them near you?'

Michelle smiled grimly. 'Grit your teeth and think of France? That's exactly what I do. I do whatever they want, and after, when I sweet-talk them, they think they can trust me because they've controlled me, and I wheedle out information and money, both of which the movement needs.'

'Aren't you afraid of catching something or becoming pregnant?'

Michelle emptied the ground beans into the top of a yellow enamel cafetiere. 'We asked London for condoms to protect ourselves, and they sent a supply. And there are ways of getting rid if we conceive, but don't mention this to anyone, Raven. It isn't legal in France.'

'I won't.' She looked up at Michelle with new respect. 'I don't know how you find the courage.'

Michelle poured hot water onto the coffee and waited. 'How do you find the courage to face a man and kill him?'

'It's a fair question. I suppose we do what we must. I've never…' She trailed off, uncomfortable with the subject.

Michelle cocked an eyebrow. 'You've never what? Oh, you mean you're a virgin?'

She nodded. 'I wanted to wait until Marcel – Maurice and I were married.'

'A man would pay handsomely for a virgin.'

She shook her head. 'I couldn't.' These girls had sacrificed their bodies for the resistance. Could she?

Michelle poured coffee and passed her a cup. 'It's easier to sleep with a man than kill him.'

'I suppose so.'

The noise of an aeroplane engine faltering made them rush to the window. The plane was trailing black smoke.

'It's coming down.'

'It isn't a German plane, Michelle. It must be American. They fly the daylight raids.' She dumped her coffee on the table untasted. 'Come on, they may need help.'

\*\*\*

The sound of the plane grew louder, coming closer, an engine stuttering. Antoine straightened from hoeing weeds between rows of onions in the garden. Chickens pecked for grubs in the disturbed soil, and a robin hopped around his feet ready to grab any unfortunate worm that wriggled to the surface.

He looked up into a clear blue sky, shading his eyes, and followed the flight line of the B17 as it descended rapidly – too rapidly, and it looked like an engine was on fire. The bomber must have been hit by a fighter and forced down within range of the anti-aircraft guns. It was going to crash land close by. He threw down the hoe, startling the robin into a whirring blur, and yelled for Florian.

Florian wiped oily hands on oilier trousers. 'Was that a Flying Fortress?'

'It was.' The sound of the plane screeching through undergrowth made him cringe. 'Is the truck running?'

'I'll see if it will start. Where are the others?'

'In town, trawling the hardware shops for saltpetre for explosives.

'Just you and me then.'

They hadn't gone far when Bonnie and Michelle stopped them. Bonnie pointed. 'It went down in the wood.'

The girls climbed in the back, and Florian stamped on the accelerator, heading for the plume of smoke rising from among trees. The truck clattered to a halt.

'Stay back, girls. If it's on fire, it may explode.'

The plane had cut a swathe through saplings and undergrowth and had come to rest against an ancient oak. A propeller had embedded itself in the trunk and the cockpit was a crumpled mess of tangled metal. One wing had been virtually wrenched off scattering its engines like confetti, one of the engines spewed flames and smoke, and the tail had broken on impact. Bombs lay visible in the bomb bay, through the torn fuselage.

'Dear God, surely no one is alive in there.'

'I told you to stay back, Bonnie.'

He climbed onto the remaining wing and clambered forward to the cockpit. The bombardier and navigator in the nose hadn't had a hope in hell, and neither had the pilot and co-pilot. 'They're dead. Nothing we can do for the poor sods.'

'What about the rest of the crew?'

Florian had wrested open the door in the fuselage. It was dark and cramped inside, and bodies were strewn across the floor. A low moan showed someone was alive.

Bonnie squeezed past and went to the low, tail end of the plane where the rear gunner would have been. She came back shaking her head. 'He didn't desert his post. He's dead, Papa.'

Three men were alive but injured. 'Florian, help me get them to the truck. They need a doctor. One we can trust.' He eyed the bombs. He knew what explosives could do if detonated. 'Hurry.'

The three men loaded into the back of the truck, with Bonnie and Michelle making them as comfortable as they could, Florian sped towards Nancy. The Nazis would be hunting for these men as soon as they found the wreckage. They'd need hiding while they recuperated, and Sofia wouldn't turn them away – it looked like the house with the big chimney was going to be fuller than ever.

Behind them, a massive explosion sent a plume of smoke and flame high into the air.

He fingered the identity tags he'd taken from around the necks of the seven dead crewmen. He'd send them to London with a request to forward them to the American Embassy. Someone, somewhere deserved to know how and where their loved-one died. With luck, if Germans came across the wreck, the explosion would hide the fact there were survivors. If it didn't, he and Raphael and Florian must bury the seven dead in a common grave. The three they'd rescued might live to go home to their families, but how many more young lives would be wasted before Hitler was defeated?

# Chapter Thirty-Nine

**Near Nancy, France. July 1943**

Bonnie scrubbed early potatoes from the garden. There was little enough food to go around, despite Sofia's careful preserving and winter storage. Feeding the household and caring for the injured airmen had become a full-time job, but it gave her space to consider her options – the airmen wouldn't need her care for much longer.

Juliette dumped another bowlful into the sink and picked up a small brush to help. 'You've been quiet of late, Bonnie. Is something troubling you?'

'The Americans we're caring for risked their lives flying over the Nazi V-one and V-two Rocket launch sites to the north. I don't feel I'm doing enough for the resistance, Juliette.'

'Feeding and caring for us all isn't enough?'

'No, well yes, but...' She tried to keep the frustration from her voice. 'You go out with Dad, if it's only driving the truck. I'm used to being active – in the thick of things.'

'From what you've told us, you've had a rough time. Isn't it time you –'.

'Stayed home and kept house? I can do so much more.'

'What do you suggest?'

'I could join the new escape route through Toulouse and the central Pyrenees. I could help the men with their plans for stopping a train heading for Mauthausen, or...'

'Or what?'

'I could become an "angel of the night" as Dad calls them, and tease information from Nazis.'

Juliette's mouth dropped open. 'Like Michelle? I daren't think what your father would say, Raven.'

'I wouldn't be able to hide my activities from him for long.'

'If I know La Fourche, he'd forbid you.'

'Forbid me? I'm a grown woman. I make my own decisions. I need to do something active.' She'd become addicted to a life of risk, and the more Dad forbade her, the more determined she would be to do it. 'Why couldn't I have been born a man? I envy the young men of the Royal Air Force who'd bombed the Möhne, Eder, and Sorpe dams.'

'Not all of them survived.'

'No, but they've done more than spike Hitler's guns, they've given much-needed hope to millions of Allied soldiers.'

Juliette sighed. 'And to the resistance, and God knows we need it after Jean Moulin's death at Nazi hands.'

'Juliette?' She paused in her scrubbing. 'Will you back me if I decide to do something Dad doesn't approve of?'

'What makes you think your father would take any notice of me?'

She smiled. 'It's obvious he likes you.'

'I like him too. He's a good man.'

'I mean, he likes you a lot. Since Mum died, he hasn't really been happy. I see him smile when he speaks to you. You make him happy, Juliette.'

Juliette gave her a wet hug. 'He makes me happy, too, but –'

'No buts. Life's too short, Juliette.'

'I'll back you if I can, Raven, but I must go with my conscience.'

'I trust your judgement, Juliette. I also trust my own.'

She'd made her decision. She might be weak compared to a man, but like Michelle, she had a weapon they hadn't. If Dad wouldn't allow her to go with him on the train derailment he was planning, she'd "grit her teeth and think of France".

***

## Near Strasbourg, France. August 1943

Antoine unpacked his satchel bombs, remembering his last, unsuccessful, attempt at stopping the convoy to the death camps by blowing the bridge over the Zorn valley. He'd blocked the canal with a sunken barge, but the bridge still stood. This time, he would take the simpler option of destroying the track and derailing the train. Then they would shoot the guards.

The others positioned themselves at intervals along both sides of the track using what cover was available; they were all armed with grenades, pistols, and Lugers, and counting the three American airmen, there were enough of them to ambush the train. He just had to stop it in the right place.

He looked along the track. The engine would travel some distance after it derailed, and the cattle wagons behind it might jackknife and topple over. It was a risky strategy; the prisoners could be injured, and once freed, they'd have to take their chances best they could, but at least they'd have a chance.

Picking what he hoped was the right place on the track, he began setting his charges.

It was more than risky; there could be women and children aboard, and it was this that had made him give in to Juliette's insistence that she came along. Once he'd agreed to her coming, he couldn't bar the other women, so now he had their safety to consider as well. At least they all knew how to use a pistol.

What made the operation more perilous was that they were carrying it out in daylight. That way, Florian had sensibly argued, they'd see who they were shooting. As he'd sensibly countered, the Nazis would also be able to see who they were shooting. Their plan consisted mainly of picking off any guards travelling on the wagons' roofs, shooting any others while they were still disorientated from the derailment, and keeping their heads down as much as they could.

He checked his watch. According to information from a cell in Paris, the train with prisoners from Compeigne for Auschwitz should reach the Zorn valley in half an hour.

The last charge laid, he reeled out the pull-cords, retreated to a safe distance, and lay flat. The thumping of his heart competed with the sound of birdsong, the shouts of bargees on the canal nearby, and the engine of a vehicle on the road.

Renoir's truck, parked a couple of hundred metres away among trees, was slow when packed with all of them. Not exactly a getaway vehicle, but it was all they had.

The slow chuff of an engine and a plume of smoke brought him back to the task at hand. 'Everyone down!' He wound the pull-cords around his hands and tightened his grip.

The train approached – closer, closer – A row of guards sat atop the wagons. Closer... The rear guard collapsed, shot, more shots rang out almost simultaneously, and two of the guards farther forward fell before they had time to return fire.

Now! He yanked the cords and ducked down as soil and shards of metal shot into the air. The engine seemed to jump off the track before ploughing a furrow across the ground. He grabbed his Luger as the wagons bucked and jack-knifed.

The train ground to a halt amid squeals of twisted metal and clouds of smoke and steam. He waited, Luger aimed. Shouts and screams came from the inside of the wagons, and the remaining guards were jumping down from the roofs.

He fired, and a man fell. Other gunshots rang out as more guards were targeted and taken out. The driver emerged from the steam, hands raised, followed by the engineer.

No one moved. Silence but for the hiss of steam and the cries of the trapped. Cautiously, he got to his feet, training his pistol on the driver. One by one, others of the ambush team moved forward weapons raised. They checked bodies for signs of life. Florian was on the far side with Adolf, Alain, Baptiste, Michelle, and Bonnie.

He kept his Luger trained on the engine driver.

The man stood stock still. 'Don't shoot. I'm French.'

'French, yet you work for the Nazis deporting Jews?'

'I need to live. My family need me working. This is my job.'

He checked the driver and engineer for weapons and lowered his pistol but kept a wary eye on them. 'Florian, all clear this side.'

'All clear here too, La Fourche.'

He threw open the door to the first wagon. Inside was a huddle of frightened humanity. He waved the Luger. 'Out, all of you. You're free.'

'Free?' The man obviously didn't trust him.

'We're French, not Germans. 'You're free to go.'

The man jumped down from the wagon. His jacket sported a roughly-sewn yellow star. The mark of a Jew. 'Free to go where?'

'That's up to you.' He pointed. 'Switzerland is a safe haven, and there are…' He paused. The maquis in the mountains were under threat themselves from the Milice. 'Many French people are partisans and will hide you in safe houses until the resistance can get you false papers, but I can only help so many.' He looked along the concertina of wagons. 'There are hundreds of you. You have a chance of survival. That's all we can give you. The rest is up to you.'

The man nodded. 'I thank God for the chance of life. God is good.'

More men crowded around. He'd underestimated the numbers of deportees that would be on the train and the enormity of the task the resistance would face providing for so many. It wasn't possible. Bonnie and Juliette were talking to a young woman with three children – he couldn't abandon the woman and her children if they had no man to care for them.

'You must go before the explosion brings more Germans to investigate. Tell your people they must go, flee.' He turned away, anxious to gather his own flock and escape. He'd played God with these people's lives, and now they must all trust in God to guide them.

***

## Near Nancy, France. September 1943

Bonnie sat with the others, crowded around the radio waiting for the BBC news. The RAF had followed the bombing of the German rocket sites in France with a huge raid over Berlin in retaliation for the bombing of London. Allied landings in Italy had the German army in retreat, and the Nazis were evacuating Berlin of all non-essential personnel. Hitler seemed to be on the back foot, for once.

The radio crackled and hummed, the voice barely audible for fear someone outside would report they were listening to a forbidden broadcast. *"This is Radio Algiers. Italy's government under Marshal Badoglio has surrendered unconditionally to the Allies and hostilities between the Allies and Italy ended early this evening."*

A cheer drowned the rest of the words.

Dad looked as if a weight had been lifted from his shoulders. 'This means there's more chance of an escape route through Switzerland and south through Italy.'

She smiled, happy that she'd had an active role in the rescue of the occupants of the prison transport. She'd spent the weeks since the train derailment cycling around the countryside delivering covert pamphlets, printed on a secret press by the resistance, and posting messages in drop boxes of surrounding cells, asking them to look out for those who'd been freed and would be needing help. Word had spread rapidly, and messages came back frequently to say another person or family had been hidden, found new papers, and helped to escape. Switzerland had been the nearest safe-haven, but it was land-locked. Reliable news from Italy was scarce, but with a possible new route to the coast, many might find new lives in England or America.

They'd derailed one convoy, but many more were heading north across France to Buchenwald. The Nazis had begun a brutal manhunt for Jews, especially in Nice, near the Italian border. The more ground the Allies made, the worse it was for the Jews of occupied Europe, and the greater the acts of resistance, the more prisoners the Nazis executed.

\*\*\*

## Near Nancy, France. October 1943

Antoine read the latest pamphlet Bonnie had left on the table. The residents of Naples, anticipating the arrival of the Allies after their government had surrendered, had risen against the German occupiers who were trying to deport them and destroy the city, as they'd done in Marseille. The Allies were still facing stiff resistance from German forces in Italy despite the surrender, and increased German military activity had been noted along the Normandy and Brittany coast, which suggested the Nazis were expecting an invasion across the English Channel.

Bonnie burst in through the door. 'Dad! Italy have declared war on Germany!'

He jumped up from his seat and hugged her. 'That's the best news I've heard for ages. To have Italy as an ally will make a huge difference to France.' He tapped the pamphlet. 'Perhaps that explains the increased activity along the north coast. Hitler's feeling nervous.'

'Or perhaps German spies have gotten wind of a proposed invasion.'

Britain had its own problems, but he understood why his compatriots had felt abandoned by them in nineteen forty. 'I wish the British *would* send ground troops to aid us.'

'Do you think that's likely after their defeat at Dunkirk?'

'I don't know, they lost a lot of men at Dunkirk, but I hope so. Italy changing sides is bound to affect the course of the war.'

'Let's hope it's the beginning of the end.'

'I pray you're right, Bonnie. I pray you're right.

# Chapter Forty

**Near Nancy, France. December 1943**

Rabbit was on the menu for Christmas dinner, or four rabbits to be accurate, stuffed with parsley and celery mixed with breadcrumbs. Bonnie was hoping they had enough food to go around. The only thing they seemed to have plenty of was Brussels-sprouts, which had flourished in the garden.

She finished helping Juliette scrub carrots from the root store and went back to her sewing. The mood was more optimistic than it had been for a while, despite the steady increase in deportations, with Gypsies now added to the list of undesirables, and the arrest of resistance members by the German counter-espionage services. They were buoyed by the increased activity by the Americans, Canadians, Australians, and New Zealanders against Germany and rumours of a British invasion of Normandy.

The escape lines had been severely damaged and had curtailed her activities, though she'd played her part in hiding hunted people and cycling into Nancy to request and obtain false identities for them. Having shed Marie Barbier as an identity, in case Maurice had compromised her, she'd also had false papers made for herself in the name of Daphne de la Haye.

With the deportation convoys now taking a more northerly route away from Strasbourg, the focus was on getting as many escapees as possible to the Swiss border, hence her sewing.

Sofia's sewing machine made the job easier and button thread made the stitching firmer. She fed the hessian under the machine's foot while working the treadle with her feet. It had been Juliette's idea to make large sacks to hide the escapees, inspired by Dad saying Renoir's lorry had been used to deliver coal and was an excellent cover for carrying explosives.

It was a genius idea. Hidden behind a few genuine sacks of coal and firewood, they shouldn't attract closer inspection from nosy Nazis, but she was glad she didn't have to travel hunched up in an oversized coal sack all the way to the Swiss border. Even with holes cut to allow a better flow of air, it would be stuffy, uncomfortable, cold, and claustrophobic.

Italy was still far from safe, fighting continued there, but if the escapees could find a temporary haven in Switzerland, it shouldn't be too long before the Nazis were driven out and a route opened. The Allies were pushing hard towards the Adriatic coast.

Dad and Florian were discussing the proposed journey. She listened over the steady clack, clack, clack of the sewing machine. It might be a chance to gather information about German troop deployment close to the Swiss border to relay to London in preparation for the hoped-for invasion; more troops tied up in the south meant fewer in Normandy.

Dad rubbed the palm of his hand beneath his missing finger. 'Most of France will be celebrating today and tomorrow, and so will the Nazis. We could drive to the Swiss border with little danger of being stopped.'

'A coal lorry out on Christmas Day?' Florian sounded unsure. 'And what about Christmas dinner. At least let the poor sods have something inside them before we truss them up like turkeys.'

Her stomach rumbled at the thought of turkey, roasted with stuffing and –

Dad shook his head. 'I'd suggest Boxing Day. We could leave straight after breakfast. It would only take about three hours to reach the border between Hégenheim and Allschwil. We can be there to give our "cargo" time to find shelter before dark.'

'True, but it will put us dangerously close to the German border, La Fourche.'

'It would.' Dad stroked a fledgling beard. 'We could take them farther south to the Risoux Forest, north of Geneva. There are partisans there who'd hide them, and it's possible to cross the border at night over a stone wall – Swiss sympathisers will take them in. It would mean an extra hour on the journey.' Dad raised his voice. 'Raven, how long before the coal sacks are ready?'

'I should be finished in time.' Her feet stilled, and the clack, clack ceased. 'I'll come with you. I can bring thread, needle, and scissors and do any running repairs, and you may be glad of a female distraction if any Nazis decide to investigate. It's surprising how useful a flash of flesh above the knee can be.'

'No –' Dad's tone brooked no argument.

'La Fourche, the girl is right. There's little danger if we travel tomorrow, and in the event of us being stopped or there being a problem with the sacks…'

'You know we're right, Papa.' She patted the knife that was always sheathed on her belt. 'I can kill a German if I need to. I'd have the element of surprise, and I've proved myself capable of killing more times than I can remember.'

Liar – she remembered the face of every man whose life she'd taken and the feel of her knife as it delivered death. They kept her awake at night or invaded her nightmares – they were someone's son. Someone, somewhere mourned their loss, as she mourned those she'd loved. War had made her a murderer, and she'd never forgive Hitler for that.

Dad agreed reluctantly, and she went back to her sewing relieved to be involved. It further delayed her unpalatable decision to join Michelle and the girls on the top floor.

***

While Dad and Florian fetched sacks filled with coal and firewood from Sofia's coal shed, and Juliette put provisions for the escapees in another sack, Bonnie explained the plan to the Jews and resistance workers hiding in Sofia's cellar. They understood the need to move on, once they had false papers, to make room for more "enemies of the Reich" who might need a refuge.

Five men, three women and two children; ten sacks.

'The children must stay quiet, especially if the lorry stops. Do they understand that?'

A young woman, Rachael, nodded. 'They're old enough to understand the need. They've become used to rushing downstairs to the cellar and staying quiet as mice every time there's a knock on the front door or a voice they don't recognise.'

At least in Switzerland, they wouldn't be living in constant fear. 'I'll make sure they are placed next to you, so you can talk to them and calm them if they become frightened. I'm afraid it won't be a comfortable journey.'

One by one, she saw them onto the lorry and helped them into their sacks, before loosely sewing up the tops. They made a game of it for the little ones, and she cut holes in the sides of Rachael and the children's sacks so they could hold hands. She prayed it would be enough. Juliette's plan had sounded brilliant in theory but in practise was a different matter.

The coal and firewood loaded, they set off for Risoux. The dusting of snow on the wooded hills turned the Vosges into a winter wonderland. The route took them through country Dad knew well, but he kept to the main road for fear of snow drifts on the mountain lanes.

It was cold. They'd done their best to ensure the children were warmly wrapped for the four-hour journey, but even with a tarpaulin thrown over the sacks to keep off the biting wind, it would still be close to freezing in the back of the lorry.

There were few vehicles on the road and little sign of German occupation. She was beginning to relax when they came upon a German military vehicle parked by the side of the road.

A soldier stood in the middle of the road pointing a rifle at them. They had no choice but to stop; it was that or risk being shot.

He waved the rifle at them. 'Out, now.'

She jumped down from the front of the truck followed by Dad and Florian. 'Is there a problem, officer?'

The man scowled. 'I'm requisitioning this lorry.'

Her heart thudded wildly. 'Requisitioning it? Why?'

'The Citroën has broken down. You French can't make reliable engines. These damn things keep breaking down.'

'Let me have a look at it.' Dad ignored the rifle and walked calmly towards the Citroën. 'I may be able to get it going for you.'

The German lowered his rifle slightly and followed.

Dad lifted the bonnet and took out the dip stick. He held it up, showing it to her and Florian, and put it back again without comment. She remembered him telling her about the Citroën factory putting the oil-level mark on the dipstick so low on lorries bound for the German military that the engines seized. What a time to come across one of them. There was no way Dad was going to get it going again, and if the German took Renoir's lorry, the human cargo was doomed.

She must act and fast, but he was a big man and could overpower her easily; seduction wouldn't work – she needed both his hands and his mind occupied. She smiled at the soldier. 'Dad's an expert with engines. If anyone can get it going, he can. You must be cold, officer. I have a flask of hot tea in the cab.'

He hesitated a moment too long. She glanced at Florian who nodded.

Her smile broadened. 'He's hardly going to drive off in it, is he, and leave me behind? Why don't you come and have a drink with me. It could take him a while.'

'I need to check your lorry. What are you carrying?'

'We're delivering coal and wood to some elderly people who have little – the spirit of Christmas.' Surely this odious man could hear her heart thumping. She pulled the tarpaulin back so he could see the sacks. *Please stay still and silent.*

A tiny whimper. She coughed loudly and rubbed her arms. 'It's so cold tonight, officer. A hot drink would warm us both.'

He took a long knife from its sheath and stabbed a sack – coaldust trickled from the slash, then another – wood.

She threw back the tarpaulin farther half-exposing the human sacks. 'You're welcome to check them all.' She tried not to hold her breath while she risked these innocents' lives. 'Or…' She parted her lips slightly and brushed back her hair. 'We could have that drink while they're… busy.'

He smiled, sheathed his knife and followed her into the cab. She reached for the flask and passed him an enamel mug, half-filled it and stopped. 'I should have asked if you're alone. I might not have enough tea to go around.'

The officer pushed his mug towards her. 'It's just me. My comrade has walked to the next town for help. I stayed with the truck.'

That was what she'd hoped. She filled his mug to the brim. 'What are you doing out here on Boxing Day.'

'I should be asking the questions.'

She lowered her head. 'Sorry.'

He sipped hot tea and softened. 'We're ordered to Italy – Italians are trying to escape into Switzerland.'

'I thought the lack of vehicles was because of the holiday. Are there many ordered to Italy?'

'It's what the Führer ordered.'

And they did what they were told. 'More tea?'

'Thank you. It's most welcome.'

She topped up his mug and put down the flask. Her hand felt for her knife. Did she need to kill this man? Dare she risk leaving him alive to probe the sacks further? She slid the knife from its sheath; she'd already gambled with these people's lives. The soldier had the mug to his lips, warming both hands on the hot enamel. It was ten lives or one; now or never. She plunged the blade into his belly and ripped it upwards. He spat tea and slumped forward onto the dashboard. Blood soaked his trousers and dripped onto the floor of the cab.

She wiped the blade on his jacket and re-sheathed it. Another nameless face to haunt her dreams.

She patted the top of one of the sacks. 'It's all right. I've dealt with the German. Only an hour now to the border.' She refastened the tarpaulin, muting sighs of relief, and walked back to Dad and Florian. 'It's done. We need to hide the body and get these poor souls to Switzerland.'

# Chapter Forty-One

## Near Nancy, France. February 1944

'What the hell is that?' Antoine stared over the parapet of the railway bridge at the monstrosity passing beneath him.

'An armoured train.' Adolf gasped. 'I've heard of them but never seen one. Apparently, they're made up from bits of trains from Poland, Czechoslovakia, and Yugoslavia.'

The angular armour-plated train, painted with camouflage greys and browns, sported gun turrets, bristling with machine guns, anti-aircraft guns, anti-tank guns, and missiles. One of the flatbed trucks even carried a light tank and a ramp for fast deployment. Troops manned the many turrets. The whole thing looked like something from a madman's nightmare.

'Hell. They can transport a massive firepower anywhere at a moment's notice. Where do you think it's going?'

'Could just be guarding the tracks. There's been a lot of sabotage on the railways.' Adolf grinned. 'We should know, we've done our share.'

'The RAF have done more, and a lot of people aren't happy about that.' He chewed a knuckle in thought. 'This thing is different. It would take a lot of explosives to destroy it.'

'One well-placed bomb, and it would destroy itself.'

'You think you could get near enough to wire a bomb with all those guards? It needs a different approach. With that firepower and troops, not to mention the tank, we'd be sitting targets, and escaping in the truck – chances are that tank would be faster than we are.'

'You're not seriously considering attacking it, La Fourche?'

'I'm thinking about it.'

'So what do you suggest?'

'We need to know where it patrols, Adolf.' He fingered his chin. 'We need poor Lucas. He had a connection in the railways.'

'You forget I went with Lucas to the station. He introduced me to his friend, Didier.'

'Could Didier find out where this abomination goes, do you think?'

'I can ask him. What are you thinking?'

'Suppose… suppose we could arrange an "error" with the points somewhere? Two trains, one track?'

'A head-on collision?'

'It would do maximum damage, Adolf, and block the track for days if not weeks.' The train disappeared into the distance, and he walked back to the truck. 'I suggest we pay Didier a visit and see if it's possible. That thing needs putting out of action as soon as we can.'

\*\*\*

Antoine bent over the map Didier had spread across the table. It was a stylised map of the railway system.

Didier pointed. 'That would be the ideal place for a collision. There's a bend, so visibility is reduced, but speed would still be fast enough to do serious damage.' He moved his finger and jabbed the map. 'Trains could be diverted here and here. Timing will be the problem – that and convincing the drivers they've been diverted for good reason. It will take some organising, La Fourche.'

'But it can be done?'

'In theory, yes. In practice?' Didier shrugged. 'I'll have to consult with stationmasters along the route. It needs to be a joint effort if it's to work.'

'Can you trust them?'

Didier laughed. 'They delay and divert trains all the while just to annoy the Nazis. They'll be eager to help. Once we know when the armoured train is due to pass, we can organise, but we may have to act quickly.'

'What can we do to help?'

'Two things. Firstly, this is between us. It must appear to be an accident, and even then, someone will be punished for it. Secondly, I'll need you on the train that will ram the armoured one to make sure the driver follows the diversion and doesn't cut his speed. We can't be sure he'll be a driver sympathetic to the resistance.'

Adolf raised both eyebrows. 'How the heck do we get into the train's cab? And more to the point, how do we get out before it crashes?'

'That's for you to work out. You thought this was going to be easy, Adolf?'

Adolf shook his head. 'La Fourche, what do you think?'

'We'll work something out, Adolf. Just one thing. Not a word about this to Raven. She is *not* coming on this mission.'

Didier straightened. 'So we're on?'

'Yes.' He wrote a number on a corner of the map before Didier rolled it back up. 'The house has a telephone. Call us where and when, and we'll be there.'

\*\*\*

Bonnie looked out of the window onto a dull February day. It was only late morning, and already the odd candle glimmered in the cottages across the street. Sofia's house had become home, a place where they could all be together, and much as she missed the solitude of Louise's cottage in the woods, she loved being here with Dad and Juliette and the others.

Dad and Adolf were up to something, their conversation stopped when she was within hearing distance, and they looked shifty, but she hadn't been able to find out what they were planning. They seemed determined not to involve her, which made her more determined to find out what it was. Things were moving rapidly, and she needed to keep abreast of events.

The RAF had dropped thousands of tons of bombs on Berlin and were bombing the industrial area around Leipzig. The Allies also fought on in Italy, giving her hope for the people, including the three American airmen, she and Dad had driven to Risoux over the last few weeks, the coal sack idea having proved successful.

However many they helped escape, it would never be enough. Lists of French Jews had been handed over to the Germans by French préfets, and arrests continued at an alarming rate. Male and female prisoners were being separated, men were detained at Compiègne and women at Romainville fort. All were bound for the Nazi concentration camps, from which no one had ever returned.

Messages had begun to come from London with the code name *Overlord,* asking for detailed maps of German installations and troop movements. Just as the resistance was most needed, the Nazis had declared all-out war on them, especially the maquis in the hills and forests. German soldiers were ordered to open fire on suspected "terrorists" and burn down any houses sheltering partisans. Innocent civilian populations were also being targeted more frequently as reprisal warnings for partisan attacks on Germans,

Sofia's beautiful home was in grave danger, as were they all.

The windows rattled to the growl of a heavy vehicle rumbling slowly along the street, followed closely by more – some covered lorries, some troop carriers, and some half-tracks. Damn Germans. She paced across the room and back to the window as the vehicles rolled past towards Nancy. Everyone seemed to be involved in something except her – what were Dad and Adolf up to?

She would find out, but if they wouldn't let her in on their secret, she'd find her own entertainment. She grabbed her coat, hat, and scarf, took a box of matches and a tea towel from the kitchen, and hurried outside. Florian kept a can of petrol in the shed, so she tipped some over the cloth, soaking it. She knew what she wanted to do, she'd heard Dad and Adolf describing the act in an unguarded moment, and if she followed those lorries, she might get the chance.

Pedalling hard, her basket full of cover-story medical items, she cycled after the convoy of lorries. As she'd hoped, they'd stopped in a wide part of the road about a mile from the village. One or two soldiers were relieving themselves in the undergrowth, so she stopped a distance away, tore the tea towel into strips, and wheeled her cycle slowly forwards, pretending a problem with the machine.

Bravado would work where stealth wouldn't. She stopped again and waited until the soldiers climbed back into the lorries, grateful that it was too cold for them to hang about outside for long. Some were drinking from canteens or eating from tins, or chatting and taking no notice of a young girl with a dodgy bicycle. Her stomach rumbled, but lunch must wait.

Not all the lorries had exposed petrol filler caps, but some had. She stopped by one and bent down, pretending to fiddle with her brakes while unscrewing a filler cap. She pushed a length of cloth into the filler tube and pushed her cycle to the next vehicle. She'd unscrewed four filler caps when her nerve failed her. Her luck wouldn't hold forever.

Striking a match, with trembling fingers, she lit the end of the tea towel and pedalled back along the line of lorries, wobbling and half-falling off as she reached the next strip of tea towel. She struck another match and lit that just as the first lorry exploded in a flash of flame and smoke.

Using the commotion as cover, she ignited the remaining two, and then pedalled furiously off the road and along a woodland track, followed by the reek of petrol and smoke as a chain of explosions rocked the convoy. A lorry wheel landed beside her and bounced along the track before careering into the trees. She must have blown up a munitions' lorry. She smiled grimly. The more damage, the better. Life – Nazi life – was expendable.

*\*\**

## Eastern France. February 1944

Antoine looked out of the truck window across the station. 'The train we want is due on the far platform in exactly thirty minutes.'

Adolf nodded. He looked more like a German than many Germans did. 'We should park the truck and get into position, La Fourche.'

'Agreed.' He smoothed his German uniform, patted the Luger at his side, and pulled the cap down over his eyes. 'I hope this works.'

'I don't see why it shouldn't. You speak German, and a train driver won't argue with a Luger-wielding Nazi.'

'I wish we could have told Florian. He could have driven the truck. As it is, we'll have to walk back in these bloody Nazi boots, and it's a long way.'

A head appeared at the window. 'It's a good thing I came then.'

'B… Raven! What the hell are you doing here?'

'I listened when you thought I couldn't hear and hid in the back.' Bonnie was shivering, her breath wreathing. 'I can drive the lorry, Dad. Just tell me where to.'

It was too cold to send her home, even if home had been close enough to reach on foot. He opened the door and helped her into the cab. Turning in his seat, he showed her the map. 'We're here. The truck needs to be there, in sight but not too close to the railway line. That's all you need to know.' He pushed the map into her hands so she didn't get lost.

'But…'

'The less you know, the fewer people will be endangered. If you want to help, bloody help! Don't argue. This is a dangerous mission, which is one reason I didn't tell you.'

'And the other?'

'We promised to keep a man's secret, so don't ask for details.'

Suitably chastised, Bonnie was silent for once. Damn the girl. He sighed. He was proud of her courage and her spirit, but keeping her safe was impossible. 'We must go, Adolf. God willing, we'll see you at the pick-up spot, Raven. Whatever you do, whatever happens, stay in the lorry. I need you to promise.'

'I promise.'

He climbed down from the truck and waited until Bonnie had started the engine before turning away. He hadn't even known she could drive. A gear crunched, and she bunny-hopped along the road. He winced. Perhaps she couldn't. Another crunch, and the lorry rumbled away.

The train was on time. Together, He and Adolf strode across to the cab and climbed aboard. He flashed a piece of paper the driver thankfully didn't ask to read. 'Inspection.'

'I don't understand German.'

'Ah, a Frenchman.' He modified his usual French with a German accent, not knowing if the driver or engineer were partisans. 'We are to accompany you for a few kilometres. The French railways are not efficient. We wish to see where improvements can be made.'

The driver put outraged hands onto fat hips. 'I follow the timetable. No one has ever had cause to complain.'

'Then you have nothing to worry about.'

After exactly ten minutes, a whistle blew and a flag waved. Right on time, the train drew out of the station. His heartbeat quickened, and he glanced across at Adolf. It was only a matter of time now.

# Chapter Forty-Two

**Eastern France. February 1944**

Antoine consulted his watch with an air of authority. 'Is this your normal speed?'

The train driver continued to stare out of the window. 'I keep to the timetable. The speed is exactly correct for this stretch of track.'

That was a relief. Any deviation from normal would throw out Didier's careful calculations.

'Very good. Continue.' He made a show of watching the engineer shovel coal into the firebox. 'Where do you stop for water?'

The engineer leaned on his shovel. 'It depends on the weight of the load we're hauling. We've already done a water stop, and we'll need to stop again at Strasbourg.'

Had Didier allowed for that? There was so much that could go wrong. Like the cargo. He'd been relieved it wasn't a passenger train, but might a heavier than normal load slow them? 'What are you carrying today?'

The man spat with ill-concealed disgust. 'Anything Hitler can steal from France.'

Adolf raised an eyebrow. 'The spoils of war, surely. You are not a supporter of the glorious Reich?'

The driver concentrated on his instruments, turning a wheel, pushing a lever. 'I'm a loyal Frenchman. I do my job.'

'And you?' Adolf addressed the engineer.

The engineer pushed back his cap and wiped sweat from his brow. 'I do what I must to feed my family. I don't have to like it.'

*La Fourche* smiled. 'So you are a partisan?'

Neither man denied it, but both would die if their plan succeeded. 'Adolf, I believe these two men are sympathetic to the resistance. I would suggest they leave the train when we do. Would you agree?'

'Indeed so. In fact, I insist upon it.'

The driver and engineer exchanged worried glances.

Ahead was the junction where the points would be changed. He fingered his Luger and saw Adolf had his hand on his.

'Hey, this isn't the right route.' The driver applied the brakes.

'You've been diverted. Keep going. Keep your speed up.' He stuck his Luger in the driver's ribs while Adolf covered the engineer. 'Do as we say, and no harm will come to you.'

The driver did as he was told. 'Who are you? What's your game?'

He consulted his watch again and dropped the German accent. 'In five minutes exactly, you will find out.'

The minutes ticked by with the speed of a snail. 'Keep up your speed.'

The engineer shovelled more coal. Five... Four... Three... His heart thundered. Two... One...

'What the...?'

He jabbed the driver's ribs hard as the armoured train thundered towards them only seconds away. 'Keep up your speed!'

*** 

Bonnie had turned the lorry around, ready for a quick getaway should it be needed, and waited, window wound down. She'd stuck her head out at the sound of trains approaching.

Presumably, whatever they had planned, Dad and Adolf were on one of them.

The two trains sped towards one another. One had troops and gun turrets on top of it. Whatever was going to happen must be... Surely, they weren't both on the same track?

She leapt from the cab. 'Papa, no! No-o-o-o!'

Four figures half-jumped and half-fell from the train and rolled down the embankment towards her. She ran forward as the trains collided in a splintering crash of twisting metal, steam, smoke, and the screech of wheels on track. The engines crumpled, leapt from the rails, and ploughed deep gouges into the ground. Carriages jack-knifed, twisted, and threw themselves into the air. Men and machines, entangled in a deathly embrace, rained down in a macabre slow-motion dance.

She threw herself to the ground, but the noise went on forever. Covering her ears did nothing to dull the screeches and screams. A huge explosion sent metal shrapnel and clods of earth into the air. She threw her arms over her head. Pain, needle sharp. Flames and smoke. Acrid air. She couldn't breathe.

Then silence.

Smoke billowed and steam drifted on the breeze. She raised her head and winced as she tried to move. If there was hell on earth, this was surely it. Bodies, or bits of bodies, were strewn around among a litter of metal. The embankment was on fire, and the acrid smell was more than coal and oil and hot metal, it was burning flesh.

'Papa? Adolf?' She crawled on her knees and one hand. The other arm didn't seem to work. Her head pounded, and her voice sounded unnaturally loud. 'Papa!' Most of the bodies wore German uniforms. 'Dad! Adolf!'

'Bonnie…' Dad's voice sounded far away.

Sobs prevented her speaking. She took a deep breath and almost choked. 'Papa.'

He got to his feet and stumbled towards her dragging one leg. 'Are you hurt?'

'My arm.'

He grabbed her. 'You promised to stay in the truck.'

'I forgot. The crash… Where's Adolf?'

He jumped after me and the engine driver. He should be close by. They supported one another, looking from prone body to prone body. Dad knelt by one feeling for a pulse. He shook his head.

'No, please, not Adolf.' She knelt too, shaking the body. Adolf's head was covered in blood. 'No, not another. Not another.'

'Bonnie, he's dead. There's nothing you can do. He must have struck a rock on the embankment or been hit by flying debris. This is on me. It was my idea. This is *my* fault.'

'My train. What have you done to my train?' The confused voice came from a short fat Frenchman in overalls.

'We used it to destroy German armaments and troops.' Dad pointed to Adolf. 'This man has just given his life for the resistance, for France. I don't give a shit about your bloody train.'

'Well, I do.'

'Papa… We need to get away, now. The smoke will be visible for miles, and there may be soldiers left alive. Once they gather their wits –'

'Who do you think will be blamed for this?' The driver waved his arms. 'If they don't find our bodies in the wreckage, they'll blame me and Gérard. While you disappear, we'll be put up against a wall and shot.'

'We have a truck along the road. I'm Raven. This is La Fourche. We can take you where you want to go or hide you in a safe house and get you false documents.'

'What about our families? After this, they won't be safe either.'

'We can do the same for them, but we must leave.'

Dad was staring at his friend's body. 'I'm not leaving Adolf.'

'He's dead, Papa.'

'Gérard and I will carry him to your truck.' The man held out a hand. 'Dominique, but my friends call me Dom. Your daughter is right, La Fourche. We must leave. Now!'

***

**Near Nancy, France. May 1944**

Antoine sat on a fallen tree trunk. The oblong of bare soil was greening with new shoots of grass. Bluebells and anemones stretched beneath the trees, and birds flitted from branch to branch, welcoming spring with their song.

He'd buried Adolf, with Dom and Gérard's help, next to the seven dead airmen, or what had been left of them. So many lives sacrificed for a freedom they hadn't lived to see. Would he, Bonnie, or any of their group live to see it? Much as he tried to justify his action with the French lives saved because of the train wreck, guilt consumed him. There had been reprisals, and he'd caused the death of a good friend.

The S.O.E would have called it collateral damage and shrugged it off as regrettable but inevitable. He clenched his fists. What gave one madman the right to cause so much pain? What hold had he over his compatriots that they obeyed his every command and turned into an army of ravaging beasts with no mercy? If he could get to Hitler, he'd kill him with his bare hands. He raked fingers through greying hair. Would it make a difference, or was there some other evil bastard waiting to step into Hitler's boots?

The world had gone mad, and there was nothing he could do about it. Nothing!

*Nothing?*

He prised himself off the log, taking his weight on his good leg; the wound had been slow to heal and it still pained him.

Nothing? He could kill more Nazis and avenge those he'd loved. He wasn't alone.

People in Northern Italy were fighting the fascists, and the Allies were driving the German army north and had bombed the Vatican, Dusseldorf, and Frankfurt. Russia and America were fighting in Europe and against Japan. Yugoslav partisans had attacked Trieste. But it wasn't all going the Allies way. The RAF had suffered huge losses during an air raid on Nuremberg, and the German army had launched a military operation against the maquis in the Dordogne and Corrèze, and more recently, in Ain and the Jura mountains.

British Squadron Leader Maurice Southgate, who'd been responsible for coordinating several maquis groups, had been arrested by the Gestapo in Paris, and hundreds of men had been deported on a convoy to Lithuania to work for the Nazi war effort.

After pleas for help from the resistance movement, Britain had sent aid and operatives to bolster their numbers. They'd received reports of vast military activity along England's south coast, and the rumour of an invasion grew stronger with each telling. Messages flew backwards and forwards across the channel, some by pigeon post, some with agents, as resistance members sent plans and maps of German airfields, fortifications, marshalling yards, and barracks. Troop movements, especially by train, were being watched with eagle eyes.

Hopes rose and were dashed on a daily basis.

He hobbled back to the house, his moment of despair and self-recrimination sated for the time being.

Juliette met him at the door. 'Quickly. There's a radio broadcast… the BBC.'

He hurried into the room to find everyone huddled around the radio. He cupped a hand behind his ear; since the train explosion, his hearing hadn't been good, and he noticed Bonnie was almost on top of the radio. The blast had damaged more than arms and legs and hearts.

*"This is London calling."* The *Trumpet Voluntary* followed before the announcement continued. *"Fighter-bombers of the Royal Air Force and the United States Air Force have today carried out successful bombing raids on German airfields and bases in France and the Low Countries. Troop trains have also been destroyed by bombers, and there have been strikes against German installations along the Normandy coast. Several radar stations have also been*

311

*destroyed along with vital infrastructure. Regrettably, there have been both civilian and Allied casualties.*"

The news of casualties couldn't quell the feeling of hope and excitement.

Florian's cheer drowned the others. 'This must be in preparation for the invasion. It must be imminent.'

He patted Florian on the back. 'We helped to get this. Our sacrifices haven't been in vain.'

Florian hugged him. Nothing could dampen their joy.

Later that day another message arrived. Over a thousand Jews, including families with small children had been deported to Auschwitz, and two thousand men, arrested for acts of resistance, were being taken from Compiègne to the Neuengamme concentration camp near Hamburg.

# Chapter Forty-Three

**Near Nancy, France. June 1944**

Bonnie's arm had healed though she had a scar where the doctor had removed a lump of shrapnel. Dom and Gervaise and their families had hidden out at Louise's cottage in the woods, it being deemed safe to use it again, though Louise and Raphael seemed happy to remain at Sofia's for the time being.

She shaded her eyes against the morning sun. The low drone had grown louder. Specks of black emerged from the sun.

Raphael stood beside her. 'Messerschmitts.'

The fighters flew over them in close formation, and the roar of engines faded into the west. 'Where do you think they're going?'

'If the Radio Londres broadcast was right, the Allies are bombing Cherbourg and Calais. They're probably looking to put some bombers out of action.'

She watched them disappear. 'Our poor boys. I wish we had an anti-aircraft gun.'

'We can send a coded message via Paris. Warn them.'

'It's all we can do, but whether it will be in time…'

'They'll have to land to refuel at some point. It may delay them.' Another low drone grew louder. 'More of the buggers.' Raphael sprinted in the direction of the shed where the radio transmitter was hidden.

She went back into the house, eager for news and yet dreading it. 'Where are the British?' She couldn't keep the anxiety from her voice.

Sofia smiled briefly. 'Patience, Raven.'

The radio was on at a low volume, awaiting the signal from London that the invasion was to begin. They'd been waiting for it for days and took it in turns to listen day and night.

*"This is London calling the European News Service of the British Broadcasting Corporation. Here is the news, but first here are some messages for our friends in occupied Europe. Les sanglots longs des violons de l'automne. The long sobs of violins of autumn..."*

Sofia jumped up. 'That's it! That's the message. The invasion will begin within a fortnight.'

It couldn't come a moment too soon.

***

The Allies entering Rome, after the Germans had declared it an open city, had been met with typical Nazi reprisals – another two thousand souls deported to the Neuengamme concentration camp.

Antoine dealt cards. Playing games helped to pass the evenings waiting for the second part of the message. They were all on edge, and the usual banter had become strained.

Florian spoke for them all. 'What's keeping them?'

Juliette took her hand of cards. 'There have been heavy seas, apparently. Not the best weather for a channel crossing.'

Bonnie sighed. 'I suppose not, but nothing is happening to stop the convoys of deportees. God only knows what they suffer in these camps.'

'You can't save them all, Raven.' Juliette's voice was gentle; she knew how much Bonnie still grieved over those she'd lost on the mountains.

Florian leaned forward. 'Hush. Listen...'

*"More than one thousand British bombers have dropped thousands of tons of bombs on German gun emplacements along the Normandy coast."*

The voice was American. Eisenhower? His heart thudded. 'It must be about to begin.'

The drone of planes continued until after dark. Fighters, bombers, heading to Normandy and sometimes the sound of flak.

The evening wore on with no one willing to go to bed for fear of missing the signal. All across France, men and women would be sitting waiting. The women brought food and drink, and they settled in for a long wait, praying to God to protect the invasion force. Young men, all willing to give their lives for freedom.

The devil could send the Nazis to hell.

It was a quarter past eleven when the final message came. *"Blessent mon coeur d'une langueur monotone. Wound my heart with a monotonous languor."*

The men threw down their hands of cards. This was the call to action. The signal for the whole resistance to sabotage whatever they could, especially the rail and communications networks, to aid the Allied invasion.

He jumped to his feet. 'This is it. This is what we've been waiting for.'

Florian downed the remainder of his drink. 'The truck is loaded and ready. Let's go.'

***

Bonnie woke to birdsong outside her window. She hurried downstairs to relieve Juliette, who'd spent the early hours of the morning listening for news on the radio.

She made a pot of tea and took Juliette a cup. She smiled; Juliette had fallen asleep in her chair.

Letting her friend sleep, she tuned the radio through the various stations. BBC, Radio Londres, Radio Berlin... Radio...

She twiddled the knob back to listen to the German. *"The invasion of Western Europe has begun. American troops landed on several beaches in Normandy in the early hours of this morning after a heavy naval bombardment. German troops are repelling the invaders."*

Could she trust a German news report?

She went through the stations again. Nothing.

It was nine-thirty, and the men were still out, the women having a late breakfast, when the BBC confirmed the invasion had begun.

Edward Murrow, an American war correspondent, read Eisenhower's order of the day. *"Soldiers, sailors, and airmen of the expeditionary force. You are about to embark upon the great crusade, toward which we have striven these many months. The eyes of the world are upon you. The hopes and prayers of liberty-loving people everywhere march with you."*

The silence at the table was absolute, a tableau frozen in the moment as Murrow read on, praising the defeats Allied troops and brothers-in-arms had inflicted on the German war machine.

*"The tide has turned. The free men of the world are marching to victory. I have full confidence in your courage, devotion to duty, and skill in battle. We will accept nothing less than full victory. Good luck, and let us all beseech the blessing of Almighty God upon this great and noble undertaking."*

As one, they crossed themselves and bowed their heads in silent prayer.

\*\*\*

Bonnie hovered close to the radio, torn away every few minutes to look through the window for signs of Dad and the others. They'd been out since before midnight, and it was now midday.

There had been reports throughout the morning from correspondents with the troops, giving an insight into the action. Dozens of square miles of invasion boats bore down on the German positions on the Normandy coast. Hundreds of troops had already been parachuted into Northern France.

The BBC Home Service came through loud and clear despite Nazi attempts to jam it. *"D-Day has come."*

The sound of a lorry sent her to the window. 'They're back!' She ran to the door and flung it open. 'Dad! It's begun. D-Day has started. It's on the radio.'

Dad hugged her and limped inside. He looked exhausted.

'Are you –?'

'Hush.'

*"Under the command of General Eisenhower, Allied naval forces, supported by strong air forces, began landing Allied armies this morning on the northern coast of France."*

The bulletin faded to music and she repeated her question. 'Are you all right, Papa?'

He smiled. 'We're all fine, Raven. We had a busy night. We've cut telephone and power wires and removed a load of screws from the clamps that hold rails onto sleepers. Any trains on those routes are likely to derail. We headed north for a bit and heard the big guns on the coast. A lot of planes came over, and we could see the anti-aircraft flak. One or two were hit, but we couldn't see where they landed.'

'They've been dropping troops in by parachute, and apparently, there are hundreds of amphibious craft landing more on the beaches.'

Florian helped himself to bread rolls on the table. 'There was a lot of German activity heading north.'

Dad nodded. 'With luck, the Allies will drive them south and east, back into Germany.'

It was where they belonged, but there were French towns and villages in the way, civilian populations open to Nazi brutality, and Nancy was one of them.

\*\*\*

Antoine yawned, desperate for sleep but glued to the radio. Montgomery was in command of the British, Canadian, and American army battalions carrying out the assault. Germany was broadcasting except on their home service – the assault spread from Cherbourg to Le Havre, but the main thrust seemed to be at Caen, and the airfield there, and there was stiff fighting.

King George VI was going to broadcast to his people at nine o'clock that evening, but now Eisenhower was speaking. *"The landing is only part of the Allies' plan to liberate Europe. I ask you to wait for the signal to rise and strike the enemy. The day will come when I shall need your united strength. Until that day, I call on you for the hard task of discipline and restraint.*

*"I am proud to have under my command the gallant forces of France. A premature rising of all Frenchmen may prevent you from being of maximum help to your country in the critical hour. Be patient. Prepare. Great battles lie ahead. I call upon all who love freedom to stand with us. Keep your faith staunch. Our aims are resolute. Together, we shall achieve victory."*

Florian leaned back in his chair. 'I, for one, am happy to leave preparing until tomorrow. I suggest we get some sleep.' He pushed himself up from his chair. 'Wake me in time for the king's speech.'

There was a general murmur of agreement from the men. He watched them go, but tired though he was, he needed to know what was happening, how best to prepare for the *"great battles"* to come. He went over his stock of supplies in his head and decided to contact S.O.E urgently for more equipment. The battles could drag out for weeks or months, and they must arm as many of the local people as they could. They needed more weapons, mortars, explosives, detonators, fuses, and ammunition, another radio transmitter, and more money and food to help Sofia with keeping them all. The invasion had been planned to take advantage of the full moon, and that same moon must be used for a drop.

He wrote a long list of requirements and hurried to the transmitter shed. Flying in a plane to drop the necessary supplies would be fraught with danger. He gave the coordinates for what he hoped was a suitable drop zone and followed it with his list. The reply came back within minutes. *"Location and request confirmed. Tomorrow at twenty-four hundred hours. Good luck."*

Twelve, midnight. Tonight, he must sleep. Tomorrow would be spent gathering dry grass and small branches to light the drop zone, and it would need all of the men to load the truck if they were to make a quick getaway and safely hide the armaments.

Juliette tapped his shoulder. 'It's nearly time for the king's speech.'

He hadn't realised he'd dozed in his chair. He rubbed his eyes. 'I'll go and wake Florian.'

They gathered around and listened in silence.

*"Four years ago, our Nation and Empire stood alone against an overwhelming enemy, with our backs to the wall. Tested as never before in our history, in God's providence we survived that test; the spirit of the people, resolute, dedicated, burned like a bright flame, lit surely from those unseen fires which nothing can quench.*

*Now once more a supreme test has to be faced. This time, the challenge is not to fight to survive but to fight to win the final victory for the good cause. Once again what is demanded from us all is something more than courage and endurance; we need a revival of spirit, a new unconquerable resolve. After nearly five years of toil and suffering, we must renew that crusading impulse on which we entered the war and met its darkest hour."* The king spoke on, entreating people to pray to do God's work in defeating evil.

*"The Lord will give strength unto his people: the Lord will give his people the blessing of peace."*

He wasn't sure he believed in God any more, but he did believe in man's power for evil, and he was determined to do his part in defeating Nazi Germany and driving the occupiers from French soil.

# Chapter Forty-Four

## Near Nancy, France. June 1944

A quarter of an hour to midnight, and Antoine heaped the last of the sticks onto the piles of dry grass that would mark the drop zone. He and Raphael were to light the fires, and Florian, Alain, and Baptiste stood ready with buckets full of water from the stream to douse the flames once the drop had been completed.

He splashed a little of their precious petrol onto each pile and replaced the can in the truck. Florian had reversed it under a nearby tree, headlights off, ready to load.

Ten minutes. An almost full moon glinted between racing clouds, now illuminating the drop zone, a narrow strip of meadow between stream and wood, and now plunging them all into near darkness. High above them, almost lost in the noise of the wind in the trees, a low droning sound told of heavy bombers flying to some unknown destination. Allies or enemy?

S.O.E would send a smaller plane, probably a Lysander, which had a large drop-tank under its belly, and it would be a hazardous trip in a sky full of enemy aircraft. Suppose the plane was late. He collected a further pile of dry sticks to keep the fires burning in the event of a delay. Suppose the plane had been shot down? How long dare he leave the beacons alight?

Five minutes to midnight. He daren't wait any longer. 'Light the fires, Raphael.' He struck a match and threw it into the first heap. The petrol fumes ignited with a *whumph*, and he moved on to the next.

'Listen!' Alain cupped an ear. 'That sounds like a Lysander.'

'How can you tell?'

'The rotor sounds like an eggbeater.'

He couldn't see the plane against the dark clouds, but he could hear it, low and coming closer. He hoped Alain was right, and it wasn't a German plane attracted by the double rows of bonfires.

Dark cloud raced past, and a black shape was silhouetted against the moon. It headed straight for them, fast and low. Parachutes blossomed and fell like field mushrooms on thistledown. He marked their descent and was about to recover the containers when a sudden whine had him diving for cover. Flak left tracers across the sky, and the Lysander banked away from the trees, gaining height as it tried to escape.

He watched, heart thumping, as the pilot took evasive action and returned fire. The German plane stuttered and banked away, and the Lysander came around for another approach.

Three more containers floated to earth. He waved, hoping his gratitude was visible against the flames, and the dark shape waggled its wings before banking west and north.

'Damn, those boys have courage.' He crossed himself from habit. *God protect you, my friend.* 'Get those fires doused before that Nazi bastard comes back.' He and Raphael ran to find the containers. They were heavy, and some took two men to carry to the truck.

The fires safely out, they hurried back to the lorry and sped away, using only the moon to light the way. First, they must hide the armaments safely, and then they must distribute them to loyal Frenchmen, ready for the signal to rise and fight as one for France.

\*\*\*

Bonnie took the washing basket into the garden and began pegging the second load of laundry onto the clothesline. It was an almost daily job, but when the sun was warm on her shoulders, and the garden smelled of roses and honeysuckle, and damp earth, it was a job she enjoyed. Life felt a little more normal doing mundane chores, and it gave her time alone to reflect.

Her natural optimism was mixed with trepidation. The Allies had liberated Bayeux and were pressing inland, but the German army had been given new and terrifying powers. They were authorised to target civilian populations during military operations, not just as punishment for aiding the resistance. No one, anywhere, was safe as the army moved north and east to counter the Normandy invasion.

The first report of an atrocity in Tulle, south of Limoge, had come last night. Ninety-nine men had been hanged two days previously, supposedly in retaliation for the murder of German prisoners by French "terrorists".

Shouting in the street made her drop her pegs and run through the garden gate. A woman was running towards her screaming.

*No one, anywhere, was safe.*

She hadn't heard any vehicles, and she couldn't see any soldiers. 'What is it, Nadia? What's happened?'

Nadia was sobbing uncontrollably. 'My sister, her husband, and their children. My parents…'

She put her arm around the woman. 'Tell me, Nadia.'

'Dead. They're all dead.'

She steered her towards the house. The door stood open, so she took Nadia inside and sat her down. 'Sofia, Nadia's had some bad news.'

Sofia knelt by Nadia's side. 'Calm yourself, Nadia. Tell us what's happened.'

'The Germans came. They surrounded the village and wouldn't let anyone out.'

Dad and the other men had gathered around by now. 'Where are the Germans? Are they close?'

'I don't know. This happened yesterday at Oradour-sur-Glane, near Limoges.'

Dad let out a tense breath. 'What did they do?'

'They gathered everyone together and separated the men from the women and children, then… then they took the men into barns, and… and… they shot them.' Nadia sobbed helplessly. 'Then… then they herded the women and children into… into the… the church.'

She rubbed the distraught woman's arm gently, her heart sinking further. 'Take your time, Nadia.'

'They threw in grenades and fired machine guns, then they… they bolted the door and set fire to the church.'

'Dear God.' Florian breathed the words into a stunned silence. 'How many?'

'Not many escaped, I don't think. One got out through a window and hid. Someone managed to get a message out.'

'How many dead?' Florian's voice was gentle.

'All of them. My sister and her husband, their children… my mother and father. Over six hundred people, two hundred of them children – all murdered. Shot. Burned alive. They burned the entire village. Oradour-sur-Glane is gone.'

None of them could speak for tears. The Allied invasion had unleashed the full brutal horror of the Nazi regime.

*No one, anywhere, was safe.*

\*\*\*

**Near Nancy, France. July 1944**

Bonnie walked alone through the trees seeking solace from the birdsong and the burgeoning life. For all the darkness and atrocities man had visited on the world, she could still find beauty in it.

But Hitler pushed poisoned thoughts through her mind. For every Allied gain, the Führer would massacre more civilians. He'd unleashed a new, terrifying weapon, a V-1 Flying Bomb, and launched it on London.

A storm in the Channel had destroyed an Allied Mulberry floating harbour, but Cherbourg had still been liberated by American troops. French resistance fighters had killed the Minister of Information, who was a Milice leader, in Lyon, and Jewish prisoners were executed as a reprisal. More people, including women and children had been deported to concentration camps and hundreds of maquis had been shot.

And while American bombers dropped propaganda leaflets and supplies to the resistance, and the Allies broke through the Normandy front, entire male populations in some areas were being deported to work for the Reich. More and more, the Nazis were targeting the resistance.

The feeling of frustration, of needing to act, was building in the house. The waiting for the call to arms was making them all edgy and short-tempered. She'd been glad to leave them for a while and soak up the peace of the forest. A small voice said, *"while she could"*. The German army would inevitably fight on, even if it did so in retreat; Hitler wouldn't allow surrender. Foremost in her mind was that Nancy and their village stood between the Nazis and Germany.

The buzzing of a bee brought her attention to a stand of cow parsley at the side of the path. The insect busied from floret to floret, intent on collecting nectar and pollen, oblivious to her and the world around it.

The buzzing grew louder, bursting into a stuttering roar, and she ducked beneath the trees as a shadow passed overhead. The buzzing stopped abruptly and was followed by the screech of tearing metal and the crack of breaking branches.

The pilot might be alive. She ran towards the sound of a falling tree and stopped short. The plane bore a German cross. Backing away slowly, she bumped into something solid.

'A Messerschmitt.' Florian's voice, steely hard, sounded over her shoulder.

'Do you think he's alive?'

'He won't be for long.'

She followed Florian towards the wreckage and climbed up to peer into the cockpit. A pale, blood-streaked, frightened face looked back. He was younger than her. 'He's just a boy. Can't be twenty.'

Florian aimed his Luger at the boy. 'He's old enough to kill, he's old enough to die.'

'But he's injured.' Her basic sense of decency cried out to aid an injured boy. She'd killed Nazi soldiers, even Maurice, but they'd been an imminent danger to her and her friends. She'd had no choice. To kill a helpless man, just a boy, went against her nature. 'Please, Florian.'

Florian holstered his weapon. 'He doesn't look as if he's long for the world.'

'Can't we help him?'

'Help him? Have you forgotten Oradour-sur-Glane so quickly.'

'No, but I'm not a Nazi. I can't walk away from an injured man.'

Florian sighed. 'Neither, it seems, can I.'

'Can we get him to the house?'

'And risk compromising it?' Florian had undone the pilot's jacket. He shook his head. 'He has a chest wound. He's bleeding heavily. He wouldn't last the journey anyway.'

She held the young man's hand. 'I'm sorry. We can't help you.'

The pilot snatched his hand away, and his face screwed in pain. 'Finish me. It's what your man wants to do. Why would a Frenchwoman help a German?'

'Because Frenchwomen are decent people. It's why we fight alongside our men to defeat Hitler and his evil.'

The youth moaned and closed his eyes. His voice had lost its strength, and his face had the pallor of a corpse. 'You can't defeat Hitler. He holds Paris, and if the Allies attack, he's given orders to destroy it utterly. There won't be a building left standing. We've already won the war.'

According to propaganda put out by Radio Berlin, the Allies were beaten. If the BBC was to be believed, the Allies were making headway, and the Germans were in retreat.

She looked at Florian as the young man's breathing grew ragged, and his chest rose and fell for the last time. She'd stared death in the face too many times. 'Would you have killed him, Florian?'

'It would have been dangerous to leave him alive had he been less severely injured. God knows, I've caused the deaths of enough Nazis, but face to face, helpless and injured... it isn't so easy.'

'What he said about Paris. Do you think it's true?'

'It would be typical of Hitler to destroy something rather than have it fall into Allied hands.'

'Do you think London know?'

'Probably, but we'll pass the message on to Paris and London anyway.'

She brushed away a tear. 'I'm stupid crying over a damn German.'

Florian put an arm around her. 'You're a good woman, Raven. It's this war that's stupid, not you.'

She buried her head in his chest and let out all the grief she'd been holding in for so long.

He let her cry, and when her sobs subsided, he kissed her wet cheek. 'Come, ma chère, we have messages to send and a war to fight.'

# Chapter Forty-Five

**Near Nancy, France. August 1944**

Bonnie stood on top of a cart with a pitchfork in her hands. Below, Raphael tossed up sheaves of wheat which she spread out to even the load. Every available man, woman, child, and heavy horse were working to get in the harvest. Wheat, barley, grapes, fruit, and vegetables. The traditional tobacco crop had long-since given way to food. What crops the German army hadn't ruined or stolen were desperately needed. Damage to the railways meant distribution of vital food to the cities was difficult, and most of France was hungry.

The French resistance in the south, formed into a more organised fighting force, was sabotaging bridges and communications, and tying down German forces, so helping the Allied invasion on the Mediterranean coast secure the ports of Toulon and Marseille, and move north. The Allies who'd landed in Normandy had fought a bitter battle south of Caen and were now pushing German forces south and east towards the Rhine having destroyed most of the German Army Group B west of the Seine.

With hopes high that the tide really had turned in their favour, there were suggestions in messages that the resistance would rise against the occupiers in the capital. If they could take Paris, which the Allies apparently had no plans to attack for fear of causing its destruction, the boost to French morale would be immense.

She firmed down another sheaf. The cart was piled high, and she was wondering how she would get down when Raphael yelled to her.

'That's enough for this load. Throw down the pitchfork.'

She speared the stubble a metre from his feet.

'Jump, and I'll catch you.'

She launched herself into the air, his arms went around her, and they landed in a heap on the ground. 'Damn, this stubble's prickly.'

Raphael laughed and sat up. 'Not as prickly as the Germans are going find life in Paris.'

'Why? Have you heard more news?'

'The resistance is planning an uprising – a lot of political prisoners have been sent to Buchenwald and Ravensbrück, including captured Allied airmen. The Paris Metro, Police, and Gendarmerie went on strike. Apparently, the whole of Paris is on strike now. Posters are all over the city calling on every able-bodied citizen to arm themselves and join the fight. Florian has distributed weapons and ammunition to people he trusts, and we have radios and enough volunteers to fill three trucks.'

She grasped the pitchfork. 'You mean we're going to Paris?'

He nodded. 'The harvest is all but in – we can afford to take a day or two off. The more people who fight for Paris, the better our chance of victory.'

Given the chance, she'd stick the pitchfork through Hitler's evil heart.

***

**Paris, France. August 1944**

Antoine had watched columns of German vehicles drive along the Avenue des Champs-Élysées. They were retreating ahead of the US Third Army, which was approaching from the south, but it hadn't stopped the Germans detonating a bomb on a barge that had set alight mills supplying flour to Paris. German units were garrisoned behind their own fortifications.

He parked Renoir's truck to help block a road. Barricades were going up in readiness for a siege, and around him people were chopping down trees and digging trenches in roads and pavements. Women and children hauled small wooden carts filled with sacks full of earth, and paving slabs, to reinforce the barricades or were transporting ammunition from one barricade to another. Several fuel trucks had been captured and vehicles commandeered, all newly painted with the emblem of the Free French Army of the Interior.

Gunfire echoed from the walls of the elegant buildings. A tank opened fire on one of the barricades. People ran in all directions, and rifle fire from balconies peppered German troops.

'Stay here, Bonnie, and keep your head down.' He climbed the barricade and ran along the road taking cover behind the trees.

The tank's gun barrel swung, seeking its next target. He took a grenade from his pocket and dashed towards the tank. He leapt up on the vehicle, pulled the firing pin, and threw the grenade into the open hatchway. The tank stopped with a loud boom as smoke and flames poured from the hatch. One down…

Several bloodied bodies lay prone in the road. A small group of people with stretchers, one a young nurse waving the Red Cross flag, dashed to recover the wounded. He retreated behind the barricade.

Dusk fell and more skirmishes broke out. The Red Cross doctors and nurses tended both French and German wounded. Vehicles were in flames and acrid smoke made him choke. They manned the barricades all night as fighting went on.

The sun rose and threw long shadows across a street filled with rubble, burned out tanks and trucks, and bodies lying in grotesque positions. He leaned on what was left of the barricade, exhausted, ammunition spent. The rate of attrition was huge.

A woman brought him water and bread. 'Eat. There is not much, but you can have what we have.'

'Thank you.' He managed a tired smile. 'We are not beaten yet.'

'God bless you.'

He sank to the ground and closed his eyes.

'Papa?'

He opened them and smiled.

She held out boxes of ammunition. 'We're running low. You look done in, Papa. Eat. I'll keep watch while you rest.'

He took the ammunition and reloaded his Luger and rifle. 'Your mother would be so proud of you, ma chère.'

'And of you.' She bent to kiss his cheek. 'Rest while you can.'

He closed his eyes again, but the sounds of boots thudding on the road and the rumble of tanks allowed little rest. The day wore on with running battles, skirmishes, explosions, and bursts of firing. He hadn't slept for two days and was flagging as the light faded to dusk again.

Florian grabbed his arm. 'La Fourche, we must hold on. The Ninth Company is here. The Second Armoured Division is on its way.'

'Thank God.' Heavy firing sounded to the south of them. People began running towards the sound. 'The Ninth?'

'Only one way to find out. Come on.'

He followed Florian and Bonnie at a run. A half-track was firing at a large group of German fusiliers and machine-gunners. People were out in the street welcoming the troops and artillery and singing La Marseillaise.

News of the 2nd Armoured Division's arrival didn't come until the next day. A line of tanks and vehicles entered the city, the bells of Notre Dame rang out, and people lined the Champs-Élysées, cheering and singing.

News of the German governor's surrender was greeted with even more joy.

'We've won, Papa!'

He hugged Bonnie and Florian. 'Yes, we did it. Paris is free.'

\*\*\*

Paris might be free, but the uprising had left a thousand resistance fighters dead and fifteen hundred wounded. Four people Antoine had driven to Paris would be returning home to Nancy to be buried.

De Gaulle's speech, praising French forces and calling upon the nation to rise against the occupiers was rousing, but more urgent than fighting was food, for the citizens of Paris were starving. With the rail network bombed or sabotaged, and the Germans having stripped the city for its own use, food was scarce.

Antoine drove Renoir's truck, one of many pressed into use carrying food from towns and villages into the city. Convoys of military vehicles carried provisions from Britain and America that had been flown into Orleans. The little the rest of the population of France had was stretched even thinner.

Driving in convoy towards Paris with other lorries, he didn't feel so vulnerable when he and Bonnie passed German armoured cars and tanks retreating eastwards, except... He pulled into the side of the road and waved to Florian and Baptiste who were driving two of the other lorries.

'Baptiste jumped down from his cab. 'What's up?'

'I'm not going on to Paris. I'm turning around.'

'Why?'

'Hitler will be furious he's lost Paris and the Allies have liberated Drancy and Romainville. If those Germans are retreating to the border, Nancy is in their path.'

'And we've had reports enough of what Nazis do when they lose.' Bonnie grabbed the radio with shaking hands. 'We should warn Sofia.'

'Tell her to get everyone out of their homes and into the forest to hide. If the Germans turn their big guns on the houses, they'll destroy the lot and kill everyone. It'll be Oradour-sur-Glane all over again. Tell her to take food, water, and the radio, but to be quick.'

He rammed his foot on the accelerator, and the truck growled into action while Bonnie relayed the message. Taking to smaller roads, he hoped to avoid the main convoy of German tanks and armoured vehicles and arrive back at the village through little-used forest tracks. He knew the area like the back of his hand, which gave him an advantage over the enemy. Checking his mirror showed him Florian and Baptiste were following.

'Sofia is spreading the message.'

'Send a message to London. Black geese approaching Nanzig.'

The lorry bounced over uneven ground. Bonnie grabbed her seat to steady herself. A message came back. "*Harass and delay. White geese circling.*" She frowned. 'What does that mean?'

'It means the Allies are on their way, but they need time to get into position.' He turned along a narrow track between trees and stopped the engine, letting the truck coast the last few yards. 'Stay here. I'll see what's around.'

He hurried through the trees until he came upon the main route. Dozens of armoured vehicles stood along the road – hundreds of troops. He melted back into the trees and checked several of the wider tracks. The forest was full of Germans.

\*\*\*

Bonnie sent another message. "*Large flock black geese in forest west of Nanzig.*" The reply was simply "*Message received.*"

Dad started the engine. 'Florian, Baptiste, and I need to reach our arms caches and do some serious damage. Bonnie, I need you to find Sofia. Keep to the trees and away from the village.'

'Be careful, Papa.'

He smiled. 'And you. Stay hidden. Sofia should have a radio with her, so message me if you need to.'

'I will.' She hugged him briefly and jumped down from the cab. Dad inched the lorry forward.

The leaves on the trees were turning yellow and gold as an early September chill nipped her ears. Sofia and the others would need shelter. There was the semi-derelict barn they'd used as a drop point. It was deep in the forest and might provide a safe haven. She pushed through a thicket of beech saplings, in the general direction of the barn.

Several times, she backtracked at the sound of guttural German voices ahead.

It took her the best part of an hour to reach the barn by a roundabout route, disguising her tracks as she went. She pushed open the barn door and was faced with a row of rifle muzzles. 'It's Raven. I'm alone.'

The muzzles lowered and Sofia rushed forward to pull her inside and shut the door. 'Thank God, Raven.'

She returned Sofia's hug. 'Are you all safe?'

'The whole village is here. What's going on out there?'

'The forest tracks are full of heavy German artillery. The Allies are coming, but we have to delay the enemy until they get here.'

'How are we supposed to do that?'

'Dad and the others are going to the arms caches. They have mortars, machine-guns, grenades. He's adamant we should stay in hiding in case they destroy the village.'

A man shouldered forward. 'We can do our share. I'm not staying here like a rat in a trap.'

'What do you suggest, Gilbert?'

'What we're good at. Sabotage. We have weapons and grenades. There are all kinds of things in this barn we can use. Jam a tank track with a lump of metal, a grenade down a gun barrel. Slash the tyres on troop transports. Soil in a fuel tank. A knife in the belly if you girls can entice one away from the others. Wire across a track to decapitate a man in an armoured car.'

She winced at the image, but it was a necessary evil. 'Then I suggest only a dozen of us who know the forest well. The rest should stay here.'

Gilbert nodded. 'Agreed.' He picked his men and two women. 'Let's go and ruin their day.'

# Chapter Forty-Six

**Near Nancy, France. September 1944.**

Bonnie shared the last of her bread with Michelle. Although the dozen chosen had been out at night sabotaging whatever they could to delay, harry, and disrupt the German force in the forest, they'd been trapped in the barn during the daytime for several days with little sleep, and less food, listening to heavy artillery and gunfire. They'd relied on broadcasts from Radio Londres and the BBC to tell them what was happening only a few miles away.

The German XLVII Panzercorps was defending the eastern approach to Nancy as well as the Moselle River crossings to the north and south of the town. The US 3$^{rd}$ Army divisions were at Metz, Pont à Mousson, and Toule, to the north, while the US 7$^{th}$ Army was approaching from the south and had crossed the Moselle near Bayon. Bombers flew over day and night, and sometimes they heard explosions as bombs fell not far away.

According to resistance reports, the river crossings were being fiercely contested with attacks and counter-attacks. Dad and Florian thought the Americans were going to try to encircle the German forces at Nancy. If they succeeded, it would be a bloody battle.

It was already fading to dusk and time to don dark clothing for the night's work. If American troops were approaching from the east, to drive the enemy into the trap, the more damage they could do to the German defences, the better.

It was a clear night, but little moonlight penetrated to the forest floor beneath the canopy of beech trees. The twelve of them spread out to cover the area. She and Dad slipped along well-known tracks towards one of the wider rides where German vehicles had been the previous night. A tank and a couple of armoured cars lay abandoned in the middle of the ride, and the whole area was eerily quiet.

She paused in the shadows, suspecting a trap, and whispered. 'Where the hell are they?'

Dad, put a hand on her arm. 'Stay here, keep watch, and keep out of sight. I'll slip along the track towards Nancy and see if they've moved position.'

Dad had been gone for half an hour when a rustle of dry leaves made her swing around, heart thumping. 'Florian... You startled me.'

'They've gone.'

'Gone?'

'The Germans. There's no sign of them.'

'Gone where?'

'If reports are right, they're in retreat, so they'll have gone east or northeast towards the border. We'll wait for the others to report back.'

One by one her friends returned, and all had the same news. The Germans had gone.

Raphael scratched his nose. 'I'll send a message to London.' He hurried away.

'They've really left?'

'So it would seem.' Dad yawned. 'We should go back to the barn with the others and get some sleep.

It was ages since she'd walked alone under the trees without fear, and much as she loved her friends, she needed the healing of silence and solitude. She looked up and down the ride. 'I think I'll stay for a while, Papa.'

'Don't be long, Raven, and take care... just in case.'

'I will.'

A crescent moon hung in the sky above the ride, stars twinkled, and a light breeze brought scents of the forest; earth, pine needles, dead leaves, cow parsley, and the pungent smell of some animal that had marked its territory, blissfully unaware of the man-made battle going on around it.

The hoot of a tawny owl was answered by its mate, and another low sound grumbled in the distance. She stopped, frozen – a vehicle? She fled from the track to the shadows as headlights lit the ride. An armoured car sped towards her followed by a jeep. By the light of headlights, she could pick out a white star in a circle on one of the jeeps. Americans?

She stepped from the shadows, and headlights caught her. A jeep stopped beside her. 'What are you doing out here, all alone, ma'am?'

'You are American!' She leant into the jeep, threw her arms around the soldier, and kissed him on both cheeks.

The soldier grinned. 'Well, ma'am, that's a real fine welcome.'

'The Germans have gone.' She kissed him again. 'They've gone! We can all go home!' Heavy artillery firing sounded in the distance followed by an explosion.

Did they still have homes to go to?

***

Antoine put an arm around Bonnie. The damage to the village was still more than apparent after two weeks of work. Several houses had been hit by mortars and almost entirely destroyed, some had had roofs blown off, and few had glass left in the windows. Sofia's house had lost its distinctive chimney and had a hole in the roof made by falling bricks. The Nazis parting shots with machine guns and missiles had been designed to do maximum damage, but no one had been injured thanks to hiding in the barn in the forest. The village had survived though it would bear the scars forever.

People were rallying around those who'd lost their homes. Florian had taken the truck into newly liberated Nancy to buy materials to board up windows and mend roofs – timber, nails, screws, tiles, and glass – and had also returned with a length of wood with a finger board pointing to *Nanzig* that he'd uprooted from the crossroads. The finger board went onto the bonfire with a cheer, but they were salvaging whatever was reusable and doing the best they could to make homes weathertight before winter.

Baptiste pushed a handcart towards him. 'Florian and Raphael are rebuilding Sofia's chimney today. Can you give me a hand carrying bricks up the scaffolding?'

'Of course. I'll catch you later, Raven.' Even now, the habit of caution was so ingrained, he never called her Bonnie unless they were alone.

'I should be going anyway, Papa. I promised to help Michelle make a huge pan of soup for the workers.'

He watched her go. Despite the upturn in France's fortunes, there was a sadness about her she wore like a veil. She'd killed... risked her life... lost people she'd loved. Would any of them be truly happy again?

He shrugged off his despond as he carried hods of bricks up the wooden scaffolding. A string of recent Allied successes buoyed him as towns across France and Belgium were liberated by British, Canadian, and American troops. In retaliation, Hitler had ordered V-2 rockets launched at London and Paris but there'd been little loss of life.

The government in exile had returned to Belgium, and General de Gaulle had formed a provisional government of the French Republic. Bulgaria declared war on Germany, and the United States First Army liberated Luxembourg. Even better news was that the Allies had entered Aachen, a city just inside the German border. The Allies were taking the battle to Hitler and had reached the Siegfried Line, the German western defences. The Allies were also making incursions across the Netherlands, and Brest had fallen.

Nancy was now garrisoned by the United States 3rd Army, who'd entered the town with little opposition but were holding off counterattacks at Arracourt. The fight for freedom continued across Europe, but more and more, the news was of German retreat and Allied advances. Not that the Allied forces were having everything their own way; an ambitious parachute-drop of troops at Arnhem had ended in disaster with huge Allied losses. Hitler hadn't yet lost his sting.

*\*\**

### Near Nancy, France. November 1944

Bonnie turned up the radio, no longer fearing enemy ears. News of the liberation of Belgium had raised their spirits. Where Belgium led, France could follow. Hitler was still bombarding Britain with V-2 rockets, but the German battleship *Tirpitz* had been sunk in a Norwegian fjord, and Metz, to the north of Nancy had been taken from German hands.

The voice of the announcer was unashamedly jubilant. *"French troops have today liberated Strasbourg, in Eastern France."*

She ran outside to find her father, who was chopping wood for the fire. 'Papa, Papa! Strasbourg is liberated!'

His smile said it all. 'German families have been leaving the area all month. Perhaps it's time to reclaim what's ours if there's anything left of it.'

'What's ours? You mean the farm?' It had been taken over by German settlers. The last time she'd been there, it was neglected and used as a fuel dump. She'd killed two German soldiers and Raphael had blown up the dump. Raphael and his friend, Jean, had gone back later and found and buried her grandparents' bodies.

'We shouldn't go alone, Bonnie. I'll ask Florian, Baptiste, and Raphael if they'll come with us. We don't know what we might find.'

They set off in the truck that afternoon, well-armed and determined to take back the farm. The blown-up fuel truck had been removed, and someone had obviously been looking after the place. Florian parked in the middle of the yard. He pointed to the piece of field next to the fence. Your parents are buried over there, La Fourche.'

She looked where he pointed. All seemed peaceful. Cattle lifted their heads to look at them for a moment before resuming their grazing. Two rough wooden crosses leaned at an angle and marked humps covered in long grass and nettles, uncared for by strangers. She took a deep breath and swallowed. She would pay her respects later.

Baptiste handed out loaded rifles and ammunition. Raphael and Florian took one each. She was more accurate with a Luger.

Dad checked the safety catch on his pistol. 'Ready?'

She unholstered hers. 'Ready.'

Raphael, Florian, and Baptiste checked the barn and took up positions behind walls and a farm cart.

Dad pushed her behind him. 'Stay back.' He walked towards the house and hammered on the front door. No answer.

She pushed past him and turned the door handle. Mémé and Pépé had never locked their door. There'd been no need until... The door opened.

The kitchen smelled musty and damp, but it was tidy and clean, and there were signs of a hurried exit – plates stacked unwashed in the sink, a half-eaten meal, a child's toy on the floor.

Dad checked the scullery and then thudded up the stairs. 'No one here. It doesn't look as if there has been for a few days.'

Her finger relaxed on the trigger. 'They were probably expecting French reprisals, Hitler-style.'

'Probably. There aren't any personal possessions – photographs, jewellery, money. It looks as if we have our farm back.' He pumped the lever over the sink. 'I'll check the well. Don't drink the water until I have.'

She nodded as Dad fetched a torch from the cupboard where Pépé had always kept it. A retreating German could well have dropped a dead sheep or human down the well in a fit of spite. She walked outside and breathed in the fresh winter air. Raphael, Florian, and Baptiste were helping Dad remove the heavy well cover. She went across to them.

Dad shone his torch beam down into the darkness. 'I think it's safe.'

'What do we do now, Papa? Do we stay?'

'Not yet, Raven. The war isn't over. There's fierce fighting in the Ardennes, and there may well be more German counter-attacks. We're perilously close to the border here, and Hitler considers Alsace and Lorraine to be German.'

'We could lose the farm again?'

He shook his head. 'I'm going to set some booby traps. Anyone coming in here will have a nasty surprise. Wait in the truck, and keep your eyes and ears open.'

She stood for a moment, head bowed, by her grandparents' graves before climbing back into the truck, keeping watch, and listening for the sound of vehicles, while Dad and the others carried equipment from the vehicle and the barn to the house. When they'd finished, Florian painted a message in German and French in large white letters on the farmhouse door.

## PROPERTY OF THE RENARD FAMILY
## DO NOT ENTER
## DANGER OF DEATH

She smiled grimly. They couldn't say they hadn't been warned.

# Chapter Forty-Seven

**Near Nancy, France. January 1945**

Bonnie peeled potatoes from the root store for supper – a mammoth task given the number of people still living with Sofia. Without the vegetable garden and the kindness of neighbours, they'd all have starved long ago.

Her optimism about an early end to the war had been dashed. Dad was right when he said Hitler hadn't yet given up on Lorraine and Alsace. He'd launched an offensive to cripple Allied airbases, recapture Strasbourg, and support his troops in the Ardennes. If Himmler retook Strasbourg, as he'd promised to do, Nancy could well be next on his list.

Dad reckoned the American and French troops in the area were stretched thin along a hundred-kilometre front.

The door to the living room stood open. The men planned while she peeled.

'The German forces pushed back to the border at Colmar are in a position to strike west and north, and there are more to the north and east of Strasbourg. Intelligence suggests they're planning to sever the American Seventh Army supply line to Strasbourg by cutting across the eastern foothills of the Vosges Mountains. There's a natural salient here on this bend on the Rhine.' The tapping of Dad's finger on the map didn't help show her which bend.

She dropped the peeler and listened harder.

'Our old stomping ground?'

'Precisely, Baptiste. We've been all over the Vosges. It's an area we know well.'

'You have something in mind, La Fourche?'

'The usual, Florian. Delay, disrupt, destroy. Do whatever we can to slow the German advance. The Allies are tied up in the Ardennes, and they need time to get support to the Seventh Army.'

'Then the sooner we go, the better.'

'Agreed. We'll load the truck and take the back roads to the old barn in the hills. We can make a base there, reconnoitre the area, and spend a few nights doing our worst.'

Chairs scraped on the stone floor, doors slammed, and the room went quiet.

\*\*\*

## Vosges Mountains, France. January 1945

Antoine looked down on the road below him. Convoys of German military vehicles crawled like ants towards the Seventh Army's position. 'Let's hope our plan works.'

Raphael, Alain, and Baptiste armed themselves with grenades, rifles, and ammunition and hid, spread out, on the uphill side of the lane ready for a quick escape. They would only have one chance before all hell would be let loose.

Florian drove up the hill and parked off a track in dense woodland above the lane they'd earmarked and the lower road the Germans were presently using. 'You get the saw, La Fourche. I'll find a suitable candidate.'

He grabbed the two-man saw from the back of the truck and hurried across the lane and down through the trees after Florian.

Florian was sizing up a tall beech tree with a thick girth a few metres from the main road. 'We can't be seen from the road, and the noise of the vehicles should mask our sawing.' He patted the trunk. 'If we get this right, La Fourche, it should do the job.'

'I've felled enough trees to know where to make it fall, Florian.' It was a beautiful tree with spreading branches that reached almost to the road, the bark was smooth and grey despite its age. Another sacrifice for their freedom. They pulled the saw backwards and forwards on the downhill side of the trunk making a cut halfway into the trunk. Another cut above it at an angle took out a wedge like a slice of cake.

Sweat beaded his brow as they began cutting on the opposite side, a little higher, to form a step to stop the trunk kicking back and injuring them. 'We're almost there.' He pulled out the saw. 'Stand back, Florian.' The tree shuddered and moved a bare inch. He put both hands on the trunk and pushed. The beech groaned, branches whipped in the air, and it fell with a deafening crash onto the road below.

'Bull's eye. Quick, let's get out of here while they're trying to get men out from under it.'

There was no way the soldiers could move a tree that size any time soon, even with a tank. With luck, they would take the quicker option of a detour. With more luck, they'd take the route where Alain, Baptiste, and Raphael were waiting.

*** 

Grabbing weapons and ammunition from the lorry, Antoine led Florian back to where the others waited. He positioned himself a distance from them, panting from his exertion, and loaded his rifle and Luger. The low growl of heavy vehicles came closer.

*Wait... wait...*

A tank rolled by followed by armoured cars, troop carriers, and a staff car. The tank reached the spot where Baptiste was hidden. Baptiste's aim was true, and the soldier looking out of the hatch slumped forward.

*Now!* As one, the rest of them opened fire. He pulled the pin of a grenade and threw it into an open-topped troop carrier. Machine-gun fire briefly strafed the area where they were hiding. One bullet silenced it. Damaged vehicles straddled the lane, and bodies lay everywhere.

*Time to go.* He threw one more grenade to disable a tank and then ran up the hill towards the truck.

Florian was already there and had the engine running. 'How long dare we wait for the others?'

It was a question he didn't want to answer. He stared down through the trees, willing Baptiste, Raphael, and Alain to appear. 'Until we see the whites of the German's eyes?'

Florian drummed his fingers on the steering wheel; he was right to be anxious.

'One of them may be injured and need help, Florian.' He opened the door and jumped down. 'Keep the engine running. I'll take a look.'

They'd known it would be a risky strategy, but they'd blocked two routes between the Allies and the advancing Germans. Someone was crashing through the trees below him; friend or foe? He slipped behind a tree and drew his knife.

Raphael appeared, breathing heavily and covered in blood.

He re-sheathed his knife. 'Where are you hurt?'

'It's not my blood.'

'The others?'

Raphael shook his head. 'Dead. Machine-gun got them, but not before they'd done a lot of damage.'

'We need to get out of here.'

Raphael nodded, took a step, and collapsed.

Not his blood? He was breathing. Could he get him up the hill to the truck? 'Raphael... Raphael!'

His friend groaned and opened his eyes.

'We can't stay here. These hills will be crawling with Germans in minutes.' The sound of machine-guns strafing the wood confirmed his fears. 'Come on. I'll help you.'

He put his arm around Raphael and dragged him to his feet, Together, they struggled up the hill. Florian jumped down from the cab and helped him get Raphael into the back.

'I'll see what I can do for him, Florian. Drive!'

The truck bounced over the rough ground and then onto a smoother lane. He knelt by Raphael's side and undid his jacket looking for blood. His shirt was wet with a dark stain. He held his hand over the wound in Florian's side to stem the bleeding. Two more lives sacrificed for freedom when the war was almost won. He was damned if he'd let Raphael be another.

***

## Near Nancy, France. February 1945

Bonnie had taken over most of Louise's household duties, as she'd barely left Raphael's side. Raphael may have been another of Louise's strays, but she fussed over him like a mother hen. Dad and Florian had brought him home rather than stay in the mountains to continue the fight, and a month on, his wound still pained him. The doctor had removed several machine gun bullets from his side, but could do nothing for a rib broken in three places. Rest, he assured them, would allow it to heal in its own time.

Their action, though it must have helped the Allies, had come at too great a personal cost, and once again, the house was in mourning.

The war ground on without them, and news came mainly via the radio. The Allies and the Free French Army had defended Strasbourg, the defeated Germans had withdrawn eastwards, and the Colmar Pocket, the last German foothold west of the Rhine, had been wiped out. The concentration camp at Auschwitz-Birkenau had been liberated, and Belgium had been declared free of German troops. At the end of January, the Red Army had crossed the Oder River into Germany and were close to Berlin. Both Dresden and Berlin had been heavily bombed.

She made coffee and took a tray of cups through to the living room. The radio was on, the rest of the household listening intently, so she slipped into a seat at the table and took a cup of coffee from the tray.

Raphael sat next to Louise. He looked pale and tired, but he was alive and recovering slowly. He managed a smile as he reached carefully for his coffee. 'Thank you, Raven.'

Florian turned up the radio, aware her hearing wasn't as good as it had been before the explosion. "*Operation Clarion is underway against Germany. Three and a half thousand Allied bombers, and almost five thousand fighters are targeting German transport infrastructure. Railway stations, marshalling yards, docks, and bridges will be destroyed to finally cripple the German war machine.*"

Sofia warmed her hands around her cup of coffee. 'Allied losses could be horrendous.'

The report continued. "*The present clear weather has opened an opportunity to inflict severe damage to the Nazi war effort. Every available Allied aircraft is in the sky over Germany – no town in that country is safe. Heavy bombers, escorted by fighters, are dropping thousands of tons of bombs on targets right across Germany. We aim to strike fear into the German heart and show the Hun we are masters of the air. Western Europe will no longer live under enemy skies.*"

The next day more radio reports were broadcast. The Allies had suffered so few losses, they were repeating the bombing to include more targets. Fighter escorts had shot down German planes, and bombs had destroyed barges, a communications centre, and several hundred locomotives, oil tankers, tracks, and rolling stock.

She smiled, it was hard not to, despite the innocents who would inevitably be caught in the flak. *Western Europe will no longer live under enemy skies.*

\*\*\*

## Near Nancy, France. April 1945

Antoine chopped the last of the winter's firewood, while Raphael stacked it in Sofia's woodstore. The wound to Raphael's side had healed, but months of forced inaction had left his muscles weak and in need of rebuilding.

Antoine's axe blows reflected his anger at recent events. March had brought more tragedy than success. A navigational error had resulted in the deaths of more than five hundred Dutch civilians during a bombing raid to destroy V-2 rocket launching equipment near The Hague.

While Hitler hid in his bunker in Berlin, the good people of Gardelegen, in Germany, directed by the SS, had herded more than one thousand slave labourers from a rail transport into a barn, poured petrol over straw, and set fire to it. Those trying to escape the flames had been shot, and the rest burned alive.

While British troops had liberated Bergen-Belsen concentration camp, the appalling descriptions of the survivors, walking skeletons, some said, made him want to retch. There seemed no end to Nazi cruelty.

Germany was being attacked from all sides, and Eisenhower had demanded their surrender. He struck the last log with a vengeance, and lumps of splintered wood flew in all direction.

Hitler would never surrender, but while the coward hid, the Soviets were advancing on Berlin from the east and the Americans were approaching from the west. The battle for Berlin was about to begin; Hitler's days were numbered, and Germany's surrender couldn't come a minute too soon.

# Chapter Forty-Eight

**Near Nancy, France. April 1945**

Bonnie scrubbed the stone-flagged floor in the living-room. Anything to keep busy and not succumb to a nerve-wracked fourth cup of coffee. The radio was on almost permanently now, turned up, so it could be heard all over the house and even in the vegetable garden outside the open kitchen window, where Dad and Juliette were weeding. Every now and again, someone would tune the radio to a different station in the hope of hearing the news they all waited for.

Dad was sure Hitler would die before he'd surrender – Hitler dead suited her fine if it brought the war to an end, though she'd rather have seen him tried and hanged for his crimes along with Himmler and the rest of the evil Nazis. Centuries ago, in England, they'd have been hung, drawn, and quartered. The guillotine would be too merciful a death…

*"The German Army Detachment under SS-General Felix Steiner is still in retreat, but Hitler has vowed to remain in Berlin to defend the city."*

Hiding in a bunker, there wasn't much else the coward could do. She splashed water onto the floor and scrubbed harder.

*"Hermann Göring is said to have asked to be declared Hitler's successor, and that, furious, Hitler has stripped him of his rank and expelled him from the Nazi Party. Berlin is now encircled by Allied forces."*

Florian trod carefully across her clean floor, leaving a trail of footprints, and changed the station.

*"The last German troops have withdrawn from Finland to Norway, and the Finnish flag has been raised on the cairn between Finland, Norway, and Sweden in celebration. We have received an*

*unconfirmed report that Benito Mussolini and his mistress have been shot by Italian partisans and hanged upside down by their feet in Milan."*

'Serves them right. I have a new respect for the Italians.' Florian had often berated the Italians for their part in the war.

'Revenge is sweet, as they say, Florian.' What atrocities would be performed in the name of justice? Did two wrongs make things right? She scrubbed harder, trying to justify vengeful thoughts. She was a resistance fighter, not a murderess.

*"German forces in Italy and Brazil are reported to have surrendered. A ceasefire has been declared. In Bavaria, the United Staes Seventh Army has liberated Dachau concentration camp."*

She stopped scrubbing and sat back on her heels. 'What those poor people must have suffered in those camps. Do you think any of our people sent to them have survived? They say millions have been exterminated like vermin. Do you believe that?'

'I do, Raven. After what the Nazis did at Oradour-sur-Glane and Gardelegen, locking people in buildings and burning them alive. I'll believe them capable of gassing millions of Jews.'

'Men, women, and children...' She brushed tears from her cheeks with the back of a wet hand and went back to her scrubbing as if she could scrub the memory of death from her mind.

At the end of April more news arrived. *"Soviet forces have surrounded Hitler's command bunker in central Berlin. It is reported that Adolf Hitler has committed suicide."*

\*\*\*


**Near Nancy, France. May 1945**

Antoine mopped his brow with a handkerchief. Hot sun burned the back of his neck. He straightened; the hoeing must wait until the evening when it was cooler. Leaning his hoe against the beanpoles, he went back into the comparative cool of the house.

The radio blared out a big band playing a swing tune. The rhythm was compulsive, and had him swaying across the kitchen to fill a glass with water. Laughter came from the living room. He smiled; laughter had been a rare commodity for so long. Florian was dancing around the table with Louise, who was having a fit of giggles. His eyes watered at such a happy sight.

The music faded to news and all eyes turned to the radio as if pictures would come out of it.

*"Reich Chancellor Goebbels is dead. It is reported that he and his wife murdered their children and then committed suicide. With Goebbels gone, General Helmuth Weilding, commander of the Berlin Defence Area, has unconditionally surrendered the city of Berlin to General Vasily Chuikov of the Red Army."*

Cheers broke out, and Dad hugged Juliette, while Florian whirled Louise in a circle almost bumping into the table.

Bonnie raised a hand. 'Hush, there's more.'

*"General Vietinghoff has surrendered his troops in Northern Italy. Martin Borman and other top Nazis are reported to have committed suicide, and German troops in Denmark, Northern Germany, and the Netherlands have surrendered to Montgomery. It is also believed that the Neuengamme camp has been liberated."*

Juliette kissed Dad on the lips. He looked slightly surprised and then kissed her back. The room burst into cheers.

Raphael cheered the loudest. 'About time, La Fourche.'

Juliette blushed in his arms and glanced at Bonnie, who smiled her approval. He was relieved, but a future with Juliette would have to wait – Bonnie had to come first, because he was all she had left of her family. He wished she had someone special in her life. Marcel had broken her heart and her trust.

\*\*\*

*"At two forty-one this morning, Germany surrendered unconditionally to the Allies at the Western Allied Headquarters in Reims, France. In accordance with orders from Reich President Karl Dönitz, the surrender was signed by General Alfred Jodf."*

The crowded room was too small to contain Bonnie's joy. She threw open the door and rushed outside into the spring sunshine, into a new day, a new dawn, a different life full of possibilities. Nothing would ever be the same again.

All along the street doors opened as people spilled out to share the news and their joy. People hugged one another and danced. Some simply sat in the shade, exhausted by years of stress, limp with relief. Husbands and wives kissed.

She felt a pang of loneliness, of regret. Part of her heart still stood on a mountaintop in the Pyrenees, watching three airmen disappear into Spanish hands. Where were they now? The Allies were still at war with Japan, and Pierre, her first love, could be anywhere in the world. Had he survived?

She brushed away tears – this was no day for sorrow.

Victory in Europe Day was declared the next day, with an official ceasefire and German surrender to the Soviet Union. Himmler, head of the SS was arrested at a checkpoint manned by liberated Soviet POWs and had taken a cyanide pill. Another Nazi too cowardly to face the consequences of his actions.

The village slaughtered the communal pig and held a celebratory hog roast – they'd all helped feed it, and now they shared it. It was a joyous occasion, with more wine than was good for them, but now the war in Europe was over… more and more, she'd felt the need to go home, except she wasn't sure where home was. And what did Dad and Juliette's blossoming relationship mean for her? She felt like a spare part, and she didn't want to come between them. They deserved happiness.

Dad cornered her in the kitchen that evening. 'I need to go back to England to look to the business. Yvonne and Rosemary have done a wonderful job in my absence, but I have no reason to stay away now.'

'What about the farm?'

'It's yours, Bonnie, to do with as you like. Your grandparents always intended you to have it. What will you do, do you think?'

'I'm not sure. I think I need to go back to England, too, for a while at least.'

He nodded. 'Cosby will always be your home, if you want that. The farm can wait until you're ready.'

She hugged him, needing to be held. So many changes, so many decisions. 'What about Juliette?'

He smiled. 'I'm going to ask her to come with us, if that's all right with you?'

She laughed. 'I think that's wonderful. She can be another of my mothers.'

He kissed her cheeks. His were wet with tears. 'You have been well blessed with mothers, my little Raven.'

She swallowed, thinking of Colette, and nodded. She would miss Louise, Michelle, and Sofia more than she could say.

*** 

## Cosby, Leicestershire, England. August 1945

Bonnie stepped onto the main street, a stranger in a familiar place. Not much had changed while they'd been in France, and a few weeks with the windows and doors open had aired the little cottage. Juliette was already making it homely.

The village was quiet, small, and she missed the bustle of a busy household, the Moselle Valley, and the trees of the forested hills. Could she settle here for a life of normality when Colette had given her life, Michelle had given her body, and Sofia and Louise had given their homes for the freedom of France? She'd done things no man or woman should have to do – what would Mrs Sibson, at the village shop, think of her if she knew?

The war against Japan went on, with heavy bombing of the naval base at Yokohama. The Allies had divided Germany between them – one area of control each for America, Britain, France, and Russia. It felt like a recipe for future animosity, but seemed the fairest solution.

Men, who looked as lost as she felt, were arriving home as Britain began demobilising its troops. The older men arrived first, and those who'd served the longest, along with the craftsmen needed for rebuilding the bombed-out towns and cities. Leicester hadn't escaped the blitz.

Some wanted to talk about their experiences, and some hardly spoke at all. For herself, she had no wish to admit she'd killed men or lost escapees on the Pyrenees. She wasn't proud of her actions; they were things that had to be done.

She hurried to the shop. Juliette was waiting for the bread and milk she'd been sent to buy for breakfast, and she'd promised to help Dad in the garden. The wilderness was being slowly tamed, and they would need to grow vegetables – rationing would continue for a while, and three months on, Juliette still didn't have a ration book.

The headline on the newspaper in the stand rooted her to the spot.

**UNITED STATES DROPS ATOM BOMB ON HIROSHIMA**

Pictures beneath the headline showed a huge mushroom cloud and a scene of total devastation. An entire city wiped out, a community lost, barely a building standing. Surely no one could have escaped.

She tucked the paper under her arm and went into the shop. 'How can people do this to other people, Mrs Sibson?'

'I'm sure I don't know, duckie. I heard about it late last night on the radio. They say anyone at the site would have been atomised, I think the word was, and those farther away have terrible burns, with their skin hanging off, and… and…' Mrs Sibson blew her nose loudly. 'They may be the enemy, but there'll be kiddies among them. What did they do to deserve that?'

'Nothing.' Any more than Ava or little Jacob had, or the thousands of Jewish children murdered by Hitler's command. Her stomach rumbled, and she wrenched her mind back to breakfast. They'd already eaten their ration of bacon. 'Can I have a loaf of bread and a pint of milk, please, Mrs Sibson.' She handed over a ten-shilling note and her and Dad's ration cards.

Mrs Sibson tore out the appropriate stamps before handing over the groceries and her change. 'I shall be glad when we can throw away our ration books, but with hundreds of thousands of men coming home, more mouths to feed, I fear it'll be with us for a long while yet, duckie.'

The war in Europe may have been won, and Hitler might be dead, but his victims still suffered under the Nazi cloud.

*** 

Another warm, sunny day greeted Bonnie as she drew her bedroom curtains. It was difficult to look at the peaceful, Victorian cottages across the brook and not compare them to the bombed-out cities of Europe and the recent devastation in Japan.

Another atomic bomb had been dropped, this time on Nagasaki, and a few days later, Emperor Hirohito had used the radio to broadcast his country's surrender to the world.

It was over. The men fighting on the Eastern front could finally come home. As every morning, she thought about those who would never go home and those, like her, who were no longer sure where home was.

A sparrow alighted on her window-sill and hopped along it, searching for spiders and bugs. She stood still, not wanting to disturb it. All that concerned it was finding food for its latest brood of chicks. It didn't worry about things it couldn't control.

She took a deep breath; she was a raven, wasn't she, in another life? She would be more raven. Life was for living, not for regret. What was the old adage? *God give me the courage to change what can be changed, the strength to bear what can't be changed, and the wisdom to know the difference.* There was much she couldn't change and much for which to be grateful.

She trotted down the stairs determined to embrace the future, whatever it brought, and leave the past where it belonged. She threw open the front door to let in the morning sun.

'Marie?'

No one in Cosby knew her as Marie Barbier. She squinted into the sun, unable to see the speaker, and shaded her eyes. A tall young man sporting a neatly trimmed beard and moustache stood on her doorstep. His face seemed familiar, but… 'Pierre?'

His face broke into the smile she remembered well. 'Yes, it's me.'

Her heart fluttered uncontrollably; her head whirled with confusion. She hadn't told him her real name. 'What are you doing here?'

'I had to find you, to see if…' He paused. 'I –'

'But you never knew my name. How did you find me?'

He took a piece of paper from his jacket pocket and unfolded it. It was the pencil portrait of Pierre she'd drawn on the train to Marseille years before. He held it towards her. 'You signed it Bonnie Renard.'

Her signature was clear. She'd signed without a thought to her false identity.

'It's taken me months to track you down, Bonnie. I… Are you…' His eyes pleaded for her love.

'Pierre… Charles…' She walked into his outstretched arms. 'I love you. I've never stopped loving you.'

He closed his arms around her. 'There hasn't been a day when I haven't dreamt of this moment. I was so afraid you'd be married. You're not married, are you?'

She smiled up at him. 'There's no one in my life, Charles, except you.' In her heart, she knew there never had been.

Their lips met in a gentle kiss. She was home at last.

The End

# Fact from Fiction

As always with my historical novels, I placed fictional characters into real historical events. The character of Bonnie Renard was inspired by the activities of girls like Nancy Wake, as told in "*White Mouse*" – (**Nancy Wake)**, and Hannie and Truus Schaft, and Freddie Oversteegen, in "*Seducing and Killing Nazis*" – (**Sophie Poldermans)**.

The courage and resilience teenage girls showed during the German occupation of Europe humbles me. They were chosen as guides by the organisers of the Allied escape lines because they looked innocent and were more likely to be disregarded by German and Vichy officials. That didn't mean that if caught, they wouldn't have been shot. They lived every day not knowing if they would see tomorrow. They seduced, tricked, and killed, and had to live with what they had done for the remainder of their lives.

There were several escape lines through France; the one I chose for Bonnie was based on the Pat O'Leary Line. The flash flood that caused the deaths of the Abrams family on the Pyrenees, was a documented event. On October 17th and 18th, one metre of rain fell on the Eastern Pyrenees. One hundred and forty-seven people died and the centre of Vernet-les-Bains, on the slopes of Mount Canigou, was swept away.

Attacks, killings, sabotage, and the treacherous escape lines are all fictional reworkings of real events. People, Jews and resistance members alike, were betrayed by collaborators and imprisoned. Tens of thousands of French citizens, seventy-five thousand seven hundred and twenty-one of them Jews, were sent to concentration camps along with Communists, gypsies, and homosexuals – in fact anyone Hitler didn't want in his world. The fact he often targeted Jewish professors, musicians, and artists speaks to me of a man who felt inferior. In total, some six million Jews died in the Holocaust.

About thirty thousand French civilian hostages were killed as reprisals to intimidate the resistance, and the brutal massacres at Oradour-sur-Glane and Gardelegen must have sent shockwaves throughout France – I had to put the novel aside for a week before I felt well enough to continue. Always, it is the ordinary people who suffer in war.

While the despots sit safely in their bunkers, those forced by law or propaganda to fight, those forced to defend their country, and the civilians who only wish to live in peace die in their thousands by terrible means. It is hard to condone bombings on civilian populations, whether they be London, Berlin, Hiroshima, or Nagasaki – ordinary people...

During World War Two, it is estimated that civilian deaths totalled fifty to fifty-five million. Military deaths from all causes totalled twenty-one to twenty-five million, including deaths in captivity of about five million prisoners of war. It is difficult to comprehend slaughter on such a scale.

Around half a million people worked for the French resistance during World War Two. More than ninety thousand of these were killed, tortured, or deported to concentration camps by the Germans. They played a major part in the liberation of France and paid a heavy price.

# Other novels by Rebecca Bryn

If you enjoyed this story, please leave me a review on Amazon, Bookbub, or Goodreads. I'd love to hear from you.

To see all of Rebecca's books, search **Rebecca Bryn** at Amazon.

## Historical Fiction

Kindred and Affinity - when faith gets in the way of love – a Victorian romance 'Gritty and real'

Revenge - The most ignominious act in Scottish history. Piracy, treachery, love, and loyalty, and the disasters that led to the union of England and Scotland. 'Another cracking adventure.'

*Tales of Love and War*

Touching the Wire - the women of Auschwitz and a man who tried to save them – IAN Book of the Year 2019, Readers' Favorite Gold Medal 2019 (also an audiobook) 'Outstanding storytelling'

The Dandelion Clock - Lovers torn apart by WW1. Connections Magazine Readers' Choice Silver Medal 2017 'Compelling and unmissable'

Under Enemy Skies – the men and women of the French resistance who stood against Hitler in Occupied France in WW2.

*For Their Country's Good Trilogy*

On Different Shores (For Their Country's Good Book 1) - a young poacher is exiled to Van Diemen's Land for life. His common-law wife sacrifices all to follow him.

Beneath Strange Stars (FTCG Book 2)

On Common Ground (FTCG Book 3) 'Truly exceptional trilogy'


*The Chainmakers series*

The Chainmakers' Daughter - the white slaves of England. Finalist Historical Fiction genre IAN Book of the Year 2020

The Chainmaker's Wife - the fight for women's suffrage and equality

The Chainmistress - hunger marches, the rise of Hitler, and the rescue of Jewish children from Nazi Germany. 'Haunting and vivid portrayal'


*Wales Rising series*

Break It Down – prequel – the Luddite rebellion – Readers' Choice Gold Medal.

Give Us This Day – the Merthyr rising

Let Us Pass – the Rebecca riots. 'Another Rebecca Bryn masterpiece'

**Mystery**

The Silence of the Stones. Alana is thrust into the centre of a 30-year-old mystery of missing children when she begins a new life in West Wales. Why is the village closing ranks against her? 'Beautifully choreographed tale of deceit, murder, and redemption.'

## Fantasy

The Child of Prophecy. Kiya is kidnapped to fulfil an ancient prophecy. Can Raphel rescue the woman he loves from a vicious tyrant priest. 'Holy cow! What an amazing story.'

## Links

Newsletter signup https://www.subscribepage.com/r4m2r0

Her facebook page is Rebecca Bryn - author

Tweet her at https://twitter.com/rebeccabryn1

and https://www.mastodon.social/@rebeccabryn

See blogs, reviews, and excerpts at https://rebeccabrynblog.wordpress.com

For new releases and deals please follow her on Bookbub at

https://www.bookbub.com/authors/rebecca-bryn-5527e97a-146a-49e7-95c7-a30b0f603c80

Rebecca Bryn can be contacted at rebeccabryn@gmail.com

Thank you for reading.

Printed in Great Britain
by Amazon